HIGH HEAT

———

ANNABETH ALBERT

carina
press

carina
press®

Recycling programs
for this product may
not exist in your area.

ISBN-13: 978-1-335-45951-0

High Heat

Carina Press
22 Adelaide St. West, 40th Floor
Toronto, Ontario M5H 4E3, Canada
www.CarinaPress.com

Printed in U.S.A.

For my dad.

I'm sorry I still haven't written you your space assassins, but I miss you every day, and I couldn't have written this one without some of the lessons you left behind.

HIGH HEAT

Chapter One

"Come on, honey. You gotta let me help you." Garrick liked to think he was good at sweet-talking, but his track record of success was in serious jeopardy here.

Woof. The dog danced away from him again. Balanced on crutches, he was limited in his ability to lunge for her. A year ago, his fast reflexes would have made his words irrelevant, but now he pitched his voice low and gentle.

"Sit? Can you sit?"

Miraculously, the dog plopped her fairly sizable behind down on his porch. She appeared to be some happy mix of pit, rottie and lab with a short brownish coat and white and tan markings on her nose and chest. No collar, which was alarming enough, but it was the bloody paw prints on his porch and scrape on her side that had him truly concerned.

He took a few steps toward her, but she quickly backed up. Damn it. It was probably the crutches that were scaring her.

"Me too, dog. Me too." Industrial gray with heavy forearm cuffs, the crutches made a heavy sound with each step. They were a necessity that made his life far easier than the underarm variety had, but he couldn't deny that they were probably intimidating to the scared dog. He needed a better plan. She was probably only fifty or sixty pounds, but he wasn't going to be able to even grab her scruff, let alone lift her.

"Can you stay?"

The dog cocked her head like she was actually listening, which made Garrick laugh for the first time since discovering her barking at his front door. Obedient even if skittish, she stayed in place while he went back into the house. He traded the crutches for his wheelchair and retrieved his phone from the dining table.

Hell. He hated needing help, had needed so much of it in the past year, but he couldn't let his pride get in the way of helping a wounded animal. His neighbor Shirley had dogs, two of them, little white yappy things. She'd have a leash and know a vet to call. She didn't answer when he dialed her number, but he could see two cars in her driveway. Probably had company, and he hated interrupting, but it really couldn't be avoided. If she wasn't home, he'd have to try another friend or his dad, but this would be quicker.

Pocketing the phone, he rolled back out to the porch where the dog waited right where he'd left her.

"Good girl," he praised, but when he scooted closer, she backed up again. "Okay, okay. I'm getting help. Stay."

He used the wooden side ramp his friends had built for him to navigate the two porch steps, then zipped down the driveway and across the cul-de-sac to Shirley's house, a neat little seventies ranch, same basic size as his own. Hers was a friendly shade of lilac, while he'd gone for gray. It was an older neighborhood of smaller homes but decent-sized yards, and close to both a park and Garrick's favorite sports bar, where he used to hang out all the time.

And the air base, but he was trying not to think about that. Gorgeous blue sky, not a cloud in sight, fresh spring air, perfect day for a training jump or two. But not this year. *Next one. You'll get there*, he reminded himself as he navigated Shirley's driveway, which had more of an angle than his.

No porch for Shirley, but the single step in front of the front door was always a challenge. He should have brought the crutches, but he'd been in a hurry. Stretching, he managed to reach far enough to rattle the storm door. "Shirley? Shirley? It's Garrick."

"What the—" The door swung open to reveal a younger man, undoubtedly one of her many grandkids, and that would explain the extra car. And of course it would be one of the gorgeous guys who starred in the pics all over Shirley's fridge—riot of curly chestnut hair pulled up, brown eyes and a lean dancer's build in a shimmery blue shirt. "You need something?"

All of a sudden, Garrick was acutely aware of his dingy sweatpants and grubby T-shirt advertising a triathlon from five years back. He'd been going through his physical therapy exercises when he'd heard the dog barking. And it had been months since he'd last worried what he looked like, so God only knew the state of his hair and face, but something about this guy made him care. And like with the dog, he did not seem to be making a good first impression, judging by the guy's scowl.

"I'm her neighbor," he hurried to explain. "From across the street? The one who built her garden beds in back. We're friends. I need her help with a dog situation."

"A dog situation?" The scowl dropped, leaving in its place a more speculative expression, one that showed off the guy's full mouth and high cheekbones. "She's mentioned you. She's resting right now though. Said she had a bad arthritis night."

"Heck. Yeah, don't wake her up. But there's a dog on my porch, a hurt stray, and I need to figure out what to do with it. It won't let me close."

"On your porch?" He gestured behind Garrick. A quick swivel revealed the dog at the bottom of Shirley's driveway, looking expectantly at him.

"I thought I told you to stay!" Garrick said to the dog, then turned back to the young man, who was laughing now. Dimples. Because, of course. "Yeah. That's it. Seems friendly enough, but I don't have a leash and I'm not sure what to do once I catch her."

"Okay, hang tight. Let me make sure Mimi and Molly are secure, then I'll get a leash and some treats." The guy disappeared into the house.

"Come on now. You don't need to be afraid." Garrick rolled toward the dog, hand outstretched. She let him get closer than she had on the porch, then started backing up.

"Cookie? Who wants a cookie?" Shirley's grandson reappeared with a black leash and a packet of bacon-and-peanut-butter-flavored biscuits. Mouth cracking into a doggy grin, the hound ignored Garrick's hand in favor of limping toward the treats.

"Guess you're Mr. Popular now," Garrick joked, following her.

"Oh, you know that word! *Cookie!* Don't you? Smart cookie!" The guy had a great voice, friendly and musical, not overpowering at all, and for a second, Garrick wouldn't have minded being the one showered with praise. Which was odd. Not the attraction—that happened some, or at least it used to. But it hadn't since the accident. Not even hookup apps or porn of any stripe held much appeal these days. But apparently golden brown eyes and bouncy hair and really bad timing did the trick.

"She knows *sit* too," Garrick provided as the dog gobbled down a treat. "Sit."

Obediently, she plopped down on the concrete driveway. *Woof.*

"Someone wants another cookie?" This time the guy was lightning fast, the sort of reflexes that would be at home on any engine crew, as he lassoed the leash around her neck, clipping it in place. He doled out another biscuit as he straightened. "She's hungry. Probably hasn't eaten in a while. Want me to get some water while you call Animal Control?"

Garrick had to laugh. "This is a small town. *Very* small town. There's no dog catcher or pound."

"None? Police nonemergency number maybe?"

"I don't think they handle stray dogs that aren't a threat. Fish and Wildlife will come for wild animals like bobcats on your property, but not dogs."

"Thank goodness you're not a bobcat." Giving a nervous laugh, the guy glanced off into the hills before patting the dog again.

"There's an animal shelter in Bend, about forty-five minutes away, but I think she needs a vet first. I'd go door-to-door to find an owner but that paw has me worried about walking her too much."

"Good point."

"Rain? What's the commotion?" Shirley emerged

from the house, walking a little slower than normal but looking pretty with her long gray hair spilling down the back of a dress dyed the colors of an Oregon sunset.

Rain. He had to be one of the Portland grandkids—they all seemed to have hippie names. Rain, Skye, Lark and so on. And he was clearly used to bigger cities than Painter's Ridge, where no one who worked for the town was coming out for a lost dog.

"Your…uh…neighbor found a dog." Still holding the leash, Rain walked over to her. The name absolutely suited his lithe frame and natural grace to his strides.

"Garrick." He offered a handshake after Rain transferred the leash to his other hand. He hadn't grabbed the wheelchair gloves he usually used for longer treks, so his bare skin met Rain's. And there it was again. Sparks, sure as a flint meeting steel, right when he could least do a damn thing about it. And because Shirley undoubtedly wouldn't appreciate him macking on her much-too-young grandson, he glanced away.

"I'm gonna get that water. You think you can hold her?" Glancing down at Garrick's chair, Rain offered the leash somewhat reluctantly.

"Yup. I'll put the brakes on." Garrick engaged the locks for his wheels. He was still getting used to all the bells and whistles on this one. It was a nice chair, far better than the old-fashioned clunky things he'd first had at the hospital. Ultralight. Racing style they called it, though that was a bit optimistic as far as he'd found. The thicker bicycle-like tires and red trim added to the sporty appearance. He'd been reluctant to give up the rental chair, get this one custom fit when he wasn't sure how long he'd need it, but the insurance, which could be a bastard about some things, had paid up.

"I don't know as I like the look of that dog. Too big. And you never know, might be aggressive." Shirley shook her head.

"Seems like a sweetheart to me." Garrick kept his tone light, not too argumentative, but the dog, who was currently twisted around trying to get at her scrape, seemed more scaredy-cat than fighter.

"Don't let Rain talk himself into keeping her here. Mimi is downright territorial over her house. And we have to watch Molly at the park. She's always goading bigger dogs."

It wasn't really Garrick's place to be preventing Rain from anything, but he nodded. "Well, hopefully we'll find the owner quickly. You've never seen this dog around?"

"No. But I can make some calls. And I'm on that neighborhood group thing." She whipped out her phone, a newer model that one of the grandkids had talked her into.

Garrick largely avoided the online neighborhood group, which tended to complain about package stealers, lawn ornament movers and inconsiderate parkers, but it might be useful for something like this.

Shirley snapped a picture of the dog and got busy on her phone as Rain came back with a mixing bowl full of water. The dog waited patiently for Rain to set it down, then gulped down most of the water, tail wagging, still paying no mind to the leash. Yeah, she was a sweetheart all right, and someone had to be frantically looking for her.

"The vet will be able to tell us if she's microchipped." Rain patted the dog on her head.

"Yes. Cherry Pet Care on Main is where I go. They

take walk-ins," Shirley added, not looking up from the phone.

"Do you want me to take her?" Rain's mouth quirked as he glanced between Garrick and the dog. "Or do you want to come? The vet might not...uh...do pro bono work on strays."

"I'll come." Garrick got it. He'd been a broke college kid once upon a time too, and Rain didn't look much older than twenty-two or so, which was a nice reminder not to go perving on his good looks again. "I'll just need to grab my wallet."

"Thanks." Relief was evident in Rain's wide eyes.

"No lost dog notices from the neighbors," Shirley reported. "And you better hurry. The vet only has short Saturday hours. You sure you're up for the outing, Garrick?"

"Nothing better to do," he said lightly, but it was true. Weekends were the worst. No physical therapy. Fewer visits from his dad, who worked long hours at his Western-themed shop, which did a ton of tourist business. Friends were busy with their own lives, and inviting himself along was far more complicated than it used to be, as was finding his own fun. The dog was the most exciting thing to happen in a while, and that was just sad. "Besides, Rain said you were feeling under the weather. You rest and check the app, and we'll handle the dog."

It felt good to take charge of something again, even if it was simply logistics for the dog. He sent Rain to fetch old towels to protect his car from the dog's wounds while he headed back to his place for his wallet, keys and crutches, which went in the holder on the back of his chair, another spiffy feature that helped. No time to change clothes though. Not that he needed to care what sort of impression he made on Rain or the vet or anyone else.

Rain met him at his car, a small SUV, with the dog waiting on her leash.

"So…dog goes in the back seat and your wheelchair in the cargo area? That sound okay?" Rain asked, not told, which was nice, especially when he continued, "Can you tell me how best to help you? Is the car too tall for you?"

A lot of people would have made assumptions and started doing things at this point, but Rain gave him space, both literal and figurative, which Garrick appreciated.

"I can stand to transfer." Pulling up even with the passenger door, Garrick demonstrated. "Tall is actually easier. If you want to fold the chair and stow it, that would be great."

"No problem." Rain wheeled it around to the back of the SUV.

"It's pretty sturdy," Garrick called as he hefted himself into the passenger seat, suddenly weirdly on edge. "It collapses by pulling on the seat cushion, but don't try to force anything."

"I've got you. Not my first time folding a chair. You're safe with me, promise."

"Thanks." Strangely, Garrick found himself nodding. He did feel comfortable with Rain, even though he was younger and a stranger and his car was old enough to not exactly inspire confidence. The gentle way that Rain loaded up the dog helped. He didn't have the brashness Garrick associated with a lot of guys his age. And he seemed good-natured, the way he'd rolled with having his Saturday upended by Garrick and the dog. All in all, Garrick could have done a lot worse for an unexpected rescuer, and despite the seriousness of their task, he found himself almost eager to spend more time with him.

Danger. Abort. Bad idea. Nice as it was to remember what attraction felt like, he wasn't up to flirting, let alone anything else, and Rain was the trifecta of probably straight, too young and way off-limits. Better he simply focus on the job at hand and not let himself get carried away with anything else.

Grandma's neighbor was hot. Like distractingly so, with broad shoulders and biceps for days coupled with a movie-star-worthy face—chiseled features and piercing green eyes and shaggy hair that danced between dirty blond and light brown. But Rain was supposed to be focusing on the dog, not Garrick, and on driving through a town he'd only visited a couple of times since his grandmother moved. She refused to call it a retirement, but buying a house had been her admitting that maybe her years on the art festival circuit were coming to a halt, and providing her fabric crafts to a nearby touristy place was more her current speed.

"So you visiting for the weekend?" Garrick asked as Rain followed his phone's GPS directions toward downtown.

"No, I'm supposed to be here for a couple of months. I took the spring term off college, thought I might see what seasonal work I could find around here, help Grandma out at the same time."

"That sounds nice. I'm sure she could use the hand."

"Eh. She's like her dog—rather territorial about her

place. It was my mom's idea, so we'll see if it sticks."
Rain did love Grandma, but so far she hadn't let him
anywhere near her sewing machine or dye buckets so he
wasn't sure how much help he was actually going to be.
"I had an interview this morning for a bartender gig—
that's why I'm dressed up—but I don't think I passed it."

"Oh?" Garrick didn't sound judgmental, merely curious.

"Yeah. It's the clubhouse at the golf course south of
town. I didn't know half the drinks they quizzed me on,
and they asked how I felt about a haircut."

"Ouch." Garrick laughed. "Yeah, don't do that. Keep
looking. Plenty of other seasonal jobs."

"You'd know, right? I thought Grandma said you
were a smoke jumper?"

"Yep." Garrick didn't seem inclined to elaborate, instead looking out the window, and Rain couldn't blame
him—he'd get the scoop from Grandma about Garrick's
injuries rather than bug him for gory details he probably didn't want to share.

"That's cool. I've got some applications in with the
forest service and other places since some of my classes
were pre-fire academy. I didn't get a slot for this year
though, hence taking a term off." He kept his voice
casual. The Portland Fire Academy was notoriously
competitive, so he was trying hard not to take it too
personally, but man it had hurt to not even make the
short list of applicants who would be considered for fall
placements. Oh well. On to the next adventure.

"You can park up here." Garrick pointed to a lot next
to a brick building with a cheerful sign with dogs and
cats on it. "And don't let it get you down, kid. Don't
give up on the dream."

Kid. Okay. So much for Hottie Neighbor. No one called him *kid* these days and got away with it. Quietly seething, he found the closest spot to the door. He might be irked, but he was still careful with the wheelchair and crutches as he unloaded them for Garrick.

"Need my arm?" He knew better than to hover, but still wanted to make the offer if Garrick needed assistance.

"Nah. I've got it." Garrick smoothly transferred from the car to the chair, then waited for Rain to unload the dog. "That's a good girl." Garrick stuck out his hand and this time the dog sniffed it, even without a treat. She seemed to be warming up to both of them, even though she was noticeably skittish as they approached the door. Once inside, she plopped down, almost like she was trying to hide behind them.

"Now, who do we have here?" A receptionist in kitten-print scrubs and pink glasses peered over her desk at them. Garrick explained about finding the dog, and the receptionist nodded sympathetically. "It shouldn't be too long a wait for the vet. I'll need a name for her though, just to start a chart."

"Name?" Garrick looked over at Rain like he might have the answer, which was nice, being consulted like that. Usually take-charge guys like Garrick didn't slow down long enough to solicit other opinions. Which Rain had.

"If they can't find an owner, you want her to have a great shot at adoption. Pick something fun and gentle for her maybe? Approachable? She looks all tough, big black dog, but really she's almost shy. Aren't you, sweetie?"

As if she knew she was being talked about, the dog crept forward to nose at the treat bag Rain was holding.

"No, you can't have another cookie," he said firmly.

"Cookie." Garrick smiled, and it was a great smile, wide and welcoming, the sort belonging to an easy charmer who probably had tons of friends. "That's it. At least we know she'll come to that. And you can put my address for now."

After the intake information was handled, they were shown to a little room with a window facing a garden and a cheery mural on the wall.

"You and your son can wait in here while I take Cookie for her weight and temperature," the receptionist said to Garrick, making Rain snort. The dude wasn't *that* old. Midthirties maybe. His messy hair and facial scruff made him look older, but he didn't have any gray yet. For himself, Rain was used to looking young. Probably one of the reasons the bartender gig had fallen through. The manager guy had sounded like he didn't trust Rain to not be slipping drinks to underage buddies.

"Not the son. Just another neighbor," Rain said quickly before she could leap to her next assumption that Garrick was the sugar daddy with the credit cards. Not that Rain would necessarily mind, but this was a small town, and Garrick had "sports-loving dude bro" written all over him.

"Ah. Well, Cookie is lucky to have you both. I'll check on a microchip while we're in the back."

"Man, I hope she's got the microchip and a nice owner on file," Garrick said as the receptionist and Cookie left, leaving Rain to take one of the seats in the room.

"Yeah, she's a great dog." Personally, Rain didn't

have as much hope of an owner—no collar, and despite a sturdy build the dog looked like she hadn't had a good meal in a few days.

"So, tell me about these firefighting classes you were taking. What certs do you have?" Garrick asked like he actually cared about the answer and not like he was just looking to kill time. Which made Rain give him a real answer, one that kept them talking about his rather eclectic collection of community college classes until a vet tech brought Cookie back.

The tech was followed by a woman around Garrick's age who had to be the vet, judging by the stethoscope around her neck. "I have good news and bad news," the vet said as she shut the door behind her. Cookie now sported a white mitt on her paw and a shaved patch around the scrape on her side, but seemed in good spirits. "Which do you want first?"

"Good," Rain said, right as Garrick said, "Bad."

"Okay. Both it is." The vet laughed. She had kind eyes and short dark hair, and Cookie was already nuzzling up to her, looking for treats. "Well, no microchip for one. No lost dog calls here either. But good news— she's been spayed and other than a large thorn in her paw and the scrape on her side, she's pretty healthy. I'd guess she's a year or two old. We've cleaned her wounds, and she'll need to keep the mitt on her paw for a couple of days. I'd like to do a round of antibiotics because the side scrape did look somewhat infected to me, but that's largely out of caution."

"What's the rest of the bad news?" Garrick sounded like a guy who had heard more than his share of it over the years, not reacting to the better news about Cookie's health beyond stretching out a hand for her to warily sniff again.

"I'm assuming you're hoping to get her off your hands, but our kennel is full of patients who need overnight care. Lydia called the shelter in Bend, and they're full as well, including foster homes that could handle an injured animal. They can stick a picture of her up on the found page, but they're not sure they can get her a place before they close tonight. A number of the rescues are in a similar boat—either they're very breed- and size-specific or they aren't taking new animals right now. I'll be honest—her size and her breeds along with the injuries are going to make her a tough placement, especially on a weekend."

"Heck." Wide shoulders deflating, Garrick studied his hands, which left Rain to pet Cookie.

"I can work on Grandma. Maybe by Monday, her owners will be found."

"She said no," Garrick reminded him. "And she's got the other dogs to think about. It makes sense. My friends in the country would be good, but they just added a third dog. I doubt they're going to be up for one more already. I can see who else might be able to help."

"How about you?" Rain turned on the sort of smile that usually brought him good luck.

"Me?" Garrick blinked.

"Yes, you. You'd be perfect." Nodding, he leaned forward, waiting for Garrick to embrace the obvious.

Chapter Two

"Perfect?" Garrick echoed Rain, only with a lot more skepticism. He wasn't sure which set of pleading big brown eyes was worse, Cookie's or Rain's.

"Yes. She likes you. And you don't have any other pets, right? No one else to ask permission from? It's perfect."

"Sure, no other pets and I live alone, but she's scared of me."

"Oh, at first, maybe." Rain waved this concern away with a flick of his long elegant fingers.

"She's a sweetie," the vet added, nodding along. "A few more biscuits and head scratches, and she'll be your new best friend. A lot of dogs are skittish around wheelchairs at first, but then they warm up."

"Maybe so, and I'm not unsympathetic to her situation." He really wasn't, and the old him would have likely given in to the twin set of puppy-dog eyes directed his way. "However, in case you didn't notice, I'm kinda…mobility impaired these days. And unlike Shirley's, my backyard is hardly suitable for a dog."

"I have an answer for that." Rain held up a hand, stopping Garrick's list of reasons why this was a bad idea.

"Somehow I'm not surprised."

"As good as she listens, I'm going to bet she's at least

somewhat housebroken. I can come walk her twice a day. And help you dog-proof today. I'll give you my cell—you can call if she has an accident or spills water or something and you need me."

"I'm not sure—"

"I'd take the bet on her being housebroken," the vet said, voice as coaxing as Rain's. "I can have Lydia give you a bag of kibble to get started, and I'll prorate our services for the wound cleanup."

"Just until the owner is found?" Neck muscles tensing, Garrick already knew he was beat.

"Yup." Rain nodded like the Blazers bobblehead Garrick kept in the truck he hadn't driven in months.

"Only the weekend," Garrick allowed. "And we'll try hard to find her owners or a more permanent place for her."

"Deal." Rain grinned widely, and damn, that was the kind of smile that Garrick would promise a heck of a lot more than canine babysitting for. Warmth spread across Garrick's chest as Rain continued, "What do you say we find the pet store?"

"Ha." Garrick had to laugh again at his big city assumptions. "We don't even have any of the big box stores in town. But the feed store will have food and stuff."

"Good. And maybe a bed—"

"The weekend. Only," Garrick reminded him.

"Sounds like we have a plan." The vet hustled them to the front before Garrick could offer more protests. He paid the nominal fee while the vet tech presented him with meds and a small sack of kibble. Judging by how hungry Cookie looked, he figured that wouldn't last more than a feeding or two.

"Add more chow to the list," he told Rain on the way

to the car. "Same brand if possible. We don't want to overly shock her system."

"You know dogs?" As before, Rain hung back, letting Garrick transfer himself to the car before taking care of loading up the wheelchair and dog.

"Oh yeah. Like I said, my friends have a trio now. And growing up, we had a sweet little terrier with a fickle stomach. Mom took her in the divorce." The memory made his stomach churn, even all these years later. "Then Dad got a cranky beagle who ate like a goat." That memory was easier, and he made himself laugh, keep his voice light. Rain didn't need to hear about his family drama. "Now he's got two old grumpy farm dogs who tolerate horses far better than humans or other dogs. I'm not an expert or anything, but I've been around them plenty."

"Good. A lot of people get scared of big black dogs like her. I don't get it, but I've seen people cross the street to avoid certain breeds."

"Like your grandma. But before you go pleading Cookie's case to me again, I'm sure there's a home somewhere out there for her." Not Garrick. He couldn't afford the distraction of a permanent pet, not when he needed all his focus for his recovery, and not when he wasn't sure what kind of life he could provide himself, let alone an animal.

"Fair enough." Rain sounded neither convinced nor like he was going to drop the subject more than temporarily. "Now, tell me how to get to this farm store place."

Garrick gave the directions to the feed store a couple of blocks over. As Rain drove, Garrick fished out his wallet, emptied his cash. "Tell you what. Cookie and I will wait in the car. You've got a sixty-eight dollar budget to get her set for the weekend."

"That might be enough for chow and a cheap bed," Rain said happily, almost dancing in his seat, and damn if making him happy wasn't fun and worth parting with the money.

"Try to get a few toys too. I don't want her chewing my couch."

"You've got it." Rain deftly parked next to a line of pickups at the farm store. He opened the windows before he shut off the SUV. "You sure you don't want to come in? It's no problem getting your chair out and we can crack all the windows for Cookie."

"Nah." Garrick wasn't about to explain that simply this amount of exertion had done him in for a while. Damn he missed his stamina. "She needs me to keep her company. You have fun. If you can't find something, Morty at customer service is a friend of my dad's. Great guy. He'll help you track down the chow or whatever."

And maybe that too was why he was staying put. He didn't need another round of questioning from well-meaning folks who'd known him his whole life, sympathy a double-edged sword he'd had far too much of the past several months. But it turned out there was no escaping his life as not even five minutes after Rain walked away, he heard a familiar voice.

"Nelson? Been a long time, man." Jimenez, one of his fellow smoke jumpers, came striding over, pretty blonde in skintight jeans trailing behind him. He was one of the rookies—

Wait. Not a rookie anymore. The new season was about to start. Jimenez would be an old hand by now, working all the fires Garrick had missed after the accident, all the jumps and climbs and everything else he missed with all his soul but couldn't show. *Keep it light*, he reminded himself.

"Hey there. Yeah, been a while. How's it going? Getting lots of jumps in? Heard you did some tourist work in the off-season."

"You know it. Gotta get my air time." Slinging an arm around his companion, Jimenez gave him an easy smile that faded into something approaching concern. "We miss you, man. Feels weird gearing up for the season without you. What's the latest word on when you'll be back at it?"

Wish I knew. Garrick swallowed hard. "Hopefully not long. I'm working hard at PT. Putting my reps in. Finally back home at my own place. Progress, you know?"

"That's great." Jimenez's voice was just this side of too hearty. "You keep at it. Chin up. I'm sure they're saving a spot for you. And if you need anything, anything at all, you call me."

Call me. Everyone said it, but he was never sure how much people meant it. Like he and Jimenez had never hung out off-duty before the accident. Was he supposed to call him for a favor now? Did the guy really want to fetch Garrick some groceries or was he simply being nice? Not knowing made Garrick frustrated with these sorts of offers, but he couldn't show it, could only nod. "Thanks."

"Okay, dog stuff obtained!" Rain came striding toward the car, wide smile still in place as he pushed a cart with a big bag of chow and a fluffy pet bed a ridiculous shade of bubblegum pink. Some of his hair had come loose, curls spilling down his face. In the sunlight, the shimmer on his shirt was more evident, making him look ready for clubbing, not a farm store.

And Jimenez, the worst gossip on the crew, went all bug-eyed. "You getting a dog?"

"Meet Cookie. She's temporary. And this is Rain. My neighbor." Garrick refused to get flustered over any assumptions Jimenez wanted to make. And it wasn't like Jimenez, who had a well-earned rep as the worst sort of love-them-and-leave-them player, was in any position to judge who Garrick hung around with.

"Ah. Gotcha." Jimenez shook Rain's hand before his companion tugged on his arm, reminding him of their errand for flowers. "We'll catch up later. And I mean it, Nelson. You call me. Can't wait to see you back out there."

"Me too." Garrick nodded even as he knew the chances of him calling Jimenez were slim. And as for getting back on the crew...well, he was trying. Every damn day. A little further. A little faster. He'd hadn't come this far to fail.

"Sorry if I cut short your conversation with your friend," Rain said as he loaded his purchases next to Cookie.

"Nah. It's okay. I'm sure he needed to get on with his day."

"Is it..." Rain started to ask something then trailed off as he slid behind the wheel.

"Is what?"

"Nothing. I was going to ask if it was hard, being around other smoke jumpers right now, then realized that was really nosy of me."

"It's okay. You can ask me about the accident. I'm not gonna bite your head off for asking questions." Garrick might be crankier these days, but he was still himself, still happy to talk to almost anyone and wasn't one to make certain topics taboo, even if he'd rather listen to his dad discuss the minutiae of new horse tack than re-count that day of the accident. And as to Rain's specific question, he had to pause, flip response at the ready. But strangely what came out was closer to the truth. "And sometimes. I mean, I love seeing my buddies. But yeah…sometimes it's…different."

Different. That was it. Not hard precisely, although it could be that too, but different. Changed. And he hated it even as he tried to ignore those feelings, the jumble of emotions better left shoved in the crawlspaces of his psyche, not strewn about for public consumption.

"I bet." Rain's look was sympathetic, but he didn't press, instead backing out of the space and heading toward their neighborhood without needing further directions. He was a quick study, something Garrick appreciated in a person. Perceptive too, not continuing down that line of conversation. "Is it okay if I park in your driveway while we unload?"

"Of course." Speaking of ignoring things, Garrick tried to squelch the weird mix of anticipation and dread at the prospect of having Rain in his space. A million years ago, he would have known exactly what to do with his Saturday, wouldn't have had dog-proofing remotely on the agenda, and would have needed a cutie like Rain for far sexier purposes. Different. That was his life now and there was nothing served by dwelling on the less-than-fun parts. All he could do was go forward. He'd make the best of this situation with the dog, same as he did any other. And if that meant enjoying Rain's company a little longer…well, he was only human, after all.

As they unloaded in the driveway, Garrick's demeanor had a certain stiffness that hadn't been there earlier—

lines around his mouth, hunched shoulders—and Rain hated it. He should have known better than to bring up unhappy topics. But he'd seen how tense Garrick was around his fellow smoke jumper. Watching them, his chest had pinched in an unfamiliar way. At first he'd wondered if perhaps it was he himself who had Garrick on edge—the whole dude bro thing of not wanting to look like he was on a date or otherwise entangled with another person of the masculine variety. And Rain hadn't missed Jimenez's blatantly speculative gaze. But then when Garrick had easily made introductions but still been oddly stilted, he'd figured that it was probably Jimenez's sympathy and offer of help. It had to be tough on Garrick, not being able to be out there with his crew.

If Garrick was a friend, Rain would know better what to say, how to distract him or get him to open up, and would be able to tell which he needed more. Not knowing made him want to try harder to get Garrick smiling again.

"Wait till you see the toys I picked for her. I found a clearance bin with some fun items," he said as he positioned the wheelchair for Garrick. A couple of years prior, his parents had had a close friend who used a wheelchair, so Rain had some experience unfolding the device. However, Paula had needed more help transferring, and it was hard not to hover as Garrick completed the maneuver.

"I'm more concerned with why she needs a pink fluffy bed."

"Everyone needs a pink fluffy bed." He grinned as he let the dog out of the back seat. "And I know, I know, the pink undoubtedly doesn't go with your style, but it's part of a plan I've got."

"I'm listening." Garrick spared a pat for Cookie before heading up the ramp to his porch, leaving Rain to follow with Cookie's new loot.

"I want to take some more pictures of her, both to find her owner, and if that doesn't work, to get her a forever home. And I was thinking about how to make her look less scary and decided to make her a pretty, pretty pink princess. Like lean into all the gendered stuff, but in a fun way that makes her seem more approachable. Pink sparkly collar, pink bed, unicorn chew toy…"

"If it gets her a home." Garrick didn't seem too put out as he unlocked the door, which was nice. "And if you had fun picking it out, then that's cool."

"Trust me. I'm jealous of the bed. And the collar." For a second, Rain forgot that he wasn't in Portland, wasn't around friends who understood him, but whatever. He wasn't making any apologies for liking what he liked. And instead of looking disgusted, Garrick looked…speculative. And wasn't that interesting?

"Not everyone can pull off sparkles." With a welcome laugh, Garrick ushered them into a small living area.

"Some of us never outgrew our princess phase." He winked at Garrick before looking around. Like at Grandma's house, the space was an upside-down L-shape with living room and dining room in a line with a sliding glass door to the backyard beyond the dining room and a kitchen to the side. But whereas Grandma's kitchen was walled off, art clutter on every available surface in the older house, Garrick's home was recently remodeled with the kitchen open to the rest of the space, clean ivory walls and light wood cabinets and floors making it look far bigger than Grandma's.

"Did you do the remodel yourself? This is really nice."

"Most of it, yeah. Got a great deal on the house because it hadn't been touched since it was built. Still had the original avocado-colored countertops and walnut cabinets with gold carpet everywhere. I worked a couple of winters for a home store in Bend, got some good discounts on materials and got lucky with some friends who could help. Demo was hella fun, bashing everything in." Garrick got a wistful expression on his face, making Rain worry they were heading into uncomfortable memory territory again, but then he shook his head, as if making a conscious choice to reach for something happy. "Man, that work party for the backyard was epic too. Come on, I'll show you why it's not the best for a dog."

Still holding Cookie's leash, Rain followed him to the glass doors. Like Garrick's front yard, which was mainly concrete and artful use of rock and gravel, the backyard didn't have any grass, instead consisting of a wide patio that ran the whole length of the house, multiple seating areas, a hot tub, a firepit, and several raised beds and trellis structures with hearty-looking plants.

"Wow. Forget the work party, you must have epic parties period. This is the most entertaining-friendly space I've seen outside of the common areas at the cohousing community where I grew up, and those are more functional—lots of vegetable gardens and benches—but this is begging for some drinks and a dude on a guitar."

"Yeah. I've had more than a few of those gatherings." Garrick's toothy grin radiated pride. "We work long, unpredictable hours as smoke jumpers, so I wanted a really chill, low-maintenance space for hanging out. Only drought-resistant plants and no grass. Sorry, Cookie."

"I think she'll be okay. There's a patch of dirt over there. If she has to come back here in a pinch, I'll clean for you. Otherwise, I'll do the walks like we talked about. Now, let's see the rest of the place, things she could get into, maybe see where you want to keep her at night. I thought about a crate, but I wasn't sure how you felt about crate training."

"It works for puppies, but I can probably keep her with me, honestly." Backing up, Garrick rolled down a short hallway near the kitchen. He sounded exactly like a dog-loving guy who could be Cookie's forever home if he'd only give it a chance. Garrick pushed open the door to a larger-than-expected bedroom.

"You took out the third bedroom and added a slider to the patio," Rain guessed. The room was about double the size of Grandma's and dominated by a large bed. It had to be one of those adjustable kinds because the head on one side was raised. A hanging metal triangle for getting up and a wheeled tray table added to the functional vibe—not a ton of color or art outside a tie-dyed duvet cover he recognized as one of Grandma's designs, and a large plant in the corner by the door, but it had a well-lived-in vibe, complete with a gas fireplace that Rain dug.

"Yeah, we bashed in the wall to the smallest bedroom. I really only needed two rooms, one for sleeping and one as an office-slash-gym, and getting a king-size bed to fit was a priority when planning the bachelor pad of my dreams."

"Bachelor dream house, huh?" Rain was trying to not be too nosy, but it was hard when he was so curious. "Never tempted to do the whole family thing?"

Another storm cloud crossed Garrick's face. Damn it. Rain had stepped in it again.

"I was engaged. Million years ago, feels like it. Nice woman. Loved her pink and sparkles, so you and Cookie would have approved."

"I'm sure." Rain sent a quick wish out to the universe that the past tense didn't mean this was a super tragic story.

"Anyway, she and her glitter-loving self moved to LA. Just couldn't stand country life any longer. And me... I got pretty damn good at the whole bachelor life thing."

"Damn. That sucks." So, not a tragedy, but still he felt for Garrick's younger self. Even if he was playing it lightly, Rain could sense his underlying tension. It had to have hurt. And the existence of an ex-fiancée was, if not definitive proof, strong evidence that he was as straight as Rain had originally assumed, speculative look notwithstanding.

"How about you? Oh wait. You're like what? Twenty?" Garrick laughed. And there he went, dismissing Rain as a kid again. Rain couldn't help bristling.

"Twenty-three. I look young, I know."

"It's the hair and cheeks," Garrick teased. "You're going to be one of those people who gets carded at forty."

"Not much I can do there. And to answer the question, I've dated. Not a ton, but some. No engagements." He was deliberately gender neutral, not particularly feeling like coming out, but also he was never very good at hiding it very long. Garrick would undoubtedly figure out that Rain marched to a rainbow beat sooner rather than later if he hadn't already.

"Good. You've got all the time in the world to wait on that stuff. Have fun. Play the field."

"You make it sound like you're ancient."

"Nah. But…my partying days are likely behind me."

"With that backyard? Hardly." Rain still wasn't entirely sure about the extent of Garrick's injuries, but he didn't see any reason why his social life should take a nosedive.

"Yeah. We'll see what the summer brings." Garrick made a dismissive gesture. "So, do you think if we bring Cookie's bed in here and put it in the corner, she'll stay if I shut the door at night?"

"It's worth a try. And I'm a night owl. If she starts howling or something, I could come back." He tried to keep the offer from sounding flirty by patting Cookie at the same time. "No people bed for you, you hear? I'd say the biggest risk is you tripping on her in the middle of the night with the crutches, so maybe leave a light on?"

"That's smart." Garrick rubbed his shaggy hair. "That's my worry too. She was scared of the crutches earlier though, so maybe she'll stay back. You see anything in here she might eat? Guess I should have you move the plant to the deck."

"I can do that." Rain dragged the plant out the sliding door before studying the rest of the room, which didn't even have as much as a throw rug out of place. "And you're remarkably clean—no socks for her to eat on the floor or things like that."

"Well I have to keep a clear floor for the crutches and the wheelchair. My dad helps, and he found me a service that's doing some cleaning too. I stayed with him for a while after the hospital and rehab facility, but I really missed my own place."

"That's cool. I've always lived with family or room-mates, but I'd be ready to be home too. It's just different being in someone else's space."

"Exactly. I know my dad worries about me falling or something, but I'm happier here."

"I feel you both. And I know you're worried about tripping on Cookie or one of her belongings. We'll stash the bed out of the way, and I bet we could train Cookie to pick up her toys if you point to them."

"The weekend. She is staying the weekend," Garrick reminded him, but his tone was less firm than it had been at the vet's.

"Yes, yes. Still bet I can teach her before I leave. Let me find the biscuits and the toys."

Forget his pretty pink adoptable princess plan, Rain was totally going to convince him to keep the dog if the owner couldn't be found. The guy seemed a little at loose ends, like his grandma had when she'd first decided to stop traveling and buy the house, and before she'd adopted Mimi and Molly as a bonded pair of siblings. They could be little demons, but they gave Grandma a structured routine that she seemed to need, the same way chores at the cohousing community kept people engaged and involved. People needed to be needed, even if they didn't always realize it, and Rain was going to prove to Garrick that he and Cookie were meant to be together. After all, Rain himself was swimming in free time until he could sort out his employment situation. He could spare the time to play canine matchmaker.

Chapter Three

"Bedtime for us." Garrick felt somewhat strange talking to the dog, but after several hours of temporary dog ownership, it was less weird than it had been. Rain had gone away to eat dinner with Shirley, then returned to take Cookie for a short walk in deference to her hurt foot. She'd taken to the sparkling collar Rain had picked out like a champ, not even protesting any and had happily gone trotting off with Rain. Even the quick walk coupled with a big dinner seemed to have tired her out. She had been dozing next to his recliner while he'd mindlessly surfed previews for shows until he too decided that it had been a long day.

He scanned the floor as he got his crutches ready, looking for any stray toys or pet spills, but the way was clear other than the stuffed unicorn that Cookie already seemed bonded with.

"Get your toy," he ordered, trying to echo the same uber-enthusiastic tone Rain had used when teaching her to retrieve her toys. Someone had clearly attempted to teach her fetch at some point because she'd been a fast study. Well, that and she'd wanted the biscuits. Showing a new stubborn streak, she stayed lying down until he rattled the treat bag and repeated the command. "Fetch. Get your toy."

Tail wagging, she complied, bringing him the unicorn in exchange for yet another little morsel. "Good girl. Now come."

Sticking the toy in one pocket and the treats in the other, he hefted himself up with the crutches. After months of casts and braces, it still felt weird not having to account for the extra bulk. There was some talk at PT of trying a new type of braces if the insurance would cover them. While he didn't like the weight of the casts and braces, he was in favor of anything that got him to his ultimate goal of getting back out there sooner.

In his room, he tossed the dog toy on Cookie's ridiculous pink bed. "Go lie down."

It took some more encouraging, but finally she spun in a circle and plopped on the bed, leaving him free to make his way to the shower in the attached bathroom. Being able to do this on his own was new too, and it was still a little unwieldy, getting set on the shower chair, making sure everything was in reach, but it beat being scuzzy. Which he'd felt most of the day next to Rain with his pretty shirt and gleaming hair. And not that he cared what Rain thought, but he still took his time in the tub, even shaving with his shower mirror. Like haircuts, shaving had become a when-he-remembered-and-could-be-bothered event.

And thinking about Rain, even tangentially, while warm and wet and soapy was a bad, bad idea. Why on earth did his cock have to pick *now* to come back online? He'd played around some on his own previously with disappointing results that he wasn't sure how to bring up to the doctors. Everyone was so focused on getting him walking again that complaining about his dick felt both petty and embarrassing. But now he was raring to go, only he didn't want to risk ending up in a slippery heap on the shower floor. Also, he didn't want to be the guy perving on the too-young dog walker who might also be a new friend. And maybe too he didn't want another disappointment.

On that sour note, he carefully exited the shower and pulled on a pair of stretchy shorts for sleeping. Emerging from the bathroom, he pulled up short in front of the bed where a very happy, very sleepy Cookie was lounging against his pillows.

"Hey! I thought I told you to lie on your bed."

Thump. Thump. Wagging her tail, she gave him a canine grin.

"That's the people bed. Yours is over there." He pointed at her bed. "Go lie down."

Helpfully, she scooted over about ten inches but otherwise didn't seem inclined to budge.

"Five minutes, okay? Five minutes and then you're going to your bed." Sitting next to her, he adjusted the bed's angle. Replacing his previous cheap king set with this setup had been a bit of a splurge, but it beat the rental hospital bed he'd had at his dad's. He was a big guy. He needed his space. And he was not prepared to share that space with a stubborn pooch.

"Go lay down," he tried again after giving her some pats, but all she did was move to the foot of the other side of the bed. Yawning and out of energy, he was no match for a stubborn dog. "Fine, fine. Let's not tell Rain that you rejected his bed selection."

Usually nights were hard—his pain level tended to spike at night in unpredictable ways, his sleep could be fitful, and his mind raced through hundreds of dismal scenarios. He'd never had an anxiety problem before the accident, but lately, calming down at night was particularly problematic. If he was physically exhausted, it was easier, but then physical tiredness tended to mean more pain, which meant more sleeplessness, which meant more time for worries to charge back up.

But that night he didn't even need to play on his phone and was asleep even before he could try again to get Cookie to move. The next thing he knew it was morning—and not crack-of-dawn morning either, but a sunny eight o'clock. A banging noise was coming from the front door.

Had to be Rain come to walk the dog. And sure enough, his phone was full of several missed messages from Rain asking about a time to come over.

"Coming," he hollered. Hell. No time to get dressed. Letting Cookie lead the way, he used the crutches to get as far as the wheelchair, then switched to the faster method to get to the door.

"Oh, good! You survived the night!" Rain greeted him cheerily. "And uh—*wow*. Um. You need me to wait a minute?"

Rain's gaze was riveted to Garrick's chest in a blatantly appreciative way he hadn't experienced in months. Damn. Felt good. Too good. And his shorts were hardly designed to conceal his body's reaction to Rain's attention if his dick decided to power up like it had last night. Abruptly, he spun away from the door. "Come on in. Sorry. We slept late. Like ten hours. I can't believe it. That never happens to me."

"You must have needed it. Did Cookie stay in her bed all night?"

"She stayed quiet," Garrick hedged, not wanting to hurt his feelings by telling him Cookie had rejected the bed but also not wanting to outright lie either. "She must have needed the rest too. You want to take her out? I'll find both a shirt and her medication while you're gone."

"Sounds great." Rain bounced on the balls of his feet before fetching the leash from the key rack where he'd hung it the night before. His hair was still up, but messier than the day before, and he was wearing silver shorts and a close-fitting pink T-shirt with several members of that pony show Garrick's sister's kids liked, and Squad Goals written under the ponies in swirly script.

"No job interview today?"

"Nope. Didn't want Miss Cookie feeling bad about being the only one in pink. I figured we could match. And I told you. I like it." Rain's eyes were defiant, daring Garrick to object.

"Hey, you wear what you want to wear." Without coffee on board, he was struggling to sound supportive and not lecherous, because *damn*. Rain looked good in pink, all warm and glowing. It made his eyes more golden, and somehow the contrast with his sharp jaw did all sorts of interesting things to Garrick's insides. While his taste in partners could be eclectic, the one unifying feature was usually confidence, because there were few things sexier than a fearless person who knew themselves and what they wanted. He'd already noted Rain's innate confidence the day before, and today's outfit choice only made him that much more appealing.

"Good." Rain clipped the leash to Cookie's collar. "We'll be back."

While they were gone, Garrick found a T-shirt of his own, black and plain because he didn't have the same need for sparkle as Rain, but man, did he appreciate glam in people who enjoyed it. As he made the coffee, he watched Rain and Cookie coming up the sidewalk at a decent trot, Rain's mouth moving like he was talking to the dog. *Cute.* So damn cute. And so very off-limits.

"We made a loop," Rain reported as they came back in. "No lost dog signs. Tonight we'll go the other direction, but I'm not holding out a ton of hope."

"What about your princess picture idea? We can send it to the shelter, maybe put it up in a few other places." Garrick retrieved two clean mugs out of the top rack of the dishwasher.

"I'll do that next." Rain unclipped Cookie before picking up her water bowl and taking it to the sink. He made fast work of rinsing and filling it with fresh water.

"But first coffee. Want a cup? Warning that I make it strong, but it's a local roaster. Very good."

"Dude, I grew up in Portland in a hippie community with a coffeehouse on-site. There's no such thing as too dark, especially if you have some sort of milk on hand."

"Of course. Milk, cream, and flavored creamer in the fridge too because my dad visits, and he's into this new toasted coconut one lately."

"I think I like your dad." Rain opened the fridge and retrieved the bottle of creamer. "Somewhere my mom is having palpitations and doesn't know why because I'm about to ingest all the tasty chemicals."

Garrick had to smile at that. "Guess I should have figured that the cohousing place would be full of health nuts. Are you vegan? It's not chilled, but I've probably got coconut milk somewhere in the pantry too. I went on a curry kick last year and went through a lot of cans."

"I float between vegetarian and vegan. Grandma's

vegetarian. My parents raised us as vegans, but the siren song of dairy occasionally pulls me in, and I'm not as close a label reader as my mom is."

"I love that you rebelled with dairy." Garrick had to laugh as he poured them both cups. "When I was your age—"

"Back in the horse and buggy days." Rain rolled his eyes.

"Yeah, yeah." Garrick wasn't sure whether to be pleased or not that Rain wanted to minimize their age difference. "I was just going to say that Lisa—the ex-fiancée—was a vegetarian, as have been some friends, and that I tried it out in my twenties. My dad acted like I'd gotten prison tats on my face."

"Why'd you go back to eating meat?" Rain sipped his coffee, lounging against Garrick's cabinets. It was nice, having him here. Easy.

"Job. Harder to be vegetarian when you're limited to food at fire camps or on base. And we burn through a ton of fuel between our exercise regimen and the work itself—the way I like to stay in shape, it's just easier for me to be able to eat a variety of protein sources. But, you know, there are vegan weightlifters and stuff, so I'm sure it can be done."

"Good. I was looking over the apps for seasonal employment again last night. You were right about some of my classwork maybe coming in handy. I filled out a bunch of stuff, both here and the positions where you have to mark that you're open to go anywhere."

"And you are?"

Rain shrugged. "Pretty much. I mean, I'll stay if Grandma actually needs help or if I get a job, but otherwise I'm pretty wide open. All about finding that next adventure. I might try again for Portland Fire Academy, but that's not until next spring."

"Why are you so keen on firefighting anyway?" Garrick had to admit it seemed like an odd fit for a hippie veggie kid with a love of pink pony shirts.

"When I was in high school there was a fire at our community. Pretty bad one. It made the news and everything. It wasn't our unit, but we all had to evacuate, and I got to watch the firefighters work for several hours. Seemed like such an adrenaline rush, what they got to do. And they were helping people. They saved most of the buildings. And uh..." Rain looked away, cheeks taking on more color.

"Hot men in uniform?" Garrick was a pretty good guesser. "I'm kinda immune to the uniforms at this point myself, but you're not going to shock me if you were crushing on the firefighters."

"Yeah?" Rain's head tilted as if he was trying to figure Garrick out. And five years ago, Garrick would have let him dangle in the wind, but he was done with closets. He'd seen firsthand how staying quiet had taken too high a toll on more than one friend.

"I'm pan. I mean, I don't exactly put it on a billboard at work, but I decided a while back that I was getting way too old to sneak around with any of my hookups or to make apologies for who those hookups were with. My best friend and his boyfriend are the two with the trio of dogs I mentioned yesterday. So sure, crush away on the hot firefighters."

"Okay, yeah, so uniforms did it for me back then. Big time. Camo. Police. Firefighters." Rain's tentative grin spread wider the more he talked. "Which is funny because I'm so not about uniforms for myself."

He gestured at his T-shirt, more of that adorable blush sweeping across his face. "And I've always liked certain things that society wants to label more femme, but when it comes to attraction…"

"Hey, you don't have to tell me how weird attraction can be." Garrick decidedly was not going to confess his own for Rain's type of person, but he could commiserate without getting skeevy. At least he hoped. Because he wanted Rain to feel comfortable around him, not like he needed to hide any part of himself, but he also didn't want to be the pervy older dude taking advantage either.

"I know." Groaning, Rain took another long swig of coffee. "My brothers think it's hilarious, my thing for hypermasculine-presenting persons. Anyway, I know that those sort of crushes were part of it when I was younger. But the adrenaline and being outdoors and helping people—that's kept me interested through the classes. I'm not cut out for a cubicle."

"Good. But uh…that whole uniform thing? If you get on with one of the seasonal forest service jobs or something, it will probably come with a dress code."

"As long as they aren't dictating my off-duty wear, I'll be fine. And if I start feeling really stifled, I'll just have fun with what's *under* the uniform." Rain's sly smile was a wicked, wicked thing.

"Yeah." Garrick barely got the word out, sputtering through his next sip of coffee, trying to shake the image of Rain in sexy underthings out of his brain and failing miserably. *Damn.* He needed to remind Rain about locker rooms and small-minded people and safety concerns with nonstandard attire, but hell if he could get two words together around the visions dancing in his head. They needed to find this dog a new home and fast. Garrick's sanity demanded it.

The shirt had been a test. Rain could admit that, especially to himself. And to Cookie, who had zero judgment as they plodded along in an evening walk. But it wasn't like some sneaky, malicious thing either. More like he'd been about to get dressed that morning, and his hand had hovered over his jeans a fraction too long. He'd wanted to wear his silver shorts. And this shirt. He'd been in the mood to smile over matching color schemes with Cookie's collar. But then there had been that moment of hesitation. Remembering, he sped up his steps, even his feet impatient with himself.

It was all because he'd had such a good time the day before with Garrick and Cookie. He'd hung around far longer than he'd needed to, teaching her to fetch and doing random tasks for Garrick like emptying the trash so she wouldn't raid it. Not that hanging out with Grandma wasn't fun, but he could listen to Garrick's stories of dogs he had growing up for hours, not to mention the parts about his job that he slipped in as well. And that was exactly why he made himself grab the shirt and shorts. Because jeans and some other less-pink shirt would have been temporarily easier, but it wouldn't have been *him*. He knew himself, knew who he needed to be to be truly happy, and if they were going to be friends, Garrick needed to see that self, all of it.

He slowed down as they rounded the corner for their own street. The way he'd figured it, either Garrick would be cool hanging out with him in his favorite shirt, the one that made him feel awesome inside, or he wouldn't, but at least Rain would know, wouldn't go getting his hopes up for a doomed friendship. So, he'd worn it, not expecting either Garrick's appreciative gaze or his surprising admission that he was pan.

"See? Bravery pays," he told Cookie. And now not only was a friendship still on the table, but also it was open season for crushing guilt-free on Garrick. "Which we're not going to do, right?"

A crush would be a bad, bad idea, even if he was already halfway there. He wasn't sure how long he was staying for one thing, and for another, Garrick seemed rather attached to that hookup lifestyle. And he had other plans for Garrick too, like getting Cookie a forever home.

"How was the walk?" Garrick greeted him as soon as they reentered the house. Cookie headed straight for her water in the kitchen. Garrick was seated in his large recliner, remote in hand, but nothing playing on the TV.

"Great. The weather this time of year is the best. You want to come along in the morning?"

"Come?" Garrick blinked.

"In your wheelchair. I'll hold the leash and manage Cookie, but you can come along."

"Maybe."

That was better than a no, so Rain rewarded him with a grin. "And it goes along with this new idea I had."

"Should I be nervous?" Laughing, Garrick gave him a look that was almost fond. "You do seem full of ideas."

"I am." Rain liked that Garrick had noticed that about him, and it made his insides light and bubbly. "And I was thinking of a trade."

"Aren't we already doing that? I let Cookie stay for

the weekend and you help." Garrick's tone was wary but not uninterested, which Rain would take as a win.

"The weekend went so fast. There's still no owner in sight, and tomorrow's Monday. Maybe we can negotiate an extension?"

"You're really set on her not going to the shelter, aren't you?"

"Well, yeah. The vet had a point—she's not going to be an easy placement, especially injured. If you foster her a little longer, she'll get time to heal."

"And for the actual owner to show." Garrick rubbed his chin. "But I can't ask you to give up part of your day indefinitely. That wouldn't be fair."

"That's where my idea comes in. I was looking over the fitness requirements for the various wildfire fighting positions, and some of those tests look tough." The hotshot crew test was more strenuous than engine work, and smoke jumper requirements were the toughest of all. The differences between the crews had a lot to do with proximity to the fire and danger level of the work undertaken—smoke jumpers went where even the most fearless ground crews couldn't go. Hotshot crews were the pinnacle of those ground firefighters—working the most dangerous parts of the front line, while engine and other crews worked farther back, trying to stop the spread of a wildfire. Each type of crew had its own requirements in terms of work experience, education, and fitness levels, and a surprising competitiveness made Rain want to be able to compete with the people working the riskiest of the jobs.

"Yup. It's hard work," Garrick agreed. His gaze swept up and down Rain, considering. "And you're worried you can't pass?"

"A little. I worry I've been coasting by on good genetics. I ran some cross-country in high school, and I did some running over the winter when I thought I might get into the fire academy, but I didn't really stick with it. None of my friends are exactly fitness buffs, and I've always done my best with being part of a group effort."

"Routine is important. As is accountability. I'm not seeing how the dog and I fit into this though."

"You totally fit." Rain bounced a little, getting into his plan again. "I keep helping you with Cookie, and you train me to meet those hotshot crew requirements. I want to aim high."

"I can't exactly run with you…" Garrick trailed off, mouth quirking, eyes contemplative. He was thinking about it, and that made Rain even bouncier, shifting his weight from foot to foot.

"You wouldn't have to. You can tell me what to do. Let me check in with you. Like you give me the plan, and I follow it, and I help with Cookie in trade for the work of coaching me."

"You really want my advice? I can be somewhat… bossy. I'm not exactly known for going easy on our rookies."

"Bring it on. Work me hard." Rain realized an instant too late that the words might have come out flirtier than he'd intended. Bossy worked for him, in a big way, but he maybe didn't need to go revealing that before Garrick even agreed. However, if Garrick noticed, he didn't let on, instead nodding slowly.

"Guess maybe the dog is growing on me."

"Not me?" Okay, that was definitely flirty, no mistake.

"You? You're trouble." Garrick made a scoffing

noise. "But if you want to hear me rattle on about fitness, I suppose I can do that. I'm going to need to do a little research about how the whole vegetarian thing impacts the nutritional advice I usually give. Doubt I can get you to crack eggs into a whey protein smoothie."

"What? You do that? Ewww." Rain couldn't help making a face as he flopped on the couch opposite Garrick's chair. "I mean, I'll keep an open mind about most of it, but no. No raw eggs."

Garrick laughed, a deep, welcome sound. "I'll do some research. If I come up with a shopping list for you, do you think you can fill it? Stuff like nut butter and some sort of vegan protein powder?"

Rain took that to be a gentle inquiry into the state of his finances. "Yeah, I've got money for food and some to live on until I get a job."

"Sounds good. Want to get me my laptop from the spare room? I'll start now while I'm thinking of it, type up some ideas."

"Absolutely." Rain had to resist the urge to dance around or maybe fist pump like his brothers would. Garrick had agreed far more easily than he'd expected him to, which probably spoke more to boredom and less to Rain's powers of persuasion, but he could dream. If Garrick helped him get in shape, maybe his next adventure was even closer than he thought.

Chapter Four

"I am strangely disappointed by the lack of ponies on your shirt," Garrick joked to Rain as he let him into the house. He was ready for him this time, already in loose track pants, T-shirt, and wheelchair gloves for their Monday morning exercise with Cookie, who was prancing back and forth like Rain was a perfectly cooked T-bone steak, all for her. Garrick shared the enthusiasm, even if he did a better job of hiding it.

"Trust me. I've got more ponies in the wardrobe. I'll remember tomorrow." Rain beamed at him, clearly pleased Garrick had noticed. "This is another of my favorites though, and I wanted long sleeves because it's still a little chilly out. I like how this one makes me feel like a mermaid."

"I can see." Garrick made a show of checking out the undulating green-and-purple shimmery pattern on Rain's slinky long-sleeve pullover as Rain twirled to grab the leash. And to show off because that seemed to be a part of his personality too. Garrick was quickly figuring out that he liked attention. Rain wasn't particularly petite or delicate in build, but somehow that added to the appeal for Garrick, showed another layer of confidence to his fashion choices.

"Did you eat something?" he asked as Rain put Cookie on the leash. "My plan is to make you do pull-ups and some other exercises at the park, get a baseline for what you can already do. You might want to eat something small now, then a bigger meal after. I've got a plan for that too."

"I had a granola bar. I'll be okay. You don't have to feed me if it's too much trouble."

"It's not. I found a vegan pancake recipe that uses stuff I've got on hand, and I'll put on a pot of coffee while I show you the rest of the information I found on-line about adding muscle while vegan or vegetarian."

"You really did research for me?" Rain's appreciative smile, slightly shy with downcast eyes, went straight to Garrick's gut and made him want to do hours more work.

"Of course. You asked me for help. I'm not going to risk giving you bad advice." That and it had been fun, a pleasant distraction with a purpose.

"Thanks." Rain looked like he might want to add more, but Cookie barked and tugged him toward the door. "Okay, okay. Someone wants us to get moving."

"Lead on. And reading nutrition blogs beats trying to find a show to hold my attention. I never was that big on TV to begin with, and now that I have all this time, it's almost torture trying to find non-stupid shows."

"We've got to get you some hobbies." Rain nodded like this was a simple prospect. All his doctors and therapists said the same thing, but so far coming up with a training plan for Rain was the most fun he'd had in quite some time. Still though, he nodded because he knew Rain meant well.

"Coming up with creative ways to whip your ass into shape doesn't count?"

"It's a start," Rain said airily as they headed down the sidewalk. "Growing up, TV was something my mom really limited. My older brother rebelled and became a big movie buff, but for me, I only really like my guilty pleasure of reality TV as background if I'm doing something else, otherwise I get bored like you."

"Well, I'm going to do my best to keep you not bored with this training idea of yours. You may regret asking though."

"Bring it on." Rain gave him a cheeky grin. "I'm not afraid of a little hard work. Or getting sweaty."

Garrick couldn't tell whether it was Rain's emphasis on the word or his own overheated imagination, but suddenly his brain was overtaken by images of Rain sweaty under far more interesting circumstances. Trying to outrun such thoughts, he picked up the pace but paused at the corner.

"After Cookie's foot heals, we'll see if she can run with you, but for now let's head in the direction of the park. We'll warm up on the way there and then I've got a list of things I want you to try."

Rain blinked before laughing. "You weren't kidding about bossy, were you?"

"Nope. Be glad you're not a rookie prepping for a fixed-line parachute jump."

"That's the thing where you dangle from a rope below a plane?" Rain visibly shuddered.

"Little more complicated than that, but that's the gist. It's a training thing, getting the rookies used to practicing proper positioning and timing while still getting assistance from the trainers."

"To be honest, I'm not sure about leaping out of perfectly good airplanes. The hotshot crew sounds more like my speed."

"Not a daredevil?" Garrick had to laugh because smoke jumping certainly wasn't for everyone.

"Not like that. Get me close to danger, with high drama and adrenaline but maybe without flinging myself out of a plane."

"It's the best feeling in the world." Garrick led the way to the entrance for the park, passing out of their neighborhood with its modest older homes to the nicer, bigger ones that ringed the park. He had to breathe deep, trying not to let the memories swamp him. "There's nothing like it. I'd done my time on engine and hotshot crews. Then I had the chance to skydive with this chick I was sorta seeing, and I just knew. Felt like coming home and brand new in the same instant. Like I was born to do it."

"So you went out for smoke jumpers after that? Free jump experience?"

"Yeah. And don't get me wrong. It's not all fun. And I take the job seriously. It's hard work. But those couple of seconds that start each jump… There's nothing on earth that can compare to free fall. It's addictive."

"I bet. I hope…" Rain slowed, voice going softer, more uncertain. "I hope you get a chance to do it again someday."

"Oh, I will." Garrick refused to be anything other than confident about this. "I'm working every day. PT again tomorrow. My therapist will be happy to hear about Cookie and me getting out more."

"I bet. Was it…" His mouth quirking, Rain licked his lips. "It's okay if you can't talk about it, but Grandma said you broke both legs? I'm sorry. I'm being nosy again."

"It's okay. And you don't have to ask her. I can talk about it. Yes, it was a fall from a tree. Both legs broke, a bad concussion, and a spinal cord injury that didn't lead to complete paralysis but has still had some lasting effects, and additional nerve issues from needing a tourniquet for a gash in my thigh."

"Wow. That's a lot. I'm amazed you survived." Rain didn't add that Garrick was lucky, which most people tended to tack on and he never knew how to respond to such sentiments.

"Honestly, me too." And Garrick knew he *was* lucky. Another inch one direction or another, and his story would be completely different. Similar falls had killed friends of his, experienced firefighters who were good, cautious climbers. But knowing that didn't make it easier to take when people handed out platitudes about luck or some greater purpose. And luck went both ways— it was seriously shitty luck to fall and decent luck to not die, and thinking too much about fortunes made his head swim. "At first, doctors said I wouldn't walk again, but I proved them wrong. I'm going to skydive again too."

"Hope so."

Needing to change the subject, Garrick pointed at the paved trail that wove through the park. "If we follow this, we'll hit various obstacles, including pull-up bars. I plan to make you do most of them."

"At your command." Rain's dark eyes sparkled, almost like he knew precisely the effect his flirty tone would have on Garrick.

"Sit-ups." Stopping at the first station, which had a

low bench in front of a sign, Garrick tried for a stern no-more-flirting tone, but he wasn't sure he succeeded. "Focus on form rather than quantity. Start with ten good ones, but five with good form is better than ten where you risk a core muscle injury. And I know you're not sure about skydiving, but even on an engine crew, core strength is vital for being able to hold a position."

It had been years, but Garrick's muscles still burned with the memory of hours and hours digging fireline, working tirelessly to build barriers against the spread of the fire. Not that they didn't do plenty of digging as smoke jumpers too, but it wasn't quite the same as working on a crew with that sole focus for days on end.

"Okay." After giving Garrick the leash, Rain plopped down on the bench and proceeded to give a first effort that had Garrick fearing for his lower back and neck.

"Plant your feet. Use the core, not momentum, and definitely not your arms pulling on your neck. Slow and steady."

"This better?" Rain tried again, two more that were more in line with what Garrick expected.

"That's it. Very good. Nice and easy." Garrick coached through his next few until Rain paused. "That's the way."

"Garrick?"

Something about his tone immediately made Garrick's back tense like he was the one doing crunches. "Yeah?"

"Are you *trying* to turn me on?" Rain looked him up and down, like that might be an actual possibility and not absurd.

"Uhhhh." Garrick made a strangled sound.

"I'll take that as a no. Maybe try being meaner?"

Rain's grin was positively devilish. "I'm just saying, I'm trying to avoid an embarrassing situation here."

"Point taken." *Damn.* On the one hand, Garrick liked Rain's directness. A lot. On the other…he could have lived a much more *comfortable* existence without knowing that apparently Rain liked orders or praise or maybe both. "Try and do another few with good form. I'll stay quiet."

"Oh, I didn't mean you had to be silent." Laughing, Rain rattled off another few sit-ups, form much better now, to the point that Garrick wondered if he'd deliberately been terrible just to get Garrick's corrections. And wasn't that exactly the kind of intriguing development he didn't need.

"Okay, okay. Next obstacle." Garrick got them moving again before Rain could flirt further.

"Good! Lunges. Those I can do." And somehow, someway, Rain made an exercise Garrick had done himself a thousand times ridiculously sexy. "No form corrections?"

"No." Garrick's voice came out too gruff. Rain knew exactly what he was doing and had too much fun doing it, especially when they made their way to the push-up station. Either Rain had avoided all push-ups in high school or he was deliberately torturing Garrick with bad form. "Ass in line with the rest of your body."

"It is." Rain waggled his eyebrows, a nifty trick while prone. "Trust me, if I was sticking my ass out on purpose, you'd know."

"Is this how you are with all your friends?" Garrick was still trying to sort out what Rain was after with the flirting, whether he was simply getting more comfortable around Garrick or what.

"How? Goofy?"

"Yeah. Goofy." Garrick rolled his eyes. If Rain didn't want to own up to the flirting, he sure as hell wasn't going to be the one to force the issue. And quite probably Rain was right—this was how he was with the world at large and not Garrick specifically. "Now to the pull-ups."

"If I can't do any..." Rain showed his first moment of true hesitation in front of the bars. "I haven't tried this in months, since I was trying for the fire academy stuff, and last time I tried I think I got like two out, maybe three. When I was a kid, I could do monkey bars all day long, but a pull-up from a static hang is harder."

"So try for two. For smoke jumpers the minimum is seven, but people don't start out being able to crank out a dozen." Then, not liking the serious expression on Rain's face, he added, "I'm not going to laugh if you can't get over the bar, promise."

"Okay. Here it goes." Rain leaped up to the bar, then dangled. But he made an admirable effort at three pull-ups, and Garrick forgot he was supposed to tone down the praise, cheering him on.

"Way to go. That's how to do it!"

"You know, if you were cheering for me, I probably *could* jump out of an airplane." Rain dropped down, but not before his shirt rode up and shorts drooped, exposing a fuzzy happy trail and some creamy skin. And the hint of a black underwear waistband that was most certainly far from boring white briefs and was going to worm its way into Garrick's brain all day, making him try to imagine what Rain had on under his clothes.

"That's awesome. Thanks." Garrick had no business

feeling as pleased as he did at the compliment or as be-
fuddled as he was at the flash of skin.

"Just facts." Grinning, Rain took the dog back, racing ahead to the next obstacle. He was trouble all right.
Trouble Garrick certainly didn't need, but hell if he
didn't want. And hell if he didn't feel more alive than
he had in months, out here, sunny morning, arm muscles pleasantly burning, prospect of feeding Rain later,
anticipation over what flirty bit of banter Rain might
toss his way next. *Bring it on, Trouble.*

Rain had seldom looked as forward to pancakes as much
as he did as they finished up at the park and headed
back to Garrick's house.

"You sure you want to make me food?" he asked as
they turned for their street, Cookie leading the way.

"Well, technically *you* are going to make you food.
I'm not sure I can manage the griddle balancing on the
crutches, and the wheelchair puts me at an awkward
angle for the counter. So we'll work together. Besides,
I'm interested to see if this oat-and-coconut recipe turns
out without eggs."

"I can help. And it'll turn out. You'd be amazed at
what coconut can do. My mom swears it's one of the
wonders of the world. She uses it for everything from
moisturizer to home remedies to all sorts of cooking."

"I'll take your word for it." Garrick laughed as he
navigated the ramp to his house. And damn, did Rain
ever like that laugh. Maybe that was why he'd been
extra flirty doing the obstacles. Getting Garrick to smile
and laugh was simply the best feeling, and bantering
with him felt natural, like shrugging into his favorite

clothes. It didn't hurt that he had a major kink for bossy people who could dole out praise along with orders.

And sure, he could try and ignore that spark of attraction and arousal, but unless it was making Garrick uncomfortable, he didn't see any reason to deny them both a little fun. He was probably only temporarily in the area and Garrick didn't do relationships, but the more time Rain spent around Garrick, the more a little flirting felt harmless. Fun, even.

After he made sure that Cookie had fresh water and chow, he helped Garrick start the recipe for the pancakes. Working together was fun and made the time go fast.

"Should we make extra for you to bring to Shirley?" Garrick asked as they measured the ingredients.

"Nah. I'll text to make sure, but Grandma was already having her cereal when I left, and she's probably elbow deep in vats of dye by now. I'm supposed to be helping, but she keeps shooing me away."

"Control freak. I sympathize. Letting people help is hard." Garrick's tone was faraway, like he had had too much experience with that.

"I bet." Rain couldn't really imagine being in Garrick's situation, couldn't predict how he'd react, but he was sure there would be a wide range of emotions involved. His parents' friend Paula had talked a little about that, as had his grandma as her arthritis had necessitated more assistance than she preferred. "I think people generally want to be helpful, but sometimes they don't know how or don't know how to not make things worse."

"Yeah, but it can be hard to know when people actually mean it and when they're simply being nice." Garrick stirred the batter rather forcefully.

"Well, I can't speak for others, but I like helping, like with Cookie and stuff. I'm not doing it to be nice or to get the free training out of it—I actually like helping."

"That's the hippie commune spirit talking."

"Yup. That's part of it for sure—how we were raised that kindness costs nothing—but doing stuff for other people feels good." Rain warmed up to the topic as he reached for the batter bowl to start putting pancakes on the griddle. The joining together to do things for others was one of the better parts of the communal living arrangement, resulting in a lasting appreciation for the joys of being useful. "You know how you were talking about skydiving and that rush? Well, when Grandma actually lets me carry one of the dye vats or something, it's a rush too, knowing she needed something and I was able to do it for her. Being the middle kid, a lot of times I got lost in the shuffle, so it's nice to be needed."

"I totally get that." Garrick nodded emphatically.

"Thanks." Others, including Rain's parents, had never quite understood exactly how invisible he could feel when surrounded by people, but he had, and that need to stand out had only gotten stronger as he'd become older. Garrick might be simply being nice, but him trying to empathize made Rain's chest expand.

"Building the raised beds for your grandma was very satisfying, exactly like you said. It's just hard to be the one needing people all of a sudden."

"I'm sure." Rain gave his shoulder a squeeze before flipping more pancakes. And that touch alone was a pleasure, the meaty feel of Garrick's shoulder, the warmth of his body. Yeah, he had it bad, but he wasn't inclined to pull back. Further, he enjoyed how Garrick relaxed into the touch, as if soaking up the contact, not flinching away.

Reluctantly, he moved away, doing a little shimmy as he got into stacking up the pancakes. Garrick made a strangled sound.

"What?"

"Shorts. Either we need to feed you a lot more or your elastic has issues."

"Ah." They'd dipped a couple of times at the park too, a particularly loose pair that went with the mermaid top, but apparently they'd dipped low enough to reveal a strip of his underwear. Just a hint of lace on the waistband really, but the way Garrick's eyes were riveted to it, one might think there was fire involved. Or maybe that was simply the heat sizzling between the two of them, some sort of charged energy. "Problem?"

"No." Garrick's gaze didn't waver and Rain didn't hike the shorts up. This was the exact opposite of feeling invisible, lost in a crowd, and the singular attention made his pulse speed up.

"Wanna see more?" He fingered the waistband of his shorts. "I'm not shy."

"That you're not." Garrick's voice was all low and husky.

"Maybe you'd like this pair as much as my pony shirt…" Rain was seconds from dropping his shorts altogether when the pancake closest to him started sizzling, that too-done aroma filling the air. Hiking his shorts back up, he saved the pancake from near doom but singed his finger in the process. "Crap. Crap."

"Did you burn yourself?" Rolling closer, Garrick's expression went from seductive to concerned.

"Not too bad." Setting aside the pancakes, he ran his finger under cold water. "I'll live."

"Bandage needed? I've got a first aid kit. God, I'm sorry. I distracted you."

"No bandage or apology needed." Rain brought both plates to the nearby table, which already had one chair pushed to the back wall to make space for Garrick. "I like the distraction. A lot."

He took the chair on the end, closer to Garrick, rather than across the table, Garrick still sputtering on about being sorry.

"Seriously, dude. Quit apologizing. I think we both could use more...diversions. In fact, I propose we start after breakfast." He gave Garrick what he hoped was a seductive and not maniacal smile. He didn't have a ton of practice with seduction, but no time like the present to start.

"*Rain*..." Garrick trailed off and cut his pancakes into rough hunks before spearing one particularly hard.

"Yes?" Rain prompted because he wasn't a mind reader. He was well aware that he could be somewhat... much for certain people, but Garrick's tone wasn't that kind of fed up.

"You don't need to show me anything. Or flirt. You know that, right? I'll help train you and keep the dog regardless of how...*friendly* you are."

Rain had to blink at this turn of reasoning. "You're worried you're taking advantage of me? Not the other way around?"

"I am the older one." Garrick nodded sharply. "I don't...ah...want you feeling obligated."

More than a little amused, Rain shook his head. "And if I don't? If I simply enjoy flirting and love being a distraction? Can I keep doing me or you need me to tone it down?" Rain didn't particularly want to dial down the flirting, but Garrick being uncomfortable was no good either.

"You do you. Whatever makes you happiest. I mean that."

That was probably as close to a green light as he was going to get, and Rain had to resist the urge to wriggle in his chair. He liked that Garrick both seemed to get him and wanted to indulge him.

"And if showing you my unmentionables would make me happy?" he pushed. Only a little. Because Garrick said he could.

"Rain..."

"That's not a no." He still made no move to stand and drop his shorts, because it wasn't a yes either, and being the diversion Garrick needed would be much more fun with him enthusiastically on board.

"It's a bad idea. Even if... Heck. I'm not sure I can—"

The doorbell cut Garrick off before he could explain further, leaving Rain to try to fill in the gaps. Bad idea because Garrick knew it was likely a temporary thing? Or because he was concerned about some stupid age gap? Or because he couldn't physically go there? Rain hadn't considered that last possibility, and if that was the case, he'd like to know more, see if there was a way for Garrick to feel good that accommodated his injuries. But he didn't get his chance to ask as Garrick quickly rolled to the door and let in an older, more barrel-chested clone of himself—dark blond hair shot through with gray, tall, big build, and Garrick's same sharp blue eyes and angular, chiseled features.

"Did I mess up the day for PT?" Frowning, the man,

who had to be Garrick's dad, asked as his gaze swept over the room, taking in Rain and the breakfast table.

"It's Tuesday this week. Crap. I forgot to send you a reminder text last night. It's been crazy with all the stuff with the dog."

"Dog?" Garrick's dad shifted his attention from Rain and the dining nook to Cookie, who was attempting to hide her bulky body behind Garrick's chair, not coming out to say hello. "Ah. I see now. Shy sweetheart. It's not a visitor?"

For a suffocating moment, Rain wasn't entirely sure that he meant the dog.

"Long story," Garrick said with a groan. "She's temporarily my dog. And this is Rain, my neighbor who is helping me out with her. Rain, this is my dad, Kenny."

"Hi." Rain gave a wave, which Kenny returned with a nod.

"I see."

"I've got the coffee on. You want to help yourself to a cup? I've still got some of that creamer you liked."

"Sure." Kenny's mouth moved like he still wasn't sure what to make of Cookie, Rain, or their breakfast. "You cooked?"

"Well, Rain helped a lot. But, yeah. There are more pancakes by the stove. And no bacon, so your doctor will thank me even if you won't."

"You with your health kicks. But guess I could eat." Not seeming too put out at the change in plans, Kenny grabbed a cup of coffee and a plate with two pancakes. He brought them to the seat opposite Rain but kept talking to Garrick. "So, if tomorrow's PT, why do you look ready for a workout?"

"I did exercise a little." Garrick was pretty close

to adorable when he preened, and Rain resolved to drag him on every outing from here on out. "I'm helping Rain train for a shot on one of the wildfire crews. Maybe an engine since he's a total newb."

"*Garrick.*" Kenny used the same long-suffering tone Garrick had when he was exasperated.

"What?" Garrick's expression was carefully innocent.

"You're still all-in on going back, aren't you? Can't leave it well enough in the past, maybe get a new—"

"Hobby. I know. And training Rain *is* my new hobby. A fun one." Garrick's grin made Rain's stomach flip even as he hated watching the conflict between father and son. "And as for going back, I told you. That's my goal. I know you hate the risks, but it's a part of me. You should understand. I bet you'd have stayed on a hot-shot crew if Mom hadn't made you quit. Some things get in your blood."

"Maybe so, but that doesn't mean it's a risk worth taking. And your mother didn't *make* me quit. You'll see if you ever settle down. It's different with kids in the picture." The father-son bickering, while not loud, was enough to have Rain eying the front door and debating whether Cookie needed a second walk.

"Hey. I am settled. Job I love. House I own. Almost got the pet thing handled too. Rain, tell him that I'm plenty domesticated already."

"Hell no. I'm not getting in the middle of this." Having a healthy sense of self-preservation, Rain quickly cleared his and Garrick's plates, making sure his shorts stayed up this time. He wondered if Garrick was out as pan to his dad. Kenny's multiple quizzical looks for

Rain might suggest so, but whether he approved was anyone's guess.

"Smart." Kenny winked in Rain's direction. "You both know I'm right. It's not worth the risks of going back, even if it ends up being possible."

Not worth the risks. The same could be said of pursuing a flirtation with Garrick, but that wasn't about to stop Rain. And he doubted that Garrick was going to be swayed by that logic either.

"We're going to have to agree to disagree. Finish your pancakes." Garrick had the tone of someone who'd had this argument a time or ten and who loved his dad, but not this topic.

And maybe Rain didn't like the risks to Garrick's life that smoke jumping presented either, but he knew the truth of what Garrick said. Firefighting was a part of that man's *soul*. So for his sake Rain hoped a comeback was possible. And to that end, if Rain could be a pleasant distraction on the road to recovery, so much the better. If Garrick was going to be Rain's cheering squad, the least he could do was return the favor.

Chapter Five

Garrick liked Rain. He liked his devious smile, liked his confidence, liked his readiness to help, and really liked his humor. What he didn't like, however, was the way Rain was under his skin, running through his dreams, worming his way into his idle thoughts, making Garrick count down the hours until he saw him again. Like right then, he was supposed to be at PT, and his body was hanging out on the parallel bars, but his mind was back on Rain, thinking about how fun the morning exercise had been, Rain managing an extra pull-up and gamely trying the extra exercises Garrick had devised for him. Rain had picked up vegan protein powder, so they'd made recovery smoothies and enjoyed them on the patio until Garrick's dad had arrived to take him to physical therapy.

His dad was using the time Garrick was at PT to do a shopping run at the big warehouse store. Garrick had ordered up extra frozen fruit and nuts.

"You feeding the neighbor now too?" His dad had looked up from the list he was jotting down to study him.

"Yup." Garrick was years beyond apologizing for who he had as a friend, and even if there was the whole age difference thing and the whole shouldn't-let-Rain-flirt thing, they were making a friendship. His dad could deal. And he knew his dad, knew he didn't object to Rain as much as the idea of Garrick setting his sights on getting back on the smoke jumping crew.

"Hope you know what you're doing." Shaking his head, his dad had headed for the store, leaving Garrick hoping the same.

And now, here he was, one foot in front of the other, still thinking about Rain. Hell, he was almost glad for the distraction, taking his mind off how this wasn't getting any easier. His balance without the crutches was still unpredictable, going from sort of okay to weaving like he was three sheets to the wind to his ass on the floor, none of those outcomes optimal.

"When do I get new braces?" he asked his physical therapist, Stephanie, an enthusiastic woman around his age with boundless energy who was currently cheering him on, hovering close by. He was ready to try anything that got him moving with a more natural gait and balance.

Glancing away, Stephanie gave a rare frown. "I thought you'd heard. Your insurance denied trying the braces with built-in functional electrical nerve stimulators. The problem is that you're already ambulatory without the assistance of a neuroprosthesis. Your insurance is balking at covering something new for you at this time."

"And paying out of pocket is gonna be a no-go?" He'd already paid from his own funds for his bed and other expenditures the insurance didn't cover, which kept cutting into his reserves.

Confirming his fears, Stephanie quoted an eye-popping sum that didn't include all the required extra PT for the system to work properly. "Also, your doctors and medical team seem inclined to agree with the insurance that the location of your injury makes any FES system less likely to show significant improvements. Right now, your best bet is to continue this course of therapy. I know you're frustrated, but the improvements are there. I see a lot more hip and ankle strength from you lately."

Garrick released a frustrated noise, which made Stephanie frown further. "Sorry. I'm just anxious to get back out there. Doctors all talk about how the spinal cord injury was incomplete, not as serious. I figured getting strength back from the broken bones would be the more important thing. And now I am stronger, but the body's still not cooperating."

"I feel you. And all spinal injuries are serious, if you ask me. Also, every person is different in how they respond. It's all very unpredictable."

He knew all about unpredictable—two nights ago he'd had vivid erotic dreams about Rain, waking up feeling energized about his chances of getting a sex life back without needing to bring the issue up with his doctor. But then last night, he'd tried indulging in a little self-loving only to get more mixed results. Was there a way to bring up that kind of variability with Stephanie? She was married with three kids and usually unflappable, but before he could wrap his mind around the question, she turned away, pointing at one of the low tables used for various exercises and therapies.

"Now, let's get you over to the table for some more stretching work." Handing him his crutches, she led the way, movements easy and efficient but not inviting more discussion either. As he was following her across the wide, open space, he heard his name called.

"Garrick Nelson! Just the man I wanted to run into today." Fred Adams was a friend of Garrick's father, had served on a hotshot crew with him back in the day, and now had worked his way up to a high level in the local forest service office. He'd been rehabbing from rotator cuff shoulder surgery, and they'd seen each other a few times at PT now. With a light jacket on and a magazine under his arm, he looked to be finishing up his session.

"Oh?" He got settled on the table, leaving Fred to pull up a nearby chair.

"You go ahead and talk to Mr. Cranky while I get him stretched out," Stephanie said to Fred. "The distraction will be good for him."

"Hey, I'm not cranky," Garrick protested.

"You're frustrated. And I get it. Now let's work on those hip flexors." She started the routine of helping him achieve deep stretches while he tried to give at least some of his attention to Fred.

"You were looking for me?"

"Yes. Look, I know you're bummed about not jumping this fire season, but I've got a proposition for you I think you'll like."

"I'm listening." *Bummed* was a major understatement, but he wasn't going to unpack all his feelings with Fred.

"So, I could use another dispatcher. It's part-time seasonal, so you should be able to work your medical appointments around it."

"To be honest, I've never seen myself doing a desk job." He tried to avoid a grimace that was as much from a particularly deep stretch as from the prospect of office work.

"I know—none of us old frontline guys like paper pushing. And I'm not saying it's the most exciting, but you know fire logistics better than almost anyone I know. You did your time on engine and hotshot crews. You'll get who you're sending out and why on a deeper level than most. You've got fast reflexes and you know how to keep a level head."

"Damn. You keep talking me up, and you're gonna write the application for me. But thanks. Your opinion, that matters to me." His chest went warm at all the compliments. Fred was right, too. Garrick was damn good at his job, which was why he needed back out there. And he had a point that it wasn't exactly like Garrick had other plans for his summer. And money would be good, especially with the insurance company balking at paying for stuff. But still he hesitated.

"We've got a good team going at headquarters. And it's not an entry-level position at all. Not much busy work. You'd have a fair bit of responsibility and autonomy. That's why I thought of you. I need someone I can trust in the role."

"I respect that. Thanks."

"You should take it," Stephanie added to the conversation, looking up from manipulating Garrick. "Your PT isn't filling all your time, and you keep complaining about being bored. And you never know, this could be the start of something great for you."

And that right there was why Garrick was reluctant. He didn't need a new career path, didn't want to take his eyes off the prize of returning to smoke jumping, didn't want a job better suited to persons more ready for a desk job. Not him. Being at a desk, on a radio while others handled the action? Torture.

"Can I think about it?" he hedged. He didn't want to turn Fred down outright, but he also legit did need time to reflect.

"Of course. But don't keep me waiting too long. I need to get my personnel set before the season gets truly underway."

"Understood. I'll let you know soon."

He kept his promise too, continuing to think even once Fred left, after trying to sell him more on the logistics, mentioning flexible hours again and the possibility of getting rides with others in the office. God, how Garrick missed driving. And his ankle strength was better all the time, but he still wasn't sure when the go-ahead to try driving would come. Damn slow recovery. Maybe the job would be the distraction he needed. Might be smarter to use that rather than overly relying on Rain's flirtations.

However, he kept his mouth shut about the job on his way home. He already knew his dad would be all in favor of him taking the job, but he wouldn't see it as temporary, a way station on his way to the job he already had and loved. His dad would be too enthusiastic, and maybe that was part of what was holding Garrick back. Regardless, it wasn't his dad he was eager to talk to about the opportunity. Surprising even himself, he was already anticipating Rain's next visit, wanting to hear his thoughts. Cookie got a fast walk from Garrick's dad, but she, too, was dancing as Rain appeared after dinner.

"You're coming? Figured you'd be too tired after

physical therapy." Rain gestured at how Garrick was already in his chair, gloves on.

"Too keyed up to rest. And I need your opinion on something."

"Me?" Rain's pleased smile had Garrick skin's tingling, almost like they'd touched. Making Rain happy was an unexpected side benefit. And even if he was already leaning towards accepting Fred's offer, he took his time laying out the prospect as they made their way around the neighborhood, a healing Cookie able to handle a faster pace now.

"So I'd still be able to keep training you. And keep up with my PT. I'm not entirely sure why I'm so reluctant."

"Because it's not what you really want." Rain offered him a sympathetic smile as he stopped for Cookie to sniff some grass. "You're afraid it will make you miss being out there even more, hearing the operations, that sort of thing. And you're not a paperwork guy."

"Exactly." That was it. Garrick's back tightened at the thought of not being in the thick of the action. That was going to be hard.

"It's okay to miss it. To get angry or grieve even—"

"I'm not angry." Garrick cut off that line of reasoning. "These things happen. Injuries are part of the job. Sure, I'm bummed about missing the season. And if I take the job, at least I'll still be helping. Being useful is good."

"Yeah, it is. But you're still allowed to have feelings."

"I know." Garrick rolled ahead a little way before sighing and slowing back down. "Sorry. I'm being ridiculous. It's a good job with pay I need, and I've pretty much known all afternoon what I'd choose. I just wanted... Hell, I'm not even sure."

"To be validated. You wanted some validation. And that's normal, and I'm totally happy to be that friend for you." Rain gave him another of those tentative smiles that went right to Garrick's gut, as surely as his sexier, more confident grins did too.

"You're a good friend to have," Garrick said gruffly.

"Anytime." Rain's voice was all happy now. Garrick liked how he didn't hide his emotions—it was generally easy to tell what he was thinking, and that was refreshing. Maybe it was the communal upbringing, but he didn't have the same reserved nature as most of the people Garrick had grown up with. Despite all the tourist dollars flowing into the region, this was still a rural community with good, solid country folk who didn't talk about things like validation and grief over having to take a job he'd rather not. But Rain did. And that was nice.

Dangerous too, how much Garrick was coming to like him. Crushing on a much younger person who wasn't sticking around when Garrick had no idea what he could bring to the table romantically was a bad idea. And yet when Rain and Cookie jogged ahead of him, he still totally tried to guess what Rain had on under his shorts. Yep. He was screwed.

"We've got a problem." Rain had walked over to Garrick's rather than text him because he was agitated enough to not want to type and needed to move. The late Friday afternoon air had a chill to it, like spring had fallen down on the job.

"Oh?" Garrick rubbed his face, and Rain realized belatedly that he might have been napping. His shirt was rumpled and he was leaning heavily on his crutches. Crap. Rain should have texted after all. Garrick was probably worn out with another PT appointment that day after his morning exercise with Rain. The guy really did work hard, and he did not need the headache Rain was about to dump on him.

"I hate to bother you, but the shelter in Bend called me. I gave them my number when I sent in the new pics. Anyway, apparently they've got a family from east of Bend who says they lost a rottie two weeks ago near here. They say, and I quote, 'She looks too dainty and girlie, but maybe...' *Whatever.* They want to see her in person."

"Where are they going to meet her?" Garrick looked rather grim at the news. Not angry or even sad, more just resigned. Which Rain hated. He didn't like being the bearer of more disappointment in a season filled with far too many of them for Garrick. It meant something that he'd come to Rain on Tuesday to talk out the job offer. Being needed like that, truly needed, was the best kind of compliment, and one he could get used to.

"Yeah. The shelter asked if I could take her into Bend today—they don't like sending strangers to private addresses for liability reasons, and apparently the family is dealing with some car trouble as well. That's why they were stopped near Painter's Ridge anyway. I was hoping I could talk you into coming along? I figure if there's a chance I'm going to be sad on the drive back, at least I could have some company for my misery."

Garrick gave a slow smile and nod. "At least you know what you need. I admire that in a person. Directness and self-awareness. And you're an extrovert like me. When I was younger, if I got in a brooding mood, I'd head to the sports bar so at least I would be around other people."

"Sub coffeehouse for bar, and that's totally me. And so you'll come?"

"Yeah." Garrick looked off into the mountains before turning to go into the house, leaving Rain to follow him.

"I don't want to bring her things." Rain was being stubborn. And petty.

"Rain…" Garrick's tone had more sympathy than censure. He transferred to the wheelchair before collecting his wallet and phone from the table. "If they're her family, she's going to have to go back."

"And if they're not?"

Drawing a long breath, Garrick took a moment before answering. "I'm not sure."

"We're not leaving her at the shelter!"

"No, we're not." His tone was calming now, the same one he used with Cookie, and Rain tried to let go of his rattled nerves. "We've established that I'll foster her, but isn't this what we want? Her to have a permanent family?"

The way Rain saw it, Cookie already *had* a forever home. Garrick simply hadn't woken up to that fact yet. "Come on. Admit it. You'll miss her."

Dark clouds crossed Garrick's eyes, and for a second, Rain thought he'd pushed too far, especially as Garrick studied the gloves he was putting on, not Rain.

"Yeah. Okay. I'll miss her. Maybe a lot. But sometimes doing the right thing sucks."

"Isn't that the truth. I hate being an adult sometimes."

"Well, I have a lot more practice at it than you, and I can tell you that it doesn't get any easier. However, you do what you gotta do, even when it hurts." That sounded a lot like a motto for Garrick's whole life, and Rain wanted to follow up on it, but Garrick rolled toward the door. "Let's go."

They loaded up Cookie and her things—which Garrick insisted on bringing, damn adulting again—and Garrick's wheelchair in near silence. The quiet continued on the drive. They made sparse conversation about Garrick's job application and Rain's continued job hunt, but otherwise they each brooded alone in their thoughts. And it was kind of nice, not needing to fill the air with a lot of chatter. Garrick seemed to understand that Rain didn't want to be alone, and he didn't need Rain to entertain him the way a lot of Rain's friends did. There was no extra tax on hanging out with him—he didn't have to be the funny, flirtatious one all the time to earn Garrick's company. He'd discovered that this weekend and liked it a lot.

"Should we take her collar off?" Garrick asked as they pulled into the shelter parking lot. "If that was throwing the family…"

"Cookie likes her pink. She doesn't need to put it away simply so they see past it. Either she's their dog or not." Tone strident, he was talking about a hell of a lot more than the dog's fashion sense.

And somehow Garrick knew because after Rain parked, he patted Rain's leg, a rare physical contact from him. "I know. I get it, okay? Collar stays."

They unloaded, and Rain was glad to see the building was one level without steps, something he hadn't thought about before making the drive and probably should have. The shelter employee working the reception desk greeted them, gave Cookie a biscuit, and led them to a little visitation room with a few chairs and tile floor.

"The family should be here shortly. They were looking at some of our other animals."

Rain sat and petted Cookie and hoped they found either their missing pet or another animal they couldn't live without. Finally, the door opened, and in came an average-looking mom, dad, and school-age kid. Country, with plaid shirts and jeans, all three, but not disreputable in the slightest. Not the totally unsuitable owners Rain had built up in his head, and his stomach sank further. This was it, and he was going to have to be nice and gracious and then start from scratch on getting Garrick a forever furry friend.

"Ursula?" The woman tilted her head, studying Cookie, who made no move to leave Rain, her usual reserve in full display as she stayed between him and Garrick.

"It's not her!" the boy wailed. "My Ursula *always* knows me."

"She's his best friend." The mom sighed. "No way would she not greet us."

"Oh." Garrick exhaled hard, a big whoosh, and Rain tried to memorize the relief in his eyes because it was potent stuff. That was what true love was—he'd been willing to give Cookie up because it was the right thing to do, but he sure as hell hadn't wanted to, that much was evident.

"I'm so sorry," Rain said to the family and meant it. "I hope you find Ursula soon."

"We're getting her a friend. For in case she comes back, right?" The boy turned to his mother, who reluctantly nodded.

"Someone fell in love with a poodle mix out in the shelter's kennel." The woman gave a tight smile. "We'll be okay. You going to keep this one if you don't find an owner? She's so shy. I'd worry about her in a big kennel with lots of dogs."

"She just takes a while to warm up." Garrick scratched Cookie's head. "Don't you?"

Cookie's answer was a canine grin as she leaned into Garrick's head.

"She's not going to the shelter." Rain gave Garrick an expectant look.

"No, she's not. And yeah, she's got a place with me. As long as she needs it." It was as decisive as Garrick had been thus far about keeping Cookie, and Rain grinned so wide his face started to hurt.

After goodbyes and good wishes had been exchanged, they headed back out to the car. Rain was carrying some new toys for Cookie in a little bag because they'd passed the shelter's gift shop, and he hadn't been able to resist letting her pick out something fun.

"We should celebrate," he said to Garrick.

"The stuffed llama isn't celebration enough?" Garrick laughed and stretched. "Seriously though, not cooking sounds awesome, but I don't want to leave her in the car, and it's too chilly tonight to sit on a patio someplace that might not care if she's with us."

"So we celebrate at your place." Rain kept his tone light, flirty but not pushy. "I have some ideas."

"Oh, I'm sure you do." Garrick groaned as he stood and slid into the passenger seat. "I'm almost afraid to ask."

"Don't be afraid. There's no biting involved. Unless you ask very nicely." Finished settling Cookie in the back seat, he stowed the wheelchair and headed to the driver's side.

"And see, that's what I'm afraid of right there."

"That I make you want to ask?" Rain waggled his eyebrows at Garrick before backing out of the parking space.

"You make me crazy is what you do," Garrick muttered.

"Come on. Tell me your ideal Friday night." Rain tried another tactic, deciding that less was maybe more in getting what he wanted from Garrick, which was more time together. And very possibly more flirting. Both because it was fun and because he couldn't seem to stop. "Grandma's out with some fabric artist friends in Sisters. Don't make me hunt down fun on my own."

"You might have to. Right now, my ideal night is pizza and wings and my hot tub, but none of that's happening. Honestly, I'll probably just reheat something and work on my plan for your workouts next week."

"Why isn't it happening?" Seemed like a perfectly reasonable request to him. "Tub not operational?"

"No, it works. And Dad has helped me use it a couple of times now, but it's a big hassle. I can't do it on my own, that's for damn sure."

"Well, luckily I'm here. And I think I've already established that I'm stronger than I look. I hammered out the push-ups you assigned me this morning. I can help. And the pizza?"

"It's hardly the most vegan-friendly food. And the place I really like in town doesn't do delivery. I've asked them to get on one of those apps, but they haven't yet."

"So? Call it in. I'll pick it up. These are minor inconveniences."

"I feel like I'm making you do a lot of extra work just to hang out with me." Garrick groaned. "Sorry. I'm not usually such a drag. Stephanie worked me extra hard in PT. I'm more sore than usual, and that's making me cranky."

"And then I dragged you into Bend. I'm sorry. I didn't think to ask if you were up for it."

"Because I wanted to be. Kinda like I'd like to be up for going out, but instead, even staying in like I want means needing a hand."

"Which I am happy to give. Seriously. I won't have to eat alone, and there's a hot tub involved. Win. Also, I'll get to see whatever this pizza place can do with crust and vegetables, and we just won't tell my mom about the cheese."

"Okay, okay. We are celebrating after all. Bring on the cheese. They do a nice vegetarian one with spinach and artichokes. I'll eat that so we don't have to make them split it down the middle. I don't need meat if I'm getting the wings too."

"Call it in," Rain ordered in his best impression of Garrick's take-charge tone, which got him laughing as intended.

They laughed their way back to Painter's Ridge, Garrick giving him directions to the little hole-in-the-wall pizza joint, which also seemed to function as a pool hall and biker bar.

"This is the best pizza in the area?"

"You'll love it. Come on, you Portland people will eat anything that falls off the back of a food truck if they call it a cute enough name. And it's not as scary inside as it looks. Want me to come in with you?"

"Nah." Rain waved away Garrick's offer of two

twenties as well. "My treat for the celebration. You rest up for the hot tub adventure."

Garrick's look that fell somewhere between apprehensive and speculative had exactly enough heat to have Rain whistling as he made fast work of collecting the food from a burly guy in a too-tight tie-dyed T-shirt that looked like one of Grandma's early designs. Rain needed to find a job and fast, but he couldn't let Garrick pay for everything. He'd been feeding him most mornings too.

Besides, he really was celebrating. Cookie got to stay and he was about to get into a hot tub with a super attractive, super nice guy. And he was already dreaming up ways to get Garrick to skinny-dip. Bring on the adventure, indeed.

Chapter Six

Garrick had had people interested in getting him un-dressed before, and hell, he'd be lying if he didn't admit he'd installed the hot tub in part because it made the road to consensual naked happy times that much more fun and easy. But few, if any, of those persons had been so downright gleeful as Rain at the prospect.

"I vote skinny-dipping. After we eat." Rain toted the food into the house, almost bouncing at his idea, which he presented in the same tone Garrick's younger self might have mentioned hot fudge sundaes.

"Laundry day or…" Garrick didn't think Rain was out to get laid, nor did he imagine curiosity about his scars was driving Rain either.

"Nah. More like I don't want to rummage through a pile of suitcases for swim trunks I hate anyway."

"You still haven't unpacked?" Garrick followed him to the dining area, Cookie fast behind them both.

"Not a high priority. Rotating stuff into drawers as I do laundry," Rain said dismissively.

"Fair enough." And that was also a good reminder that Rain wasn't about putting down roots. "And I've said before, you wear what makes you happy. Not some-thing that you hate."

"So that's a yes to my idea or more of a keep-your-underwear-on compromise?" Rain set out the pizza and plates with the same efficiency as his tone, easy as if he ate here all the time and not like they'd only known each other a week. He slid into the chair to Garrick's left and started dishing out the food.

"How about the compromise?" Garrick tried to sound like that was practical and not like he had any interest in seeing Rain's underthings. And honestly, he wasn't sure whether he was more concerned his dick would misbehave while skinny-dipping or that it wouldn't.

"Oh man. This is *good*." Rain dug into the pizza with an almost orgasmic intensity, nostrils flared, eyes wide, mouth lush, and suddenly Garrick's worries about his dick being offline were unfounded because *damn*. He wanted more of that look and he wanted to be the cause of it.

"Yeah, it is," he said gruffly as he helped himself. The pizza was exactly as he remembered—chewy crust that wasn't too thin, like some local places', creamy pesto-laced sauce, briny artichokes, and fresh spinach. "This is what I was craving. Thanks."

"I'll brave the big, scary biker dudes to get you more of this anytime."

"They're not so bad." Garrick laughed, then sobered as he remembered that Rain wasn't him, wasn't from around here, and was wearing a lavender sweatshirt with a delicate pattern and slim fit. "Did someone hassle you? Maybe I should have gone—"

"Chill. No one gave me a hard time. And I could handle myself if they did."

"Okay." Garrick had picked up on what Rain had been trying to say in the car—he wasn't changing for anyone, and his style was a part of him, something essential, not a costume he put on for kicks. And Garrick could be worried for him in certain situations, but he wasn't going to lecture and potentially make Rain uncomfortable. That was the last thing he wanted.

"I'm regretting getting you the wings." Rain's voice was mischievous, not particularly grossed out, but Garrick still set aside the one he was eating.

"Vegetarian thing or..."

"Or. My feelings about the source are...mitigated, you could say, by you licking sauce off your fingers."

"Is this like the me-giving-orders thing?" Garrick's abs tightened at the thought of unintentionally turning Rain on again.

"Oh yeah." Rain's grin was an easy, friendly thing, not especially seductive, more like he was having great fun flirting and enjoying being around Garrick, which was more than a little infectious.

"I'm not sure whether I should put them aside for later or eat even slower and torture you more."

"Torture. Always choose torture." Eyes sparkling, Rain grabbed another piece of pizza.

Self-conscious now in a way he wasn't used to being, Garrick took more pizza himself. Unlike Rain, who could make eating something he enjoyed sound like a low-key orgy, he didn't really know *how* to be seductive while eating outside of the unintentional. And he still wasn't entirely sure whether turning Rain on was a good idea.

Leading them both on seemed like a recipe for disaster, yet he couldn't deny how good the flirting and banter felt, especially when he gave in and did eat another wing, and Rain did an exaggerated swoony sigh simply to make him laugh. It was a lightness he hadn't had in months.

"Now tell me how to help make your hot tub dreams come true." Rain managed to sound all fairy god-mother-y as they packed the leftovers away. Garrick enjoyed how he managed to make the offer sound fun but not cheesy and how he always did it like that, defer-ring to Garrick to know what it was he needed or how he wanted things done.

"I can undress myself fine. Slow. But fine." No way was he asking Rain for help undressing. Mainly be-cause Rain's hands all over him sounded like an awe-some idea, but also a prelude to something a lot more intimate than whatever flirty friendship they currently had going. The warier parts of Garrick weren't ready to go there. Yet. "It's the getting in and out of the tub where I need a lot of help. I just don't have the hip or ankle range of motion or the balance."

"Well, that's what I'm here for. My folks have a smaller one on their deck for…close friends, and there's a bigger communal one that the community operates for everyone."

"Close friends?" Garrick had picked up on Rain's cagey tone there.

"They're poly. As are a lot of their friends. And one of their good friends a while back used a wheelchair—I helped her some, so that's how I knew how your chair folded and stuff."

Ah. That made some sense—he'd been wondering how Rain got to be so insightful about what Garrick both needed and didn't. "That's cool. I've been around poly people before. Fun dates."

"Is there a type of person you haven't dated?" Rain laughed.

Garrick pretended to think a moment. "Not really. But I'm probably not quite as...active as you're picturing. The fire season keeps us plenty busy, and in the winters, pickings outside of the ski tourists can be slim. It's a small town."

"And you've dated your way through it. I feel you." Rain shook his head, amusement still dancing in his eyes. "Anyway, you want me to go check out the tub and you can get undressed at your own pace in here?"

"Yeah. That sounds good." Smooth too, the way it took the pressure off Garrick needing to be fast. "There are towels in the hall bath—grab a couple, please."

"Sure thing."

Grateful to not need to demonstrate his new painstaking way of undressing, he retreated to his room. His grabber tool helped him with his slip-on shoes, and he wriggled out of his pants sitting on the bed. He'd let Rain have his no swim trunks thing, but he left his own black boxer briefs on, at least for the moment. And because crutching across the deck in the chilly evening air was likely to be a slow effort, he shrugged into his old fleece robe, which was in the closet next to various castoffs from parties past—swimsuits, towels, assorted robes and cover-ups that weren't his, unclaimed stuff he kept meaning to donate—and his hand paused near a silky emerald robe.

Pretty. Sexy. It was a dangerous idea, but the vision of Rain in the garment slithered through him, warming him way more than his own wrap. Unable to shake the thought, he draped the spare robe around his neck before carefully making his way out to the hot tub.

"Hey, Skinny-Dipping King, I brought you something," he said as Rain stood from where he'd been sitting on one of the deck chairs. He already had the cover off the tub and the water bubbling. Cookie was napping by one of the loungers, already bored with the proceedings. "Someone left this here several parties ago. Thought you might like to borrow it."

He tossed the jewel-toned robe at Rain, who easily caught it.

"Oh *nice*." Rain smiled, his shyer, pleased one that he usually kept hidden behind his wider, flirtier front. "I'm going to try it on."

Apparently, the whole no-modesty thing the other day wasn't a fluke because Rain pulled off his sweatshirt right there, not even sparing a glance at Garrick. His chest was more muscled than Garrick might have expected, with intriguing fuzz across his pecs. Still in his pants, Rain put the robe on before Garrick had a chance to truly look his fill.

"It feels amazing. Forget the tub, I might want to bond with this all night."

"It's yours then."

"Really?" Rain's whole face lit up, making Garrick want to buy up all the silky garments in the area.

"It's been a couple of years at least. Doubt its owner has missed it and they probably didn't enjoy it as much as you seem to."

"I do like it." Rain twirled once, robe flapping in the night breeze, before pushing down his black pants, some sort of slinky workout material that were nominally track pants but that clung to his ass in all sorts of good ways. And—

"Sweet Jesus." Garrick's voice went gruff and his

eyes flew open so wide it was a wonder they stayed in his head at all. Damn. He should have been better prepared and braced himself, but maybe there was no preparing for Rain in sheer, lacy black briefs that while covering the essential bits left little to Garrick's already overheated imagination.

"You like." Rain's grin was both surprised and mischievous. "Like not in a 'you do you, Rain' way, but in a turn-on-for-you sort of way."

"Yeah." Garrick didn't bother denying the obvious. "I've always had a weakness for…pretty things on other people. Like I'm not much on wearing glitter or glam stuff myself, but put someone else in it…and yeah, I can get into that."

"*Good.*" Rain took a step forward, robe swishing about him, but Garrick held up a hand.

"I can appreciate without taking advantage. I've got some self-control."

"And if I want you to take advantage?" Rain's voice was low and seductive now.

Garrick's breath caught, anticipation thrumming low in his gut. And then, because he'd been standing so long, his crutches wobbled, ruining whatever response he could have managed.

"Hot tub time!" Switching on a dime, Rain managed a sort of cheery bossiness that was exactly what Garrick needed right then. "Let's get you settled."

Somehow Garrick managed to explain the help he needed in actual words despite the proximity of Rain and his underwear, which was something of a feat, right up there with actually getting into the tub. They managed though, Rain proving that he might be benefiting from all the workouts, and Garrick showing that perhaps all the exercises Stephanie put him through in PT were doing something.

And it was worth it when he was finally in the water, one of his favorite things, right up there with skydiving. He'd had a vision for this space rooted in entertainment possibilities, but his love of water was a lifelong thing, and he let out a deeply satisfied noise as he arranged himself in one of the seats.

"Much better." Smiling, Rain let his robe flutter to land on one of the nearby loungers, leaving him in only the sexy underwear before he gracefully slid in the water opposite Garrick. "Now this is nice."

"Yeah it is. Thanks. Damn. This is exactly what my muscles need after this week. Maybe I need to listen to Stephanie and add some swimming into my routine, even if getting in and out of the pool is a challenge. She has me do hydrotherapy some, but the therapy place has a pool with a lift chair."

"You should try the swimming. I'd help, even get over my dislike of swim trunks for you."

"That's quite the offer." Garrick had to laugh at Rain's exaggerated sour expression.

"Hey, I get *you* in trunks out of it. I'm going to bet you were one of those super wholesome high school guys. Football and lifeguarding. You look like the type who would live at the local pool between sports practices."

Garrick had to laugh because Rain had captured him pretty darn perfectly. "Add in river raft guide the summer after high school before I got on with an engine crew. I've always loved the water. My dad has a place in the country north of town, kind of a small hobby ranch with a couple of horses and other animals, and there's a pool."

"Sounds nice."

"It is. Hell of a place to grow up. There was a time when it looked like he might lose it in the divorce. Some lean months, that's for damn sure. But it was worth it to get to keep it."

"I bet. I'm sorry about the divorce. I bet that was hard as a kid. Does she live around here?"

"Eugene. About four hours or so away, but when I was fourteen, it sounded like the ends of the earth. I stayed put with Dad, and she and my sister moved. She's still there, working at the university, and my sister married a local guy, so she's there too with her kids. We visit some though—they came to Portland when I was hurt. So it's not awful, but..."

"Still sucks," Rain guessed, rather accurately as usual. "But I'm glad you have your dad."

"Me too. When it warms up a bit more, I'll show you his place and we can swim if you'll help me into the pool. No skinny-dipping, but Cookie can run free there, make friends with the old cattle dogs he's got these days."

"I'd love that. It's a deal." Some of Rain's usual clump of curls on top of his head—the sort of half-ponytail, half-bun thing he seemed to excel at—had escaped, clinging to his face in damp tendrils that made him look at once both younger and more irresistible. "Dang. You like the water extra hot. I'm gonna sit on the edge for a few, okay?"

"Sure. Assuming you want to do this again, I can lower the set temp."

"You know I totally want a repeat. This is a sweet

setup you've got here. And it's fine. Don't change anything. I'm just not used to it yet." Rain effortlessly used his triceps to push up and out of the water, sitting on the little deck that rimmed the tub. And, holy hell, the water had rendered his briefs all but transparent, clearly outlining a cock that was either half-hard or genetically blessed or possibly both. Trying not to stare, Garrick moved his gaze to the patio lights, but not before Rain let out a knowing laugh.

"You can look. Promise you're not gonna offend me." Rain's voice was almost a dare, and Garrick had to wonder if he was actually overheated or if he wanted the excuse to show off.

"That's not what I'm worried about." Garrick made himself look at Rain's sweaty, glowing, mischievous face, which honestly was as arousing as the underwear and anything underneath it.

"I think you like watching. And that's quite all right because I like showing off."

"That much is a given." Garrick snorted. "But I'm not sure where you get that I like watching. I'm not like…a perv." At least he hoped he wasn't. It was true that Rain sort of grabbed his attention and didn't let go, but he'd tried to not be too obvious in checking him out over the past week.

"That's not the kind of watching I mean and you know it." Rain sucked on his index finger before trailing it down his sternum, proving his point, damn it, because Garrick was fucking riveted. "You…enjoy me. I see you. When we're working out or whatever. And it's not pervy. It's a massive turn-on, the way you watch me."

"Maybe it's just me…restless. Bored," Garrick countered, eyes still locked on Rain's fingers. "And I like *doing.* I'm a guy of action. All this waiting around as part of my recovery, it makes me punchy."

"Oh, you can do. Feel free to *do* all you want." Rain circled his finger around one of his nipples, the barest graze, an almost idle touch except Garrick knew damn well it was calculated. "But, I'm simply saying…if you like to look, then you can look. All you want. At anything you might like."

"Anything?" Garrick almost didn't recognize his own husky whisper.

"Anything," Rain confirmed, more of that dare in his voice. "I even take requests."

"That so?" This was a dangerous game they were playing, and he knew it. But there was also safety in it. This was flirting. Nothing more. Not making out where there might be…expectations. And damn it, it felt *good.* Warmer than the water, more relaxing than the bubbles. Simply *good.*

"Yeah. Got any?" Rain ran a finger under the waistband of his lacy briefs, stopping right before he reached the erection pushing at the wet fabric. "I've seen you around other people. You don't look at them like you look at me. It's fucking addictive and I want more of it."

"Tell me how the underwear feels on your skin," Garrick asked in hushed tones.

"Yessss," Rain hissed out a breath. "I'd tell you to come find out… But I'll let you stay all comfy over there. They feel silky. Clingy, but not in a bad way. You looking at me has me hard, and they're stretchy, pulling against my cock but not constricting."

Rain ran his fingers up and down the length of his covered cock, deliberately pulling on the material, but not freeing it either.

"What makes you like that style so much?" Garrick liked listening to Rain almost as much as he was enjoying the show. Also, conversation made it easier to ignore what they were sliding toward.

"They're mine."

"Uh-huh." It was a more serious answer than Garrick had expected, so he leaned forward, waiting to see if Rain would continue.

"It's my thing. Not my family's or my friends' but mine. I don't have to share it with anyone else. It's something I can do just for me, my own little sexy secret under my clothes that I get to choose who sees."

"I like that. Thank you for letting me see."

"Mmm. I like you seeing." Rain stretched, resuming his touching. "And that's the other part of it—it's simply sexy. I saw some show in my teens, some reality TV thing, and there was a dude wearing sexy panties as a joke, but all I could think was that I wanted that to be me. So I bought some, discovered that jerking off in them was a huge rush, and kept on buying when I could."

Garrick groaned at the mention of Rain jerking off and all the images that inspired. "You have a collection? Different styles?"

"Let's just say that I do my own laundry for a reason." Rain's laugh echoed through the still night before he dropped his voice again. "And if you're nice, I'll show you more of my favorites."

Ran had continued stroking through the fabric, breath hitching every now and then in the sexiest sound Garrick had ever heard.

"I'd like that." Clearly, Garrick's tongue had divorced

itself from his brain, but damn did he ever want to see what else Rain owned.

"Can I slide them off? Wanna show you something else I like…"

"Yeah. Do it." That Rain was asking for permission short-circuited what was left of Garrick's brain. Even as he played at being the show-off siren, he still seemed to want Garrick in charge, which was heady stuff.

"I like to do this." Rain wiggled out of the briefs, then wrapped them around his fist, a sexy little cocoon for his cock, which was indeed a nice size, uncut with an oval head and thick shaft.

"Show me. More." At this point, no way was Garrick backing off this game, not now, not with desire curling low in his belly, the potent hum of arousal in his veins that only increased as Rain began to stroke himself with the silky fabric.

"Good. So good." Garrick offered praise, both because he knew now that Rain liked that and because it came naturally, encouraging Rain, directing him. "Slow down now. Make it last."

"Please." Rain made a needy sound, somewhere between gasp and moan, and even though it was soft, it still made Garrick's nerve endings sizzle with new awareness.

"Not yet." Sternness came easier now, a desire to maximize Rain's enjoyment boiling deep inside him.

"It's too much." Rain's fast breathing said it was anything but, said he was enjoying this every bit as much as Garrick.

"You can do it," Garrick encouraged, keeping his voice soft but steady. "Gonna feel so good for waiting."

"Need it." Begging seemed to come easy to Rain

as his eyes fluttered shut, face tensing along with his shoulders and arms. The tension vibrating off him was as sexy as his stroking, which he kept speeding up, then slowing down, like he was trying hard to follow directions.

"I know. Show me." Garrick scooted slightly closer, not close enough to touch, but wanting more of that delicious energy rolling off Rain.

"God. Now." Head falling back, Rain's whole body strained as he stroked with the fabric, dick peeking out of the silky folds.

"Not yet. Tell me how it feels." Yeah, he was being pushy, but Rain's voice all strung out like this was even better than the sight of him jerking off.

"Good. So good. Like I'm going to die from it, but also like I never want it to end. Like…it's a blizzard of pleasure, and I'm trying to soak it all up, but it's almost too much. So much." Rain managed a lot more coherence than Garrick could have had the situation been reversed.

"Keep soaking it up. As much as you can. Draw it out."

"Yeah." Rain's face squished up as he bit his lower lip. The thrum under Garrick's skin was louder now, a deep buzzing, and he stroked his own stomach and thighs, letting the good feelings build in him too.

"That's it."

"Please. Please." More of Rain's hair tumbled loose, damp tendrils clinging to his face and neck as he panted.

"You're doing so well. So hot. Hottest thing I've ever seen."

"Can't. Hold. Back." Rain sounded almost alarmed at the prospect, so much so that Garrick couldn't help reaching out and touching one of Rain's feet under the water, needing that contact.

"Go ahead. Come for me, baby," he urged right as Rain shot all over his fist and the fabric, not shouting but breathing hard, whole body twitching.

"Oh my god." Cleaning off his hand and stomach, Rain threw the underwear to the ground and flopped back against the deck, dreamy grin on his face. "Wowza. Did we really just do that?"

"Uh. Think so." Damn. This was probably when he needed to be regretting things, but it was pretty hard to regret something so hot. And fun. So much fun. Giving Rain orders and praise might be his new favorite thing, watching how he responded.

"And now for your turn." Rain slid smoothly back into the water, advancing on Garrick with a gleam in his eye that had Garrick both anticipating and dreading in equal measure.

Chapter Seven

"We should talk." Garrick uttered Rain's three least favorite words as he held up a hand, effectively making Rain sag back into the hot tub seat opposite him.

"We don't *have* to talk," Rain countered, not wanting to hear some big proclamation that they couldn't do that again. "That can just be…a fun commercial break so to speak. No need to make a big deal out of it or you to go all guilt stricken over it."

"I'm not. I like sex, and it's not something I make a habit of feeling bad about as long as *you* feel good about what happened."

"Me? I'm fantastic." Rain made himself grin even as he still didn't like Garrick's serious face. "If you're not feeling terribly guilty, then what would be so wrong with a little harmless making out next? Let me make you feel as good as you made me feel."

"I don't… *Fuck*, this is hard. Maybe you're right. We don't need to talk about it. That was hot as fuck. Thank you for letting me see that." Garrick sounded oddly stiff and formal, thanking Rain for the single sexiest experience he'd had.

"Feels like I should be thanking you, what with your sexy-ass voice. I love it when you get all growly and commanding. And I'm totally down for letting you watch again sometime. Anytime you want."

"Rain..." In all the different ways Garrick had for saying Rain's name, this one was the most pained, like he wanted to say more and couldn't. Fuck. Maybe they *did* need to talk.

"Maybe I should be the one feeling guilty. I kinda... came on strong. Did I steamroller you into something you're...not ready for? Not like a guilt thing but something else?"

"God, the last thing I want is you feeling guilty. No. You didn't take advantage of me. I loved it."

"Good. But I sense a *but* there..."

"I...ah...haven't been with anyone in a long time. Since before the accident." Garrick looked over Rain's head at the patio lights, cheeks going pink even as he avoided eye contact.

"I see. And you think it matters to me? Your injuries? Because it really doesn't. You're sexy as hell, exactly as you are."

"It matters to me," Garrick ground out, and Rain couldn't tell whether he was more frustrated with Rain for pressing or with himself. "I can't... A lot of things I could do before... I can't now. And most of the time I'm okay with that. But sometimes it fucking sucks, especially when I don't even know all my limitations, can't predict what will work and what won't."

"Ah." Rain finally got enough subtext from all Garrick's dancing around the issue to have a better idea what they were talking about. "The neurological part of your injuries...it's affected your cock in some way? Fuck. Now I feel like we should have talked more first, if you couldn't enjoy it."

Garrick made a frustrated sound. "I told you. I loved it. I enjoyed every moment of watching you, I mean that. And as for the spinal injury's effects, it's…weird. Like I got super turned-on watching you, and my cock got hard at a couple of points, but I just know from… uh…playing on my own that it doesn't always stay that way. Or…cross the finish line every time, if you get what I mean."

"What does your doctor say? Like the meds they have for that, they don't work on your sort of injuries?"

Garrick mumbled something unintelligible while studying the bubbling water. "Haven't asked. No clue on meds."

"Okaaaay." Rain drew out the word, because if it were him, he'd be calling the doctor right away at the first sign of difficulty. But maybe that wasn't fair—it was a personal issue, and he got where a big, tough guy like Garrick might be embarrassed admitting to a problem. "So, that's where you start."

"You make that sound so easy. 'Hey, Doc, about my dick…'" Garrick made a dismissive hand gesture, sending droplets of water Rain's direction.

"Actually, exactly like that. You think you're the first guy with a misbehaving dick? I'm sure they've heard it before."

"Not from me."

"You could message your doctor if you don't want to bring it up face-to-face? Like that's how I handle getting tested on the regular—I just use the scheduling app and never actually talk to a person. I go in, get the blood drawn, and the results show up online."

"That's actually not a bad idea. My neurologist's office does have one of those apps. I just… I fucking hate the idea of needing…help getting it up." He made another frustrated gesture, this time sending water Cookie's direction and making her bark before settling back down. "Sorry, Cookie. And sorry to you too. You're sexy as hell and the last thing you need is a guy with a…how did you put it? Misbehaving cock. The old me would have had a hard time not shooting, watching your little show."

"The you right now is pretty darn awesome," Rain said firmly. "And you said you felt good? You enjoyed it, right? I mean, I'm sure an orgasm would be great too, but if I made you feel pleasurable things, that's cool. And it's a start."

"But you see now why we can't do that again. A repeat would be a bad idea."

"Nope, don't see that at all."

"I can't guarantee I could get off no matter what we tried. At the risk of TMI—"

"Please. Give me all your TMI." Rain scooted close enough to bump shoulders with Garrick. "Seriously, dude, I'm not put off by this, and the more information you give us to work with the better."

"Ah. Okay. Well, it's…unpredictable. Sometimes it works fine. Others, not so much, and it's not a matter of a tighter grip or sexier porn or heated lube—all things I've tried, mind you. Or like toys versus no toys. That sort of thing."

"You've experimented. That's good. You can report all that to the doctor."

Garrick made a gulping sound. "I might need to get out of the tub before I drown one of us accidentally. And trust me, after you help wrestle me out of the tub, you're not going to want any more sex talk anyway."

"Okay. Let's get you out. But not before…"

"Before what?" Garrick asked, turning toward Rain, giving him the perfect opportunity to ghost his lips over Garrick's. Not a deep kiss or even a particularly sexy one, but a kiss nonetheless, one that left a lingering impression of Garrick's soft, wide mouth, stubbly cheeks and surprised intake of air.

"That. Because I'm not done with the sex talk. Or you."

"Tell me that when you're all cold from the night air." Adorable blush sweeping across his cheeks, Garrick rubbed his mouth like he was trying to believe Rain had actually kissed him.

"I saw the fireplace in your room. I'll wear my new sexy-ass robe, and you'll warm me up, and we'll keep talking. Now enough excuses."

"Okay, okay." Garrick explained how to position himself to best help, and working together, they got Garrick dry, into his robe, and back on his crutches, limbs wobblier after the long soak.

Rain grabbed a towel to dry himself enough for the robe to not stick to his damp skin.

"Fuck." Garrick took a fast seat on the lounger next to Cookie. "Damn it. Hadn't thought about the water turning my legs to soggy breadsticks. Might need the chair."

"Coming right up. And I'm gonna flip that fireplace on when I dash in."

"I can't decide whether you're damn determined to get in my bed or simply cold," Garrick said once Rain produced the chair, and they made their way across the patio to the double doors to Garrick's room.

"Can't both be true?" Finally drier but still cold, Rain

slipped the satiny robe on and stood near the fireplace. Cookie gave him a snort and went and hopped up on the big bed.

"Hey! What about her bed?" Rain pointed at the almost-pristine princess bed in the corner.

"She likes it. Promise. And she sleeps there some. But somehow she decided her place is the other side of the bed." Garrick shrugged as he transferred to the bed.

"You're too nice."

"As evidenced by the fact that I'm not sending you home like I should." Garrick groaned as he stretched his legs out in front of him. "Cookie, go lay down. Rain wants your spot." Shooing the dog off the bed, Garrick patted the place she'd vacated. "This isn't like a…seduction. Swear I've got better game than this, but if you were serious about wanting warmed up, you can come over here under the covers. I might even manage some of that talking you're so keen on."

See, this was what Rain really liked about Garrick. He never stayed truly grumpy all that long, and he had a generous nature.

"I don't think you're trying to seduce me. Your bedding on the other hand…" He dove under the covers to come up near Garrick, buried under a pile of downy blankets and comforters. "Forget you, I'm going to make out with my new robe and these sheets. Damn. Which ex was into the high thread counts? I want to thank them."

"You're such a hedonist." Garrick gave him a fond pat on top of the covers. "And my sister got me new sheets that fit this bed—the base is split adjustable so it took different sheets than my old setup. She said she wanted to spoil me."

"Damn. Write that woman a thank-you letter." Rain whistled low as he made a show out of getting comfortable. "You can do it after you email the doctor."

"I guess I kind of need to, don't I?"

"Yup." Rain flopped his head onto Garrick's shoulder. "Even if it's not for me. Dude, it's clear that you loved sex prior to the accident. Don't give it up if you don't have to. If it's as easy as some pill or maybe a gadget…"

Garrick started coughing. "Not sure about *gadgets*."

"Hey, you said you owned toys. It would just be one more thing to play with. I'm sure you could find some way to still be all bossy and badass while ordering me to use it on you…" Giving a shaky laugh, he shifted against the sheets. "And okay, now I'm all turned on again. Which was not my intent. But damn. Anyway, yeah. My dick is making the point for me—any of that can be sexy if it means we get to get off together."

"Okay, okay. I'll message the doctor tomorrow. But uh…" Garrick made an awkward gesture between them. "Us dating or whatever is probably still not the best—"

"Or whatever." Rain cut him off before he could go too far down that unhappy trail. "We're friends. Friends who work out together. And friends who are going to figure out how to get off together. Because that would be fun. And maybe if you're *really* nice to me, the sort of friend who gets to see more of my underwear collection. And oh, feel free to order me to jerk off again sometime. That was fucking hot."

He was intensely aware of wearing nothing under the silky robe, memories bombarding him.

"God. Keep talking like that and my nerve endings might spontaneously decide to cooperate. You're something else, you know that?"

"Too much?" Rain asked carefully. He'd been told that a lot over the years—too loud, too colorful, too femme, too silly, too fun.

"Just right." Garrick pulled him close enough to kiss his head. But when Rain cuddled closer, intending to kiss his mouth again, Garrick gently pulled back. "Not that I don't want to kiss you. I do. God, I do. But I don't want my mouth writing checks my body can't cash and frustrating us both."

"Sex isn't just orgasm count for me. Sometimes kissing and not getting off is fine by me. Ignore my hard-on and give me a good-night kiss. Please?"

"Good-night? You're going?"

"My grandma will probably be home soon." That and Rain didn't want to overstay his welcome. This had already been a damn near perfect evening, and he could tell Garrick was tired, like actually physically worn out, not just tired of the talking. There would be time enough for Rain to show Garrick that not all make-out sessions required orgasms for either of them. "I don't want to stay out all night and worry her, not without telling her—"

"Fuck. Somehow I forgot about Shirley. She's going to kill me for fooling around with you—"

"No, she won't. And I'm not planning to sneak around. She knows we're friends and thinks it's great. Now exactly what type of friend, that's between us, but I'm not really into being some dirty secret. Been there, got the T-shirt, not going to go there again."

"Fair enough." Garrick scrubbed at his hair. "I'm not planning on hiding anything either. I don't ever want to make you feel bad, Rain. I mean that."

"Appreciate that." This time when Rain leaned in to kiss him, Garrick let him, and it was a sweet, sweet kiss that felt like the cementing of a deal. At first it was Rain kissing Garrick, a soft press of their mouths together, but then Garrick groaned and deepened the kiss, nipping at Rain's mouth until he let him in, tongue making Rain's toes literally curl against the impossibly soft sheets. They kissed long moments until they were both breathing hard when Garrick released him.

"Oh, damn. I'm supposed to get dressed after that?" Rain both groaned and laughed as he hefted himself out of the bed, determined to keep his promise even if he wanted more of what Garrick had on offer, like years and years more kisses like that, yes please.

"Don't strangle your dick." Laughing like a teenager, Garrick flopped back against his pillows. "Rain?"

"Yeah?"

"I'm glad we're friends. Lock up when you leave?" Garrick yawned.

"I'm glad too. And I will."

And as he locked up and left, Rain's cock might have been aching for another round or seven, but his heart and footsteps were light. He couldn't help but hope this was indeed the start of a great friendship, and that he could convince Garrick more naked time was exactly what they both needed.

Garrick almost spit water across the break room when he glanced at his phone's newest text message.

How'd it go at the dick doctor? :) :)

Rain's text was about as unsubtle and direct as the rest of him, and it made Garrick laugh out loud to the empty room, which was undoubtedly Rain's intent. He'd been doing a lot more of that since Rain came into his life, laughing and feeling light and hopeful, and he loved it. He was, however, glad he was alone in here for the message and not at his desk out in the main office. So far it was day three on the new job. His had been the fastest government hire Garrick had heard of—application last Wednesday, a day after talking to Fred, and here it was, the following Thursday. Most of what they had him doing right now was all the new hire paperwork and required trainings and reading of manuals, so he was understandably taking his time on this break, eating his snack and composing a fast response to Rain about his neurologist appointment that morning.

Neurologist is referring me to a urologist—an actual dick doctor, fucker. I'll tell you more when you come over tonight. Are you eating with Shirley? If not, I saw a recipe using lentils as taco filling we could try.

They'd been eating together some nights, and Garrick found he looked forward to seeing Rain more each day. He'd seen the recipe in a cooking magazine in the doctor's office and taken a picture of it, and simply thinking of Rain had made him relax, temporarily forget the reason for the appointment. Because of damn course it hadn't been as easy as a single email, and his doctor had wanted to see him in the office. Which had meant a lot of talking to the posters of spines and nerves in the exam room, avoiding looking directly at his doctor, a matronly neurologist who made him feel like he was trying to discuss his sex life with his mom.

But thinking about Rain had helped. They'd had a few more kisses in the past week, each sweeter than the last, and simply hanging out reminded Garrick why he needed to have the talk with his doctor. Not that Rain pushed or even teased that much, letting Garrick have space to sort out the whole doctor thing, but he was so damn sexy and fun, even when he wasn't trying that hard to be. They'd moved their workouts to earlier to accommodate Garrick's new schedule, and even bleary eyed, Rain was still the cutest wakeup call Garrick could imagine.

Right as he finished his snack, one of his coworkers came in.

"Another day of training videos?" Tucker Ryland was something of a friend, a local who'd been ahead of Garrick in school, and while they'd both started on engine crews, Tucker had quickly gone the Forest Service route, working as Burn Boss on controlled burns and helping manage unexpected wildfires too. More of a family guy than Garrick, he commanded a ton of respect in the firefighting community. And honestly, his word had probably meant as much as Fred's in getting Garrick hired so fast. He'd been Garrick's ride in that morning as well, and as much as Garrick disliked needing favors, he was good company.

"Yeah. That and lots of reading."

"It will get easier when we have more for you to do. I've got a scheduled burn coming up, and you'll be helping me with coordination."

"Sounds great." And it did. Anything more active would be awesome, make him feel more a part of a team again.

"First though, I've got my own paperwork—stacks of the applications for entry-level forest technicians. It's harder than you'd think to find people wanting to do

grunt work like digging line and mop-up duty. Everyone wants to be on a hotshot crew these days."

"True facts. I'm training someone right now who
wants a place on a frontline crew. But...actually this
might be a good fit for them. It's another temporary
seasonal gig?"

"Yeah. Variable hours, like most of these openings.
Competition for full-time hours, that's fierce. But I'll
do what I can to get people plenty of work. Your rec,
that would mean something to me. And it's good, honest work out there in the field. I'd put in a good word for
them if a spot opened up on an engine crew or something else with more action."

Another thought crept into Garrick's mind as he
mulled over talking Rain into trying for the job. "So...
uh...you or someone on your level would technically be
the supervisor, right? I wouldn't want any...issues with
continuing to train with this person. We're...friends."

"I know you, Nelson. Friend or *friend*?" Tucker
laughed.

"Um. Maybe both?" Garrick itched under his ear. It
wasn't really a coming out thing that had him antsy as
much as not wanting to screw up a potential opportunity for Rain that he could really use, both as experience and to get some money in.

"And no, you wouldn't be the direct supervisor to
anyone on the cleanup crew or anything like that. You
being...social shouldn't be an issue as long as it doesn't
affect the work. Fred's not a huge fan of dating between
crew members, but God knows that happens enough. And
this isn't even that. Just stay professional on the clock,
and I don't see a problem. I appreciate the heads-up."

"Thanks. I'll mention the opportunity then, see if he

can get you an application in quickly if there's not already one in the queue. Rain's been applying for a lot of seasonal stuff."

Tucker's eyes went wide as Garrick got specific on gender, but if he was truly shocked, he didn't offer any commentary on that either. Like most of Garrick's friends, he undoubtedly had *some* idea that Garrick was pan, even if they'd never had a formal conversation about it. He wasn't one of the party or bar scene friends, but he'd probably heard something over the years. "Sounds good."

And now he had another reason to look forward to seeing Rain and Cookie after work, especially once Rain texted that he was staying for dinner, and it wasn't long after Tucker dropped him off that Rain appeared on the porch in a Bear Bait T-shirt under an unzipped hoodie and silver shorts.

"I'm not sure that you should be wearing that shirt," Garrick said between laughing. "At least not around here. The actual bears might get ideas. I imagine it makes you pretty damn popular in the Portland bars though."

"Oh I don't wear it *out*. Just for you. Because I knew it would make you laugh, and I knew you were stressed about the doctor business. Heck, the shirt even made Grandma laugh."

Garrick had to cough at that, still not sure how he felt about Shirley knowing about his and Rain's…flirtation. But he supposed it was indeed a good sign that she didn't seem to have an issue with Rain's sexuality.

"Are you coming for Cookie's exercise?" Rain glanced down at Garrick, who was in his chair, his work clothes and shoes still on. "It's okay if you're too tired after your long day. Doctor plus work. That's a lot."

"I'm not tired," Garrick lied. Actually, he was exhausted even though he'd mainly relied on his chair that day. He guessed his body was still getting used to the hours. "But I am hungry. How about I start the lentil recipe I mentioned?"

"Sounds great." Rain leaned down to brush a kiss across his cheek before hooking Cookie up to her leash. "I'll be back soon. She's all healed now, so we can run a little."

After switching out of his shirt into something more comfortable, Garrick made quick work of chopping vegetables at the table, then transferred them to a skillet with a can of lentils. He was just checking his taco seasoning to make sure it was vegetarian when Rain came back in with Cookie, breathing hard and looking sexy all flushed and wide-eyed with his hair falling out of its topknot.

"Tell me about work," Rain demanded as he undid his hair.

"Uh." Garrick blinked, momentarily mesmerized by Rain's hair, unrestrained for the first time, curly and wild and longer than he'd thought. He wanted to feel it on his skin, and the rush of desire made him a little lightheaded. "Sorry. Work. Yes. That. Mainly boring. More workplace safety videos and insurance paperwork, but there's actually something you might be interested in."

"Oh?" Rain bundled his hair back up, then washed his hands. He set the table while Garrick told him about the position Tucker had available. "Yeah, I could give that a try. Would you be my boss though? I don't want to have to sneak around."

"No sneaking around. Just being professional. I... uh...kinda mentioned to Tucker that we were...*social*." He figured Tucker's word was as good as any for describing the weird limbo land he and Rain occupied of not dating but also not platonic either.

"You did?" Rain's small, pleased smile was all the confirmation Garrick needed that he'd done the right thing not trying to hide whatever they had going from Tucker. "Maybe we can be more social after dinner. Did you get anything...interesting from the doctor?"

"No prescription yet. She wants me to see a urologist because apparently there's a couple of different kinds of pills they usually try first, but there's also some tests the urologist can do on function." Somehow it was easier talking about this with Rain than the doctor herself.

"That's great news. That means there's options for you." Rain nodded enthusiastically as he retrieved the condiments Garrick had set on the counter for their tacos.

"And the urologist's office called already. They actually have an opening next week. But I need a favor." Garrick took his plate and started drowning his share of the taco filling in cheese and salsa.

"Sure. Anything." Unlike Garrick's ode to cheddar, Rain more sedately added a green salsa and extra cilantro to his portion.

God. Asking anyone for a favor was hard but especially Rain, even knowing he'd agree. Garrick took and swallowed a bite before figuring out how best to word his request.

"Can you give me a ride to it? I'd kinda rather not

involve my dad and have to explain what the latest appointment is for. I told him today's was for a neurologist follow-up, and he was cool. And he'd be fine with the other but..."

"You'd rather not talk about your sex life with your dad. I get it. I love my parents, who were always super open with us about stuff like that, and I still wouldn't want them knowing everything about my private time. Does he know you're pan or should I be more careful around him?" Rain had seen Garrick's dad on several occasions, and while Garrick was pretty sure his dad had no idea what to make of Rain, he was his usual affable self around him, lecturing Garrick but polite to Rain.

"Just be yourself. I told him last year. Prior to the accident. A friend of mine on the crew was out, and a few more of the other rookies were various flavors of LGBTQ and I was just...tired of hiding it. Tired of it feeling like it was an open secret among most of my crowd, but not something I ever talked about outside it."

"I feel you. There comes a point where not talking about something becomes almost this deafening roar, and you just want to get it out there."

"Exactly. And anyway, there was Jacob, out and not getting hassled, and there was my other friend, stupid in love with Jacob but not really out, and it created... tension. I *knew* they had feelings, and I kinda tried to prod them in the right direction by making like I might go there with Jacob. And I wanted my other friend to stop being such a dumbass and just live his life already. Finally, they're together now, and it all worked out, and somewhere in the whole thing, I ended up coming out as pan to more people, including Dad."

"You're a good friend." Rain leaned over and squeezed Garrick's biceps. "And your dad? How'd he take it?"

"Dad was okay. Tried to chalk it up to the fact that I love sex and have always made no bones about that fact, but I tried to explain that it wasn't about being… I dunno…indiscriminate, but a legit way that attraction works for me. Like how I'm wired thing and not a 'Garrick wants to double his dating pool' thing. I'm not sure if he truly understood that part, but he wasn't mean about it either."

"Good. I meant what I said about not wanting to be a secret, but I can also understand if you need to…tone it down around him, keep the peace."

"Nope." Garrick leaned over and kissed Rain's head. "I'm not sure exactly what the hell we're doing, but hiding isn't a part of it. I like you exactly how you are, no toning down required."

"Good." Rain patted his hand. "I like that. And thanks for the job lead. You might not know what we're doing, but I think what we're doing is awesome. You're a good guy."

And as they sat there at the dinner table, Garrick had to hope that he wasn't going to be the one to let Rain down, the one to dampen his glittery free spirit or break his big, generous heart. He tried not to ask the universe for too much—a chance to do his job again mainly—but now he added a little, quiet request to get a chance to be what Rain needed.

Chapter Eight

"Are we at the point yet where I get to tell you that you look smoking hot in those work shirts of yours? And that compliment might get me a kiss hello?" Rain batted his eyes at Garrick, not trying to hide his admiration for what crisp cotton and a row of buttons did for Garrick's buff chest and forearms, especially with the collar buttons open and the sleeves rolled back.

"Someone's in a good mood." Garrick waved him into the house. Cookie was dancing around like an extra in a rap video, preventing Rain from leaning down and claiming that kiss.

"I should be. Put my application in online last night and got a call this afternoon for an interview Monday. Your friend is fast."

"Good." Garrick's smile was genuine and wide, but his eyes were tired, shoulders more slumped than usual.

"Did you overdo it again today? You had our morning exercise, PT with Stephanie, then work. You must be bushed." Rain rubbed one of Garrick's meaty shoulders.

"Nah. I'm okay. But because it looks like it might sprinkle, I think I'll stay in. I'd rather avoid needing to dry the chair if it gets wet."

"What? It's not designed for underwater use?" Rain

joked, but honestly, he wasn't sure what it would take for Garrick to actually admit he was tired and sore. "And yeah, I wouldn't be surprised if we got some weather before morning."

"Did you already eat? My dinner was a sandwich, and I was contemplating making some sort of dessert while you walk."

"Yeah, I ate with Grandma and now she's off with her Friday night friends. As to dessert, I have ideas…" Rain grinned because he was more than happy to volunteer himself as dessert, but he could be good too. "Sorry. Not trying to tease—"

"Liar." Garrick laughed and shook his head.

"Truth. I'll walk Miss Impatient here, and you see what you can find, but seriously, dude, if you need rest—"

"What I need is a way to make a brownie mix vegan so you can have some." Garrick waved away Rain's concerns.

"Use flax seed to replace the eggs." Rain liked how Garrick always tried to accommodate Rain despite his own omnivorous tastes. "And thanks for adapting the recipe."

"I try. Now get going before it rains."

A bitter wind greeted Rain and Cookie, and they'd barely reached the halfway point when the skies opened up in a way they seldom did this time of year, pelleting them with a harsh, driving rain.

"Come on, Cookie. Let's run!" But even racing back to Garrick's place at top speed, they were both soaked by the time they reached the porch.

"There you are." Garrick was waiting for them in his chair, stack of fluffy gray towels in his lap. "I was worried."

"It's just water." Rain didn't like him worried, didn't like adding to the tightness around his eyes, but he'd be lying if he didn't admit that Garrick's caretaking felt damn good too. They worked together to dry Cookie enough to let her into the house.

"You're shivering," Garrick pronounced as Rain straightened from toweling off the dog. "You need a hot shower. How about—" A torrent of more rain cut Garrick off. "Crap. You want to avoid the mad dash across the street and shower here? I'm not sure what I've got clotheswise that you'd like, but you left your robe here last week. I hung it up in the hall bath for you."

"That works." Warmth spread across Rain's chest. *His* robe. That Garrick had so easily assigned ownership of the elegant garment to him, that meant something.

"If you need shampoo or whatever, there are toiletries from various guests under the sink." Garrick all but herded Rain toward his guest bathroom. Apparently, worrying over Rain had given him a fresh jolt of energy because he didn't seem anywhere near as tired now. His concern was super cute. Rain didn't usually get fussed over like this and it was nice. "And I'm going to turn the fireplace on for you."

"You're spoiling me."

"You deserve it." On that warm note, Garrick left him to peel off his soggy clothes. Damn. Even the sexy purple underwear he'd worn hoping for a chance to tease Garrick had gotten soaked.

Cranking the shower to hot, he rummaged under the sink to find a bodywash from the eclectic collection that was too big to simply be his mom and sister visiting. He picked a fun beachy scent, hoping it didn't have a bad association with one of Garrick's exes, and took his time in the shower. The warm water pounded his chilled skin until he was nice and warm and relaxed. When he exited the shower, the aroma of brownies greeted him.

"Go ahead and crawl under the covers if you want," Garrick called. "I'll bring the snack and my laptop."

"Sure thing." Rain scampered across to Garrick's room, where he had to smile at how Garrick had readied the space for him. The fire was going, lights dimmed, and bed covers turned back. Grateful, he kept the robe on and slipped beneath the puffy mountain of covers, continuing to towel off his hair. He needed a comb, but his fingers would have to do.

"I could get used to this," he teased as Garrick placed his laptop and a plate with two brownies on the rolling tray table next to his side of the bed.

"Good. But if you want milk, you'll have to get it yourself. I've learned the hard way not to attempt uncovered liquids in the chair, but I did make sure Dad brought in some coconut milk with the rest of my groceries if you want it."

"Nah. I'm staying put. But thanks."

"Anytime." Garrick transferred to sit on the edge of the bed.

"Wait. You're way overdressed." Rain gestured at Garrick's work clothes.

"You just want me naked."

"Guilty. But don't make me come over there and do it with my teeth. Or rather do exactly that. Please."

"Okay, okay. I'm on it." Garrick used a nifty grabbing tool to pull off his shoes, then wiggled out of his pants and shirt, leaving him in blue boxer briefs.

"Now that's more like it. Although I can't believe you turned down my kind offer of assistance..." Giving a flirty wink, he couldn't help leering as Garrick climbed under the covers. Damn. Those muscles.

"Trust me, I'm amazed at my restraint too." Laughing, Garrick arranged himself as easily as if they planned a cuddle party like this every weekend. Rain scooted closer while Cookie found her way to her bed with a mighty harrumph.

"I thought you're not much on TV." Rain gestured at the laptop.

"I'm not. But every time we work out, you keep talking about all those reality shows I never watch. Pick one to educate me on all the pop culture I'm missing."

"Yes, Grandpa. I'll show you what us youngsters are into these days." Rain deliberately made his voice more country, earning another laugh from Garrick, who tossed an arm around him and hauled him closer so that Rain could scroll around the laptop. The warm weight of Garrick's arm on his back made him tempted to suggest porn, but he didn't want to ruin this cozy little cocoon by bringing up sex too soon either. He picked a show he thought Garrick would appreciate—ridiculously fit people attempting wacky obstacle courses. "Here. Maybe you'll get more ideas for my workouts, but I draw the limit at dodging inflatable pylons."

"Hey, if you have your way, you'll soon be dodging burning debris. Don't make light of things that improve your reflexes. They might be the one thing keeping you alive."

"True that." Maybe he should have gone for a lighter show, one with relationship drama or petty squabbles, but before he could change the selection, Garrick pulled him in tighter, settling him against his chest, and Rain decided he could endure even the worst TV if it meant getting to stay right there as long as possible. Garrick smelled like the woodsy aftershave he favored on the days when he shaved, but he already had some sexy stubble going, and his body was warm and solid behind Rain. He started absently finger combing Rain's still damp hair.

"I love your hair down like this."

"It's kind of a wet mess." Rain's face heated at the compliment. As much as he enjoyed dishing them out, getting them always felt weird.

"Beautiful mess." Garrick blessed him with a kiss on the top of his head, and yeah, he wasn't moving, not even for brownies, but eventually partway through the second challenge Garrick stretched and retrieved the plate, feeding a bite to Rain.

"If you keep taking such good care of me, you're not getting rid of me anytime soon."

"Good." Garrick kissed the side of his head. Him free with the kisses like this was worth any number of rainstorms. Hell, Rain would happily endure snow—

Wait. He probably wouldn't be here come winter, a sour thought that took a little shine off the present coziness.

"Why the frown? Are the brownies that bad?"

"They're fine. You did good." Returning the favor, he pressed a kiss to Garrick's neck. Might as well enjoy it while he had it.

"And no pressure, but you're welcome to sleep over if you want to text Shirley."

"You're blushing." Rain had to laugh before he sobered. "You're sweet enough to not want her to worry about where I am, but you're...embarrassed?"

He had been a walk on the wild side for enough people to not like feeling like a secret people were ashamed of, and some of that must have crept into his voice because Garrick gave him a kiss on the head.

"Not in the way you're thinking. More like I still feel like I'm too old for...whatever we've got going. I like your grandma a lot, and I don't want her pissed at me or thinking I'm taking advantage."

"If anyone's taking advantage, it's me." Turning his head, Rain finally claimed the kiss he'd wanted since Garrick opened his door. Garrick's lips were warm and soft and tasted faintly chocolaty, but even better was his groan as he took over, teasing Rain's mouth until he opened for Garrick's questing tongue. Damn but the guy could kiss, especially like this, an intoxicating blend of tightly coiled restraint and sweet surrender. Unlike most of their shorter kisses over the past week, this one went on and on, no rushing and no breaking away either, just the press of their mouths and slide of their tongues until Rain was trembling, actual shudders racing through him.

"Cold?" Garrick stroked down Rain's arms and torso, hands leaving a cascade of sparks wherever they touched, like the animated trails of a magic wand. And magic was definitely the right word for what this was, this sweet, this sexy, this slow, and this perfect.

"Not cold. Burning." Rain tugged him down for another kiss, this one long enough to wallow in Garrick's roving hands, especially when he got bold and slipped one under the lapels of Rain's robe. Garrick stroked his chest, a reverence to his touch that made Rain feel singularly special, heating him more than the shower or the fireplace could ever do. Making an encouraging noise, he stretched, letting the robe fall open more.

"Fuck. You are so sexy." Garrick danced his fingertips down Rain's sternum, circling his navel, skating close to Rain's straining cock without actually touching it.

"You make me feel that way." Rain preened, trying to get Garrick's hand where he wanted it most.

"Good." Instead of going straight for Rain's cock, Garrick touched everywhere else—hip bones, thighs, nipples, ribs, big blunt fingers everywhere and yet nowhere at all.

"More." Rain's voice had reached the husky and demanding stage, and he backed it up with a kiss that left them both breathing hard, Garrick's head resting against Rain's as he tangled a hand in his hair.

"Rain…" Of all the ways Garrick had of saying his name, this was the most intimate, almost pained with a palpable need to it. Sexy as fuck and Rain could listen to it all night.

"Yeah?" There was little Garrick could ask for that Rain wouldn't give him, especially if it meant more kisses and heated touches and needy noises.

"I want… Can I jerk you off? I really want to touch you, make you come apart for me." Garrick stroked Rain's stomach again, this time letting his fingertips graze the shaft of Rain's cock.

"Uh-huh." Like he was turning that down. In all his wiggling around, he'd felt what he was pretty sure was Garrick hard and wouldn't have minded some mutual playing. However, he wanted to let Garrick drive this encounter, and if what he wanted was to focus on Rain, well, Rain wasn't exactly going to turn down that sort of attention.

"Oh fuck, that feels good." He arched his back, meeting Garrick's firm grip as he took charge of Rain's cock, big hand creating a snug channel for Rain to fuck up into before he gentled his touch back to light, teasing strokes.

"Yeah, it does." Garrick groaned right along with Rain. He alternated between a purposeful rhythm and something much more playful and meandering, driving Rain out of his mind. All his scattered thoughts, the show on the laptop, the snores of the dog, everything faded until his entire being was focused on Garrick.

"Want…"

"Tell me." A sexy growl rumbled loose from Garrick's chest, making Rain clutch at his arms. He wanted to touch Garrick, wanted to make him feel this good, but he also didn't want to ask the wrong question and risk derailing something so damn good. So instead, he gripped Garrick's arms like a fucking lifeline, connection and salvation and torture all at once.

"Want more." He bucked his hips, chasing more of Garrick's caresses, moaning as soon as Garrick gripped him tightly again. "*Fuck.* But don't want to come. Don't want it over."

"I've got you." Kissing the side of Rain's head and ear, Garrick established a slow, devastating pace that felt like climbing steps at a lighthouse. Up, up, up, circling and circling until he wanted to expire from all the delicious energy coursing through him.

"Fuck. That…it's too much. Need…" Writhing against Garrick, he tried to force a faster pace. Fuck waiting. He needed in a way he wasn't sure he'd ever needed before.

"Sssh. Let me give you this. I'll get you there, baby." If anything, Garrick slowed his touch, each stroke making Rain's control crack further, each endearment taking him apart more and more.

"Yesssss." Even with the slowness, heat still licked at his balls, made his thighs tense. He might come, exactly like this, not the race to the top from earlier but a total body release, everything he had sinking into Garrick, into this moment.

"That's it, sweetheart. Let go." Garrick's encouragement got him that much closer, made him gasp and make inarticulate needy whimpers.

"Need to come."

"Soon." Releasing a harsh chuckle, Garrick seemed to vibrate with tension, every breath mirroring Rain's harsh pants.

"Please."

"You're not the only one who wants this to last forever. Damn, you are so, so sexy." Finding Rain's mouth for another kiss, Garrick slowed down further, making the orgasm that had seemed imminent a few seconds ago retreat, a butterfly just out of reach.

"Crazy sexy more like. *Please.*" It was all too much, the drag of the silky robe against his skin, Garrick's dirty talking voice, and his devastating touch.

"Not like you don't know you're hot as fuck. Especially like this." Twisting his grip, Garrick did something with his palm that had Rain seeing stars, shards of light erupting behind his eyelids, making him clutch at Garrick that much harder.

"More."

"Yeah. Okay." Garrick's breath was coming as fast as Rain's now, him sounding like giving in to Rain's demands was a surrender of sorts, as if he was as far gone as Rain was.

"That's it." Rain was close to weeping, fingers digging hard into Garrick's arms, so damn grateful when Garrick quickened the pace. His hips bucked, chasing every stroke.

"Fuck. Like that. Fuck my fist." Teeth grazing Rain's ear, Garrick tightened his grip, making them both moan.

"Don't stop."

"Not gonna. Come, baby. Come for me." Like he had a direct line to Rain's brain, Garrick sped up, fast hard strokes that had Rain's balls tightening again, this time tipping over from close to inevitable, pressure building to that point of no return that made the whole world go bright and wonderful.

"Fuck. Fuck. *Garrick*." He shot so hard he was pretty sure at least one volley landed on Garrick, the rest painting his abs and chest with messy stripes. Still shaking, he grabbed for the towel with rubbery fingers. Next to him, however, Garrick was breathing like a marathon runner on that last hill, whole body tense.

"Can I…" Garrick shoved a hand inside his boxers.

"Fuck yes. Tell me how to help." Making fast work with the towel, Rain pressed firmly against Garrick, both to give him something to rub against and because he was damn greedy, wanting to soak up all Garrick's pleasure.

"Touch my arms like that again. Please." Now that was an unexpected request, but Rain happily complied, stroking Garrick's forearms and biceps.

"This?"

"Yeah. Harder. Like when you were about to come. Damn. Fuck that was hot." Garrick's eyes were squished shut and his hand on his cock was barely moving, but his body stiffened as soon as Rain grabbed his arms harder with his fingertips, gripping rather than stroking.

"Yeah, it was. Never came so hard before." He didn't even have to pretend to be back in that moment as his whole body still tingled and his breath came as little gasps and sighs, which apparently ramped Garrick up too as he moaned softly whenever Rain made a noise. His free hand drifted through Rain's hair, holding him close. Wanting to do more, Rain pressed a kiss to Garrick's neck, licking up a rogue drop of sweat and teasing along its contours.

"Oh hell. That. Yeah. Kiss me there again." Garrick shuddered as soon as Rain did it, using his tongue to tease all along Garrick's neck, trying to find more places that made him moan and curse. Eyes still shut, his body was as rigid as a stack of textbooks. "Need…"

"Anything." Acting more on instinct than anything else, Rain dug his fingers into the meat of Garrick's biceps right as he nipped at the curve of Garrick's neck, the spot that had seemed to get the biggest reaction from his attentions.

"That… Fuck. There. Right there." Garrick went impossibly stiffer, then the tension seemed to recede in waves, leaving him flushed and shuddering. Rain felt like he had witnessed the solar eclipse, exhilarated and awestruck and incredibly grateful simply to be there.

"Wow." He pressed a flurry of softer kisses to Garrick's neck and shoulders. "Did you…?"

"Appears so. Weird as fuck. It was like my arms and neck as much or even more so than my dick, like my biceps were buzzing, pleasure and pressure gathering there instead of my abs and cock like I'm used to. And then I was coming."

"I'm glad. Arms. Neck. Whatever does it for you, I'm happy to go there."

"Not sure if it would work a second time." Garrick frowned, flopping an arm over his face. "Doubt it's like…magic. Doesn't seem to work like that, at least not in what I've found so far. It's unpredictable. Pleasurable, but not necessarily duplicable. Don't get me wrong, I enjoyed the hell out of that, but it's not…"

"A cure. I get it. I'm not the dick whisperer even if I feel like a fucking rockstar right now. And I'll take unpredictable. Getting you off, making you feel good, it's worth any amount of trying and uncertainty. And hell, trying is *fun*. If I can make you come by touching your arms, I bet there's other brand-new erogenous zones waiting for us."

"You're something else." Garrick peeked out from under his arm to give Rain a fond smile.

"I try." Pushing his arm gently out of the way, Rain gave him a quick kiss.

"I know." Garrick returned the kiss, more tender and lingering. "You make me want… Damn, I wish I'd met you…before. Back when I could have given you everything you deserve."

Rain pulled back enough to glare down at Garrick. "I deserve *this*. And so do you. I don't need anything else in bed, promise. This is awesome. I mean, I do think you should keep the doctor appointment, but that's for you. For me, I don't need you to be anything other than this. That was seriously top ten sex of my life. If it gets much better than that, I might pass out from good feelings."

That got a laugh from Garrick, who tugged him

close again. "Okay, point taken. And fucking you near-unconscious just went on my bucket list."

"Damn. Now it's on mine too. But I'm also okay if it takes…some practice to get there. Or creativity." He kept his voice light but firm. He wasn't giving up on sex with Garrick simply because things weren't as straight-forward as with some partners. Uncomplicated could be nice, but it was also a bit boring. This was a challenge, but not an unwelcome one at all, and taking it on with Garrick made him feel close. Connected. Bonded even, like they were on a team with a common goal and like they got to share something special together.

"You and your ideas." Garrick gave an exaggerated groan even as he gave Rain another quick kiss.

"I do have good ones." He preened. Like how Garrick had made researching vegan workout tips his new thing, Rain was totally going to look up more ideas relevant to Garrick's condition because hell yes he was going to get that response out of Garrick again.

"Yeah, you do." Garrick's smile as he agreed was enough to make Rain's feet wriggle happily against the sheets.

"Did you mean it about sleeping over?"

"Of course. I mean, I can't guarantee a repeat…" Garrick yawned, that tiredness from earlier reappearing. He'd probably be asleep before the next episode started, and strangely, Rain was looking forward to sleeping next to him even more than the earlier sex.

"I don't need a repeat. Just this." And for now, that was absolutely true. All he needed was this thing with Garrick and the job he hoped to land next week, and maybe that would be enough adventure for one summer, enough to stay put.

Chapter Nine

"What the heck is that and why do I think you're about to stab me with it?" Out of all the unusual things Rain had produced, the spiky object with skinny needles sticking out from a mass of thin yarn had to be right up there on the list of surprises. Shortly after they'd arrived at the doctor's office, Rain had dug a small pouch out of his half-sized messenger bag, which Garrick had assumed was mainly a water bottle and wallet-toting device since Rain didn't always have pockets.

"It's my knitting." Rain's tone was almost bored as his fingers flew around the needles. It was almost hypnotic, the way his hands kept moving even as he looked up at Garrick. "Told you. I like to have something to do with my hands. Sock knitting is great because it's so portable. I keep meaning to bring it over to your place, but someone keeps distracting me..."

"I'd say sorry, but we both know I'd be lying." They'd spent most of the weekend together, playing with Cookie, exercising, and baking banana bread they shared with Shirley, who as Rain predicted didn't seem upset about Rain's sleepover Friday. She'd been working with vats of dye on her patio, and Garrick had passed an enjoyable few hours watching Rain attempting to help her hang up fabric to dry and her micromanaging Rain's efforts. "Did Shirley teach you to knit?"

"Her and Mom both. I was a squirmy kid who needed distracting. And I can tell from how full this waiting room is that we're going to be here awhile. I'm not a fan of magazines or daytime TV, so I'm happy to work on these socks for Grandma's birthday."

"You're going to hand-knit something and then just give it away?" Garrick wasn't a stranger to crafting of various kinds as his dad worked with different artisans at his Western-themed store, but generally he associated it with money-making efforts. And in Rain's case, he would have figured he'd knit as a personal expression sort of thing, more color to add to his wardrobe.

"That's how it works. If you stop looking at me like I'm a space alien, I might knit you something next."

"I'm not staring! I'm impressed, that's all." He wasn't lying—the stitches flying off Rain's needles into something that actually resembled a sock for a human foot was pretty nifty. "And you don't have to make me something—"

"Right now I'm picturing a muzzle in a nice cable pattern. Of course, I don't *have* to. I want to. Maybe a hat so you can remember me."

Garrick opened his mouth to say that he didn't need to remember Rain, that he was right here, but then he remembered that Rain wasn't meant for this place on a permanent basis, that winter would inevitably come and he'd be on to his next big thing. He'd scored the job with Tucker Ryland on Monday, but like Garrick's position, it was seasonal part-time, and there was no guarantee Rain would even finish the season. The thought made his neck ache enough that he had to rub it.

"Nervous? Don't be." Rain lowered his voice. "Like I said in the car, I'm sure this doctor has heard it all before. And that's a good thing."

"Jesus. You're so…"

"Normal? Because this is." Rain continued calmly making tiny stitches on his project, a counterpoint to everything churning through Garrick.

"Maybe I should be the one knitting."

"Maybe so." Rain thrust his spiky circle into Garrick's hands. The yarn was slippery but softer than it looked, and it felt surprisingly nice on his skin. Maybe Rain was turning him into a hedonist along with everything else. "No time like the present to learn."

"Pretty sure my hands are too big," Garrick grumbled as he tried to make sense of which way the needles were pointing.

"Yes, Hercules. You're big." Rain gave him a pointed look that had Garrick's skin heating. He had a way of making Garrick feel like they were the only two people in the room, like nothing else mattered other than this happy little bubble where Rain was moving his fingers this way and that and couldn't care less for who might be watching. It was…refreshing. Nice. Needed. It reminded him of all the hours spent repairing smoke jumper gear, the little tiny details that had to be exactly perfect. Like now, his hands had always felt too oversized for the work, but there had been something soothing about that work, weirdly relaxing. And it worked here too, Rain's bossiness and his own hopelessness at juggling needles and yarn distracting him until his name was called.

"You want me to come back with you?" Rain asked in a whisper. "Would that help?"

"It's entirely possible you might talk more than me." Garrick drew a deep breath. Inviting Rain along to the exam room seemed...significant somehow. But it wasn't like Rain didn't already know all of what Garrick needed to explain to the doctor. And for all Rain said this appointment was about Garrick and his sex life in general, there was only one person Garrick wanted to get horizontal with presently, and making sure Rain was satisfied was important to him in ways he couldn't really explain. "Sure. Come on. Bring the knitting."

Rain gave him that small, pleased smile that never failed to make Garrick's stomach flip. Everyone else got Rain's devil-may-care grin, the wide, welcoming one, but Garrick alone earned that private one, got to see that vulnerability from Rain. As they followed the nurse, Garrick had a brief moment of second-guessing when he had to navigate balancing on the scale, but it wasn't like Rain hadn't seen him wobbly before. And if the nurse, a pretty young thing with red hair, wanted to have an opinion on Garrick's choice of companion, that was on her.

She'd probably briefed the doctor—a slim younger guy with dark hair and *Doctor Hu* embroidered on his white coat—on Rain's presence, because he didn't seem at all surprised to find Rain in the exam room with Garrick. And honestly, Rain did make it easier, prodding Garrick to explain more than he might have if alone, and joking enough to keep the energy in the room from getting too heavy.

Dr. Hu was the kind of person who listened intently, leaning forward on his stool, smiling and nodding, a sort of scientific intensity to his interest, reducing Garrick's fumbling explanations down to impersonal data.

"I know you probably don't want to hear this, but you're lucky—a best-case scenario sort of situation. Incomplete injury, enough nerve function to retain continence, some mobility returning, and even the occasional ejaculation. The erectile dysfunction you're experiencing is incredibly common in situations like yours, and again, luckily, treatable."

Lucky. There was that word again that Garrick hated so much. He didn't like feeling caught between gratitude and doom, self-blame lurking no matter which way he turned.

"Common meaning *normal*." Rain nodded enthusiastically. Another word that Garrick was coming to hate. There had been nothing normal about his life since he fell from that tree, and hearing that others shared his issues wasn't much comfort as he was trying to defy the odds.

"Exactly. And just like you've learned to deal with the mobility challenges, there are a variety of strategies you can employ here. It helps to have a mindset that not all sex needs to be penetrative." Dr. Hu's eyes darted toward Rain, and Garrick would have chuckled had he been less uncomfortable. For his part, Rain looked like he was seconds away from whipping out his phone and taking notes. Garrick tried to listen as Dr. Hu went on, talking about different things to try like various medications and external vibrators of certain frequencies, but it was hard to get past the buzzing in his brain that kept protesting this was not normal, not something he wanted to deal with.

"Are the pills kind of like my crutches? Something I might not need with enough time?" It would help if he could treat this like the PT, a necessary waystation to get his life back.

Dr. Hu frowned for the first time since he'd entered the room. "You're expecting to not need the crutches? Is that the prognosis your neurology team has shared with you? Because your chart... That's not precisely the conclusion I'm drawing."

"I know what the chart says. But I kept the leg when that was in jeopardy. I walked when they said I wouldn't. I'm going to return to smoke jumping. Beat predictions. I'm still in intense PT—I have to believe more improvements are coming."

"Ah. Well, while I'm optimistic for you, I'm also a realist. The medicines—and other interventions—might simply be a part of your new normal. We'll schedule regular follow-ups, but assuming you keep in good health with stable blood pressure, there's no reason to put undue pressure on yourself to...perform to certain pre-injury expectations."

"Thanks." Garrick didn't appreciate that viewpoint, but growling at the doctor wasn't going to solve anything, so he shoved his increasingly sour mood down. He'd simply have to prove this doctor wrong too, along with everyone else.

Resolved, he attempted to pay attention to the rest of the appointment, managing a laugh when Rain did in fact take notes on his phone about the specific medicine Dr. Hu wanted to try first.

"You've got the most important element for success—a supportive partner. You're both very lucky."

Not that Garrick didn't agree that Rain was worth the praise, but he'd had more than enough of that word, and his tone came out surly. "Yeah."

Rain gave him a censuring look, making Garrick feel worse for making him deal with this in the first place. Dr. Hu wrapped up the appointment, and then it was time for Rain to drive Garrick into work. Rain's first day was tomorrow, and he chatted about that as they got underway.

"So do you want to pick up your prescription after work? I can pick you up if you need a ride."

"Tucker's taking me home. I'll get to the pharmacy at some point."

"Okay." Rain drummed his fingers against the steering wheel. "You know it's normal to be frustrated, and if you want to talk about it—"

"I don't. And I'm tired of hearing what's normal. None of this is. You can drop the fake cheerfulness. I know this is a pain in the neck for you too—"

"It's not fake. I've told you, I like helping you, but this isn't even about that. I like you. I freaking love sex with you. And I'm genuinely excited—for both of us— that you get to have more of it. And if it takes a visit to the pharmacy to make that happen, then that's hardly a hassle. I've had worse dates." At the next stoplight, he gave Garrick a reassuring grin, one that made guilt snake up Garrick's back.

"Sorry. You don't deserve my bad mood."

"No, *you* don't deserve your bad mood. But I do understand it. It's okay. You can be a little grouchy."

But it wasn't okay, and even after he was at work, he continued to feel bad that he'd been snappy at Rain, who didn't deserve it, and Rain could say it didn't matter all he wanted, but Garrick had noticed his smile drooping around the edges.

"So, your friend starts for me tomorrow, and then

next week we've got that controlled burn. Looking forward to it?" Tucker leaned on Garrick's desk, expression far more friendly than Garrick was feeling. But he'd been a dick to enough people that day, so he made himself smile.

"You know it. But what's up with the weather? Rain all last week and wind this one. Are we going to be able to proceed?"

"Of course. Where there's a will, there's a way, right? Might have to improvise somewhat on ignition, but what would be the fun in things going according to plan?" Tucker had a jovial laugh, the kind that made others want to join in, and Garrick felt some of his tension slipping.

"Huh. You sound like Rain." And it made Garrick think. Maybe Rain did have a point. Perhaps improvising could be more fun than Garrick had let it be thus far. And determination had gotten him this far. He wasn't going to back down from a challenge, even if that challenge was trying to be the person Rain deserved. As Tucker laid out plans for the controlled burn, Garrick made some of his own, hoping ignition wouldn't be an issue for either of them.

Rain was hot, tired, and utterly exhilarated after two days of orientation for his new job. He liked being outdoors, liked the prospect of regular income, liked his coworkers, and liked learning about forestry in a more hands-on way than his college classes. As entry-level technicians, they would be doing a lot of forest maintenance—brush hauling, debris removal, trail grooming—while they waited to be needed in case of emergency. He hated the dress code and wasn't crazy about being dirty, but that was to be expected, and as he waited outside the headquarters office, he had plans to remedy that situation as soon as possible.

Even though his immediate crew boss as well as the Ryland guy who had hired him both knew he was friends with Garrick and giving Garrick a ride home, he didn't want to overly call attention to their friendship, so he waited patiently, working another few rounds on his socks until Garrick appeared. Keeping his greeting friendly but professional, he helped him load up his bag, chair, and crutches.

"You look exhausted." Garrick frowned. "I had this idea, but...you look too tired to walk Cookie, let alone be up for a date."

"Date?" Rain perked up. "You want to go on a date? I wasn't aware that we did that."

"We kinda have a Friday night thing going," Garrick pointed out. "And I had this thought, but it definitely falls under date territory, not a friends thing."

"Keep talking," Rain encouraged, mentally figuring out how much coffee he could get away with prior to dinner to make him appear sufficiently awake, because he truly wanted to know what Garrick had in mind. A date. Now that was new. And whatever had motivated it, Rain liked it, like Garrick sounding more energetic than he had the past few days.

"Okay. Well, I need to visit the pharmacy, and for *reasons* I'd rather not do that in town. If we go into Bend—"

"I am one hundred percent in favor of any evening that includes the pharmacy." Rain hoped his smile wasn't too lecherous, but he'd been worried that maybe Garrick didn't want to try the new meds or at least not with Rain. It wasn't that Rain wanted more sex—seeing Garrick on a daily basis, hanging out with him and the dog, making food together and working out, all of that was important and plenty fun too. However, he knew that Garrick wanted more from his sex life and Rain really wanted that for him too.

"Yeah, I figured you would be. And because I've been a major grump and it's the end of your first week of work, I thought maybe I could treat you to dinner. I know a spot you'll like—very inclusive and big vegetarian side of the menu. Way I see it, you're probably itching to get out of uniform."

"You know me too well. Yeah. Let's get home, take care of Cookie, and let me shower and change. Then onward to the pharmacy and dinner."

"And after…if you're not too tired…"

"I'm not," Rain lied, because he'd down a six-pack of energy drinks if it meant finding out what Garrick was being cagey about.

"So the restaurant is downtown, and right nearby is this…upscale adult shop. Boutique sort of place. Not skeevy."

"You had me at adult shop." Rain laughed, already liking where this evening was headed. He turned into their neighborhood, anticipation starting to gather at the base of his spine. "You want to add to your toy collection? I saved the notes in my phone about which frequency vibes the doctor said might help—"

"Well that, but also I want you to pick something for you. You like to show off, right?"

"And how. But you don't have to get me anything. Let's focus on you—"

Garrick's groan cut him off. "Which is kinda exactly

what I don't want to do. I've been thinking about this idea off and on for a couple of days now. I love the idea of you picking out something you want me to watch you use. Something you find sexy."

"Ah." As he parked at Garrick's place, Rain was starting to see the appeal of this idea. It was a great way to get the pressure off Garrick with waiting to see if the meds worked, and going to the store together could be fun in and of itself. "But you don't have to get me anything. I've got some money—"

"Rain." Garrick stopped him with a hand on his thigh before Rain could exit the vehicle. "Let me do this? Let me do something nice for you. I want to see you enjoy yourself."

"Yeah, but you're getting dinner. I don't want you thinking...you owe me or something else weird. Because you don't. Yeah, you've been moody, but the way I see it, you've got good reason."

"Fair enough, but what do you have against presents? I've noticed it before. That's why I said it was a date—not friends going fifty-fifty on everything. Me wanting to do something special together. Spoil you a little."

"You do that a lot already." Rain's voice went thick and rough.

"Yeah, and I like it. I mean, I know this thing is casual, but it doesn't mean I don't care for you. And you're always telling me how much you like helping me. Well, it goes both ways."

"Okay." Rain set his hand on top of Garrick's, studying their intertwined fingers. "We can have your date. And I'm not trying to be unappreciative. It's more...it's rare for me to get things that are just for me. Growing up with two brothers, almost everything was shared, from clothes to toys to books, and everything else was shared with the community at large." As much as he liked the values he'd learned growing up in the community and always having friends at the ready, this was the less-than-great part, the way nothing had ever felt entirely his own. Coupled with those feelings of invisibility he'd struggled with, it had been tough to count on being heard and count on things he cared about sticking around.

Garrick nodded like he was waiting for Rain to continue, so he did, even if the memories were making his stomach churn. "If I outgrew something, someone else down the hall could use it. My mom's big on decluttering. Things I liked had a way of ending up with new owners."

"I feel you. Not with possessions so much, but with people for sure. Things I liked had a way of not sticking around." Garrick's voice was soft and distant, as he was undoubtedly thinking of his parents' divorce and the ex-fiancée. "So I get it. It's hard to trust, even with something small."

"Exactly." A lot of the tension left Rain's shoulders. Garrick understood him on a level he wasn't sure he'd ever been understood before. "I became pretty good at getting stuff for myself. And with most of my friends, I'm the one giving. People don't...exactly go out of their way to do nice things for me. And when they do, it feels...strange."

"Well they should." In an unusual move for him, Garrick leaned in and gave Rain a fast kiss. "And maybe it will feel less weird if you practice."

"When you put it that way..." Rain returned the kiss, slower and deeper, trying to convey what he couldn't find the words for, that this meant something, something more than simply a fun outing. Garrick cared, and he wasn't afraid to say it or show it. Garrick's choice of careers alone showed that he was courageous, but this, the way he was forging ahead despite some disappointments, was true bravery on some deeper level. "Bring on the date."

He wasn't sure he'd ever be worthy of Garrick's sort of heroism, but hell if he didn't want to try.

Chapter Ten

"Well, that's done." Garrick sounded like he'd vanquished a dragon as he locked his prescription in Rain's glove box. He was both cute and exasperating at the same time.

"Was it really that hard?" Rain gave him what he hoped was an encouraging smile. "Not like the pharmacist made you wear a big sign or something, and she didn't even give you much in the way of embarrassing warnings."

He had completed another few rows on his sock while they waited at the pharmacy, but the big box store wasn't that crowded for a Friday night, and the way he saw it, they'd been lucky to draw a nice, motherly type of pharmacist who had been chatty about everything other than the subject of their visit.

"Nah." Garrick stretched as Rain headed the car toward downtown Bend. "You're right. This isn't a big deal to anyone other than me. And I'm making too much of it. It's hard, letting go of all the messages in my brain saying real guys don't have trouble getting it up."

"Real guys." Rain snorted. "You know as well as me that that's a toxic myth. And you're talking to the guy wearing purple lace underwear. Fuck real-men-don't messages. Life's more fun when you stop caring about that shit."

"Truth. And now my brain is stuck on visions of your underwear."

"Play your cards right and I'll show you." Waiting for a red light, Rain gave him a wink. After a few days in regulation forest service clothes, showering and putting on some of his favorites had felt so good, made even better knowing Garrick would appreciate his efforts. He'd grabbed this particular pair already anticipating the heat in Garrick's eyes. And since Garrick seemed to have a thing for his hair, he'd pulled only half of it up, leaving most of it spilling down over the shoulders of his silver sweater. He'd added boots and skinny black jeans, a decision he was already regretting as the tightness combined with Garrick's admiring looks had him wiggling around more than was probably socially acceptable. But like he'd told Garrick, fuck acceptable. He was determined to have a good time with this unexpected date night.

The restaurant Garrick had picked had a discreet rainbow sticker in the window next to their menu, and the atmosphere was the sort of sophisticated-yet-quirky that Rain really dug with a mixed adult crowd—lots of friend groups and various pairings likely on dates. The interior was long and narrow with lots of wood and metal details, but the server led them to a table on the expansive back patio where they had more room for Garrick's chair and more fun people watching for Rain. Cocktails in a huge variety of house specials came in mini mason jars and the menu was full of dishes meant to be shared. And as promised, the menu was about equally divided between imaginative vegetarian fare

and bacon-infused everything else. They ordered zuc-
chini fries as an appetizer and were discussing what
else to split when two tall, buff guys stopped in front
of their table.

"Garrick, my man!" The older, bigger one looked like
an escapee from a motorcycle gang, while the younger
one wasn't that much taller than Rain but ripped in a
way that implied he could take almost anyone in a fight.
And all the muscles and confidence undoubtedly meant
these were more of Garrick's smoke jumper friends.

"Linc." Garrick nodded at the bigger guy. "And
Jacob. This is Rain."

"Hi." Now this was suddenly more interesting because this was the pair that Garrick had mentioned a
few times, the one he'd tried to use jealousy on to force
them to admit their feelings. And Rain was acutely
aware of their twin scrutiny on him, his hair going all
itchy on the back of his neck and his sweater seeming
to shrink to corset tight. He'd lectured Garrick about
telling societal expectations to go fuck themselves, but
it was easier said than done, especially when these were
friends whose opinion Garrick valued.

"You owe me a twenty." Jacob bumped Linc's arm
before turning toward Garrick. "We've been worried
about you, dude. But my theory for your lack of texts
was that you were…occupied."

"Guilty. And sorry. I've been a crap friend to everyone. Didn't want to bug you—"

"It's not bugging. We like helping you." Nodding enthusiastically, Jacob rested a hand on Garrick's shoulder.
Rain resisted the urge to flick it away. Barely.

"Yeah, whatever you need," Linc added.

Garrick sighed, and Rain felt his frustration low in

his own gut. Had to be tough, the push-pull between friends wanting to help and him wanting a return to a normal that might not be coming.

"I know. And it's appreciated." Garrick managed a smile more genuine than the one Rain might have. "Anyway, I ended up with this dog. Big black rottie mix. I'm not sure how she does with other dogs, but she should meet your mutts at some point."

"Absolutely."

"We'll have you over soon." Jacob's voice, like Linc's, was almost but not quite too cheerful. "And later in the month we're having a thing for my birthday. Family. Friends. Grilling. My mom's making chocolate cake. You can bring your…new friend too."

"Sure. I'll see what our schedule is like." Garrick smoothly changed the subject into a brief discussion of his dispatcher work and Rain's new job before his friends had to move to let a server by and used that excuse as a reason to leave them to their dinner.

"You should go to the party," Rain urged once they had moved on. "Even if you don't want to take me, it would be good for you to see more of your friends."

"Why wouldn't I want to take you?" Garrick frowned, but Rain's stomach did a happy flip at how easily Garrick included him. "You're the one who told me you don't want to be something secret."

In Rain's limited past dating experience that request wasn't always honored, but he nodded. "I don't. I just meant if it was…easier."

"Honestly, having you along, that *would* be easier. Introducing you around, that sort of small talk, it's better than a bunch of questions about how I am and when

I'll be back and hearing endless stories about how the season is going."

"Point taken. And I'm happy to be that kind of buffer." And he was happy, period, to be Garrick's date, to be someone he was so willing for people to assume he was in a relationship with. It had meant something when Garrick had asked him to go back with him at the doctor's office. He might be deeply uncomfortable discussing his present sex life, yet he was far more secure in his pansexuality than Rain would have guessed, and it made Rain all warm, being with someone like that.

For the rest of the meal, he tried to keep that cuddly feeling close, bask in how good being with Garrick felt. It couldn't last—nothing ever did—but while he had it, he was determined to fully enjoy it. After the food, they leisurely made their way to the store Garrick had mentioned, window-shopping along their way back to the car, ducking into a pet boutique for a new type of chew for Cookie, and collecting cupcakes for later at a bakery.

On the edge of downtown, the adult store had an unconventional, funky vibe—part lingerie, part sex toys, and part an impressive array of head shop items amid assorted Oregon kitsch in an older log-cabin-style building. The aisles were narrow, not necessarily laid out for a wheelchair to navigate, but Garrick, who had clearly been there before, managed, leading him to the cases of sex toys in the rear of the store. A curvy younger woman with cat tattoos up both arms and a trio of nose rings was working the counter and took an immediate interest in them. Or rather in Garrick's biceps, which she couldn't seem to stop staring at.

"We've got a bunch of buy two, get one sales right

now. And let me know if you need anything unlocked. I'm here to help!" She smiled directly at Garrick's pecs and ignored Rain completely.

Garrick, though, seemed oblivious to her flirting, waving her away, posture stiff like it had been in the pharmacy. "We're fine. Just browsing."

Once she was back behind the register, though, Garrick relaxed considerably, joking with Rain and pointing out different sexy options while Rain looked at egg-shaped vibrators that had the right frequency. He'd pick something out for himself as he'd promised, but he wanted to make sure they also purchased some things that might help Garrick.

"Hey." Garrick crooked his finger, motioning Rain closer, so he could whisper. "You like the black thing the mannequin is wearing over there?"

"Uh-huh." It was a sheer short robe over matching silky panties that would feel amazing on his cock, and simply admiring the outfit had his blood rushing south, more so because Garrick supported his kink. He'd had partners before who seemed to get off on Rain's like of lingerie, but Garrick seemed to appreciate it on a more intimate level than he was used to. He shared it but also wasn't a chaser or some other type of user just out for a walk on the wild side with no regard for Rain as a person.

"Add it to our basket. It can join your other robe at my place." His filthy grin had Rain regretting his tight pants again.

"Okay. Sure." He was trying to get better about the whole present thing. Maybe he had absolutely no use for a sugar daddy, but Garrick was simply trying to have a little fun, and he didn't need Rain's whole emo thing of making this more than what it was. It was a nice gesture, not a commitment, and Rain needed to remember not to get attached merely because Garrick enjoyed being generous. And even if the way he seemed to understand him was absolutely swoon-worthy, Rain would do well to keep his healthy sense of self-preservation.

But all the inner lectures in the world were futile when a still-grinning Garrick pulled him close when he deposited the outfit in the basket on Garrick's lap. Fuck. Even his touch alone made Rain's knees rather literally wobbly. Swoon-worthy indeed.

"I can't fucking wait to see you in that. Might not even need—"

"Hush now. You can take your meds while I get changed. Deal?"

"Guess it would be a waste of a copay not to try it." Garrick's mouth twisted as he absently toyed with the end of a leather whip.

Needing him to smile again, Rain raised his eyebrows. "You got other kinks you want to confess?"

"Nah. I've fooled around with some stuff, but nothing serious. I mean, I wouldn't be averse to spanking you next time you try to shortchange your push-ups, but pain isn't a regular part of my fantasies."

"What is?" Rain was still considering the display of toy options. Maybe he could get Garrick to give him a hint as to what he should pick.

"Lately, the whole fucking you near-catatonic thing. Preferably with you wearing something sexy." Seductive grin back, Garrick shrugged. "What can I say? I've got simple tastes."

"Ha. I like it." And he did because it gave him an

excellent idea of what direction to go with the toy purchase. "And this?"

He pointed to one of the packages in the locked case, loving how Garrick's eyes went wide as he nodded. Damn if he wasn't starting to absolutely live for those sorts of reactions from Garrick, body already counting down until they were alone.

A million years ago, Garrick had been a horny teen, reckless and spontaneous with a single-minded intensity that made sex both fun and an almost physical necessity. And he'd spent most of the past year worried that those feelings were gone for good, that spontaneity was never going to be a thing for him again, that headlong rush into an encounter simply not possible. But Rain kept proving him wrong.

As it turned out, spontaneity wasn't a literal mad dash for the nearest horizontal surface, but rather an energy, a bubbling, swirling, sexy vibe that followed them from the adult store to the car to the drive back to his place, them ramping each other up with little touches and heated looks and sharing fantasies and stories. It carried them, even through the mundaneness of unloading and greeting Cookie. Right before Rain took Cookie out, he pressed Garrick's pill bottle into his hand, a wordless suggestion that rather than killing the mood seemed simply part of it, part of this intoxicating mix of anticipation and need.

So he used their absence to swallow the medication before he could talk himself out of it, and soon they were sprawled on his bed, lights low and fire going, that rush he'd craved still sweeping them up. Rain was half on top of him and it felt like the only thing that mattered in the whole world was keeping this make-out session going. Each kiss was a revelation, snowflakes to marvel at, each unique and special and worth slowing down for.

"Fuck. I love this." Lips kiss-swollen, Rain grinned down at him before claiming another kiss. They were still clothed, and somehow that added to the excitement, made those first touches on skin that much more potent. He worked a hand under Rain's sweater, memorizing the warmth of his back, the flex of his muscles, the way he hissed as Garrick stroked his spine. His tight black jeans had slipped down enough to expose a line of silky underwear for Garrick to play with, fingers dancing over the waistband before dipping under the elastic.

"Purple, huh? Forget the new outfit. I wanna see these."

"Coming right up." Eyes sparkling, Rain scampered off him to stand next to the bed.

"Give me a good show." Leaning back against the pillows, he luxuriated in the delicious feeling of being this turned on and not in a hurry. Rain's eagerness, both to please and to show off, was heady stuff.

"Go-go dancer, I'm not." Rain laughed as he yanked his hair the rest of the way down, shaking it free and making Garrick's fingers curl, wanting to touch it again. His easy movements belied his words, shimmying a little as he raised, then lowered his sweater, flash of skin and treasure trail.

"Maybe not, but you're damn sexy. Go on," Garrick encouraged.

Emboldened, Rain pulled the sweater up and off, a smooth gesture that revealed his increasingly toned chest and arms, all their workouts paying off. His dark nipples pebbled up as they were exposed, and Garrick had to resist the temptation to call Rain over so he could taste and touch. Soon. But first, Rain's little show was too fun to miss, especially when Rain spun, showing off his ass.

He lowered his pants by increments, revealing a silky pair of dark purple underwear with lace inserts playing peekaboo with Rain's smooth skin. When he stepped out of his pants and turned back around, the fabric outlined his hard cock in a way that had Garrick needing to lick his lips, especially the way Rain's cockhead poked out of the waistband, as if it couldn't wait to get in on the action.

"Leave them on," he urged as he opened his arms to welcome Rain back to the bed.

"I want to play with our news toys." Giving a sassy butt wiggle, Rain retrieved the bag from the store, dumping the contents next to Garrick before climbing back onto the bed. "You're overdressed again. You remedy that and I'm going to sort out the battery situation."

Garrick liked how Rain seemed to have picked up on how Garrick wasn't crazy about help undressing. Not to mention he enjoyed the sight of Rain wiggling around in the purple undies as he made quick work of his shirt and pants. As soon as he sat back against the pillows, Rain was on him, lightly straddling his waist without putting all his weight on Garrick. Mischief in his eyes, he held one of the egg-shaped vibes in his hand.

"Hey, what happened to your show?" Garrick's laugh had a nervous edge, even to his own ears. But he didn't push Rain away, curious to see what he had in mind.

"We're getting there." Vibrator still off, Rain rolled the egg down Garrick's arm, tickling.

"Not fast enough."

"Chill and let me have fun." With that, Rain did two things simultaneously—flipped on the buzzing sensation and captured Garrick's surprised gasp in a deep kiss. Then he proceeded to trade kisses and touches, rubbing Garrick's arms and pecs, stopping and lingering on places when Garrick inhaled sharply. He'd been hard most of the make-out session, but something about the deep pulsing vibration made him more aware of his cock, made the kisses feel more urgent, amplified the feel of Rain on his lap. And when Rain circled one of his nipples with the vibe, Garrick couldn't help a moan.

"Fuck. Okay. That's good. Weird but good."

"I knew you'd like it." Smirking, Rain repeated the move on the other side.

"Smug much?" Garrick's voice was rougher now. Damn Rain and his big ideas. This *was* working.

"You like it and you know it."

"Not as much as I'm gonna like this." Not about to let Rain have all the fun, he plucked the egg from Rain's grip and mimicked his moves, caressing his arms and chest.

"Oh, that's no fair." Rain took on a dreamy expression when Garrick rubbed across his nipple. Pulling Rain toward him, Garrick upped the ante, licking one while rubbing the other, loving the sounds Rain made. "Fuck. You…mmm."

"How about this?" Wanting more of those happy noises, Garrick trailed the vibrator down Rain's abs, tracing the outline of his cock through the thin fabric. Hips bucking, Rain cursed low as a bead of moisture appeared on his cockhead.

"Fuck. Can I try that on you?" Rain reached for the

egg right as Garrick was doing complex geometry to decide how best to get his mouth on Rain's cock without toppling anyone to the floor.

"I'd rather suck you," he said even as he handed the vibe over. "You could turn around and let me do that while you do whatever experimentation—"

"Experimentation? Ha. This is an introduction. Your cock and I are just getting acquainted, and you are not going to distract me with your mouth."

Garrick wanted to protest but then Rain's hand was on him. Even through his boxer briefs it was intense, a warm, firm pressure that had him moaning. The first few touches, Garrick was all up in his head, trying to figure out if it felt the same or different than before his injury, but then Rain yanked his boxers down and all scientific inquiries took a back seat to how damn good it was. Rain had bigger hands than his slim frame would indicate, long elegant fingers, and his grip was tight and sure as he stroked. And then he shifted, releasing Garrick's cock to trail the vibrator down the shaft. The buzzing resonated through his body, settling low in his balls, a deceptively strong pleasure.

"Damn. That's…something. Wow."

"Good." Rain took that as permission to redouble his efforts, alternating stroking with his hand and exploring with the vibrator. He kept adding slow, lingering kisses to the mix and other caresses with his free hand, an onslaught of sensations that both overwhelmed and thrilled Garrick, body tensing. His eyes kept drifting shut, but when he opened them next, Rain had a playful expression that said he was moments away from adding his mouth to his efforts with Garrick's cock. The thought alone had heat gathering in unexpected places, vibrations seeming to intensify.

"Wait. Don't want to come this way," he panted, breath as out of control as the rest of him. "Want to watch you with your other new toy."

"Mmm. Not sure what I like more—knowing you were close or that request." Rain stretched seductively, setting the vibrating egg aside.

"The request. I want to see." He managed to sound more commanding than pleading but it was a near thing.

"Okay, okay. I got the batteries in both parts." Rain held up the toy, a space-age-looking black plug with a wide, flared, forked base and curved shaft that was more artsy than phallic. Its main appeal was the wireless remote that came with it that controlled its impressive array of features—internal rotation, vibration in both the shaft and base, pulsing patterns, and warming. The base was designed to tease both the rim and the balls while the curve in the tip looked ready to massage the money spot. Anticipation swirled through his veins as he couldn't wait to see its effect on Rain.

"Hand me your sexy panties," he said as Rain pushed them down and off. "I've got plans."

"Oh? Not into gags, but otherwise feel free to surprise me." After handing over the underwear, Rain slid a condom on to the toy and lubed it up with the ultra-long-lasting stuff they'd bought.

"Come here." He tugged Rain close for another kiss as he stroked and squeezed the globes of Rain's ass. "You want my fingers first? Warm up?"

"Too impatient." Rain scooted backward as he rose up to his knees. Garrick was torn between asking him to spin so he could watch the penetration and wanting to keep studying Rain's expressions. Then Rain's tongue darted out to lick at his full lower lip as his torso twisted, and no way was Garrick going to miss watching Rain's face.

"Oh. Fuck. It's not even on yet, and..."

"That's it," Garrick encouraged. "Tell me how it feels."

"Good. Bigger than this thing looked in the package. Damn. I'm teasing with the tip and it feels like a freaking traffic cone."

"Go as slow as you need to."

"Yeah. Fuck. Been a while... Oh *yeah*." Rain's eyes went wide and his mouth slack as he must have found something that worked. Damn. He was the sexiest fucking thing Garrick had ever seen. He started a leisurely stroke of his cock, not trying to get off, just amping up all the good feelings from watching Rain.

"Good?"

"And how. Here." Rain pressed the remote into Garrick's free hand. "Have fun."

"I intend to." Garrick started by sending soft pulses, enjoying how Rain wriggled around.

"More. It's all the way in now. Fuck. So full."

"This?" Garrick flipped on the internal rotation thing. Rain's eyes practically rolled back in his head, which made Garrick's whole body throb.

"*Yes.* Oh my god. Only premium toys from now on. Fuck."

"You want more of the fancy features?" Pressing the button for heat, Garrick could tell the moment Rain started to feel it because his hips started rocking.

"Jesus. It's warm." Biting his lower lip, Rain hovered

his free hand over his cock. "Which should be weird, but somehow…"

Rain trailed off in a series of moans as Garrick increased the vibrations. This. This was exactly what he'd fantasized about all week, watching Rain let go like this, seeing him enjoy each new sensation. It was a hell of a show, turning him on on multiple levels.

"Can you come from this?"

"Maybe." Rain rocked his hips more deliberately now. "Never done it hands free… Fuck. Need to touch."

One hand still holding the toy in place, Rain started stroking his cock in earnest. Batting his hand away, Garrick wrapped the discarded silky underwear around his shaft and slowly stroked, making sure his thumb grazed the exposed tip on each upstroke.

"Okay, you keep that up and it's going to be over fast." Little beads of sweat appeared on his forehead as Rain breathed hard.

"You like that?" Taking a quick second to turn up the vibrations and rotation, Garrick jacked him faster now.

"Ung. No fair. No fair." Flailing, Rain bent forward, bracing a hand on Garrick's chest. The pressure of his hand felt almost electric, making tingles radiate down Garrick's arms. Getting Rain to shoot all over him became his new number one goal, and he stroked faster, until Rain's eyes drifted closed. His breath came in harsh pants. "God. More. Like that."

"That's it, baby. Let go. Let it feel good." Toying with the vibration level again, Garrick put it on a pulsing pattern.

"I think…oh man. Almost too much."

"You can take it," Garrick encouraged. Abs tight and neck straining, Rain was shuddering now. He had to be close, and simply knowing that excited Garrick to new heights.

"Think I'm...oh fuck. Yes. Need to come. Now."

"Do it. Come for me." He barely got the words out before Rain was coming with a shout, painting Garrick's chest with creamy stripes as his orgasm seemed to go on and on. Finally, he pulled away, collapsing next to Garrick as he withdrew the toy.

"You have to try that at some point. Never come so hard in my life." Rain was half panting, half laughing as he struggled to catch his breath.

"That's awesome. And you are so fucking beautiful when you come." Merely the memory of Rain's sounds had Garrick needing to resume stroking himself. Felt good, being this hard, this tense and ready. Letting Rain go first had absolutely been a brilliant idea.

"Oh, yeah. Do that." Rain snuggled in close, licking Garrick's neck as he danced his fingers down his arms, making the tingles in those locations that much more intense. Rolling away long enough to find the egg vibrator, Rain captured his mouth in a blistering kiss while touching the vibrator to his arms and pecs. Tension gathered in Garrick's limbs, arms going almost too rigid to keep stroking, but he couldn't stop, not now.

"I'm close," he panted against Rain's mouth.

"That's right." Rain pinched one of his nipples while vibrating the other, mouth finding Garrick's collarbone. He was everywhere Garrick needed him to be, and the buzz from the vibe seemed to be everywhere too, snaking throughout him as his muscles tensed even more.

"Fuck. What are you..." Whatever he'd been about to ask died on a moan as Rain raked his teeth across Garrick's shoulder. "*Yes.* That. Right...there..."

And then he was coming, hard, almost painful waves of pleasure as everything went hot and tight and impossibly good before rendering him spent and shaking with the aftermath of it.

"You weren't…kidding. Nothing…that intense." He pulled Rain up for a kiss, trying to regain control over his brain while continuing to wallow in how damn good it felt.

"Fabulous. I'm investing in fifty more of these things." Rain set the egg vibe aside as his finger idly trailed through their mingled come on Garrick's chest. "You shot, but it sounded almost like it hurt."

"Did a little. Weird." The shooting had been an unexpected bonus, another level to the orgasmic sensations. It didn't happen every climax anymore, but when it did, he noticed it more now, the pleasant ache in his balls, the receding tension in his abs, the increased sensitivity of his cockhead. It was all wonderful, and he struggled with how to explain it. "My muscles get more tense right before, almost painful as it hits, but it's a *good* hurt. Deep. And then more limp after. Like an hour in a hot tub relaxed. So good."

"I'm so glad. And see? Meds are awesome." Rain kissed his cheek.

"Pretty sure that was more you than the pill, but yeah, I'm maybe a convert." As much as he wanted to praise Rain, he had to admit it had been nice, not worrying about the erection disappearing and whether it was the pill or the situation or both—the intense climax and getting to share that with Rain had been more than worth any hassle over the meds.

"Me too. That and I'm now a believer in pricey toys. Damn. I'm not comatose, but it's a close thing."

"Good." Garrick held him close, blood still thrumming, both with the aftermath of what they'd done and new ideas for getting Rain even more worn out.

"You hang tight and I'm going to clean up and grab you a towel." Rolling away from him, Rain released a huge yawn. "It cool if I crash here awhile?"

"As long as you want." And wasn't that the truth. There was no one, absolutely no one, he could think of whom he'd rather share this experience with. It wasn't simply sex and it wasn't merely getting back something he'd lost. It was deeper. More connected. *Shared.* Like a journey they got to go on together, exploring and discovering and drawing closer together. He knew full well it was dangerous, getting attached to Rain, getting used to him being here, but hell if he could pull back now.

Chapter Eleven

"Fisher? Rain? Dude! You awake?" One of Rain's fellow entry-level forest technicians snapped him out of a pleasant fog where he'd been reviewing his entire underwear collection, trying to decide what to wear next time he and Garrick were likely to fool around. Not today, though. This controlled burn project called for long hours for both of them, and Rain would be out here most of the rest of the week on cleanup duty with his crew. He needed to pace himself, and Garrick did too. He'd be lucky to sneak in a few workouts and Cookie's exercise time, let alone another lengthy sex fest. Luckily, he had his memories of their weekend keeping him warm and far from bored as he waited for their next assigned task. They'd been digging fireline most of the day in preparation for the controlled burn and were nominally on a break, hence the daydreaming.

"Yeah, yeah, I'm here." He pulled at the collar of his forest service shirt, which he wore over a plain black T-shirt. As hot as he found other people in uniforms, he couldn't wait to peel off his yellow and green duds later and get into something truly comfortable. Like purple lace...

No. Couldn't be thinking about sexy times while trying to carry on a conversation with a guy who looked ready to audition for a farmer-of-the-month calendar, an earnest young guy with a clean-cut appearance and can-do attitude who blushed every time someone said a curse word.

"Boss wanted to see you." The guy spoke over Rain's shoulder like eye contact might be more than he could muster.

"I'm on it." Rain strode over to where his crew chief was standing with a couple of the more senior members of their group.

"Good work today, Fisher." O'Connor, the crew chief, was an older woman who'd been with the forest service a long time and was now in charge of all the new forest techs Ryland had hired. "I've noticed…"

Hell. Here they went. What had she noticed? He hadn't worn nail polish since starting the workout regimen with Garrick, was wearing strictly regulation clothing, and had every last strand of hair up inside his helmet. "Yeah?"

"Oh, nothing bad. Only that you love the tech. Anytime some new piece of equipment comes out, you get a shine to your eyes. I was thinking Bosler here could train you to be our backup radio person."

"Yeah, I could do that." Working the walkie-talkies and sat phones sounded awesome, especially because it meant that he might get to hear Garrick's voice sooner than at the end of the day.

"Good. Bosler will show you the ropes." O'Connor left him with Bosler, who started by showing him the variety of devices he was carrying. Bosler was retirement age, a former smoke jumper well versed in radio work and dispatch duties, who'd come back to do some hand crew and forest management work part-time.

"The key is keeping track of all the chatter, deciding what the boss needs to know right away and what can wait a second," Bosler explained. "And also knowing who to call for what when the boss needs to get a message out in a hurry. The burn boss is setting up for ignition now, with senior hotshot crews in position as well as the hand crews that have been digging line all day. Dispatch will be waiting to hear that we're ready."

"Got it."

"Well, go on then." Bosler handed him the radio. "Tell Dispatch our status."

Okay. Maybe this was weirder than he'd thought because he couldn't exactly warn Garrick that it was him, and he didn't particularly want to reveal their close friendship to Bosler right off.

"Headquarters? This is hand crew four-five-one reporting line is complete from anchor point to anchor point."

"That's good, four-five-one. We're expecting ignition soon." Garrick's voice was warm, and if he recognized Rain, he wasn't saying. It was nice, though, having him on the other end of the radio. Reassuring as the big blaze was about to head their way. This was a first for Rain, being this close to a wildfire, even an intentional one. As the blaze approached, another fire would be ignited inside the firelines they'd dug, both blazes hopefully meeting and burning each other out without crossing any fireline or causing hotspots to flare up outside the designated area. They would stay back while the burn occurred, letting more experienced personnel manage the containment of the blaze, but then they'd move in to clean up and look for hotspots.

Working with Bosler, he relayed more information to Garrick as needed, taking messages back to the boss as well. It was far more interesting than standing around and waiting for the action to get started. And it was kind of neat, working with Garrick in this way, listening to him juggle information incoming from various crews and make decisions alongside Ryland as to who needed to be where in advance of ignition and after the blaze was underway. It reminded him of town-hall-style meetings at the community growing up, lots of details and ideas flying around and the need to pay close attention to keep up. Too bad he didn't have his knitting to keep him focused.

But what he did have was people counting on him, the crew chief and his fellow workers, and the time before ignition passed quicker now that he had a purpose. After all the hours of prep work and all the logistics that went into planning, the actual burn was over relatively quickly, a fact he marveled at much later when he was driving an exhausted Garrick back home.

"It was so fast."

"The real deal is often even faster moving—whole towns gone in a matter of minutes. That's fire. And that's why we do the controlled burns, so we have some say in how and when it happens."

"Yeah. You were great today. Hearing you…that was so cool. You're good at this."

"Eh. It's just a summer job, you know?" Garrick didn't seem to want the praise, but he really was good at the job, and Rain was sure he wasn't the only one who had noticed.

It was late enough that Garrick's dad had been en-listed to walk Cookie after he closed up at his shop, and his truck was still there when they pulled into Garrick's drive.

"Heck," Garrick muttered. "There goes my plan of asking if you wanted to shower here."

"It's okay," Rain assured him as he exited the SUV.

"I've got that." Garrick's dad met him at the back of the SUV, removing the wheelchair before Rain could. To Garrick, he said, "Dog seemed lonely, so I stuck around, made you a chili for dinner."

"Thanks. See you later, Rain." Garrick sounded both grateful and tired, and Rain should have been glad he had his dad for help, but in actuality he was feeling a bit summarily dismissed. And he'd become rather used to being the one walking Cookie and fussing over Garrick, so much that he missed it. His grandma had a pan of vegetarian enchiladas waiting for him, though, so he couldn't simply head to his room to sulk.

"How about we don't tell your mom I used real Monterey Jack?" She laughed as she made him a plate. She'd eaten earlier, but she settled herself opposite him with a big mug of herbal tea. "And you're back earlier than I expected. No dog walking? Or canoodling?"

He had to snort at that. "Garrick's dad is there. So no."

"Might be good, an evening on your own." She nod-ded sagely. "Do some laundry, watch a movie with me? You can work on those socks I'm not supposed to know about until next month."

"Yeah. I guess." Then, realizing he sounded rather petty, he forced himself to swallow back his emo mood. "Sorry. I'm happy to spend time with you. Guess I've been wrapped up in Garrick, huh?"

"Not that that's a bad thing." She brushed her gray hair off her forehead with dye-stained hands. "But some space…that's healthy too. Especially since neither of you are exactly the settling-down type. You're a wanderer with itchy feet and he's a player with a roving eye. But it's a cute summer fling, as long as no one gets hurt."

"Yeah," he said weakly. Grandma wasn't wrong. But it still turned his dinner to toxic sludge in his belly, made him push the plate away.

As long as no one gets hurt. Her words kept echoing in his brain as he showered and ran a load of laundry and sat through a comedy about a group of senior citizens running a hotel, churning out more rows of the sock to avoid ruminating too much on that assumption. Did he need to pull back? Should they cool it off after going hot and heavy so fast? Was he asking for a broken heart? And God knew that the last thing he wanted was to dole pain out. Hurting Garrick would suck.

Maybe Grandma was right and space was good. But then as he was getting ready for bed, his phone dinged.

Lying here wondering what you changed into. Sorry for the fast exit. Would have rather eaten with you TBH.

Rain couldn't help smiling to his empty bedroom. Funny how a single message could relax him so thoroughly, chase those pointless anxieties away.

No sexy panties, sorry. But I am wearing your favorite pony T-shirt. And no problem. I understand. You need time with your dad too.

He used the wait for a reply to put away his laundry in drawers, suitcases now empty and neatly stacked in the corner. Eventually he'd need them again, but until then he wasn't going to get caught up in worries he was giving too much of himself. Holding back simply wasn't his style.

Darn. Was hoping for a sexy pic ;) LOL. JK. Hoping you get some rest. Tomorrow is a shorter day for me, so I'm going to make a stuffed pepper recipe and have it ready when you get off work. I'll make enough in case Shirley wants to come too.

See? That was sweet. And it was impossible to hold back with a guy that sweet who pushed himself to make vegetarian food for Rain, who was nice to his grandma, who made it clear over and over that it wasn't simply about a sexual connection for him. They were friends. Friends who cared. And hell if Rain could turn that off simply because of a risk of future pain.

"Damn weather, fucking with all my plans," Garrick complained to Rain as he got settled in the SUV. Rain's workday had been cut short as well, skies opening up and hindering all the mop-up efforts his crew had been engaged in. The past few days, they'd had limited time alone together, and Garrick had been looking forward to a nice long outing with Cookie and Rain. Being outside would help with this cooped-up feeling he kept having. Even though the controlled burn had been challenging, it had still meant long hours in one place for him. But now high winds and precipitation meant another long night of trying to find something worth watching. "I'm so bored of being bored."

"But luckily, you have me." Rain gave him an indulgent smile, apparently not going to let Garrick's bad attitude get him down. "And I am full of good ideas."

"That you are," Garrick had to admit. And honestly, sex wouldn't be a terrible plan B for the night either—getting Rain off in some new and creative way could go a long way to jump-starting his mood. "Okay, surprise me."

But sex didn't seem to be Rain's highest priority as he arrived back at Garrick's after his shower in comfortable sweats, a rain jacket, and toting a big bag. He didn't look like a person dying to get laid, and indeed, after a fast walk for Cookie while Garrick got the towels ready, he produced a large rectangular box from his bag.

"We're playing a board game?"

"Not just any board game. Remember how my parents limited TV? We're playing the game that has produced years-long sibling grudges in my house. Epic battles. Brother against brother violence. Entire chore regimes hung in the balance over this game, man, and when I saw it at Grandma's in a closet, I knew it would be the perfect distraction for you. And then after I kick your butt at the game, we're going to watch this not-half-bad movie she had me watch earlier in the week, only I'm going to teach you how to knit during it so you can gain two new boredom-busting hobbies tonight."

"I thought we agreed when you tried to show me the sock thing that my hands are too big?"

"No, *you* said your hands were too big. I heard your complaints and raided Grandma's craft room for some bigger needles and chunky yarn. You'll be fine," Rain said airily, as if Garrick had a burning desire to craft and he was doing him a favor, making that happen.

"I'm not sure…"

"Grandma sent cookies." That got a woof from the actual Cookie lurking nearby, making them both laugh before Rain continued, "You must have impressed her with the stuffed peppers if she was motivated to bake for you. And I'm only sharing if you give this a try." Rain started setting up the board game on Garrick's dining table.

"I'd rather give *you* a try," Garrick grumbled, thinking again about the sex option. Rain was a lot less bossy when he was strung out and begging to come.

"I told Grandma not to wait up." Winking, Rain patted his arm. "Win the game and I'll wear whatever you want for the knitting lesson. And then after…"

"Yeah?" Suddenly Garrick was a lot more invested in the board game. "I… I've missed you this week. I mean, I know I see you every day, but…"

"I know what you mean." Rain leaned over and gave Garrick a lingering kiss. "Don't tell Grandma but I sleep better over here."

"Well, I do tell better bedtime stories…"

"I'm counting on it." That got him another kiss, this one far sweeter than any cookies Rain could produce. With other people, kissing had usually functioned like an express train to the bedroom, but with Rain, kissing was more like…conversation. Nuanced. Hello kisses and goodbye kisses and give-this-a-try kisses and wait-till-I-get-you-naked kisses. Sometimes sex followed, but often via a more meandering route, and he could honestly say he was coming to appreciate the more scenic route. Even when it came with board game tokens.

"Okay, so you're going to have to help me here. I'm not really much of a gamer guy."

"You don't say." Rain gave him an exaggeratedly pointed look. "I've already figured out that you were one of those kids they couldn't keep indoors. Roaming around your dad's farm. Sports. Scouts and clubs, too, I bet."

"Guilty. We owned some video games, but they could never hold my attention. Even now, buddies have tried to get me into this first-person shooter game, and honestly it's boring. And sports are great to play, but watching them can drag unless I'm at a bar and trying to... *Anyway*, how about you explain the rules to me?"

"Nice change of subject. And you can go ahead and admit your sports bar patronage is in direct correlation to how good of a pickup joint it is. Even Grandma knows you're a player. She was joking about it the other night."

Rain's tone was offhand, but it hit Garrick like a well-aimed dart. How could he explain that he wasn't really a player? He'd been that guy a lot of years, true, but now it felt like a discarded coat, something that no longer fit. He wasn't ashamed of that past, but maybe he wasn't that guy anymore. Hadn't been even before the accident, if he was being honest. But now...all those years of fast living seemed so very far away. And it wasn't precisely a lack of words that kept him from speaking up. More like it seemed Rain had already reached a conclusion and Garrick didn't want to try to talk him out of it and end up looking stupid.

"Right now, only one I'm playing with is you," he said at last, tone light. "And I've been at the bar for trivia night. Tell me this is more engaging than that."

"Poor baby. Nerds invading your sacred space." Rain

laughed as he put the finishing touches on the game.
"Now think of this like football. Or capture the flag as
kids. It's all about strategy and misdirection."

"Okay." Garrick let him continue explaining the
rules, liking how into it Rain got as he warmed up to
his role as the teacher. As they got started playing, he
had funny stories about his brothers and managed to
distract Garrick into bad decisions with his side of the
board more than once. He was deceptively competitive, and if Garrick had expected him to go easy on him
since he was a newbie, he was quickly proven wrong.

"You're out for blood," he complained as Rain
mowed down another chunk of his defense.

"My brothers were even more ruthless." Grinning
like a pirate, Rain was adorably animated, and despite
his initial grumpiness, Garrick found himself sucked
into the game.

"Okay, so maybe this isn't terrible," he allowed. "No
idea why this is more engaging than a phone app or
video game."

"It's the pieces. Holding them. The tangible aspect."
Rain licked his lips as he nodded, mischief in his eyes.
"That and I'm good company."

"Yeah, you are." Garrick wanted to kiss him but
didn't want to upset the arrangement of the board, so he
settled for rubbing Rain's arm. Eventually, the cookies
came out, along with mugs of a tea that Garrick hadn't
been aware he had. Shifting from playful to intent on
winning, Rain narrowed his eyes as he considered each
move, a general surveying his surroundings.

"You would have made a hell of a quarterback."

"Ugh. No." Rain made a sour face. "High school
sports were *so* not my thing. As much I can appreciate

a tight ass in uniform pants, locker rooms are the worst. And I'm not a violent person. Smacking into other humans for fun isn't my idea of a great Friday night."

"Ha. Not violent? You're slaughtering all my pieces. Remind me to never cross you." On the floor under the table, Cookie made a snorting noise in her sleep like she too didn't believe Rain's assertion of being all peace loving.

"Me? Scary? This is me trying to hold back. I wouldn't *mind* if you won. But I keep getting carried away."

"You're cute." Garrick didn't think he was about to go out and join a tabletop gaming league or anything, but he had to admit it was a pleasant way to pass the evening, even when Rain ultimately won. "Damn. I mean, congrats. Good game. But I was looking forward to the naked knitting lesson possibility."

"Me too." Rain wiggled his eyebrows at Garrick. "Let's pretend you won. You get all cozy in your recliner and get the movie up, and I'll slip into something suitably distracting for you."

"Okay." Garrick wasn't going to turn that offer down. But he also hadn't been thinking it through because when Rain emerged from the bedroom in the little robe and black panties set they'd bought in Bend, all his remaining brain cells toppled over like pieces on the game board, surrendering to Rain's superior firepower. "Damn. How am I supposed to concentrate on yarn with you looking like that?"

"You like?" Rain gave a little turn before retrieving the bag with the yarn and needles. The outfit was a delicious contrast between silky, flimsy fabric and Rain's increasingly buff muscles, black lace details making his creamy skin look that much more edible. But he seemed utterly determined to get Garrick a new hobby, perching on the arm of Garrick's chair and talking him through the basics again.

Cookie fell asleep again next to his chair and the movie droned on. The whole scene was almost unbearably cozy with just enough of a kinky vibe to be fun. Like with the board game, Rain in teacher mode was captivating, the way his whole body seemed to glow when he was excited about something. Garrick still wasn't sold on knitting, but he could happily listen to Rain all evening. Still, though, he couldn't resist slipping a hand under the edge of the robe, stroking Rain's bare back.

"Hey, now. Time for that later." Stern look firmly in place, Rain made a clucking noise and undid Garrick's last several stitches, which were lumpy, gnarly things compared to Rain's neat work. "You need to pay attention."

"I *am* trying." He had to admit there was a certain satisfaction when he did get it right, the moment when he seemed on the verge of some breakthrough to a smooth rhythm like Rain had. It wasn't so much the yarn and sticks that held his focus as much as the promise of that rhythm—like hammering out exercises, the very monotony a good, mind-clearing thing.

"I know. And you'll get more comfortable with it, promise. Knitting in public is a great conversation starter—I've met several friends that way. And someday you may want to woo someone with something more than bad pickup lines at a sports bar."

Garrick had to laugh at that, both because Rain wasn't wrong and because if he wasn't mistaken, Rain's voice had a jealous edge. Maybe he didn't like thinking about a future where they weren't together any more than Garrick did.

"Maybe all I want to do is woo you." He tugged Rain into his lap, letting him sprawl across Garrick in an inelegant but cuddly heap.

"Okay, sweet-talker." Rain had that small, pleased smile Garrick liked so much. And he offered Garrick a slow, thorough kiss as a reward. "More lessons later?"

"Sure." He gently loosened Rain's hair from its tight knot, letting it cascade down over Rain's shoulders. "Later."

And then they were kissing again, more intentionally now. Finally free to do the touching he'd been craving all evening, he swept his hands all over Rain's arms and torso. Rain stretched like a cat and arranged himself more comfortably, bodies pressing together in the tight confines of the big chair. His hair was still slightly damp and smelled like sweet wildflowers. Everything about him drove Garrick wild and not simply physically. Sure Rain was hot as fuck, but he was also funny and caring and smart and fierce and a whole pile of other things that Garrick liked so very much.

As the kisses grew more heated, Garrick wished he had a way to freeze time. He wasn't sure when he'd last been this happy, this content. Years, probably. He wanted to bottle all these feelings and sensations up, save them for later, save them for cold, wet nights that wouldn't come with a lap full of warm, vital Rain. But he couldn't think too much about that murky future, not with Rain moving increasingly urgently against him, little encouraging noises escaping his throat. They had tonight and that counted for an awful lot, and he was damned determined to make the most of every opportunity to savor Rain.

Chapter Twelve

Rain was quite possibly going to die of sweetness overload. Like for real, a person couldn't be expected to endure such endlessly hot kisses. Not that he wanted to stop. Making out with Garrick in his recliner was the best thing that had happened to his week, and he happily wriggled against him, trying to soak up the most possible good feels. He wasn't trying to get off, not yet, simply wallowing in how damn perfect this night had been. His favorite game. New sexy outfit. Chocolate cookies. Knitting. Garrick, who for all his reluctance had actually been a pretty good sport about all of it and was now kissing Rain like it was his sole purpose in life.

"We should...find...the bed," Rain suggested in between more kisses, not sure how much longer he could hold out and pretty confident that Garrick didn't want spooge on his favorite chair. Also, Rain was in the mood for something more mutual if Garrick was interested in that.

"Damn. I don't want to move. But I guess we should. I did promise you help sleeping." Garrick offered him a meaningful leer. "And sadly, I can't carry you to bed from here if you pass out after you come."

"The risk is real." Rain chuckled as he reluctantly moved off Garrick. "And I want to make you sleepy too."

"Watching you—"

"Is not what I have in mind. Not that I don't love showing off for you, but I love it when both of us have a good time." He kept his voice light, not wanting to put pressure on Garrick but wanting him to know how much he enjoyed their time together too, enjoyed touching and tasting and watching Garrick just as much as he enjoyed showing off for him.

"Every time with you is a good time. I mean that." Garrick reached for his crutches then shook his head and transferred to the wheelchair instead. "And you already have me all jelly-legged simply from all that kissing. I don't have to come to enjoy the hell out of being with you."

"I know. And I agree one hundred percent. I feel the same way. But I'm not going to lie, I've got a whole long list of things I'm still dying to try with you. If you're game."

Garrick took on a thoughtful look, then finally nodded like he'd finished some equation in his head. "I've got a wish list too. Let me get some water, and you tell me what fantasy we can make come true before sleep."

Rain correctly assumed that Garrick's request for water was him deciding to take a pill, and he hung back while Garrick did that, choosing instead to herd Cookie toward her princess bed. "Sorry, Cookie. I get the people bed tonight. Humans only."

He arranged himself in what he hoped was a seductive posture on the bed as Garrick came in and pulled off his shirt. Damn. Rain was never getting tired of that chiseled chest. Moving to sit on the side of the bed,

Garrick used his grabber tool to remove his shoes. Not content to watch, Rain draped himself over his bare muscled back, dropping kisses on his neck and shoulders.

"Mmm. You're the best kind of distracting." Garrick leaned into the contact.

"I try." Holding Garrick's broad body close, he licked his neck, thrilling to the shudder that swept through Garrick. He kissed and licked his way up from Garrick's collarbone to his ear, flicking the lobe with his tongue. "How would you feel about fucking me?"

"In theory? Fuck, yes. Thanks to your show with the toy, I have dreams where I get to fuck you, get to feel you come apart for me."

"Well, then, let's make your dreams come true."

"Not that simple. I'm not sure precisely how best to make it happen. My hip and knee strength still isn't one hundred percent."

"Me on top." Rain couldn't keep the excitement out of his voice. "And if that doesn't work, we can try something else. But I'd like to try, see if we can make it good for you."

"And you." Garrick captured his hand and kissed the knuckles. "I'm trying to not feel bummed that I can't fuck you through the mattress—"

"I love being on top. Seriously. It's my favorite. You know me by now. I like being watched. I'm not crazy about being on all fours because I don't get to see the other person, see their reactions, and I don't get off as hard as I do on top."

"Seriously?" Garrick sounded uncharacteristically vulnerable, so Rain hugged him tighter.

"Yup. And how. Let me show you? I promise you that your goal of me near passed out is still on the table."

"Good." Garrick turned so that he could pull Rain half into his lap. Going happily, Rain settled with his arms looped around Garrick's neck, happier still when Garrick claimed his mouth in a soft kiss.

"I want you so much," he confessed. And it was true. Nothing about their break in the action had dulled his earlier desire. If anything, the time spent talking always made him want Garrick that much more. Whenever they talked about sex, it was clear that this meant something to Garrick, that he cared about it being good for Rain, and his willingness to be brave and open up about his feelings and fears was an unexpected turn-on.

"Show me." Garrick gently set Rain aside so he could finish removing his pants and then arranged himself sitting back against the pillows. The head of the bed was slightly inclined which made for a fabulous angle for Rain to straddle Garrick and kiss him until they were both breathing hard, right back to where they'd left off in the living room. Holding Garrick's scruffy jaw in his hands, he plundered his mouth until Garrick growled low and reclaimed control, nipping at Rain's lips, the sort of aggressive licks and bites that made Rain's cock throb.

Testing to see how much weight Garrick could handle on his thighs, Rain undulated his hips, a gentle grind of his slippery underwear against Garrick's hard cock. Delicious shivers raced up Rain's spine as Garrick gripped his ass, encouraging him.

"Fuck. Love this outfit on you. But want to feel your skin too." Garrick plucked at the waistband of the panties. "Leave the robe on if you want, but lose these."

Slithering out of the underwear, Rain took the interruption as an excuse to dig the lube and a condom from the nightstand. He tossed them on the bed, then resumed straddling Garrick.

"Now where were we?"

"Right here." Pulling him close, Garrick kissed him, tender at first, then more intense. It was all-consuming, the way Garrick took charge of his mouth and senses, like he had a cheat sheet for how to turn Rain on, one kiss at a time. He tasted sweet as his tongue fucked its way into Rain's mouth in a way that left no doubts about how into this Garrick was. A soft, needy whimper escaped Rain's throat as he resumed grinding against Garrick. He had to gasp each time their bare cocks bumped against each other.

"God, I could almost come from kissing you like this." Groaning, he rested his head against Garrick's, focusing on how each movement of his hips made his cock pulse.

"Better not." Garrick reached for the lube bottle. "This okay? Wanna feel you."

"Oh, yeah." Rain wasn't turning down a reason to feel Garrick's big hands on him. Hell, just watching Garrick slick up his fingers had his insides all flippy with anticipation. And then he pulled Rain close with one arm while his other hand reached around. "Oh, *hello.*"

Garrick laughed, but Rain leaned into the contact as he traced soft circles around his rim. He claimed Garrick's mouth for another kiss right as Garrick pressed in. Like with kissing, he seemed to instinctively know what Rain liked, going for two fingers and steady pressure, not so much teasing. The stretch was so fucking welcome, exactly what he'd been craving, even before

Garrick connected with his gland. "Okay, you're damn good at that. Too good."

"Damn. You feel amazing." Garrick did this scissoring motion with his fingers that had Rain moaning hard against his mouth as he fucked back onto Garrick's hand, trying to get more of that blunt pressure against his spot.

"Fuck, yes, it does. So good." His cock leaped against Garrick's, the contact adding to the overall sexiness of the experience.

"Can't wait to be inside you." Garrick stole another kiss as he continued to fuck Rain open with his fingers.

"How about now?" Never exactly known for his patience, Rain was even more insistent than usual, voice rough and needy. Enough kisses and grinding and Garrick's magical digits and this was all going to be over far too quickly. "Wanna try your cock before I come on your fingers."

"Now there's an image." Garrick smiled wickedly right as he rubbed against Rain's gland a final time before withdrawing his fingers. Rain grabbed for the condom and lube, getting Garrick slicked up and ready in record time.

"Uh-huh. But I like this picture more." He winked at Garrick as he moved into position, holding Garrick steady with one hand.

"Fuck. Me too." Eyes wide, Garrick kept his gaze locked on Rain, and he felt seen in a way that transcended sex. He paused, drinking the moment in for several seconds before gradually lowering down.

"Damn. You're bigger than that toy, that's for sure." Bigger than Garrick's fingers as well, his cockhead providing an insistent stretch that forced him to descend more gradually, working Garrick's cock with little rocks of his hips.

"Ha. Sweet-talker. Go slow as you need."

Still impatient, he pushed through the burn, seeking that moment when everything got bright and wonderful again. Like now. The moment Garrick slid deep enough, broad cockhead producing perfect pressure against his spot. All he could do was moan.

"Oh. Right…there."

"Fuck. You're so damn hot." The wonder in Garrick's eyes was like a drug to Rain, making him preen. He moved more freely now, sliding up and back, each long motion a fresh wave of pleasure.

"Can… Tell me how it feels to you?" He was intensely curious about Garrick's side of the experience, not wanting to dwell if his sensations were somewhat diminished, but wanting to know nonetheless. Needing it good for him so badly, he slowed while waiting for Garrick's response.

"Feels amazing. Hot. Tight. And…" Garrick trailed off on a moan as Rain tensed his inner muscles, gripping and releasing his cock. "Yeah, show-off, that too. Damn."

"Want to move faster." Knowing Garrick was feeling all the pleasure made him bolder. Needier. More driven to get them both off.

"Do it. Fuck me." Garrick rested his hands on Rain's hips, encouraging him. Stretching, Rain luxuriated in the freedom of this position, how damn good Garrick's gaze locked on his felt, warm and urgent. Made it so damn easy to ride Garrick fast and hard until they were both groaning. He didn't want to come yet, but when Garrick moved to stroking his torso, he couldn't hold back a hungry whimper.

"Yeah. Like that. Fuck. Touch me. Please." Nothing was stopping him from reaching for his own cock, but somehow it was so much hotter when Garrick did it.

"Mmm. Love it when you ask nice." Chuckling, Garrick ran a single finger down the length of Rain's straining shaft.

"For real. Come on. Please."

"Gonna come all over me?" Giving in to Rain's begging, Garrick gripped his cock firmly, matching Rain's rhythm.

"Yeah. Yeah. Want it." Falling forward slightly, he braced himself on Garrick's broad chest, which made Garrick groan, head falling back.

"Go hard as you need it." Voice rough, Garrick sounded as strung out as Rain felt. "It's good. So good."

"Fuck yes it is." Drinking in the verbal encouragement, he moved faster now, fucking himself harder against Garrick.

"That's it. Like that, baby."

Simply the sound of Garrick's voice, so low and gruff, along with the way his face was scrunched up, pleasure contorting his rugged features, had Rain riding the edge, balls tightening, abs and thighs tensing.

"Close. Are…" He backed off the question at the last moment, wanting Garrick to come with him in the worst way, but also not wanting to pressure him. This alone was so good, so perfect, so right. And it wasn't simply the physical—Garrick's solid body under him, hard cock providing exactly the pressure Rain craved—it was the way Garrick looked at him, like Rain was the answer to every deep question he'd ever had. Made Rain feel like he was flying, made it hard to back off the rising pleasure, carrying him higher. "Damn. Need…"

"Whatever you need. Wanna feel you go." Garrick stroked his cock faster now, other hand urging Rain on. "Harder."

"God. Right…" Fuck. Forget flying. This was a headlong tumble into climax, one he was powerless to stop, moving harder and faster against Garrick, chasing every last good feeling. "Oh, fuck, Garrick. That's…"

And then he was coming, intense spurts all over Garrick's fist and chest that made him dig his fingers into Garrick's chest, trying not to collapse from the waves of pleasure.

"Yeah. Yeah. That's right. Damn." Garrick didn't seem to mind Rain's death grip at all, eyes going hot and needy, as he moved Rain onward with his hands, keeping the fuck and all the amazing sensations going.

"Do that. Want you…" Summoning the last of his energy, Rain got into it, moving against Garrick as he raked his fingers down Garrick's chest again, more deliberately now. Garrick was tense under him, even the tendons of his neck straining, and Rain couldn't resist leaning forward for a well-placed nip.

"That's it. Like that." Garrick stiffened further, face somewhere between pleasure and agony, voice rough. "You… Perfect… *Fuck.*"

Oh, that was *it*. Shuddering, Garrick slowly went slack, all that tension rolling away, leaving them breathing hard together. Rain made a halfhearted attempt to swab at the come on Garrick's chest with his underwear before he collapsed against him, head settling on Garrick's shoulder.

"See? Closer to comatose." He didn't even have to fake his yawn because damn that had worn him out in the best possible way. "We did good."

"Damn right. Fuck. I didn't think I was going to be able to... And then it just kinda...happened." Garrick sounded both amused and amazed.

"I'm so glad. Not that it's...like a requirement or something, but damn, I love getting you off." Rain pressed a kiss to his cheek.

"Same." Groaning, Garrick held him close as their breathing gradually returned to normal. "That...that was what you like?"

The vulnerability was back in his voice, an uncertainty he seldom had that hit Rain square in the chest. God, the things this man made him feel...

"Oh yeah. *You* are what I like. Everything about you." And then, because that was way heavy, he had to laugh and add, "And the sex doesn't suck either."

"Gee. High praise. And right back at you." Garrick smiled at him, a tenderness in his eyes Rain wasn't sure he'd had from anyone before. "You... You're special, Rain. I hope you know that."

"I do now." His voice was soft, and he had to hide his face in Garrick's neck, not wanting to reveal quite how much those words meant to him. Garrick made him want, made him *dream*, things he'd thought weren't meant to be his. All the things he'd told himself that he didn't want, now those dreams came crashing back into him, one after another. It was almost too much, that kind of hope requiring a bravery he wasn't sure he possessed. And he could tell himself those feelings weren't real, that it was only good sex and friendship, but right then, all he wanted was to hold Garrick close and pretend if only for a while that this was real, that Garrick was his, and that all those impossible things were within reach.

Chapter Thirteen

"I suppose we have your neighbor to thank for today's good mood." Garrick's father chuckled as he unloaded Garrick's wheelchair and crutches from his truck. He wasn't wrong. Garrick was in a good mood, had been for weeks now, maybe more so this morning because Rain had slept over again last night. They'd played another round of Rain's favorite game and made popcorn and talked late into the night, like kids at a slumber party. Okay. Maybe an adults-only party, because there had been sex too, but that hadn't been the whole focus of the evening nor was it why he'd been all smiles on the way to his PT appointment.

"Rain did a personal best in pull-ups this morning." Because they'd had to park farther back in the lot, he settled himself in the chair with the crutches in their holder.

"In actuality or is that some sort of newfangled slang?" His dad seemed more amused by Rain's presence than anything else. He could get a little awkward around Rain, as if he wasn't precisely sure what to make of him and his role in Garrick's life. The way Rain disarmed him was sort of cute as his dad was a stout pine tree normally, unflappable and confident, a natural people person and leader.

"For real. It was a good workout. We barely made it back before you showed up. Thanks for that, by the way. Rain had to get to work or he would have given me a ride. I'm off today, but he's on brush hauling duty."

"He sure is a helpful...friend. Almost makes your old dad expendable. Along with your friends too. I keep hearing from people that they've barely seen you."

"Oh, I'm never getting rid of you." Garrick laughed as they made their way toward the building. "And I'm seeing people tomorrow actually. Birthday party for Jacob out at Linc's. Great chance for Rain to meet folks and for me to prove that I'm still alive and kicking and not purposefully ignoring anyone."

"Ah. Never would have figured Linc for..." His dad shook his head. "Never mind. Hope it's a good party. You got a present for the birthday? I got some nice belts in last week. Or I could do up a gift card."

"Gift card is a good idea. Thanks." His dad might be old-school Western to the core, but he *was* trying, and Garrick wanted to give him credit for that. He also wanted to reassure his dad more that Rain wasn't about to shove him out of Garrick's life, but then they had to pause to let a group of people pass through the wide double doors of the medical complex and the moment passed because his dad was clapping him on the shoulder, already moving away.

"See you after your appointment. I've got your grocery list and mine, so I shouldn't get into too much trouble."

"See to it." Garrick waved him away before he checked in to his appointment. Good mood still swirling along with some excess energy from that morning's outing, he was ready to get to work. But, to his surprise, Stephanie was accompanied by a stuffy-looking dude in a white dress shirt and skinny mustache, and they led him to one of the little private exam rooms in the back of the facility, not the main PT room with all the equipment.

"What's up?" His stomach churned, already not liking whatever this interruption to his routine was.

"This is Alec. He's from the billing department," Stephanie explained.

"Oh, f—*crap*. Am I behind on copays? Thought I had you guys on autopay."

"No, you're largely caught up." Alec glanced nervously at Stephanie. "That's not what we need to discuss. It's more about going forward. That is, looking at both what your personal goals are as well as what the insurance is willing to cover and what your clinical team recommends."

"I'm afraid I don't understand," he admitted. Alec and Stephanie's uneasy faces were giving him a complex, so he looked away and studied a poster illustrating correct posture for carrying boxes and other bulky loads. "I come. We do the work. I haven't missed an appointment yet. Goal hasn't changed. Get me back out there."

"It's not that easy." Stephanie gave a pained sigh. "I wish, I really wish it was. But what Alec is trying to get at is that he's been fighting the insurance on your behalf several weeks now. They want to stop covering intensive PT. And we've been working with your neurologist to try to get them to reconsider, but we keep running into brick walls."

"What does that mean? They're not going pay for more PT? Why?"

"The insurance looks at what is medically necessary." Alec continued to frown, mouth twisted like he'd rather be discussing colonoscopy options than having this conversation with Garrick. "That is, they need the medical team to regularly review your care plan and to state that your condition can be reasonably expected to improve with the current course of physical therapy."

"But that should be easy, right? I'm still not at one hundred percent. I don't get why they wouldn't think it's necessary."

"It's the 'reasonably expected to improve' part." Stephanie's voice was soft but weary. "The whole care team has been worried for a while that your personal goals may not be realistic. I know the neurologist has explained to you the slim chances for total recovery. And your attitude of wanting to defeat those odds is so, so admirable, but—"

"I'm not here to be inspiring." Garrick wasn't sure whether he was madder at her and the rest of his medical team for not believing in him or the insurance company for putting all of them in this position. "If I'm hearing you right, what you're saying is that the insurance doesn't think I'm going to have significant improvements from where I am now, so they don't want to pay for what we've been doing. Okay. So I pay out of pocket."

"It's a lot of money. A lot. And we can discuss that option, but the insurance *is* willing to cover some things on an adjusted care plan—for example, more occupational therapy for things like learning to drive with hand controls, counseling to help with your adjustment, and more limited PT to maintain your current level of mobility. Part of why I didn't want to hit you with this over the phone or let Alec explain this to you alone is that everyone on your team—our head of PT, me, the neurologist, and the orthopedist—want you to take some time to seriously reflect on what your treatment goals are from here on out."

"You said I was making improvements. As recently as a few weeks ago, you said you'd seen some progress."

"Yes. Incremental progress. You are way stronger than when you started. Your balance has improved as your hip and ankle strength has improved. Your initial breaks have healed about as well as could be expected. You're so much better at navigating with the crutches now. The problem is that the spinal injury is going to have a lasting impact, one that all the therapy in the world can't erase. I wish it could."

"But it was incomplete. Everyone said it was best-case scenario in a lot of ways." The urologist's words about luck rang in his ears, along with that doctor's skepticism for him giving up the crutches. Fuck luck. Fuck it hard. Did no one believe in him? *It's almost been a year.* That was what the neurologist had said at their last appointment, like Garrick didn't know that, like he could forget, like that mattered when he was willing to work as hard and as long as it took.

"Incomplete doesn't mean nonexistent." Stephanie's eyes were shiny, as if she were working to not cry, and Alec didn't look a lot better. "And it doesn't mean you can't have a full life—"

"I *have* a full life. One I'm enjoying greatly at present other than the whole not smoke jumping thing. I don't need a motivational speech here. What you guys are really saying though is that I'm not going back to work. And that's not simply an insurance decision, but the whole team believing it."

Both Alec and Stephanie slowly nodded.

"Maybe a second opinion…" Once when he was eight or nine, he'd jumped farther out into the deep end than he'd been planning, and he'd had this terrifying moment when the side of the pool seemed so very far away. He hadn't been at all sure of his ability to make it to the wall and had started to sink lower in the water. This felt like that sort of moment, everything hanging in the balance, him needing something to cling to, even the idea of more doctors, more tests. *Something.*

"Yes. You can go back to Portland, to the medical school or even to Seattle or San Francisco. That's absolutely an option. And you should probably pursue that before committing to paying out of pocket for anything. But I've done hours of research on your case, hoping to find something I could point you toward, some device or procedure or therapy that would get you the breakthrough with mobility that you're wanting."

"I…" His ears rang, his voice echoing like it was coming from an empty tunnel. He'd done the same research. He'd *had* doctors in Portland. But damn. He needed that life buoy, could feel his panic rising, throat closing and palms sweating.

"Do you need a minute? Some water?" Stephanie made a shooing motion at Alec, who bolted from the room. Putting her hand on his arm, she leaned forward. "This is a lot. I know. We don't have to try and do a full session after hitting you with this, but maybe some stretching and some hydrotherapy would help?"

"Maybe." Swallowing hard, he accepted the water

Alec returned with moments later. It wasn't either of their faults, and Stephanie and him, they went back well over six months now. She might be his healthcare provider, but she was also something of a friend. He didn't like seeing her so upset on his behalf. And there was absolutely nothing that would be served by storming out or raging.

So, he let her dismiss poor Alec, who looked relieved that Garrick wasn't making a scene, pale skin blotchy and head bobbling as he made his escape. And then he let her lead him to a quiet corner in the main therapy area, put him through some basic stretches before she took him down to the hydrotherapy area. Usually they'd do more exercises in the warm pool, hard work with the weight belts or range of motion moves, but today Stephanie went easy on him, using the first available excuse to leave him to do his own thing in the empty pool, no other people around.

Nominally, he was supposed to be doing easy laps, but instead he floated aimlessly, staring up at the ceiling lights until his eyes blurred. This was what he'd forgotten that day he'd panicked in the deep end—floating until a solution appeared was always a valid option. Except unlike then when a lifeguard had spotted him and jumped in with assistance to make it to the side, no answer was forthcoming, no rescue from his internal flailing.

What if I never skydive again? He ducked under the water, but the thought followed him down. He'd known for months now that that was what the neurologist believed. No one had lied to him other than himself, his daily mantra that he was going to prove every one of the doubters wrong. Fuck the whole thing about function regained by six months predicting overall prognosis. He'd had the appointments, heard the facts and projections, and chosen to maintain his unshakable belief that he was going to succeed. Sheer determination had carried him thus far. It couldn't let him down now. He wouldn't let it.

Except... Doubt, that fucker, had a hold of him, sure as a nasty undertow. Reality—the friction between his optimism and indisputable facts—couldn't be avoided forever. He stretched out, trying to find that floating numbness again. Hell, trying to find himself, trying to gear up to smash this latest round of doubts. But he kept smacking into reality. Cold and large, increasingly undeniable. And not unfamiliar either. Certain fires he'd fought had required an acceptance of available data and gut instinct, knowing when to pull back, when even all the conviction in the world wasn't a match for the will of the fire, and reality mandated that he adapt and change course. Fuck, how he hated those moments. And this...this might be one of them, and hell if he knew what to do now.

The only thing worse than Rain being in a funk himself was Garrick being in one and not wanting to admit it. He'd been strangely distant when Rain had arrived to walk Cookie after work the day before. Not mean or snappy, but a sullenness that wasn't usually there. However, he'd denied being down, instead claiming tiredness, which was when Rain knew something was up because it usually took Herculean efforts to get Garrick to admit to being worn out. But he'd let Garrick have his privacy and his brooding time and had returned to

Grandma's to watch another comedy with her while he quietly worried about Garrick.

But he'd had hopes that Garrick would either snap out of whatever was bringing him down or talk to him about it. Neither happened, though, and now they were on their way out of town to the party at Garrick's friends' place in the country. Ordinarily, their silences while driving were the good kind, either broken up by random observations and Garrick's commentary on Rain's music selection or stretching out, contentment and anticipation mingling. Comfortable. However, today there was nothing comfortable about Garrick's closed-off face and stiff posture.

"Are you sore from yesterday's workout plus PT? We can always leave early if you need to." Rain tried to sound upbeat but flexible.

"I'm okay." Garrick sounded anything but, and Rain groaned. The empty rural road stretched out in front of them, a gorgeous summer day with blue skies, but the storm cloud over Garrick's head didn't seem to be going anywhere anytime soon.

"I'd ask if you want to talk about it, except you quite clearly don't. So, instead I'll ask if there is anything I can do?"

Garrick paused like he was actually considering a real answer, then sighed. "It's okay."

"Nothing?"

"You sleeping over tonight?"

"If you want, sure." Rain refrained from pointing out how Garrick hadn't seemed exactly open to that last night.

"Slept like utter crap last night. Maybe...you being around might help."

"Good. I'll plan on it then."

"Thanks. And sorry. I know I'm being difficult. I'll work on being better."

Rain wanted to tell him that he'd prefer Garrick to *talk*, not worry about how to hide his grumpy mood, but then the GPS bleated for him to make a turn into a long gravel driveway. A small, low house with a cheerful porch sat back from the road, and a number of vehicles were already parked off to the side of the drive, which meant Rain had to park farther from the house than he'd like. All the gravel and uneven, scrubby terrain was going to be hell on the wheelchair, something he wouldn't have thought about a few weeks ago, but now he'd learned to always be looking for accessibility issues.

"How do you want to handle it?" he asked Garrick. "If you're up for me helping push, we can probably get the chair to the porch or—"

"I'll take the crutches. It'll be slow going, but I don't want to tear up the chair. And I don't want... Yeah. Better this way." Garrick nodded firmly, tone resigned, as if he'd had some internal discussion that Rain hadn't been privy to.

Which was frustrating because Rain wanted to help and couldn't do the best job at that if Garrick wasn't communicating, but he also wasn't about to start an argument right here or try to make Garrick's bad mood about him when he was pretty sure it had nothing to do with their relationship, especially given the sleepover invite.

And he tried hard not to hover as Garrick painstakingly made his way across the yard to the house. All he could really do was carry the seven-layer vegetarian dip and chips they'd brought and hope for the best. There was little actual grass though, not much to cushion Garrick if he fell, and barring fluffy grass, Rain would have given a lot for a paved path of some kind right about then. As they reached the porch, the door swung open and the guy Garrick had introduced as Linc came out.

"You made it!" He frowned as he watched their approach. "Hell, I didn't think about your wheelchair. Do you need me to fetch it from the car for you? Need help with the steps?"

"I've got it." Garrick gave his friend a tight smile. Rain knew from experience with Garrick that steps, even three flat, wide ones like these, were among Garrick's hardest challenges. He preferred to take his time and have his space doing steps and not have someone crowding him like his overeager friend was doing. Linc kept close, acting like he could catch Garrick if he fell, hands moving restlessly like he was tempted to steer.

Good luck with that. Rain hung back, waiting until Garrick was safely on the porch before he followed after the two of them.

"You did it." Linc had a relieved smile as he opened the door to the house. "And you brought your friend… Ryan, was it?"

"Rain." He gave the guy a nod, more concerned with finding a spot where Garrick could sit than shaking hands.

"Right. Rain. Jacob? Garrick and his friend are here," Linc called as they entered the small house, which was teeming with people, several of whom turned to call greetings to Garrick. A tall blond woman plucked the food from Rain's hands and spirited it away to the kitchen.

"Dude! You came!" Jacob bounded off a sofa where some tween boys were playing video games on tablets. He motioned for Garrick to take his place. "Sit, sit."

"Nah, man, I'm not going to take your spot." Garrick protested even as he was still breathing hard from the stairs.

"Take it. Please. I need to go play host, not get sucked into another round of the game. And speaking of hosting, what can I get you guys to drink?"

"Did your sister bring sparkling water like usual?" Mouth twisting like he was trying to smile and failing, Garrick settled heavily on the couch, tucking crutches in next to him. Rain asked for the same before perching on the arm of the couch.

"You didn't want a beer?" he asked in a low voice. He'd seen Garrick have a drink on a few occasions now, and he thought maybe that might relax whatever funk he'd had going on the way to the party. "I'm driving, but you go ahead."

"Gotta be able to navigate the steps and back to the car. Hard enough. Can't risk a buzz and my tolerance is for shit lately." Voice a rough whisper, he grimaced again.

"Ah. Gotcha. And a pain pill would also be a no go until later?"

"Yeah. Haven't needed one of the heavy hitters in weeks. But maybe when we get back…" He trailed off before raising his voice and getting that almost-smile in place as a woman stopped in front of them. "Jenna. I hear you made cake. How have you been?"

"Good." The woman, who turned out to be Jacob's mother, made small talk with them a few minutes until a minor kitchen emergency merited her attention.

"Okay, so who else here do I need to know?" Rain kept his voice down, even though the kids on the other end of the couch were paying them no mind.

"Heck. I should introduce you around." Garrick made like he might stand, but Rain kept a firm hand on his shoulder.

"Chill. People can come to you. And I'm having fun people watching. But I want the inside scoop before I make my way to the kitchen to find us some food."

"Okay." Garrick nodded, his ready agreement another sign that he'd already overdone it. He played along with Rain, though, pointing out various family members of Jacob and people he knew in the smoke jumper community. Rain could have guessed which ones were smoke jumpers on his own—they were the buffest, most confident ones in the room. The party had spilled over to a deck beyond the kitchen, but Rain had been right as various people kept drifting their way over to say hello to Garrick. Smaller kids ran through the place along with a pack of dogs that made him glad they hadn't tried to add Cookie to this chaos. But it was fun chaos, a lot of people and food and a welcoming atmosphere.

"You ready for some food?" he asked Garrick right as Jacob arrived with drinks.

"Yes, go get food. And while you're in the kitchen, make sure and admire the new deck. That's my birthday present." Jacob had a fond look for Linc, who was deep in conversation with some of the smoke jumping crew. Rain didn't really envy him the new deck, but he did know a pang over that glance. Damn. Everyone needed someone who thought that highly of them and who wasn't afraid to so readily show their heart.

Jacob's mom assisted him in loading up a plate for

Garrick, helpfully telling him which dishes were vegetarian for himself. She was chatty, and by the time he made it back, Jacob had stolen his perch on the couch arm and was in the middle of a conversation with Garrick about another upcoming controlled burn. Not wanting to interrupt, he handed Garrick his plate, then took a seat on the rug by the couch, close enough to contribute a little to the work talk and close enough for Garrick to tangle a hand in his hair after he was done picking at his food. He idly played with Rain's half-bun and the escaping strands while he kept up his end of the conversation with Jacob, who kept glancing at Garrick's roving hand with undisguised curiosity.

Nice as the contact was, not to mention being publicly claimed like that, Rain still worried because he'd never seen Garrick without an appetite before, especially given that the party food contained many of his favorites including wings. Speaking of cute affection, Linc ruffled Jacob's hair on the way to let in more guests, a group that included the cocky smoke jumper he'd met that first day he'd known Garrick. A bunch of people called out greetings to Jimenez's group, and they made their way over to the couch, where handshakes and backslapping bro hugs were handed out.

"Nelson! My man!" Jimenez had a particularly hearty hello for Garrick. "Looking good. How'd that lost dog turn out?"

"Pretty good." Garrick gave a wry smile. "She's mine now. Spoiled rotten, but she's a great dog."

"Excellent. And you? How are you? When are we going to see your ass back in gear? Getting awfully quiet around the base without you talking smack."

"I…" Garrick had already fielded a wide variety of

questions about how he was, most with brief yet polite replies, but something about this one seemed to stump him. "Not happening."

"What?" Jimenez frowned along with several others standing close by.

"I mean, I'm not going back to smoke jumping." Garrick's voice was loud enough to make the other swirling conversations around them stop, all eyes on him.

"What?"

"Since when?"

"What happened?"

"Really?"

The questions came from all directions, and Rain sure as hell had some too, but he was more concerned with how Garrick's eyes were flat, no light at all, and his skin grayish, like he might need to hurl soon.

"I...need to get out of here." Garrick used his crutches to stand, then pushed past several open-mouthed people to make his way to the front door, which banged closed behind him.

"I should go after him." Frowning, Linc headed after him, but Rain got there first.

"Let me."

"Me and him, we go way back. Grade school even." Linc's eyes narrowed like he was readying more of a case for himself, then his head tilted, considering. Rain stood firm, meeting him hard stare for hard stare, and Linc must have seen something satisfactory in Rain's gaze because finally he nodded. "Go on then."

Not that Rain needed permission, but he appreciated not needing to battle a crowd of well-meaning folks to get to Garrick. He didn't have to go far to find Garrick as he was still on the porch, sitting on a bench at the far end.

"Fucking steps. Can't even storm off properly. Not to mention I didn't drive here myself."

"If you need to leave, we'll leave." Despite wanting desperately to touch him, Rain hung back, trying to figure out how to give Garrick what he needed most right then, whatever that was.

"I should go apologize first. Explain. Fuck. I hate this."

"You don't owe anyone an explanation. If you want, I'll go make a quick goodbye. Then you can call Linc or whomever when you're ready."

"You're too good to me." Some of the fight went out of Garrick's voice, leaving him sounding utterly exhausted. Worn out. Rain couldn't not reach out now, and he rubbed one of Garrick's concrete-pylon-tense shoulders.

"You should know by now. There's not much I wouldn't do for you. We're totally hide-the-bodies friends."

"Totally." Garrick gave him a weak but grateful smile. "And yeah. I know it's not the best, but I just want out of here."

"Quit worrying about other people," Rain said sternly, continuing to rub his shoulder. "I'll make it happen for you."

And he would because making excuses was easy. Fixing what was wrong with Garrick, though, that was going to take some work. And talking. Lots of talking. This time he wasn't letting Garrick out of the conversation either. One way or another he was getting the whole story.

Chapter Fourteen

"I'm just so fucking pissed." Garrick finally had enough silence, enough of the quiet compassion coming from Rain's side of the car, to feel slightly human again, less of the burnt-out-hull feeling he'd had sitting on Linc's porch. Still, though, he surprised himself by speaking, especially by acknowledging the feeling he'd been running from ever since the day before.

"Good." Eyes on the road, Rain nodded sharply.

"Good?" That hadn't been the response Garrick had expected from his hippie, free-spirited lover at all.

"Good. Be angry. You've been bottling stuff up far too long. It's okay to let it out."

"But you don't need me unloading on you…" The long list of things he was mad about welled up in him again, making it hard to breathe let alone talk.

"Dude. That's exactly what I'm here for. I can take it. Get mad."

Garrick had a brief flash of himself as a young teen, and his mother telling him to stop being so dramatic and needy. *No one needs your bad mood.* Expressing emotions was not as easy or as cathartic as Rain made it sound. It was risky and more than a little scary. People counted on him to be fun and upbeat, not an emotional downer. But somehow the words refused to stay put any longer and came tumbling out.

"Insurance doesn't want to pay for my current schedule of PT. Fucking sucks. They blindsided me with this BS yesterday. Apparently, there's some question about 'medical necessity' given that my whole fucking team thinks this may be as good as it gets for me."

"Ah." Rain didn't leap in with a quick suggestion that Garrick prove them wrong or pay out of pocket. Just that. *Ah.* And somehow that made Garrick madder.

"You're not surprised. Hell. Does *anyone* think I can beat the odds anymore?"

"Do you?" Rain's tone was thoughtful.

Oh, now that was uncalled for, putting it back on him like that, and Garrick made a frustrated growl.

"Yes. No. I don't know. It's…the odds." Just getting those words out stung like a scrape. "They're small now. Most big improvements with spinal cord injuries happen in the first six months, some within the first year, and rarely more within eighteen months. Walking again, that was huge. I thought… I really believed after that that I could come the rest of the way back."

"But now?" They were nearing town, same small streets Garrick had known his whole life, but they'd somehow never looked bleaker even with what looked to be a spectacular sunset looming.

"Time isn't on my side," he admitted. Whispering helped, like kids sharing ghost stories under the blankets, easier to speak his fears aloud. "My PT says I can still expect incremental progress. Incremental. That's not going to be enough to get me back out there smoke jumping. I want to tell her to go to hell, that I will have that big breakthrough, run again. But…"

"Yeah?" Rain prodded when Garrick went silent again.

"There's optimism and then there's reality. And reality is what I haven't wanted to face for months now. It's easier to believe, really believe, down deep that I'm going to be different. The exception. The odds breaker. But at a certain point..." He swallowed hard, not sure he could continue.

"And that's where the anger comes in," Rain guessed. "You're mad about having to confront those odds."

"Yeah, exactly." He exhaled hard. "I'm fucking pissed that all my hard work and belief hasn't been enough. It's so unfair."

It was the first time he'd said that word aloud, and it banged its way out of his brain, seeming to echo through the small SUV. *Unfair. Unfair. Unfair.*

"It is," Rain agreed as he turned down their street. "It's entirely unfair."

"Other people have it worse." He tried to backpedal, but the anger was still there.

"It's not the pain Olympics. Sure, other people have shitty deals too. Lots of unfairness to go around. But that doesn't negate the fact that this is unfair and it does suck. You're right. You worked hard. You had a good attitude. You did everything you were supposed to. Anyone else would be mad and sad and pissed off about the unfairness of it all."

"I'm lucky to be alive." God knew he'd had enough people telling him that over the past year.

"You can be lucky and grateful and still unlucky in this instance, in how the recovery odds worked out. You're not getting what you wanted most. It's understandable."

"Well... I don't know about that. I've got a good life. House. Family. Friends. You."

"Me?" Rain sounded both surprised and pleased.

"Yeah, you. I mean, for now. But we've got a good thing going here and I don't discount that."

"I agree. It is pretty awesome. And you can have a good life and still be mad because you wanted to return to smoke jumping."

"Yeah. I did. I really, really did." His voice broke right as Rain pulled into his driveway. This. This was what he'd been running from. The heavy weight of failure. He'd tried and tried and it wasn't going to be enough. People had been trying to tell him that for a while now and he simply hadn't wanted to listen.

"I know." Rain shut off the engine and grabbed Garrick's hand, held it tight. And he didn't speak, didn't offer up platitudes or try to joke the heavy silence away. Just him. There. Holding on. And somehow that presence, that simple acceptance of his pain, undid him.

"In the pool yesterday, I kept thinking how I didn't know that would be my last jump. I didn't slow down, didn't take a minute, didn't *know*. I didn't know what was coming. I didn't know I'd miss it this much. *Fuck*." He didn't even realize he was crying until his hand came away wet when he scrubbed at his eyes.

"It sucks," Rain agreed quietly, still squeezing his other hand. "It does, and I'd give anything for you to get to skydive again. I know how much your job meant to you. It's okay to be sad at that loss. You take as much time as you need coming to terms with that."

Stupid tears still falling, he nodded, unable to do anything other than cling to Rain's hand and replay his favorite jumps in his mind. Free falls that lasted extra long. Stunts he'd done for fun and maneuvers he'd pulled off for work. Gorgeous vistas stretching out in front of him. Perfect landings. Let himself really miss it in a way he hadn't before. *Loss.* That was what Rain had said, and that was what this was. A loss. One he wasn't sure he was ever going to get over.

"We should go in," he said at last when he trusted his voice not to fail him again. "Hell. I know it's early, but all I want to do is go to bed."

"All right. Let's make that happen." Releasing his hand, Rain made quick work of unloading Garrick's chair and crutches. He handled greeting Cookie, immediately putting her on the leash and racing down the driveway. "Back in a flash."

And he was, returning when Garrick was still sitting on the side of the bed, not having gotten any further than taking his shoes off. He could hear Rain making sure Cookie had food and water and then he was there in the bedroom, crawling up behind Garrick.

"You don't have to stay. I know what I said earlier, but…" Sighing heavily, he studied his hands. "I'm a major drag tonight. I wouldn't want to be around me either. And you weren't wrong about my maybe needing a pain pill after all that walking. Can't mix that with…you know. And not exactly in the mood for fooling around anyway."

"Garrick." Rain wrapped him up in a hug from behind, one of Garrick's favorite things that he did, pressing himself all along Garrick's back. "I'm not staying for sex. I'm staying for *you.*"

"Why?" The word came out way more plaintive than he'd intended.

"Because we're friends. And I care about you a lot. You said you didn't want to be alone, and I don't want you alone either. I'm staying because I think you could use a friend right now, even if you don't want to talk

Annabeth Albert 207

anymore. I can simply hang out, make you some of those vegan brownies you like, fetch the pain meds. Whatever you need."

"This." He leaned into the hug. "I need this. Feel like I don't deserve you though."

"Hush." Rain kissed the side of his neck. "You're having a rough time. You're allowed some bad days."

"Don't want to be…needy." His mom's complaint echoed again.

"You? You're the least needy person I know." Rain laughed. "Let me take care of you, okay? You know how you're always talking about liking to spoil me."

"Not doing a very good job of that tonight," he grumbled, but he still didn't pull away from Rain's steadying embrace.

"Well, let me try for once. Okay?"

"Well, if it involves brownies…" He managed something of a laugh. "But not yet, okay? I…this right here. This is good."

"Yeah, it is. And I'm here for it. Here for you. As long as you need." Giving him another soft kiss, Rain helped him out of the nice shirt he'd worn for the party. By the time Rain joined him under the covers, both of them in their underwear, he was so weary and wrung out that he was close to tears again. Which Rain seemed to recognize, holding him close as Garrick continued to wonder who he was in a world where he could no longer count on being able to touch the sky.

Rain woke up with a stiff neck and a warm body pressed against his. The sore muscle was understandable—he'd fallen asleep in a weird position on Garrick's shoulder and apparently never found his own side of the bed.

But the warm body, now that was a nice bonus, worth a pinched nerve or two, especially since it came with a hard cock pushing against his hip. Not that Rain was going to assume that it was an invitation, not after last night's emotional bender, but he also was only human and couldn't deny it was a turn-on, being wrapped up by Garrick's bigger body.

"Mmmph." Garrick made a cute little huffing noise into Rain's hair, holding him closer before dropping a kiss below his ear. "You awake?"

"Am now." Rain had to chuckle. Outside the light was still faint, but they'd fallen asleep pretty darn early. "You having a hard time staying asleep? Need something?"

"I've been up awhile, watching you and Cookie sleep. You're both adorable, by the way. And neither of you moved an inch when I went and showered."

"Did you now?" Rain stretched, figuring his chances of getting lucky were getting higher by the second. Garrick smelled like he'd taken the time to shave and a quick brush of his jaw confirmed that. And his breath was minty, as if he'd brushed his teeth too. If he'd done all that, odds were good that he might have taken a pill, not that Rain was going to ask. This was too lovely of a wakeup to risk ruining by embarrassing Garrick, who could still be touchy about the meds.

"Uh-huh. Couldn't stay asleep any longer. My body's rarely been one to need crazy amounts of sleep. And someone was being all sweet, using me as a body pillow." He snaked an arm down Rain's front, more deliberately seductive than when he hadn't been sure Rain was awake. And Rain honestly wasn't that surprised that Garrick wanted sex—it was a natural reset button after the past few days. Sex was a great equalizer like that and Rain had used it for similar purposes in the past, so he was happy to be that sort of distraction for Garrick.

"I am pretty cute." He bumped his ass backward. "You planning on doing anything about it?"

"Maybe. It's early. Cookie's still snoozing."

"Well, by all means. If the dog approves…"

Garrick's answering chuckle confirmed that this sort of light banter was what he was after that morning. Later there would be plenty of time to talk more seriously with him, but if he needed easy and sexy, then Rain could be that too. He rolled slightly, intending to end up face-to-face, but Garrick caught him up in a bear hug as he turned, using the momentum to wind up flat on his back, Rain stretched out on top of him.

"This okay?" Rain's weight was more fully on Garrick than usual.

"Pretty sure that should be my question." Garrick's eyes sparkled up at Rain. "This is awesome. And goes along with a sexy thought I had in the shower."

"Mmm. Tell me."

"Easier to show you." Shoving his hands down the back of Rain's underwear, Garrick grinned, all sinful promise and playful energy. It was a fairly boring pair of underwear as far as Rain's collection went—silky sky blue boy-cut shorts—but Garrick didn't seem to care as he growled low and massaged Rain's ass.

Eager to be skin to skin, Rain happily helped by wriggling as Garrick pushed the fabric down. The scrap of fabric fluttered to the floor as Garrick pulled him tight, cocks dragging together. Rain barely had time to appreciate the sensation before Garrick's mouth found his. His lips were hot and urgent, and Rain loved him like this, all demanding and cocky, sure in his ability to drive Rain out of his mind.

Kissing him was like a hit of top-quality espresso—warm and smooth with an undeniable kick that revved him up like nothing else. Tasting like mint and rising need, Garrick used his tongue to fuck his way into Rain's mouth, setting a driving pace that had Rain moving insistently against him. Every thrust of his hips had their cocks rubbing together, delicious friction.

"Lean up."

"Am I hurting you?" Rain struggled to sit up quickly.

"Only in the best way possible. Wanted to do this." Garrick wrapped his big fist around both their cocks at once.

"Fuck yeah. Lube?"

Not having to stretch that far, Garrick grabbed it from the nightstand. "Your wish is my command."

"Can my wish also be for more kisses?" Curling forward, he tried to give Garrick space to move his hand, but still coming in close to claim another kiss.

"Of course." Like magic, Garrick raised the head of the bed, which made the kissing a lot easier. Their tongues tangled as Garrick slid his slick grip up and down their shafts.

"God. So good." Rather than add his hand to Garrick's efforts, Rain used the opportunity to stroke Garrick's shoulders and arms, loving how that made him groan more. It was a simple pleasure, making out and rubbing off like this, but the emotions churning inside him were anything but ordinary. Big. Expansive. Like his heart could scarcely hold all of what he was feeling for this man.

Somehow, the day before had drawn them closer together, like they'd forged their way through battle together, stronger for confronting Garrick's dragon-sized fears and loss. And it didn't hurt that Garrick kissed him as if he were the center of the universe, all his attention zeroed in on Rain. His free hand roamed everywhere—Rain's hair, his chest, arms, waist—leaving little sparks of electricity in its wake.

"That's it." Garrick's head tipped back as he groaned. "Fuck, you feel so good."

"You're the one with magic hands." Laughing, Rain claimed another of those toe-curling, planet-moving kisses until it seemed the very gravity in the room shifted, something bigger than themselves holding them together.

"Damn." With glassy eyes and slack mouth, Garrick looked as awestruck as Rain felt. "Kiss me like that again."

"This?" Pushing Garrick back against the bed, he held on tight to his upper arms and shoulders as he kissed Garrick with everything he had, every big feeling, every scary thought, every intense sensation all funneled back into the kiss. Garrick's hand sped up on their cocks, but still Rain kept kissing him until finally Garrick broke away, breathing hard.

"Fuck. Love that pressure. Feels like you're going to leave marks."

"Sorry—"

"No, you're not." Garrick laughed wickedly. "And I love it. Want more. Mark me all you want."

Still grinning mischievously, Garrick did something new with his hand—tighter grip, twistier stroke, *something*—that had Rain not sure how much longer he could hold out himself. It was so good—the kissing, the touching, Garrick's voice, the press of their hard cocks together—all of it making his balls tighten and his abs tremble.

"Not…fair. Damn it. Too close."

"It's okay, baby. Want you to come." Garrick accelerated his efforts right as he stole another kiss, the insistent thrust of his tongue enough to get Rain perilously close to the edge.

"Gonna…"

"Do it."

Rain's climax was barreling into him, full steam ahead, but hell if he wasn't going to try to get Garrick there too. Dipping his head, he sucked hard at the spot where Garrick's neck and shoulder met while his hands gripped his biceps firmly.

"Oh fuck. Me too. Me too." Garrick panted and shook as Rain finally lost the battle with holding back his own orgasm, coming all over Garrick's fist. Triumph mingled with pleasure as his consciousness gently floated back to earth, his head finding its favorite spot on Garrick's shoulder.

"Did you…"

"Yeah. It's weird when I don't spurt like before, but trust me, feels good. Better than good. And getting you off…that's everything to me." Garrick kissed the top of Rain's head.

"Excellent." Rain gave a happy sigh and snuggled in closer while Garrick wiped off his fist. "I like making you happy. If me coming makes you happy, then count me as totally willing to take one for the team."

"It does. And you do. You really, really do make me happy." Garrick's tone went from sex-drunk to more somber as he held Rain tight. "Thank you for yesterday. You were... That's a real friend, being there for me like that."

"Always." He tried to echo the gravity in Garrick's voice, heart beating faster, but he wasn't able to crack a joke here either. He liked Garrick too much to not be honest, even if it was scary. "I... I want to be what you need. I care about you. A lot."

"Thanks. And you are. I guess...maybe I simply needed to melt down. Grieve, silly as that sounds—"

"It's not silly at all. It *is* a form of grief—you're facing losing something really important to you."

"Yeah. But this morning, waking up next to you, you still asleep and all cuddled up against me, my first thought was 'I'm going to be okay.' And I am. I've survived other disappointments before. I'll survive this one too. And you being here, that helps."

"Good." Rain liked hearing that, both that he'd helped and that Garrick recognized that he'd get through this.

"Do you need to help your grandma today? I don't want to monopolize your time—"

"Monopolize away. She's at a craft fair in Sisters. I'm never gonna turn down more time with you." Across the room, Cookie was finally stirring, which meant Rain would have to leave this cozy nest soon enough.

"Same. And I was thinking, there's this long paved path over at the resort we could try with Cookie. Getting out, getting away from my head, that's what I need. Then I can come back and worry about what to text Linc and Jacob."

"Don't dwell on that." Rain sat up and gave him a stern look. "The only one you owe an explanation to is yourself. And for what it's worth, I'm pretty damn impressed with you right now. Not that there's one right way to cope with this, but you're plowing ahead. That's admirable. If your friends can't see that you're coping as best as you can, then that's on them."

"You're pretty damn impressive yourself, you know?" Garrick stopped him when he would have left the bed, pulling him close again, tender expression in his eyes.

"Yeah." But instead of preening, as they kissed, he felt anything but smart. He was losing his heart to this guy, risking a sort of heartache he wasn't sure he'd ever had before. The thought of one day not having this was terrifying, but he seemed powerless to stop the surge of emotions that happened every time their lips met.

Chapter Fifteen

"I can't believe I let you talk me into this." Garrick shook his head as Rain searched for a parking space, circling several blocks near the park in Bend they were aiming for. "Actually, correction. I can't believe you got my friends on board with this. I never thought the day would come when I'd see Linc at a Pride event."

"It's not even a parade. No one's asking him to march or hold a sign," Rain said reasonably as he finally found a spot to park his SUV. "It's a little one-day festival. And we should support it. I've had fun at Portland Pride for years now. It's nice that this area is organizing its own."

"Yeah, it is."

"And all I suggested was that when you called to talk to Linc, you mention getting together for this. Jacob's the one who ran with the idea."

"It wasn't a terrible suggestion," Garrick allowed. And having a purpose to his call other than apologizing for his abrupt exit from Jacob's birthday party had been nice. He'd gotten the apology out, though, not that Linc had let him really own up to his behavior, trying to excuse it as Garrick being under a lot of stress. And he'd been a bit too hearty on the return call, reporting that Jacob liked the idea of getting together for food at this thing and working out a time to meet.

It felt like even his oldest friends didn't know quite how to deal with him now, and while Garrick appreciated them making the effort, it was still exhausting, trying to manage their helpfulness along with his own jumbled emotions. And he knew perfectly well what Rain was doing too by suggesting things like this outing—trying to keep him busy and distracted and unable to dwell too deeply on the new reality where he likely wouldn't be returning to smoke jumping.

Each day since Jacob's birthday had been a little easier, but he still wouldn't say he was over what Rain gently called a grieving process. He didn't like that word precisely because he knew others wrestled with far greater losses, but there was a certain amount of working stuff through, coming to an acceptance, a place where he wasn't so mad at the world and dumb luck and himself all together. And sad. There was a fair bit of that too. He was going to miss it—all of it, the jumps, the adrenaline, the race against time, the tree climbing, hell even digging fireline.

And it was undeniably weird seeing Linc and Jacob socially like this, not for work, and for what was for all intents and purposes a double date. A year ago, he wouldn't have expected any of this. And as he rolled along next to Rain on the wide sidewalk, he tried to shake the surreal, floaty feeling.

"Oh my god, I love your shirt," Jacob greeted them with his eyes glued to Rain's Bear Bait shirt when they met up at the entrance to the part of the park with the festival. Or maybe Jacob's eyes were for Rain himself, who did look super hot in the tight T-shirt, purple shorts, and hair in a rare braid instead of his usual bun. And every time Garrick saw the braid, his brain went straight to sex, because Rain had let him comb his hair out after a shower, which had led to making out, which had led to them almost being late to this thing and Rain leaving his hair down in the rush to get ready.

"I want one," Jacob continued, and Linc made a sort of growling noise, which only made Jacob laugh. Damn. Garrick had waited a lot of years to watch Linc get his comeuppance and it was more than worth it. "What? It's fun. And don't make me covet those matching I'm His/He's Mine Disney Pride theme shirts we saw a minute ago."

"On second thought, Rain's shirt is delightful. Buy seven. No way are we doing matching anything."

In a stage whisper, Rain leaned into Garrick. "I triple dare you to get them matching pajamas for the holidays."

"Maybe so." Thinking about winter made Garrick's back tense. Rain would likely be gone then and who knew where or if Garrick would be working. He'd keep it summer as long as he could.

The event was set up along a paved path, three rows of maybe thirty or so booths and food carts making a triangle, the center of which housed activities for kids and families. At one end was a stage where a folk singer in a long skirt was singing. Shirley and some of her crafting friends had a booth filled with rainbow tie-dye shirts, and they stopped there to say hello before continuing on to the food. Shirley had on a Free Grandma Hugs button and appeared to be having a great time.

"Are you sure you don't need my help loading up afterward?" Rain asked.

"No, dear. I've got my trusty wagon. We've been through many a festival together. You have fun with your friends."

"So much for my mom's insistence that Grandma couldn't make it this summer without my help," Rain grumbled as they walked away. "They're visiting next weekend for the Fourth of July, and I guarantee you I'm going to get a lecture about how I'm not doing enough for Grandma."

"It took me a solid six months of asking before she let me build her the raised beds out back. Some people are just super independent. I know she likes having you around." That niggling worry about winter returned, this time stronger. How much longer would Rain want to stick around if Shirley didn't need him? Was hanging out with Garrick enough of an inducement? Garrick knew full well he was finding the forestry work rather boring, with a lot of brush hauling lately as they were between controlled burns and no unexpected fires had cropped up yet. *Just a little longer*, he asked the universe. No way was he ready to worry about how in the hell he was ever going to let Rain go.

"Hey look! A pet-toy booth!" Jacob led the way to a display of rainbow collars, leashes, dog T-shirts, and more.

"They have baskets of toys at home. Baskets." Linc gave a helpless groan as Rain and Jacob loaded up on organic heart-shaped dog treats and little plush squeaker-filled toys that were bound to get destroyed in thirty seconds. "And the teenagers who watch our dogs when we're gone long hours are always bringing more toys too."

"You've had a lot of call-outs recently?" .

"Oh. Sorry. Maybe shouldn't have mentioned..." Linc rubbed at his super-short hair.

"It's okay." God, Garrick hated this. "You can talk about work. I promise I'm not about to flip out again."

"Okay." Linc exhaled hard and looked away.

Maybe this part would get easier with time. He had to hope so because, man, he'd rather get his back waxed than endure too many more of these awkward conversations.

Still meandering toward the food, Jacob and Rain next stopped at a booth featuring temporary tattoos, bumper stickers, and other small souvenirs. The two of them bonded over their lack of permanent ink but admiration for tattooed individuals. It was nice, watching Rain from a distance like this, not keeping him all to himself like usual.

Seeing how easily he made friends with Jacob reminded Garrick how damn special he was and how lucky he was that Rain chose to hang out so much with him. Of course, some of that was undoubtedly Cookie and her appeal, not to mention Rain's desire to make a hotshot crew driving their morning workouts, but he stuck around enough other times, even without sex, that Garrick figured he was doing something right to earn more time with someone this fun and appealing.

"What are you going to do?" Linc asked, interrupting his quiet appreciation of Rain's charms.

"Do?"

"Yeah, now that you can't... Is there disability? Or do you think you can keep doing the dispatch job? Maybe work for your dad? Jacob and I were talking earlier. You know you can ask if you need...anything, right?"

"Ah." Garrick could tell by Linc's pinched expression

that he was getting at the question of whether Garrick was okay for money. Which was nice, but this was the sort of future looking he was trying not to do. "I'm okay. Medical copays are finally calming down. Adams says he can use me all season at least. Guess I'll see about after. No way in hell am I cut out for either the ranching or the retail life with Dad. Love the man, but we'd go crazy working together."

Not that his dad hadn't offered. He'd finally told his dad about the physical therapy news, and while he'd been sympathetic, the relief had been clear in his eyes. Not that he wanted Garrick injured, but he also hadn't made any secret about not wanting him smoke jumping anymore. Which made Garrick less inclined to hear his offer to come work in his store with him. Maybe someday he'd come around to that, but for right now, forestry and wildfire fighting were still in his blood. At least working for Adams, he got to stay connected to the community in some meaningful way. It might not be the thrill of frontline danger, but it was still good, honest work and a whole lot more appealing than folding shirts and polishing buckles for his dad.

"Feed me now." Laughing as he exited the booth, Jacob flopped against Linc, and the glance that passed between them was so intimate that Garrick needed to look away. He refused to be jealous that they got each other, the sort of happy ending other people aspired to. They'd worked damn hard to get to this place, and if Garrick's neck went a little tight, well, that had more to do with those questions rattling around in his head about how long he might have with Rain.

Because damn if he didn't want it all. Sometimes, like now, he looked at Rain and his chest ached with the force of wanting him so much, wanting him and his jokes and the way he made Garrick feel so alive, even during one of the most challenging times of his life. *I might be in over my head.*

"The noodle truck has huge plates of veggie pad thai. You want to split that and I'll get you a couple of chicken skewers to supplement?" Rain asked as they surveyed the food offerings.

"Sure. I'm easy."

"Yeah you are." And just like that, Garrick earned his own look, one that made sweat gather in the small of his back, warmth pooling low in his gut, all from Rain's heated gaze, which was full of all sorts of promises Garrick was going to hold him to later.

They found an accessible picnic table after Rain collected a few other dishes for them to share, and Rain took a seat on the bench closest to Garrick so they could share the food while they watched the stage. Their fingers and shoulders kept brushing in a cozy, familiar way that made his skin tingle with awareness. On the stage, a different singer was covering a seventies ballad, one about coming home that Garrick's dad was always humming, and when Rain smiled at him, for the first time in a long time he was so happy he almost couldn't hold it in. He had to laugh simply because being here, in this moment felt so damn good. Being here like this, it was easy to pretend that everything might work out after all. In that instant, with Rain's smile filling him up, it was impossible to wallow in what was lost when he had so much right here.

Rain's laughter mingled with his own, and Garrick shut his eyes, inhaling deeply, drinking in every drop of happiness, as long as he could, as long he had it. For right now, right here, this person and all this contentment was his and he was holding on to both as long as he could.

This was the strangest, best double date Rain had ever been on. They were sharing a picnic table in view of the stage, and mid-bite of pad thai, Garrick offered him an unexpectedly tender look, one that made Linc and Jacob and everything else fade away. Not for the first time, he wondered how in the hell he got so lucky as to have this guy so happy to spend time together.

He hadn't been sure how Garrick would react to his idea of trying Pride together, wasn't sure how far the boundaries of him being out extended, but he'd been game enough for going, and there was something really nice about being here, knowing others probably read them as a couple, and being free to touch and preen. *Yes, he's mine, all mine.* And at least for right then, it was true.

"You guys are damn adorable." Linc gestured at how they were sharing food. They'd done what they always did eating out—chose a few things to share, then some meat on the side for Garrick. They'd fallen into that pattern early on, and it worked for them because they both liked having a number of things to sample. It wasn't about being cutesy, but if it gave them more of the happy couple vibe, he wasn't going to complain either.

"You could take pointers," Jacob suggested with a laugh. "Don't come between Linc and his steak. And we have shared food. But he's right. You guys are cute. Tell me you're sticking around, Rain."

"I—"

"Don't bug him about that," Garrick answered for

him, rolling his eyes at Jacob's rather obvious match-making. Which was fine because Rain wasn't sure how he would have answered. *Was* he sticking around? He didn't know. A few weeks ago his answer would have been far different than it was these days. All he knew was that Garrick made him damn happy and he wasn't giving it up, not yet.

"What? I'm not being *that* pushy. But I know how hard it can be to find work after the fire season. I did some work with the winter crews last year though, and while driving a snowplow and trail grooming isn't the most exciting, it beats working one of the ski lifts if you ask me."

"Nah. Ski lift isn't the worst. I'd rather do that than wait tables again. Tourists, man. They tip worth shit." Garrick's observation led to the three of them debating various seasonal employment options while Rain thought about staying, what that might look like. It wasn't the first time the thought had crossed his mind, and he let himself daydream about snow. Surprisingly, the thought didn't make his skin itch as much as make him curious. Would Cookie like the winter? Could he coax her into a cute pink parka? Which holidays did Garrick celebrate?

It was a nice little improbably cozy fantasy, one that wasn't likely to come to pass. Garrick would get tired of him eventually if nothing else, but for a minute it was a pretty little picture.

"What are you smiling about?" Turning his attention back to Rain, Garrick gave him an indulgent look, the one that usually meant he'd be up for whatever idea Rain had. However, this time Rain simply shook his head, not willing to let his fragile fantasy into the world. Jacob had it all wrong—the worst thing wouldn't be some boring job. Rather, it would be Garrick laughing at the prospect, not wanting him. And this day was simply too nice to ruin by inviting rejection.

On the stage, a troupe of young dancers had replaced the folk singer. They weren't particularly coordinated, but they made up for a lack of talent with a lot of earnest enthusiasm. Rain and the others applauded loudly as they finished their first number.

"Bet this is a far cry from Portland Pride. There you've got all the parties and parade and professional acts, right?" Garrick asked.

"Oh, I've been." Jacob laughed. "It's way more of a hookup scene than—hey, why are you glowering at me? I didn't say I wanted to go back!"

He bumped shoulders with Linc, more of their easy comfort with each other. Rain couldn't help but wonder what that would be like, years with one person, shared history and jokes, fake jealousy and real, deep feelings.

"It's fun," Rain agreed, mind still on Jacob and Linc and how nice that might be to have. "But this is cute and fun too. It's nice to not have a huge crowd of people and all the vendors seem really happy to be here. Lots of local flavor."

He *could* have slid in something about the company and how that was the real draw for him, but he wasn't that smooth, not then, not with a throat this tight and Garrick looking at him like he was a few minutes from ditching them for the big city experience.

They finished up their food and returned to browsing the booths, Jacob trying to goad Linc into a temporary rainbow tattoo and Linc threatening to get Jacob's name instead in some cheesy location, their banter filling up any silences between him and Garrick.

"Hey, it's your favorites!" With Linc and Jacob distracted by the tattoo selection, Garrick pointed at a pink T-shirt with Rain's favorite pony characters and a Morning Sunshine slogan. "You should get it."

"Or maybe that one." He pointed at a different shirt with a single pony and Daddy, I Want a Pony under it in swirly font.

"Behave." Though Garrick's mischievous smile said he wasn't truly opposed to Rain getting the shirt.

"You're almost elderly enough to be someone's sugar daddy, old man," Rain couldn't resist teasing. Not that he'd changed his mind about wanting one of those, but Garrick could get uptight about the age difference every now and then, and teasing him was a good way to get him to lighten up.

"Ha." Garrick captured his wrist and tugged him down so he could whisper closer to Rain's ear, "Bad boys get spankings. Might want to be nice."

Oh yeah. Delicious heat spread through all his muscles, molten butter and sugar leaving him all bubbly and craving more. "I'm getting the shirt."

"You do that." Garrick winked at him, and damn if Rain didn't want a teleporter to zap them both right back to Garrick's bedroom, where he could make him carry through on all the sexy threats in his eyes.

As he paid for his purchases, another singer on the stage was crooning about love lasting only a single night, lyrics hitting Rain square in the chest. He didn't want a single night, not anymore. Hell, he was starting to think he might never get enough of this man and little moments like this one.

Chapter Sixteen

"Are you sure about this?" Frowning, Garrick studied his handiwork, not at all convinced it was ready for public consumption. And truly, he wasn't at all sure about this whole day, lacking Rain's easy confidence.

"She's going to love it." Rain plucked the lumpy little purple-striped pouch out of Garrick's hands and dropped it in a gift bag. Garrick had actually managed to complete a knitting project of sorts—a small drawstring pouch that held a bottle of local lavender essential oil and a gift card. It was far from perfect—lumpy with some unintended eyelets, and the cord was possibly the best knitting of the whole piece, but Rain kept insisting Shirley would appreciate the gift.

"If you say so." Privately, he was rather proud of the lumpy little project. What had started out as admittedly something to get in Rain's good graces had become an activity he genuinely got some satisfaction from, to the point that he'd worked on the project several times without Rain being around. Rain himself did the best job of distracting Garrick when the nights got long and lonely, but the hobby didn't hurt.

"Guess we should head out." Garrick's gaze flitted across the street. Any moment now people would start descending on Shirley's backyard for a combination birthday and Fourth of July celebration.

"Calm down. You're nervous about meeting my family, which is cute, but I'm pretty sure they're going to love you." Rain put the finishing touches on his own gift. The handmade socks had turned out beautifully and he'd paired them with a foot cream from the same little gift shop where Garrick had found the lavender oil. They'd had a number of fun outings recently in addition to Pride, trying different parks and paths with Cookie and exploring shops and restaurants.

Garrick knew keeping him busy and distracted was a lot of the motivation behind their explorations, Rain on a mission to keep him from the melancholy that threatened to reappear whenever he was idle too long. So busy was good. Knitting lessons. Rain's workouts. Eating out. Work, taking on a few more hours. Playing with Cookie. Getting better at Rain's board game. None of it exactly made up for what he wasn't doing, but he didn't like dwelling on that, preferred to focus on making fun memories with Rain. There would be plenty enough time later to let the disappointment back in.

"I still say I'm too old for you, and your parents are going to give me the evil eye." Meeting the parents had never exactly been Garrick's favorite thing, and even if Shirley seemed cool with their friendship, he wasn't convinced Rain's parents would feel the same.

"They are not driving down from Portland to lecture either of us. Although I do talk about you enough that they're curious. Besides, it's going to be a big party. No one's going to be that focused on us." Rain grabbed both gift bags and the carrot bread they'd made together.

"If you say so," he grumbled as he settled into his chair for the trip across the street.

"Don't make me drag you back to bed, get you in a better mood." Rain's tone was anything but threatening. "And if you truly hate the party, we'll simply slip away early, come back here and make our own fireworks."

"Now that sounds like a plan."

"Of course, I'm kind of digging this whole small town Fourth of July thing too. The parade was fun."

"Yeah?" Garrick had lived here his whole life, so the old-fashioned parade and festival was comfortable and familiar. He'd figured Rain would be bored though, but to his surprise, Rain had been into it, waving at the floats of kids and civic organizations. "I'll save enough energy for the town firework show tonight then. You'll like that."

"I will. But Cookie won't." Rain laughed, then frowned as they encountered Cookie lurking at the door. She had a baleful look for them, as if she sensed she was about to miss out on some fun. "Wish Grandma would let us bring her to the party. Her dogs can deal."

"Her house, her rules." Garrick shrugged as he pointed and ordered Cookie to her living room bed, a big flowered cushion Rain had found at one of the shops that carried his grandmother's textiles. "And she was nice enough to invite my dad too. She doesn't need Cookie adding to the chaos."

"Did you tell your dad that the burgers are black bean?" Rain followed him out the door and down the driveway.

"I promised him a steak next week." The presence of his dad made this even more of a meet-the-family thing. Not that he had an issue being a couple with

Rain, but he also felt a certain…pressure to make sure the party went well. .

"Rain!" Two tall curly-haired guys with Rain's brown eyes exited a hybrid SUV. The older one had glasses and a spiky-haired, shorter friend hanging on his arm. "Come here."

"You drove on your own?" Rain hurried over.

"Three hours or more in the Prius's back seat listening to one of Mom's self-help audiobooks?" The younger brother did a comical shudder. "I think not. You'll note too that we beat their drive time."

Brotherly hugs and introductions were exchanged, and Lark, the older one, introduced his friend as Harper, while the younger one, Skye, studied Garrick with undisguised speculation. Skye was full of stories about summer college classes while Lark and Harper were both nursing students with summer internships at the same Portland hospital where Garrick had initially been treated for his injuries. All three—or okay *four*, Rain included—made Garrick feel even older.

Rather than navigate the front steps, they went around to the side gate where the backyard was decked out for the party—tie-dyed table linens, a beanbag toss game for the younger kids, coolers with drinks, various types of lawn chairs scattered around, and a truly impressive array of food. A fair number of people were already there—neighbors along with some of Shirley's fabric arts community and a few assorted cousins. Her yappy dogs were underfoot as usual, but Shirley herself looked rejuvenated in a rainbow-dyed dress and twin gray braids down her back.

"My boys!" She handed Garrick her phone so that he could take pictures of her beaming with all three brothers. As he was giving it back, Rain's parents arrived. His dad was shorter than Rain's mom with Shirley's longer nose and sharp features, while the mom was almost as tall as Rain's brothers with a riot of curly hair held back by a woven band. Her lean muscles gave the impression that she must live at the yoga studio. She brought carob hemp seed cookies and an appraising stare for Garrick.

"So...this is your new friend, Rain? The one we've heard so much about?"

"Uh-huh." Rain nodded enthusiastically and made the introductions, heaping on the praise for Garrick's rescue of Cookie and his work with the forest service.

"You know I read the most amazing article recently about clinical massage and cannabis and chronic pain in spinal cord injuries. Fascinating stuff!" Rain's mother enthused, bending to be more on Garrick's level.

"Mom. He can't do cannabis. Drug testing for work." Rain rolled his eyes.

"Yet another reason it needs widespread acceptance." Far from put off, Rain's mother spent the next few minutes making an impassioned case for alternative healing including CBD oil and acupuncture.

"I think I've seen enough needles," Garrick demurred.

"Just say no to her brownies," Rain whispered in Garrick's ear when his mom got distracted by a question from Skye. "Also, this is how she shows love. When she met Harper, she was full of nonbinary resources. When she volunteers to run a 10k race for spinal injury awareness, that's when you'll know she really likes you."

"Noted. And she's nice. But I'm still not trying acupuncture."

"Not gonna get any flak from me there." Rain

glanced away toward the gate. "Your dad's here! Can't wait to hear what *he* thinks of Mom's baking."

"Warn him about any...*special* ingredients." Garrick waved at his dad who strode over. Looking patriotic in his usual blue jeans and a red plaid shirt, he carried a small casserole dish with potholders.

"Brought some baked beans," his dad said by way of greeting. "Left out the bacon I usually use."

"The hardship." Laughing, Garrick pointed to the food table. "Put it over there, then come and let me introduce you to Rain's family."

Rain's mom shifted topics to the virtues of a low-sodium diet, much to the befuddlement of Garrick's dad, but Rain's dad got him talking about his horses and store. Lark shared information about a horse rescue operation closer to Portland, and the group settled into easy small talk before everyone helped themselves to heaping plates of food.

Eventually, it was time for cupcakes and presents. Shirley exclaimed over each gift, including Garrick's lumpy pouch.

"The gift card is from Dad, too," he added, trying to get attention off his knitting abilities. His dad's eyebrows went up, but he didn't say anything about Garrick's new hobby.

"Now, don't you go getting embarrassed," Shirley admonished, holding the pouch up. "It's a fine first effort, and we all have to start somewhere."

"Honestly, I'm amazed Rain has stuck with the knitting as long as he has." Rain's mother's tone was joking, but Rain stiffened next to Garrick nonetheless. His chair was close enough that Garrick could reach over and squeeze his arm. He had enough experience himself with familial teasing to be sympathetic toward his plight.

"And he's actually good at it," Lark joined in, leaning forward on the glider swing he was sharing with Harper. "Most hobbies only last days with him. Look at those socks, though. They're actually wearable."

"High praise." Rain moved his hand like he was about to flip Lark off, then apparently thought the better of it, tucking it back by his side.

"Come on, dude. You know you never stick to anything." Lark didn't seem ready to drop the subject, typical older sibling, voice light but there was a bite there as well.

"I do too." Mouth pursing, Rain gave his brother a hard stare.

"Rain's done an amazing job sticking to his workout program all summer." Even if he was loath to wade into a family squabble, Garrick felt honor bound to defend his person.

"Boys. And Rain, you know we love you." Rain's mother had a long-suffering tone as she played peacemaker. "It's a compliment. You're a good knitter. Now, if you could only apply that dedication to the rest of your life."

"Maybe I already have."

Even as Rain said the words, little doubts prickled up Garrick's back. Rain was a lot of great things—loyal, affectionate, funny, hardworking—but his history with staying power wasn't the best. He'd confessed to changing his major a number of times and even his interest in wildfire fighting felt as much like an occupational fling as a genuine calling. *He'll move on from you too.* Most days Garrick could ignore that worry, live for the moment with Rain, but right then his gut churned. Damned reality again, forcing its way past his good mood.

"And maybe Mom will go to a cheese expo." Skye laughed. This was clearly an old sibling argument, and even if there was some truth to it, Garrick frowned.

"Hey, at least you'll be able to take the knitting with you when you bounce on to your next adventure." Lark shrugged. And there it was, Garrick's biggest fear—Rain wouldn't stick around. Couldn't. The siren call of something shiny would come his way. Garrick had known this ever since they first met, but lately things had become more complicated, his heart wanting things his brain knew damn well were impossible. He liked Rain. So damn much. But he couldn't deny that all the like in the world wouldn't be enough to hold Rain here.

"I'm so sorry that not all of us have had our future completely mapped out since we were ten." Rain's retort did nothing to relieve the tension in Garrick's neck.

"At least I have a plan." Lark looked like he wanted to say more, but his mother clapped her hands. She quickly thrust another gift at Shirley.

"Next present!"

The tiff died away, replaced by softer brotherly teasing about beanbag toss skills and gorging on the cupcakes. However, even hours later, Garrick still hadn't forgotten. He and Rain had driven to a good vantage point for the town fireworks, not wanting to get caught up in the crowds at the fairgrounds but still wanting to see the show.

Sitting on the rear hatch, Rain rested his head on Garrick's shoulder. The stereo was softly playing as the first of the fireworks exploded in the clear night sky, soft breeze tickling their skin. One of life's truly perfect moments, and Garrick wrapped his arms around Rain, trying to memorize his beachy scent, the solid feel of his muscles, the softness of his hair. But through it all, he couldn't shake the knowledge that someday soon Rain would move on, and it was going to hurt like hell when he did. Even knowing that, though, he still couldn't let go, couldn't do anything other than hold Rain close, hope memories like this were enough to soften the inevitable heartache.

"Damn. How about you tell your friend in Dispatch to call us back in on account of this sun?" Bosler wiped the sweat off his forehead with a paisley bandanna. He was splitting radio duties with Rain this week, but at the moment they were all knee-deep in brambly brush, a weeklong fire prevention cleanup project.

Rain paused in his hauling of branches to consider how best to reply. The other people on his crew had picked up on his friendship with Garrick—inevitable, really, what with them riding together so much. But he couldn't tell whether Bosler was trying to joke with him or if he was trying to make some underlying point.

"Eh. It's not so hot," Rain hedged. "You need a water break? I've got extra trail mix bars if you need one."

"Appreciate the offer, but I'm good. Just wish they had us working in a shadier part of the forest this week. I'm still recovering from the holiday weekend. How about you young guns? Who overindulged?"

"Our prayer group did a booth at the Fourth of July festival and then a camping trip with some rock climbing." Zeb, the earnest farmer guy who made Rain's teeth hurt with his wholesomeness, spoke first.

"Hope you had a good time. My family came down

for my grandma's birthday. The festival was fun too—great work from all the volunteers."

"Sounds like fun all around." Bosler nodded as he got back to work.

Honestly, though, Rain was happy to be back at work. Too much family togetherness all weekend. Too much teasing from people who should know better, who should have his freaking back, but instead wanted to act like he was still aimless and sixteen. He was still salty at his brothers because Garrick hadn't seemed to know what to make of their heckling, alternating between defending Rain and being a little more distant than usual.

But now his family was all back in Portland and life could get back to normal. At least everyone had seemed to like Garrick. That part had been nice, families mingling, feeling like it was a real, solid adult relationship and not some random hookup. Maybe finally his mom could believe that people other than Lark the perfect were capable of managing their own lives. God, he loved Lark, but he had a way of making Rain doubt himself, worry that maybe Garrick could do a lot better than him, worry that maybe he didn't have what it took to hold on to something this good. Because when it was good, like on the Fourth, watching fireworks together, it was spectacular, and that was even before they reached the bedroom.

"Crew four-five-one?" The radio on his belt crackled right as Rain was in the middle of a sexy daydream about when he might next get to sleep over at Garrick's.

"This is four-five-one." Damn. He hoped he sounded normal. Not that Garrick might care, but with Bosler and the others looking a little closer at him, he didn't need any extra teasing. He'd had enough of that this weekend.

"We're pulling you in."

A cheer erupted from the people closest to Rain, but he held up a hand to silence them.

"Yeah, hang on there. We're not sending you home."

"You're not?"

"We've got an elevated fire risk warning with a small fire to the south of us. You're being redirected to dig line as a precaution. Crews are en route to the fire, and we're hopeful for quick containment, but we're going to act accordingly and get our crews in place."

"Understood."

"Tell your crew chief she can contact Ryland with questions about the logistics. You all might be in for a long day."

"Got it."

"Good. You take care now. Tell the crew to look sharp."

"I—*we* will." The reminder to be careful might be directed mostly at Rain, but he tried to stay professional. He wanted to ask Garrick how he was getting back if Rain was out late, but he refrained. Garrick would get a ride—Ryland or his dad or another friend. Even Rain's grandma had given him rides a couple of times. He'd be fine, but Rain still knew a pang for the early evening he'd been hoping for, the two of them and Cookie and no family members bugging them.

"Do hotshot crews spend so much time digging?" he asked some hours later as sweat ran down his muscles, every muscle screaming in protest. He swigged water along with the others who were taking a moment, but the sky was hazy with heat and smoke and they couldn't afford too long a break. Nightfall was coming and they'd been told they'd be making the long drive back to base soon. Meanwhile, the fire command was debating whether this fire was adequately contained or whether they needed to set up a fire camp and other infrastructure needed for a longer fight.

"Oh, we all dig." Bosler laughed. "But they see more real action for sure. You got a taste for the front line, kid?"

"Someday, maybe. I applied all around but didn't have enough experience yet, I guess. This job will help."

"Well, they're hiring hotshots for the second half of the season down in the LA area. Those jobs sometimes last into November. My brother's a crew chief down there. You want me to pass him your application?"

"You'd do that for me?" Rain hadn't been under the impression that Bosler liked him that much, but the older man nodded.

"Sure I would. You've got that look about you. Hungry. You'd do well. God knows you've been spending your summer getting ripped. How many pull-ups you up to now?"

"Did a personal best of ten the other day. I could probably pass the fitness test for a hotshot crew, yeah."

"You train with Nelson, right?" Zeb asked. "I need to find me a personal trainer. Next season, I'm gonna make a hotshot crew here for sure. Not California, though." He gave a comical shudder. "Couldn't pay me to leave home. Gonna marry my girl, stay local. California, that's too far."

"Nah. I've done seasons all over the West." Bosler gave a dismissive gesture like he was older than dirt, which wasn't too far from the truth. Rain worried about him some, long hot days like this. "It's a good crew my brother's got going there. You let me know, Fisher. I'll put a word in for you. Hard worker like you and a thirst for the big city life—you'd probably be happier with their culture for sure."

"Thanks." Rain wasn't entirely sure whether Bosler meant the area's lack of nightlife or a more subtle reference to him being queer, but he also seemed perfectly willing to help Rain get a prime chance at career advancement, so Rain wasn't going to question his motives too closely. Instead, he thought about the chance at a hotshot crew the rest of the shift.

A few months ago, he would have leaped at it, for sure. Excitement? Danger? New place? Closer to a city? Yes, please. Sign him up. But now...

Everything was different now. Confusing. Brain muddled, he finally made his way home, stars already out and twinkling. Garrick's living room light was on though, and Rain could see the shadow of the TV. Even dragging as he was, he still wanted to make sure that someone had seen to Cookie, so he sent Grandma a fast text that he was at Garrick's place.

Already in bed, dearest. Food in the fridge, she texted back as he crossed the street.

"Damn. You look like crap." Garrick shook his head when he answered the door.

"Gee. Tell it to me nice, will you? I do have some ego, you know." And okay, Rain could admit it, he'd wanted to see Garrick, too, not simply check on Cookie. Garrick's welcoming smile was better than any post-work drink.

"I know, baby. And I'm happy to see you, I am. But you look about ten seconds from falling over. Have you eaten?" Leaning heavily on his crutches, Garrick had clearly been home longer than Rain. His hair was damp, the scent of his shampoo filling the night air, and he'd changed into sweats.

"Snacks. I'll get some food. Just wanted to see if Cookie needed a w-a-l-k." He spelled out the word since she was right there, looking eager.

"You need dinner more than she needs out. Come on in. Let me feed you." Garrick headed toward the kitchen, leaving Rain and Cookie to follow. "My dad was here. We took her out for some nice exercise. And guess what he brought?"

Garrick grabbed a short rope from the counter, tossed it to Rain, who examined it. "Leash?"

"Not just any leash, it's a specially designed wheelchair lead. He said your brother gave him the idea. We tested it out and she did pretty good. Now I can take her out on my own! Isn't that great?"

"You're not going to need me anymore?" A strange, empty feeling opened up in his chest. He hadn't realized how much he counted on their twice-daily interactions until that moment.

"I'm always gonna need you." Garrick gave him an affectionate look, but Rain wasn't convinced. "This is just for in a pinch. Nights like this one, or if you get called to work a fire camp. Backup plan. And since it looks like Cookie isn't going anywhere, I need to make sure we don't impose on you forever."

"Okay. That was nice of him." It was the right thing to say, but Rain still couldn't seem to shake his unease. Garrick admitting Cookie was his forever should have had him smiling, but he couldn't seem to manage that.

"Tell you what." Garrick studied the interior of his

fridge. "I'm going to make you a nice big cold drink—you need to hydrate—and you're going to go shower off fast and climb into the hot tub. I've got a package of that tofu brand you like, and I'm going to scramble that and make you some toast."

"Don't you want to do the tub with me?"

"Nah. Too much hassle tonight. Let me take care of you?"

Rain was too tired to put up much of an argument and the offer was too damn tempting. "Okay."

But that empty feeling persisted through his shower, the weird energy he'd had all day, especially since his conversation with Bosler. And now the feeling seemed worse, here where he wasn't precisely needed but was always welcomed by the sweetest guy ever, who was right now cooking for Rain while Rain floated in the center of the hot tub.

He could take it. Take that chance at a hotshot crew. Nothing holding him here. Except maybe for everything.

Splash. He narrowly avoided sinking to the bottom of the tub. Fuck if that thought didn't scare him, make every muscle in his body tense. Could he really pass up the chance? Should he even tell Garrick? Hell. He hated that there wasn't a blueprint for him to follow. People like Lark had it so damn easy. He'd known he wanted to be a nurse practitioner forever, been in love with Harper several years now, probably had a plan in place for their future too. But not Rain. All he'd known was a passion for adventure and a restless soul. Could he live with himself if he stayed?

"Baby, the tub is supposed to relax you. Not make you ready to do battle." Garrick laughed as he wheeled out onto the deck, plastic plate balanced on his lap. "You look so damn fierce."

"Sorry."

"Don't be sorry." Garrick set the plate on the nearby picnic table. "Grab a towel. Come eat. Your shift go okay?"

"Yeah, it was fine." Rain ducked his head, not wanting him to see the half-truth in his eyes. He wasn't telling him about Bosler. Not yet. Maybe not ever, not with Garrick looking at him so tenderly. His eyes were soft, mouth open and inviting as he motioned for Rain. He was every damn thing Rain had ever wanted. Only a fool would walk away from this, but the question remained, the one he'd had all damn week—could he trust it? Trust himself? Trust Garrick? He simply didn't know and that fucking sucked.

Chapter Seventeen

Garrick had been trapped before, true no-win situations in the midst of a fire, had had midair malfunctions, and knew how to keep his cool in all manner of scenarios. So he had no reason to be freaking out right then. Except he totally was.

"Cookie? Want a biscuit? Cookie? Come on, girl!" He kept his voice light and encouraging even as his mind raced. One second he'd been adjusting the wheelchair leash and the next Cookie had been sprinting away from him, top speed, like this was some fun new game. Except it wasn't and Garrick seriously didn't know what he'd do if he couldn't catch her.

Rain was working late, so he'd thought he'd do him a favor and give Cookie her exercise. However, they still hadn't worked out all the kinks with the leash system. She wasn't used to walking that close to the chair or on that short of a lead, and he wasn't used to the extra pull of her as he wheeled himself. He was confident they'd eventually work it out, but first things first, he had to get her back.

Funny how life could change in a few short months. He couldn't imagine life without Cookie now. He counted on her company on the nights when Rain wasn't around. Hell, he'd been talking about putting in a strip of some sort of grass for her out back, getting opinions from Linc and Jacob about what they did for their pack of beasts. Talking dogs had been a nice way to smooth over the tension after his abrupt exit from the party. He'd really rather not call them or his dad to come help him catch Cookie, but he might not have a choice.

Damn it. He'd lost sight of her now. They were at the park but near the edge, by all the houses. Crap. He patted his shirt for his phone and—

Fuck it all. He'd left the phone on his dining table as he'd been adjusting the new leash.

"Cookie? Cookie?" he called again to no avail. Damn it. No choice but to head back now, have Shirley put a red alert on the neighborhood board, and call someone to come help him. He raced back, wheeling hard, glad he'd remembered his gloves at least. Almost home, he narrowly avoided crashing into Rain in Shirley's driveway.

"Damn. What's up with you?" Rain jumped out of the way. He was still in work clothes and had tired eyes, but right then, all Garrick cared about was help getting Cookie back.

"Cookie. Got away from me. At the park. Need help. Please."

"Okay. Okay." Rain clapped him on the shoulder. "We'll get her back, promise. Let me tell Grandma— Wait. Look!"

He pointed toward Garrick's place, and heart in his throat, Garrick spun around. There on the porch lay Cookie, looking for all the world like she was waiting on *him.* Her fur was dusty with muddy clumps and she was chewing on some mangled tennis ball, but she was *there*.

"Cookie. Stay!" he called as he hurried over, Rain fast behind him.

"Got you." Rain lunged for Cookie's sparkly collar, which was looking a little worse for the wear after her adventure. "And you got yourself all dirty, girl. Bath time?"

"Don't think I can do it myself," Garrick admitted, patting Cookie's head with a still shaky hand. "And you seem bushed. I'll call Dad, see if he can help me take her to the groomer they've got part time at the feed store."

"I can handle a bath for her. You don't need to call anyone." Rain sounded all indignant, eyes all but shooting sparks at Garrick.

"Okay, okay. But you're going to let me make you dinner afterward. Let's hurry her into the bathroom before she can get dust everywhere."

"On it." Rain scooped up Cookie like she was a sack of potatoes instead of fifty-odd pounds of dog. He clomped to the bathroom, heavy tread saying he was in a mood of some sort. "Now stay. Neither of us is gonna like this, so let's make it quick and easy, okay?"

Still frowning, Rain deposited Cookie in the tub, then stripped down to a very basic pair of black boxer briefs.

"Laundry day?" Garrick tried for some levity but didn't get a laugh from Rain, who peeled them off with far more force than usual.

"Work pants chafe with lace. Sorry if you were expecting something sexy."

"I wasn't." Staying in the bathroom doorway, Garrick held up his hands. "You know I don't require...a certain wardrobe, right? I like you every which way."

"I know." Rain huffed out a breath.

"What's wrong?" Garrick asked as Rain dug under the sink for the bottle of dog shampoo they'd bought last trip to get dog chow and then never used.

"Dunno." Rain hopped in the tub with Cookie, who seemed rather bemused with the whole proceeding. "Guess I'm mad at myself for having to work late. And mad that you needed to take Cookie out on your own. You could have waited—"

"Hey now. I appreciate your help. So much. But this—" he gestured between them "—doesn't come with chore expectations. She's my dog, and I need to be able to take her out on my own because you've got a life too. I never meant that I expected your assistance indefinitely."

"Obviously." Rain's voice was way harsher than his gentle hands as he soaped up Cookie.

Garrick tried to figure out where he'd gone wrong here because Rain was certainly acting like Garrick was trying to shove him out the door. Heck. Was that it?

"You know I love having you around, right? I sleep so much better when you're here, and I actually eat a real dinner, not simply a sandwich, on the nights you're over too."

"Glad to be of service."

And now it was Garrick's turn to get irritated. "Are you only with me because you think Cookie and I need taking care of? I mean, I know we both enjoy doing things for each other, but if you're thinking I need... dunno...some sort of full-time keeper, I'd like to know that now."

"Nah." Some of the ire seemed to leave Rain as his shoulders slumped. He carefully rinsed Cookie with the spray attachment. This had to be the weirdest damn location for a state-of-the-relationship talk. Not being able to kiss some sense into Rain was particularly irksome.

"Why are you in this thing then?" Maybe it was ego but Garrick needed more than monosyllabic answers.

"Uh, you have to ask? You're sexy as fuck. You make me feel…special."

"Good." Garrick liked knowing that because he did try to show his appreciation for Rain as a person he cared a lot about.

"Even when I'm feeling lousy, like the other night, you make me feel sexy. Wanted. And you take care— wait. That's not really the word. You *pamper* me. Like I'm the princess instead of this one." Tone lighter now, he ruffled Cookie's head. "I like it. A lot. And yeah, I do like returning the favor, helping you out because you do so much for me from cooking to workout plans to making me rest. Guess I worry about not being able to do anything in return to make it worth it for you."

"You. You make it worth it for me. I'd want you around even if you couldn't or didn't want to do favors anymore."

"Thanks." Rain quickly rinsed his own body before grabbing two towels from the rack. He toweled off Cookie first, who still managed to shake enough water off to get Garrick damp too, and then wrapped the other towel around his waist. "I appreciate that. And sorry. I'm just in a weird mood. Ever since… Never mind."

"Oh no, you do not get to tease me like that." Garrick stopped him with a hand on his arm when Rain would have breezed on by. "Seriously. What's going on? Something at work?"

"Sort of." Gently breaking loose from Garrick, he chased Cookie into the bedroom, herding her onto her bed. "There. You can dry off before you get anything else wet."

"You were saying?" Garrick prompted.

"It's nothing. Just that Bosler—older guy on our crew—has been after me to put in for a hotshot crew down in California. His brother is a crew chief down there, and he thinks I'd have a good chance of getting the job."

"And?"

"Well, obviously I'm not taking it. Like I said. It's a weird mood. That's all."

Fuck. Garrick had known this was coming eventually, but still wasn't ready, didn't know what to do with the dull ache spreading out in his chest, the heaviness taking over his limbs. But he did know exactly what he had to say. "You should take the opportunity."

"What the ever-loving fuck?" Rain whirled on Garrick, who moments earlier had seemed intent on proving that their relationship was way more than the trading of favors. Except maybe it wasn't, not if Garrick could so easily cast him off. "You want me gone that badly?"

"No!" Garrick held up his hands again, like Rain was the one being unreasonable here. "Of course not. Didn't I just get done telling you how much I like you around?"

"I don't know. Did you?" Yeah, he was being childish, but damn. He *hurt.* He'd expected Garrick to thank him for not going, not…whatever the hell this was instead.

"We have a great time together. You know that. I love having you around. Cookie does too. I'll miss you like hell, but we both know that hotshot crew slots are hard to come by. If this is really your dream, then you need to go for it."

"I'm not sure," Rain admitted, brain whirring like an overloaded motor. He'd thought about little else for days now and still wasn't certain. He'd thought he'd had his answer—Cookie and Garrick needed him here. Only now he wasn't sure about that either.

"You've been working out like it's a second job all summer. I've seen plenty of smoke-jumping rookies less determined than you. You've added muscle, overhauled your diet, gained strength and flexibility—"

"Yeah, well, you're a good trainer. You could probably do it professionally—anyone would be ripped following your orders."

"Thanks. But you've put in the work, not me. You said you wanted to be on a hotshot crew. What's changed?"

You. Us. Everything. Those words froze in Rain's throat, refused to budge because what if that wasn't enough of an answer for Garrick? What if he was disappointed in Rain changing his mind?

"Spot might open up here," he said instead, pacing in front of the bed. "It's only July. There's a few more months—"

"California's burn season is longer, and their crews are always way bigger."

"Why the fuck are you so hell-bent on me going? You want a medal for training me enough to earn a spot?" He stopped short of accusing Garrick of living vicariously through him, swallowing back caustic words he wouldn't be able to recall, but seriously, he did have to wonder why this seemed to matter so much to Garrick.

"Of course not." Garrick waved away the accusation. "As someone with a lot more experience than you, though, I know how rare it is to get a hand up like Bosler is offering. You get a few years of hotshot crew experience—"

"*Years.* You want me gone for *years.*" Rain's voice came out flat and lifeless.

"I don't *want.*" Eyes wide and pained, Garrick's face softened. "What I want has absolutely no bearing on this though. This is your future. Your career, if you play your cards right."

"But it could—your opinion, it could make a difference," Rain said softly, pausing his pacing near the fireplace. "What you want, that matters to me. Making you happy, that's important."

"At the expense of making yourself happy? No, thank you. That's a recipe for a short and bitter relationship." Garrick had stripped off his wheelchair gloves and was twisting them in his hands, worrying the leather.

"Like it's got a ton of longevity to start with. You're ready to kick me to the curb."

"Stop that. I am not. But you have to do what's best for you here." Garrick stopped twisting long enough to slap the gloves against his thigh.

"Ask me to stay, Garrick." Rain sank onto Garrick's side of the bed, putting their faces at the same level. "If that's what's in your heart, then ask me to stay."

"I can't do that." So much for eye contact. Garrick wouldn't meet his gaze. "It wouldn't be fair to you. You'd be miserable. I've known all along that you're more of a city person."

"So? Ask me to stay anyway." *Ask me.* His ribs ached from the force of his wanting. Maybe that's what this was—he needed Garrick to desire his presence enough to be willing to ask him to stay. That would be proof that Garrick truly wanted him, that he wasn't going to cast Rain aside when he got to be too much. "Maybe you mean more to me than any amount of nightlife. Maybe I'd stay if you asked."

"I appreciate that. I do. God, you don't even know how much." Garrick scrubbed at his short hair. "But for how long?"

"How long what?"

"How long would you be happy if I asked you to stay? How long until this place started to grate on your nerves? This job? Me? Tell me you wouldn't resent passing up this opportunity if another one doesn't come along."

"I…" The denial was on the tip of his tongue but didn't come. *Fuck it.* Why did this have to be so hard? All he wanted was a reason to stay, and Garrick wasn't giving him that. "I don't know. I mean, I figure if I start hating this job too much, I can find something else. Don't worry. I'm not intending to freeload."

"That was hardly my worry." Garrick gave a bitter laugh as he reached over and patted Rain's knee. His hand was clammy and cool, not warm and reassuring like usual. "Jobs aren't all created equal. Trust me. I know. And any job that excites you enough that you've been getting up extra early simply to train for it, you owe it to yourself to chase, others' wishes and wants be damned."

I've been up early for you. But he couldn't admit that, not with Garrick being all adult and reasonable here. He didn't want to look even more like some kid with a hopeless crush while Mr. Older and Wiser was trying to push him out of their cozy little nest. Maybe Garrick had a point that he wouldn't know whether the hotshot crew was for him unless he tried it, but figuring out *whether* he wanted to try—that was the whole damn quandary he was in. And all he needed—the one thing he *wanted*—was for Garrick to ask him to stay. Then he would, and that would settle it as far as he was concerned. Everything else could work out if Garrick could simply admit he wanted Rain to stay.

And if he didn't, well then, there wasn't really much point in staying, was there?

Garrick grabbed his hand, but Rain didn't squeeze back.

Fuck. Rain had known better than to get attached. He really had. But here he was, well and truly attached to this man, who didn't seem to want him, at least not the way Rain craved him more than he did ice water in the July sun. Garrick simply didn't understand. Rain would *happily* commit to a future together, if only Garrick would ask. He'd stay. He'd give up whatever.

"I can't stay here." He pushed away from the bed, dropping Garrick's hand.

"I know. That's what I'm trying to tell you."

"I mean right now. This minute. I can't have this conversation with you with me in a towel. You want me to try for this job. So I guess I will. But damn it, I really thought you wanted me here."

"Rain. I do. I want you so bad my hands are shaking with it." He held one up and he wasn't lying.

"Then—"

"But I'm not going to ask you to stay in Painter's

Ridge. I like you too much for that. I like us too much for that. I'm not going to taint my memories of what we had—"

"Fuck memories. You could have *me*. You're so damn afraid that I'm going to leave someday that you're shoving me out the door right now to ensure that I don't get a chance to break your heart later on. That's fucked up, man."

"You've got it all wrong. I'm not going to let you mortgage your future for me. It would be disastrous, and I know it. If that means letting you go, then that's what I have to do." Garrick's jaw was firm as ever, but his eyes were glassy.

Hell. If he cried, then Rain was going to cry, and then they were truly going to have a mess. If Garrick wanted to play martyr, let him. He stalked off to the bathroom to find his work clothes, pulling them on with robotic hands, brain still back in the bedroom with Garrick.

"Don't go."

"What?" Rain's heart leaped, rest of him scarcely daring to hope.

"Don't go. I said I'd feed you dinner. Let's not ruin what time we have left together. We always knew this was a fling—"

"Did we? Did we really now?" Still buttoning his shirt, Rain whirled on him. Hope, whatever there had been, died a swift, merciless death. "So this was always only casual for you? Even the last few... You know what? Never mind. Clearly I'm the idiot here. I thought... And it doesn't really matter what the fuck I thought. You're the one who's made up his mind."

"Rain." Garrick's face might be anguished, but his

voice was all be-reasonable-now tone that had Rain ready to claw at the walls. "Don't leave angry—"

"You'd prefer a party? A nice little civilized going away get-together?"

"Is that *such* a terrible idea? Ending things as friends—"

"Fuck. You. You know how you like me too much to ask me to stay? Well, I like you too much to end things like that. And I definitely like *me* too much to settle for a few more days or weeks or something when I know damn well we could have had more if only you'd fucking ask me. Which you won't. So yeah. Leaving."

One boot on, one in his hand, he hopped to the front door, almost tripping on Cookie's unicorn toy. He'd known better. He absolutely had. And he'd still had his heart broken by the nicest guy he'd ever had the privilege of knowing. Fuck it all to hell. The absolute last thing he wanted to do was cross the road, knowing full well that Garrick was watching him go, knowing that Garrick was hurting too, and knowing that this was well and truly over if he went. And still he walked.

Chapter Eighteen

"You look like shit." Garrick's dad had pats and head scratches for Cookie but only a skeptical look for Garrick, eyes narrowing.

He'd known that asking his dad to come by early before taking him to his neurologist appointment would likely invite questions he didn't want to answer, but it had been two days since he'd seen Rain. Forty-eight long hours. More now. And Cookie was pining even worse than him. She alternated pouting and watching the door with sulking on her bed, ignoring his offers to toss a toy for her and plodding along when he carefully took her out on his own. Rain had done the responsible thing, texted to make sure Garrick had a plan for Cookie, but no way was Garrick calling him over on some pretext of the dog missing him too much.

So he'd sucked it up and asked his dad to come, hoping the visit and a brisker walk on a longer leash would perk her up before he had to leave her for the day. Somehow he'd gotten through work yesterday. He assumed Rain had too, since he hadn't called in sick, but it had been Bosler on the radio his whole shift.

"Sorry," he said to his dad. "I did shower but didn't feel up to a shave."

"No kidding." His dad clipped Cookie's longer, re-
tractable leash on her and headed for the door. "Come
on. Come along, you can tell me what's really wrong."

"Not sure I'm up to—"

"Yes, you are. I've had enough of my own company
this morning, and I didn't rush chores at my place so
that you could continue whatever funk you're in."

"Fine." Pulling on his gloves, he transferred to his
chair and followed his dad out and down the ramp.
Sparing a moment to notice the lack of Rain's car at
Shirley's, he made it to the end of the driveway before
he gave in to the urge to talk to someone. "Rain and I
sort of…ended things badly."

"Ah. I had a feeling that was what it might be. Saw
him leaving across the street right as I pulled in. If it
helps, he didn't look much better than you. Same kicked
dog expression."

"Not helpful. I don't want him suffering. That's the
last thing I want. Things are…complicated. He's got a
chance at a hotshot crew in California. You know as
well as me how hard it can be to work your way up to
the top crews."

"That I do." His dad turned the corner toward the
park, setting a nice pace that had Cookie wagging at
least. "And so, you're…what? Jealous that he gets to
be on the front lines? Guess I can see that, how that
might be."

"What? No." The denial came so fast it was almost
a reflex, but then he forced himself to actually think.
His dad did have a way of seeing things that sometimes
Garrick missed. But he didn't like this suggestion at all.
"That's not it. I mean, do I wish I were back out there?
You know that I do. Still struggling with that."

Glancing over, his dad quirked his mouth, considering. Not saying a damn thing, but making Garrick's brain work that much harder. Fuck it. Was he pushing Rain too hard to do this? He honestly wasn't sure of anything at this point. He didn't *think* his own unfulfilled desires were that much of a factor in him pushing for what he knew was the right thing to do. He couldn't be the one holding Rain back. He just couldn't.

"He's been working all summer to get in shape to get a chance at a frontline crew," he said at last, trying to work it out in his own head as much as to convince his dad.

"So he's raring to go, then. You guys breaking up... probably inevitable, don't you think? And for the best."

"What do you mean?" A rather unsavory thought crept into his head. "Is that some sort of gender-based commentary?"

"Gender?" His dad turned to give him a wide-eyed stare.

"Don't play innocent with me. I know you've had... thoughts on Rain being a guy."

"Maybe at first." His dad shrugged as they entered the park. He let the leash out further for a happy Cookie. In the distance, a group of kids was playing at the sprinkler pad. "Not gonna pretend he wasn't something of a surprise. But you're well past thirty now. Long past the age where I get a say in who you're with."

"Damn right." Garrick had to work harder to keep up with his dad's long strides.

"Now, do I think it's a harder row to hoe, out here in the sticks, knocking boots with another man? Yeah. It is. But times change. People change. Look at Lincoln. Him and Jacob were in the store the other day, spending that gift certificate plus some. They seem happy enough. And that's all I've ever wanted for you. Happiness."

Now that was a speech. One that made Garrick's throat clog up and his eyes sting at how hard his old-school dad was trying. How much he'd changed from when Garrick was younger and seriously afraid that coming out as pansexual might tank their close relationship.

"Thanks. And Rain does make me happy. So happy." Merely thinking about Rain and all the little things he did had Garrick sighing all over again.

"And that's what I meant. It's for the best. Distance never works, you know that."

"Yup." It wasn't only his parents' marriage that hadn't been able to survive questions of long-distance love. His efforts with his ex-fiancée had all been for naught in that regard too.

"And staying…that's its own can of worms. Happiness has a way of drying right up when someone is where they don't want to be."

"I *know*. And that's what I told him." The kids in the sprinkler were dancing around now, some sort of move that was in an ad or show he'd seen recently. Rain would know which one. Heck, Rain would probably join the kids in trying it. Damn. Garrick missed him so damn much already.

"See? You said your piece." His dad's tone was emphatic, and he was barely breathing hard at the brisk loop they were making around the park. "You asked him to stay. If he can't, then it's best to make your peace with him going."

"Ah… I didn't exactly ask him to stay. I knew better. More like I told him to go." Fuck. Now he was going to second-guess this all day. Should he have asked Rain? Admitted how much he wanted him to stay at least? Fuck. He had no clue.

"That's smart too. If you knew he'd say no, no point in putting yourself out there."

"Maybe I was afraid he'd say yes." Garrick had to admit the thought that had kept him up the past two nights.

"Ah. That's the risk, isn't it? Like I said, last thing you want is someone where they don't truly want to be."

"Yeah," Garrick agreed weakly, slowing down his pace to let his brain catch up.

"I know it sucks right now, but this is the right move. He's a city kid. We both know how that story ends."

"Isn't that the truth." And there it was, the real answer to all his uncertainty. He knew it was only a matter of time before Rain moved on, whether Garrick asked him to stay or not. It wasn't simply that that letting Rain go was the right thing morally, but it was also inevitable. Whether he fought against it tooth and nail or whether he accelerated the process, it was still going to happen. And if that made him a coward, so be it.

Banana bread. The craving had hit a little while ago, along with the idea that it might help this empty feeling inside him, and as Rain studied Grandma's cupboards, he was willing to try damn near anything to get that hole inside him gone.

"Where's the loaf pan?" Rain called out to Grandma, who was on the patio, bundles of fabric spread out on the picnic table, dye bottles at the ready, and dogs lounging in the sun.

"Hmm." Her mouth quirked. "Your mother organized my cabinets while she was here. Put a bunch of things aside for donation."

"Because of course she did."

"Be nice. She means well. Check the boxes in the garage waiting for a trip to the donation place."

In the crowded garage, he found a neatly labeled stack of boxes of random items. In addition to the loaf pan, he rescued his favorite of Grandma's coffee mugs, an oversize one with a rainbow handle and cheery sunrise on it that he'd given her several years ago. It had been a dollar store find, true, but a cute one. And it was a silly thing to get sentimental over, but he was already in a rather emo mood.

Still, it went to show yet again that there was no point in getting attached. Things moved on, went on to find new homes to bless, and he could try to snatch favorites back, but eventually everything moved on. Like Garrick, who was either too afraid to keep Rain around or simply not as invested as Rain was in their relationship. Something.

Rain kept saying he was done trying to figure him out, but here he was, mind back on their fight as he mashed bananas with an almost alarming amount of force. He whipped the batter hard enough that he was legit sweating by the time he put it in the oven. But the last thing he wanted was more time alone with his thoughts, so he went out to the patio while he waited for the bread to bake. "Need a hand?"

"No, sweetie. I've got this. You worked another long day yesterday. And you're baking us a treat." Her tone was warm, not dismissive, but it still prickled at Rain, made his neck tense.

"Why don't you ever need my help? It practically takes an act of Congress to get you to let me help you."

"Pardon?" Grandma blinked, undoubtedly at his petulant tone, which sounded whiny even to his own ears. She pulled herself up to her full height, looking him straight in the eye. Damn, she was scary when she wanted to be. "Am I supposed to need your help doing something I've been doing since before your father was born?"

"Mom said..." Whoops. This was dangerous territory. Time to backtrack. "Never mind. More that I thought when I came for the summer that you'd want my help with your work. I kinda figured you might need me for more than the occasional yardwork or dye pot lifting."

"Your parents have a way of getting ahead of themselves." Her gaze was still steely. "My newest arthritis medicines have been working so well that I haven't needed much help, which is something I'm happy about. Point of pride, I guess you could say. I always have been independent to a fault. But I certainly didn't mean to hurt your feelings."

"You didn't," Rain was quick to lie.

"I did, and I'm sorry. But it's not that I don't *want* your help—want and need, those are two different things."

"How so?" To Rain's mind, if someone needed his help and then accepted it, that was them wanting him around. Simple. He had years of memories surrounding growing up in the community, tasks that needed doing, praise doled out for doing the work that benefited the group. Somehow, he'd come to crave that feeling of being needed and wanted all at once.

"Want is way more about choice. Preference, not requirement. Freedom. Want is getting to do what's enjoyable simply because it's appealing, not because you need assistance doing something you've done fifty years on your own."

"Oh." A vision of Cookie's new leash leaped to the front of his mind, along with the memory of the melancholy that had been chasing him ever since. Maybe not being needed wasn't the worst thing in the world. Maybe it was possible to be not needed but still very much wanted. Maybe. Want required trust though, which was in damn short supply for him right then.

"See, when I don't need help, I can still do what's *fun*, like dyeing a few shirts with my favorite grandson." She passed him a squeeze bottle.

That made sense, made him think of all the fun he and Garrick had, and if everything wasn't beyond fucked up, he'd be chomping at the bit to go tell Garrick about his realization, apologize for being pouty. Maybe it was a good thing to not be needed as that created more room to be wanted.

But even if Garrick did want him around now, he'd made it clear that want didn't necessarily extend to a future together, and Rain simply wasn't sure he could give him a few uncertain weeks.

"Lark's not here," he felt honor bound to remind Grandma as he pulled on a pair of gloves and started applying dye. He was still pleased though, a warmth spreading across his face.

"Oh, you're all my favorites in different ways," she said airily, causing the warm feelings to abruptly stop. Figured. He wasn't special on his own, was just another grandson, one who was more than occasionally the annoying one, the one who was too much for people. And just like that he was back to worrying that maybe his parents were right all along and he was best in small doses. Maybe it wasn't so much Garrick being a coward about commitment as the inevitability of him not wanting Rain as much as Rain wanted him.

Hell. He didn't know, and going around and around on that point had him using way more dye than needed for the shirt.

"Are you going for a certain dark look with that shirt or is something else on your mind?" Grandma asked.

No way was he opening up about the fight with Garrick, not right then, but there was the other thing. "If you don't need me—"

"But I do *want* you," she interrupted, voice firm but kind. "As long as you want to stay. I mean that."

"I appreciate that, Grandma. I've got this chance though, to make a hotshot crew." He explained to her about the California opportunity, skirting by his argument with Garrick in only the vaguest of terms to conclude, "If I was needed here, it would be an easy choice to stay. But since I'm not, I guess I can't turn down this chance."

"Sure you can." She shrugged, like it was that easy. "You won't, of course. But you could."

"What do you mean I won't?"

"Ever since you were little you've had a taste for adventure. You're like me in that regard—you like moving on when things get boring. Took me forever to decide to buy this place, stay put awhile. Even now I see listings for festivals elsewhere and I get itchy feet."

"It's not that I'm bored here," he protested. "I mean, my job isn't the most interesting a lot of the time, and neither you nor Garrick truly needs me around, but I'm not like…unhappy."

"Of course you're not unhappy. You've got my charming neighbor and his biceps distracting you. You don't have to be unhappy to want that adventure you've been craving. I imagine this one, going off to fight fires on the front lines, seems like the sort of thing you've been waiting for."

"Maybe." He wasn't so sure anymore what he'd been waiting for. For years now he'd wanted his real life to start, something important and all-consuming, and yeah, an adventure. Spinning his wheels in Portland certainly hadn't been it, bouncing from dead-end jobs and trying on different majors. Losing out on the fire academy had certainly stung, and part of that was losing that sense of direction that goal had provided. He'd been so sure that was going to be his big adventure, and then it wasn't. And then all summer making a hotshot crew had been the next big thing. But now the chance was here and…

He simply wasn't certain. Maybe Grandma was right, and this was simply who he was—a person who moved on. A free spirit, like her. Everyone else seemed to believe it about him too. And attachment fucking sucked, that much was indisputable. He'd let himself get attached to Garrick and Cookie, and like always, attachment led to heartbreak. Whether it was a coffee mug or a stubborn boyfriend, things had a way of moving on, and there was no shame in wanting to be the one to leave first.

But then wasn't he just as cowardly as Garrick? Running from commitment because he might get hurt if he stayed around? Fuck. Why couldn't someone have the answers for him?

Even the fresh baked banana bread didn't quiet the questions in his head, nor did helping Grandma clean up from her dyeing marathon. He was trying to get the remaining blue dye off his arms when his phone buzzed.

Garrick. He almost didn't answer, not sure what Garrick could say that could make a difference. But what if he had the solution to all the roiling in Rain's brain? And more importantly, what if he *needed* him?

But when he answered, it turned out none of those questions really mattered because what Garrick said was "There's a fire. Big one. Forest Service is calling all hands on deck. I need a ride, and you need to be ready to roll."

Fuck. What if the only thing worse than too much time on his hands to think about where his life was headed was no time at all?

Chapter Nineteen

"Okay. Let's go." Rain arrived at Garrick's place, all business in his forest service work uniform, smears of blue dye on one arm and messy hair, which he bundled up under a hat as he waited for Garrick to come down his ramp. "Is Cookie going to be okay?"

"Yeah, I've got Dad coming over in a few hours to check on her. If we're gone overnight, he's going to take her to his place. He'll keep her separate from the farm dogs until he sees whether they can make friends."

"Good." Rain came around his SUV so he could load Garrick's chair and crutches. He'd also quickly packed a backpack with some snacks and other provisions in case of an extended shift.

Being in the field—even if it was at a fire base camp along with Fred Adams and Tucker Ryland and the other bosses—was something he generally enjoyed and had missed since his accident, and if he wasn't twisted in knots over Rain, he'd be looking forward to the challenge. The fire camp they'd set up for interagency coordination was about an hour away, and Ryland was having his crews meet up there rather than go thirty minutes or more in the other direction to headquarters first.

Several hotshot, engine, and smoke-jumper crews

were already either en route or on the scene as fire management teams had been working since the early morning hours on developing an attack plan. This fire, while in a remote location, had the potential to do some real damage if it was allowed to spread toward rural communities potentially in its path. The less experienced hand crews like Rain's would dig fireline some distance from the fire while the other crews worked on the more challenging spots closer in.

"I've got the GPS on my phone set." Garrick plugged it into the dashboard. God, this was weird, acting like there wasn't a Crater Lake–sized gap between them, acting like this was simply another workday commute when the truth was he'd been begging rides from Ryland and his dad for several days now. Avoiding Rain was so much easier than this, being close enough to touch and smell and not knowing a damn thing to say that might relieve this awful tension.

"Were you dyeing fabric with your grandma?" he asked at last as the miles ticked by and the silence became oppressive, a heavy weight that seemed to make him hyperaware of each breath and each small movement of Rain's, like how he was drumming on the steering wheel.

"Yup. Shirts. Big sale coming up in Klamath Falls in a couple of weeks. She's excited about a weekend away. I volunteered to watch her bratty dogs, so I'm hoping it's before I get a call about California."

"Ah. You...uh...put in for that hotshot crew?"

"Not yet." Rain's jaw had a stubborn tilt to it as he studied the road ahead. "But what else am I supposed to do? Thought that's what you wanted me to do."

"I was just asking. I didn't say to not do it!"

"Of course not." Rain sounded more resigned than disappointed, which honestly made Garrick feel even worse.

"What did your grandma say about the idea? Can she spare you?"

"Ha." Rain snorted, more of that bitterness to his tone. "She says to go, says I need to chase my big adventure like I've always talked about."

"See? She's not wrong. This is a good chance for you to do exactly that."

"Yeah." Rain's sigh was so empty that Garrick's chest hurt.

"Does it help if I admit that I'm going to miss you like crazy? I already do. Cookie too. She's been pouting for days now."

"Poor Cookie. Could…could I come take her out maybe? Cheer her up with a run?" Rain neatly avoided acknowledging Garrick's admission about his own missing him.

"You're welcome anytime. You know that." But Rain's answering frown said maybe that wasn't true. Maybe Rain didn't know that Garrick would happily squeeze every last drop of togetherness out of his remaining time in the area. His conversation with his dad came filtering back into his brain. A clean break might be the easiest and smartest thing, but hell if Garrick could seem to stick to it. "I want you around. For Cookie but for me too. I meant it. I miss you."

"Damn it. I—"

"Turn left in 900 feet," the GPS bleated, cutting off whatever Rain had been about to say, and after he made the turn, his tone was a lot less soft.

"It'll just make it hurt that much more when I do go."

Garrick couldn't argue with that, but being with Rain had a way of making all logic and good sense fly out the window. The scenery outside was much more rugged now, signs of civilization few and far between, and a haze hung over the forest. Something about being out here, only the two of them, made him more honest than was probably wise. "Maybe it would be worth it."

A muscle worked in Rain's jaw as he took several long moments to consider this. "You're always going to be worth the heartache. I wish it didn't have to hurt so damn much though."

Damn it. Something broke loose inside Garrick's chest, and he needed them to not be in this car, the road needing Rain's primary attention. He needed to be able to hold and touch him, try to take away some of that pain in his voice.

"Come over. After this is done, come over. Please."

Rain opened his mouth, but the stupid GPS interrupted again with another turn and then they were at the fire camp—a collection of makeshift tents and old logging structures repurposed by the forest service. Trucks and equipment from several different agencies also occupied the clearing, and activity buzzed, people barking orders, personnel putting on gear, others checking on equipment and studying maps. It never ceased to amaze Garrick how fast the interagency logistics crew could get a camp together, even in the middle of nowhere like this. Trailers had already been brought in for food, hygiene, and for admin to work out of.

"Wow." Rain's wide eyes mirrored how awed Garrick had been the first time he'd seen an operation like this in action.

"Rain." Garrick didn't want to let the moment pass,

not when they might not get another one for who knew how long. "I mean it. Come over. Let's talk."

"Maybe." Rain bit his lip and glanced away.

Fuck. Now Garrick would have to live with that non-answer, wondering whether they'd get a chance to talk or not. And there was no time to advocate for a better answer either. Ryland met them at the car to help him get to the operations trailer that was housing Dispatch for the various crews and agencies. While flat, the ground was still uneven and rocky, but Ryland arranged it so that they could pull close to unload so he didn't have to walk far with the crutches to his station. At least the trailer had a floor for his wheelchair to roll on.

"All set?" Rain asked, eyes flitting to all the activity outside the trailer, clearly itching to be out there. Or maybe he simply wanted done with Garrick, which was a far more depressing thought.

"Yeah. Good luck out there." Garrick had no hold on him, no reason to ask him to stay a minute, no choice but to let him go.

No choice but to let him go. That might as well be his mantra right then. He had no choice but to let Rain go, let him be free to chase adventure. *We both know how that story ends*, his dad had said, and Garrick had felt that truth down to his bones. He did know how the story ended, both his own with Lisa and his dad's with Garrick's mother.

Hell, here it was, over twenty years after his mother had left and his father had barely dated in all that time, preferring instead to throw himself into his business and his property. *Is that going to be me?* The future stretched out in front of him, as endless as the forest surrounding them. He could see himself and Cookie, alone against the world, like his dad and his horses, and just as bitter about relationships and risk.

But watching Rain stride away, he questioned everything about that future. Did the story have to end with Rain walking away for good? With it hurting so much? He'd assumed the pain was simply inevitable for both of them, but what if it wasn't?

For the first time he contemplated what it would take to choose a different path, not the straight line to heartache but a rockier trail with more uncertainty. More of that risk his dad had counseled against, but maybe more reward.

Perhaps the real question, and the one he should have been asking himself all week, was whether he was brave enough to put his heart on the line or whether for the first time in his life, he was going to accept being a quitter when it came to getting what he truly wanted.

The smoke, even this far from the fire, made the air hazy and clung to Rain's nostrils, astringent and omnipresent, overriding the usual forest scents of dirt and pine. The forest was noisier too—chainsaws whining from every direction, and planes and helicopters going by overhead. Airtankers and helicopters had been dropping retardant and water all afternoon, and he'd heard numerous reports that Garrick's old smoke-jumper buddies were being deployed close to the fire. This was day two of the firefighting effort, and he'd grabbed a precious few hours of sleep in a tent with Zeb and Bosler, whose snores mingled with the drone of the chainsaws off in the distance.

He'd seen Garrick briefly in the distance when he was grabbing a sack lunch to take out with him. He'd been deep in conversation with Ryland, so Rain hadn't headed over. Not that he would have known what to say even if he'd been free. Garrick wanted to talk when this was all over. Said he missed him. Implied having him around was worth the coming pain. And damn did Rain want to go to him, even if talking ended up with them in bed and no words spoken. But as to whether that would be the right call for either of them...

Well, he simply wasn't sure. And hours of backbreaking digging in the hot sun hadn't provided much of an answer either. Presently, they were working to provide an outer perimeter for a planned burnout—a controlled burn from some of the firelines toward the approaching fire, depriving the wildfire of fuel. Crews would then come through and attack hot spots—cutting open smoldering trees, spreading water, covering other hot spots with dirt. It was hard, messy, hot work, and he'd give half his underwear collection for a shower and a chance to wash his hair, which was bundled up under his helmet and adding to his sweatiness.

"I'm worried about O'Connor." Bosler came over to him, mouth pursing and gaze darting back to where their crew boss was sitting near a stump. "She keeps saying she's fine, but I think she's overheating or something else medical is going on. She's dizzy even if she won't admit it, and her color's no good."

"Crap. Should we call for assistance?" There was a first aid tent set up at the fire camp and medics on-site staffing it. He and Bosler had been sharing radio duties as normal, but he was the one with it at the present.

"Come over with me. Let's try to get O'Connor to agree before we go over her head."

"Good idea." He followed Bosler over to her. Bosler

had been right—O'Connor's color was a mix of pale and blotchy red patches, and she was sweating even harder than Rain. His limited first aid training had the hair on his neck prickling, unease gathering low in his belly. This wasn't good. "Hey, Boss. You feeling okay?"

"Fisher. I take it Bosler's been telling tales?" O'Connor's voice was weary with a thready quality that worried Rain further.

"He thinks I should put a call in for some medical assistance for you. Tell you what, how about you let me call simply to put his mind at ease? We'll get you checked out, Bosler can hold down the fort, and then you can be back out here with us once they get you hydrated or whatever else you might need?"

"You're probably...right." O'Connor blew out a pained breath between her teeth. Damn. Rain did not like where this was heading. Might simply be heat exhaustion, but it could also be her heart or something more serious. "Maybe...some electrolyte drink. Keep... having floaters in my eyes too. Never had heat...do me like this."

"Okay. I'm going to radio in." He was more than willing to take her nominal agreement that hydration could help as permission. "Base? This is hand crew four-five-one requesting medical assistance."

"Four-five-one, we copy. What is the nature of your emergency?" Garrick's voice was warm but concerned, and no matter what issues lay between them, Rain was damn glad he was on the call. Not only was he reassuring, but he was also good at his job. He'd get them help.

"Our crew boss is ill." He quickly relayed O'Connor's symptoms to Garrick. "I don't think she can walk back to the hard line rendezvous point."

"Copy that. I'm paging medical now to see what our options are. Despite this heat, wind conditions are a big concern today. See if she'll drink some water, and I'll be back in a second with a plan. Hang in there."

Simply knowing Garrick was working on the problem helped. His last words felt personal somehow, a message to bolster him. After Rain ended the transmission, Bosler urged O'Connor to drink, which ended up being a mistake because she promptly threw it up.

"Sorry. Guess… I…am…little sick." Her breathing was more labored now, and Rain wasn't waiting for Garrick to get back to him, reaching for the radio even before she was done talking.

"Base? Four-five-one here with an update. Water was a no-go. The boss is vomiting now. She doesn't report pain, but her breathing is getting rough. What's the ETA on that assistance?"

"Copy that, four-five-one. We've got medics heading to you via truck, and we're trying to get a helicopter for medical evacuation."

"That's good." He couldn't keep the relief out of his voice. He didn't like not knowing how to help himself, didn't like coming up against the limits of his rather sparse training, and he was seriously regretting not getting an EMT certification when he'd had the opportunity. Several others had stopped working, a small group gathering to see what was up. "And the rest of us?"

"Rather than pull the whole crew, your orders are to continue on. Bosler is your acting crew boss."

"Copy that. I'll let him know." He wanted to keep Garrick on the line but tempered that impulse. Garrick could help them best if he wasn't tethered to the call. Taking a deep breath, Rain went back over to Bosler.

He'd simply have to work through the fluttering pulse of anxiety on his own.

"Okay, back to work, everyone. Help is on the way." Bosler waved the onlookers away. "And no one else get dehydrated. Drink your fluids. More than you think you need. Fisher, you keep a lookout for the medics and keep listening to the radio chatter."

It felt like a decade passed, but in reality, it wasn't that long before the sound of a motor nearby cut through the forest. Two medics arrived with a stretcher for the boss. The older of the two, a woman with short gray hair, frowned as she took O'Connor's vital signs.

"Damn this wind and smoke. Hopefully we're able to rendezvous with the helitack crew, get her airlifted to Bend," she said to him and Bosler, adding to his worries that this was more serious than simple heat exhaustion. "You did the right thing, calling for us."

"Good."

They didn't take long loading up O'Connor, which let them get back to work on the fireline. He kept the radio though at Bosler's request, and incoming messages were all about the shifting wind and changing fire conditions.

"Think they're gonna call us back before the burnout?" he asked Bosler after relaying another update.

"Could be." Bosler's eyes were on the increasingly smoky sky. "Say a prayer for the smoke jumpers dealing with this. Bet some end up treed or worse. Wind. It's the devil."

Rain's thoughts flashed to Linc and Jacob, hoping that they and the rest of Garrick's friends were safe, realizing on a deeper level the sort of danger Garrick had lived with on a daily basis. It was rather humbling, knowing that the smoke jumpers were out there doing the impossible so that the hand crews like Rain's had a better shot of success. And likewise, it made their work that much more important too, made it necessary that they complete their line so that the burnout could happen as scheduled, reducing the risks for everyone.

Trust. They all had to have it—trusting in each other to do their jobs, all part of the same effort. Without trust, everything would fall apart.

Kind of like a relationship. All members of a relationship had to trust each other. And maybe that was where he and Garrick were having trouble. Garrick didn't trust him to stick around, that much was clear. But, if he were being fair, he wasn't exactly trusting Garrick either, not believing him when he said he wanted Rain around or when he said he'd miss Rain. He'd discounted all of that when the whole summer Garrick had done nothing other than give him reasons to trust. He was the sort of person who meant what he said, who followed through, and why should this be any different?

Because it's scary. Funny how being this close to a raging wildfire wasn't as scary as opening his heart up to another person, truly trusting them, and being willing to risk pain. *Maybe it would be worth it*, Garrick had said. And he had a point—there was a place where the benefits of being with someone outweighed the risk of hurt. He could see the outline of that place now, a shimmering mirage of a future he desperately wanted and was afraid to hope for. Could he do it? Could he offer up that kind of trust?

"Four-Five-One, this is base, do you copy?" His

radio crackled with Garrick's voice coming in loud and strong.

"Roger that, base. Go ahead." He wasn't sure whether to hope Garrick could hear that he'd been thinking about him or not.

"The fire's turning. We need to get your crew out of there ASAP."

Oh crap. No more daydreaming. His spine stiffened, muscles coiling.

"No burnout?" He was already on it, racing toward Bosler, who had been checking the crew members on the farther end of the line.

"No time." Garrick's voice was clipped, a tone Rain recognized as him trying not to get emotional. Damn. He must be seriously worried for them. For Rain. Rain's pulse sped up as Garrick continued, "Your orders are to get back to your hardline anchor point, follow the riverbed."

"Copy that. I'm advising Bosler now."

"Good. We're extracting crews as quickly as we can along the river. Priority is going to a couple of serious injuries first. Please advise if you run into problems."

"Will do."

"Rain—" It was the first time Garrick had ever used Rain's first name on a transmission and it made his heart leap up into his throat, made it hard to keep listening, given the emotions that swamped him.

"Yeah?"

"You guys be safe, okay? Move fast. No stupid risks, but *move*."

"Got it. We'll make the river."

"Stay in contact."

"Roger that." He had to fall back on his training because simply hearing Garrick worried was enough to make talking difficult. Garrick *cared.* And maybe he cared about all the crews, but there was something extra there, an urgency in his voice that said far more than the actual words he used.

As he helped Bosler round everyone up and start hustling toward the river, he kept coming back to that point. Garrick cared. He remembered the day when they thought they'd found Cookie's owner. Garrick had been willing to let her go because it was the right thing to do, but it didn't mean he didn't care about her. And maybe that was what he'd been trying to tell Rain in his own roundabout way—he was willing to let Rain go because some mixed-up code of ethics said that was the right thing to do. But he didn't mean he didn't care. He might even love Rain, might want him that much, but he'd been willing to let him go because he thought he had no choice.

That was who he was. The guy who did the right thing, even when it was hard, even when he didn't want to. That was the guy Rain cared so much about. In some weird way, him being willing to let Rain go made him care that much more, now that he saw it for what it was. It wasn't Garrick caring too little. It was him caring so very much. And that realization had him moving that much faster, made his movements that much more urgent. Garrick wanted to talk, and suddenly, he had so much he wanted to say to him.

No way was he missing the chance to see if they could make this right. His hand landed on the radio. The temptation to say something was almost overwhelming, but he needed so much more than a quick transmission. Trust. Came back to that. He had to trust that it wasn't too late for them. Had to trust that Garrick would listen. And he had to trust that he could get through this.

His crew slipped and slid over rugged terrain, helping each other, climbing over felled trees and scrambling down big boulders. The smoke was getting thicker, more cloying. They needed to stop, put damp bandannas over their mouths and noses. They didn't have the full masks like the hotshot crews closer in. Those crews would also have the fireproof shelters to deploy in an emergency if they were unable to outrun the fire. Rain's crew wasn't supposed to be this close in, and the fear from some of his crew members was a palpable thing, clear in their wide eyes and jerky movements.

"Come on, come on," he urged. They just needed to make it to the river. Garrick was counting on him. And so was his crew—he'd worked all summer with these people. He knew Zeb had plans for a spring wedding, and there were so many other stories he'd heard during their long hours together as a crew. He wasn't leaving anyone behind. Even Bosler moved with haste, far speedier than he looked. Like Rain, he was right there, helping people over rocks, cheering them on as they approached the river.

The sound of rushing water was quite possibly the best thing he'd ever heard, and it spurred them on, pushing through the brush to reach the pebbled banks. As the last crew member stumbled out of the forest, Rain made the mistake of turning around. The fire was ever closer, thick smoke and glowing embers. They had some measure of safety here at the river—a hard line the fire couldn't cross. However, they were also well and truly trapped now and had to hope the smoke didn't overwhelm them. Rescue couldn't come soon enough.

Chapter Twenty

Staying still was the hardest thing Garrick had ever had to do. He'd had to do his job under challenging circumstances before, but nothing compared to the hell that was knowing Rain's group was in serious danger and all he could do was pray they made it to the river in time. And really, it wasn't nothing, but all he could do was continue his job—getting the other crews to safety as well, deploying the medical assistance needed, coordinating with the other dispatchers for the hotshot and engine crews.

"Base? This is four-five-one." Never had Rain's voice on the radio been so welcome and never had Garrick's gut churned so hard. If they weren't to the river yet...

"Copy that, four-five-one. Go ahead."

"All crew members present and accounted for. We're at the river. It's smoky as hell and we can see the fire now, but we made it."

"Thank God." He couldn't even pretend at professional distance right then, resting his head on the desk for a long moment before he regained the ability to speak. "We're going to get you out of there, okay? It may take some time, but help is on the way."

"Good. Is there any word on our boss?"

Typical Rain, caring about others even as his own life was in peril.

"Helitack crew was able to get a chopper in the air before the fire turned. She's at the hospital in Bend. Medics said she was stable. You did the right thing, calling for help."

"Roger that. We better conserve battery power."

"You do that. But keep checking in as you're able. I'll update with an ETA on extraction."

"Got it." Rain sounded like Garrick felt—like he was desperate to add something personal but didn't dare. There was too much unsaid between them, too much uncertainty for a public channel. He wasn't going to rest easy, though, until that crew was back, until he could lay eyeballs and hands on Rain.

"Did four-five-one make it to the river?" Ryland asked a few moments later, stopping by Garrick's station.

"Yep." Garrick had to swallow hard, merely thinking about how close they'd come to not making it.

"Good. That's your friend, right? Glad for you both that he made it out. I…uh…not sure what I'd do in your shoes." Ryland looked away, and not for the first time, Garrick wondered what was up with his personal life. Garrick couldn't recall ever knowing him to date much, and despite their commuting together all summer, he had shown a deft talent for avoiding any talk about his life outside work. Garrick wouldn't wish the anxiety of the past few hours on anyone, but he'd also rather have Rain, have that risk of pain, than not at all.

And the power of that realization had him restless, needing to see for himself that Rain was okay, even as he forced himself to focus on work, taking the latest fire data and working on a plan for which crews to send where and relaying all the information he'd gathered from the multiple hand crews on the line, not only Rain's.

For the first time since he'd been on a hand crew himself, all those many summers ago, he felt truly helpless. All he could do was handle the flow of information. The final call on who to send where was on Adams and Ryland. The actual fieldwork was up to others, and he had to trust in their abilities to carry out assignments.

But hadn't that always been the case? He'd felt invincible as a smoke jumper, on top of the world, at the peak of his skills, but really he'd only been as good as his crew, as the support personnel, as the other crews, the interagency coordination, all of it working together. The idea that he'd been in charge of his own destiny was merely an illusion, one that didn't give enough credit to others.

And that made him think all the more about Rain and their fight and where they were in their relationship and how much he could truly expect to control.

"What's the status of being able to extract?" he asked Ryland some time later after he returned from a meeting with Adams and other brass. "I've been in contact with crews all along the river waiting for news, but so far, everyone accounted for."

"The wind and smoke are finally cooperating. We've got airtankers flying in now, dropping water. Helicopter crews will be next, starting with the highest priority evacuations, and we'll have other crews walking out where that's a safe option." He clapped Garrick on the shoulder. "We'll get your guy out. Promise. And once we do, I'm sending you for some rest. Even if the worst

of the fire is past, cleanup is going to be some time. We
need to pace ourselves."

"Understood."

He busied himself with staying in contact with the
various hand crews waiting, relief coursing through
him each time he got to hear Rain's voice with updates.
They were tired and hungry and banged up with the real
worry being all the smoke, but they were alive and Garrick was intent on keeping them that way.

Then finally, late in the day, temperatures dipping,
word came that the hand crews were starting to return.
The food truck geared up for the onslaught of raven-
ous firefighters, while Garrick braced himself against
a tidal wave of emotion. Taking a long overdue break,
he rolled out onto the trailer's small makeshift porch—
a narrow platform with a couple of steps. Studying the
crowd of returning hot and dusty people, he looked
fruitlessly for Rain.

"Garrick!" There he was, hopelessly rumpled, wet
boots and dirty face, and the best thing Garrick had
ever seen.

"Hey you." People were everywhere around them—
in line for food and medical attention and talking in
clumps of threes and fours. All his attention was on
Rain, but he was also acutely aware that they were far
from alone. "You made it out." He had to swallow hard,
simply thinking again about how close the long day had
come to a different ending.

"I did." Rain regarded him solemnly, their eyes having a deeper conversation than their voices were capable of.

"Ryland's making noises about people getting rest.
I think he's going to send me home soon, at least for a

break before my next shift. Would you want me to see if he'll let you go too?"

"I'm staying." Despite him looking dead on his feet, Rain's voice was firm. "Sorry. There's nothing I'd like more. But my crew needs me. We've already lost our boss, and Bosler's trying to fill the gap, but word is that they'll be sending us out on mop-up duty first thing in the morning. I should probably crash in Zeb's tent again."

"Yeah." Garrick would have said the same thing in his shoes. Duty first, even when it sucked. "I'll catch a ride with someone else heading back. I talked to my dad. Cookie is living the life of luxury at his place. Even went to work with him today."

"She'll still be happy to see you."

"Hope so." Garrick tried to keep his voice light, but it was hard with his heart hammering like this. "And you? You gonna be happy to see me when this is all over? Gonna come over?"

"It's probably a terrible idea—"

"Rain." Garrick wasn't above begging. "We need to talk."

"Yeah, we do." Mercifully, Rain nodded. "I've got… so much to say. And you're going to listen?"

"I will." He held Rain's gaze as he promised. "And I get it. You want to see the fire through. I do too, as much as Ryland and Adams will let me. We can wait. And that's what I should have said sooner. You do what you have to do. I'll be waiting for you. As long as it takes. I mean that."

"I'll find you then."

Throat tight, all Garrick could do was nod. He couldn't tell him everything right then, but he could tell

him that he'd wait, could put that much on the line. And
he would. He'd wait for Rain, wait for their talk, wait
for a chance to make this right between them. There
was so much he wanted to say, and most importantly,
he wanted to keep his promise to listen to Rain, really
and truly listen this time with his whole heart and without old fears ringing in his ears.

Rain probably should have showered first. Eaten some
hot food that included a vegetable. Last few days, being
a vegetarian had meant a lot of bread, a lot of rice, and
far more cookies than prudent as the staff of the food
truck had tried to keep him and the other non-meat
eaters in enough calories to keep their energy up. And
a change of clothes wouldn't have been a bad idea either. He stank of smoke, probably would for a week. He
might never get the scent out of his car or hat.

   In short, he was a mess, but he'd promised Garrick
days earlier that he'd find him, and somehow keeping
that promise seemed more important than anything else,
including the sleep he desperately needed. The interagency coordinators had dispersed the fire camp even
though the cleanup efforts would continue in the coming weeks, sending everyone home to rest and regroup.

   He'd talked to Garrick briefly earlier. Wait. Was that
yesterday? All the days were starting to run together.
Regardless, Garrick had been around sporadically the
past few days, a few stilted conversations here and there.
But Rain had a feeling that Ryland and Adams had
made him getting rest a priority, since he couldn't exactly pile in a tent like Rain and the rest of the hand
crew guys, and he'd been among the first admin people dismissed as they disbanded camp, catching a ride

back with a woman who'd been working in the medical tent. In any event, their eyes had met through the crowd of people, and he'd seen that promise to find him reflected there, and his heart had sped up. He couldn't not come to Garrick's house, even though night was starting to fall. The late hour and his physical condition be damned. He needed to be here.

Excited barking greeted him as Garrick opened the door. Cookie acted like Rain had been gone a decade, dancing in circles, practically howling with happy noises and all but climbing him like a tree.

"You came." The look in Garrick's eyes was everything, warmth and tenderness saying he'd made the right choice to come here first. "I got in a couple of hours ago myself. Made a big pot of lentil soup in case you came hungry."

"You have no idea."

"Oh, trust me, I do. I wasn't even burning energy like you guys in the field and I still ate two dinners—steak at Dad's and then the soup here. Showered for a good half hour too, but that was a while ago. There's plenty of hot water if you want to shower while I heat up your soup."

"Yeah. That sounds good. Perfect, really. I'll text Grandma that I'm at your place. Gonna take off my boots right here on the porch."

"You do that. I spoke to her earlier myself. I'll make sure there's towels in the guest bath for you."

"Weird. Feels both like I was just here and like it's been years," he admitted as he unlaced his boots in between giving Cookie more pats.

"I know. Me too. I… I'm glad you came. So glad." Garrick's eyes were full with an emotion Rain couldn't easily name. He had to look away quickly lest his own gaze give too much away.

Rain wasn't sure that warm water had ever felt so good. He soaped up three times simply because he could and washed the dust out of his hair twice before he was willing to get out from under the pounding spray. It took a ton of conditioner just to get his mess of hair to loosen up. When he left the shower, his favorite robe was waiting for him along with a pair of purple satin underwear he'd left at Garrick's some time back. Seeing them there made his stomach give a happy little flip. He found a wide-tooth comb under the sink and continued working out the tangles in his hair on his way out to the living area.

"Damn. I feel more human now. Thanks. Feel more like me." He tightened the belt on his robe.

"Figured you might be craving something like your robe. I'm not…it's not some kind of come-on. Promise."

"I know. And we're probably both too bushed, and I know we need to talk, but I'm not sure I'd turn down a come-on. Just saying." He gave Garrick a wink as he settled at the table in front of a steaming giant bowl of soup.

"Isn't this one of your mixing bowls?"

"Maybe." Garrick held out a hand as he rolled up behind Rain. "Let me finish your hair while you eat?"

"Sure." Rain gave him the comb. They'd done this before, Garrick combing out his curls after a shower, but there was something different about this time, a greater intimacy somehow. Adding to that effect, Garrick was infinitely gentle as he worked on Rain's hair, working in small sections. His fingers felt so good, even incidental contact on Rain's neck and scalp, that Rain kept leaning into the contact, like Cookie seeking more pats. Damn. He'd missed this so much.

"Poor hair. That helmet really did a number on you." Garrick deftly braided the detangled hair, something Rain didn't always have patience for on his own but Garrick seemed to enjoy doing for him.

"That and the same bun days on end." Rain laughed because that was better than letting the tenderness of the moment swamp him. "The soup is really good. Thanks for making it."

"There are chocolate muffins from your grandma too. She's worried about you, even if she won't admit it aloud."

"You left me some?" He raised an eyebrow, hoping to get another chuckle out of Garrick because being back here, bantering like this was as soothing as the soup and hair care.

"Come on. Cut me a break. I'm not that much of a chocoholic." Finished with Rain's hair, Garrick had moved to his side, big glass of ice water in front of him.

"Yeah, you totally are. But you're cute about it," Rain teased between more sips of soup.

"And I share." Garrick rolled over to the counter and returned with two muffins, plunking one down next to Rain.

"That you do. You're generous. It's one of the things I lo—*like* most about you."

"You still like me?" Garrick's voice was serious, and that was all it took for the banter to evaporate and them to be right back in the awkward place, where there was both so much unsaid and too much that had been already said, all the baggage of their previous argument showing up like an unwanted guest.

"Yeah," he admitted, voice as grave as Garrick's, no more kidding around. "Not like I could hate you, not even if I tried."

"That makes one of us. Maybe I hate me enough for both of us. I've been so damn mad at myself, but I simply couldn't see an outcome where hating myself for letting you go didn't happen."

"And now?" Rain had been so sure that he didn't have any hope left in him, but there it was, that bubbly sensation in his chest and tremor in his hands.

"Now, I'm still not sure. But I meant what I said at fire camp. I want to listen to you. Really listen." Reaching out, he rubbed Rain's shoulder, a contact as welcome as his words. "And I don't have all the answers, not by a long shot, but I do know that I want to work this out. I missed you so damn much."

"Me too. I missed you and I hated myself for missing you that much."

"I'm sorry." Garrick's hand was as heavy as the emotion in his eyes, but Rain wasn't running from either the contact or the intense feels. "I never wanted to hurt you."

"Yeah, you kind of did," Rain had to point out. "You thought it was the right thing to do and that you didn't have a choice, but I told you it hurt, asked you to not, and you still pushed me away. Which made it hurt more, not less."

"I fucked up. And I wish I had better words than simply another 'I'm sorry.' But I am sorry. Truly."

"I believe you." Rain couldn't keep a yawn in any longer, belly full of warm soup and soul heavy with both this conversation and days' worth of exhaustion catching up with him. "I don't know where we go from here, but I believe you."

"Do we need to have a map tonight?" Garrick laid his hand on top of Rain's on the table. "We're both wrung out. Can it be enough to say that we both want to work this out—whatever that takes—and that we'll figure it out, together?"

Rain had to think for a moment because the urge to get all the answers was almost as strong as the need for sleep. But if they were going to have to talk, really talk, emotional heavy lifting, then he wanted to curl up in Garrick's arms one more time first. If that made him selfish, so be it.

"Can I sleep here?"

"You have to ask?" Squeezing Rain's hand one more time, he pointed toward the bedroom. "To bed. We'll talk in the morning, promise. We're both off, so we can go out with Cookie—"

"*Cookie.* Darn it. Forgot all about her. Do I need to find clothes for a fast walk?"

"Dad helped me with her when he dropped me off. No more excuses—bed."

"Okay, okay." Too tired to even worry about the dishes, he followed Garrick to the bedroom. But somehow after shucking his robe and climbing under the puffy bedding, his mind started racing, disjointed flashes of the past several days combined with future worries about him and Garrick along with the present awareness of Garrick stripping down to boxers and joining him under the covers. He shifted restlessly against the sheets.

"Problem?" Garrick rolled so that his arms were open for Rain to snuggle in against him, which was nice but only made the revving in his pulse that much stronger. Garrick smelled like his soap, no trace of fire, and Rain reveled in the clean, familiar scent.

"Tired. So tired. But my brain won't shut off."

"Oh, I know the cure for that." Garrick waggled his eyebrows at Rain before he pulled him closer. Giving Rain ample time to object or roll away, he slowly lowered his mouth, gracing Rain with the sweetest, softest kiss he'd ever known. "This okay?"

"More than." Rain tugged him down for another kiss. God, he'd missed this man so much, been so worried he'd never have this again. First the argument, then the fire. The fear had been real, and he pushed all of that into the kiss, into the way he clung to Garrick. He needed this on some primal level, had needed it for days, and now that he was getting it, all he could do was moan and kiss Garrick harder.

Luckily, Garrick seemed to need it every bit as much, claiming Rain's mouth with aggressive nips and licks that had Rain writhing against his big, hard body. Wanting to lose himself in this, he rolled to his back, taking Garrick with him. They didn't kiss like this very often, Garrick on top, but Rain loved it, loved all his heaviness and bulk and the way it chased out every rogue thought until the only thing he knew was this kiss, this moment right here.

"Still good?" Garrick asked as he kissed his way across Rain's still-scruffy jaw to tease his ear and neck.

"Fuck, yeah." Rain wasn't as sensitive there as Garrick but it still felt electric, each little lick a fresh wave of arousal. Shifting on the bed, Garrick kissed a determined path down Rain's neck and chest, pausing to flick at each of his nipples with the tip of his tongue, little teases that had Rain groaning. But then Garrick continued south, licking down Rain's sternum, sexy intent clear in his eyes.

"Hey, I didn't mean—"

"I did." Garrick dropped a kiss right above Rain's underwear, hooking his fingers in the silky purple fabric. "Damn. You are so fucking sexy in these. Please?"

"I'd kinda rather something for both of us." Rain's gasp as Garrick continued to lick along his waistband called him a liar. Did he want Garrick's mouth? Well, of course. That was like asking if he wanted frosting on his cake. But getting oral had always made him feel weirdly on display and like he should be doing more for the other person. For all he liked showing off, being this kind of focal point made his neck itch. Want battled with unease in his gut.

"This is for me too." Garrick stroked his thighs, big thumbs caressing Rain's hip bones. "I've been dying to do this. Trust me?"

"I do," Rain said quietly, relaxing by degrees under Garrick's intent gaze, his warm breath that close to Rain's cock an undeniable turn-on. "I just like getting you off too."

"You do. A lot. If anything, our sex life is always about *me*, what I'm up for, what I can do, and what I need. Let me do this for you? Please?" He lightly kissed Rain's straining cock through the thin fabric. Yeah. Rain wanted this, wanted to see what Garrick had in mind, and that want trumped his initial reservations, made him groan.

"Like I could say no with you asking all sweetly to suck my cock. Do it." Plenty into the idea now, he helped wriggle out of his underwear when Garrick tugged them down. Laughing, Garrick peppered the shaft of Rain's cock with little kisses.

"Been a while since I did this, so tell me if I do it wrong." Still teasing, he traced a meandering path along the underside of Rain's cock, barely there touches that had Rain struggling not to buck his hips and had him moaning softly.

"Ha. You know exactly what you're doing. And no such thing as—*fuck*." He lost track of what he'd been about to say as Garrick finally took him in his mouth, tight, hot suction that was the definition of perfection. "That. Just do that."

Humming happily, Garrick swallowed his cock deeper, setting a slow, shallow rhythm with a lot of tongue action. And okay, it was hard to worry about being the center of attention when it felt so damn good, little bursts of pleasure that skated up his spine. Garrick seemed to know exactly how to tease all the most sensitive places, and his hands stayed active too, one hand holding Rain's cock steady while the other roamed all over his torso, dual onslaught.

"Fuck. Damn. You get any better…damn."

"Good?" Garrick looked up, eyes sparkling.

"Fuck you. You know it is. Too good."

"Excellent." Garrick seemed to take his words as a challenge to redouble his efforts, sucking hard while his hand jacked the base of Rain's cock. The movement of his fingers made his balls tingle, made his legs start to tense. It had been too long and much as he wanted to savor this, his body seemed to have other plans.

"Damn it. Close. Don't wanna…" Words were failing him, moans and whimpers escaping instead as Garrick did this thing with his tongue around the head of

Rain's cock that had him clutching the sheets to avoid grabbing on to Garrick.

"I want you to. Get close. God, I love your sounds." Garrick upped his game even further, faster strokes of his hand and mouth, tighter suction, and he moved to using his free hand to play with Rain's balls and the patch of skin beyond them, skirting close to his rim and making Rain moan more with the memory of how good Garrick fingering and fucking him could be.

"Garrick. Please. Need to—*fuck*."

"That's it. Come for me. Do it," Garrick pulled back long enough to urge. As he went back to sucking Rain, he used his tongue to milk the underside of Rain's cock, glorious pressure that made his vision blur and every muscle tense.

"Oh God. That. Right there. Gonna…" He didn't get much more warning than that out before he was coming. He expected Garrick to pull back, but Garrick stayed with him, stroking him through the climax and swallowing around his cock, a sexy, lewd noise that coaxed out a last wave of pleasure.

"Too sensitive," he gasped at last, pushing at Garrick's meaty shoulder.

"Good?" Garrick had a wicked, knowing smile as he returned to lying next to Rain.

"Damn you. You finally did it." Rain's voice was sleepy, his whole body heavy and lethargic now, orgasm having chased the last of his restless thoughts away. "I'm dead. Done in. But I owe you—"

"Nothing. You don't owe me anything. Just you, here. That's everything. All I need, promise."

"Gonna hold you to that." As his eyes fluttered shut, Rain wanted to believe him in the worst way, wanted to believe that he could be everything Garrick wanted, everything he needed, wanted to believe that they could be that for each other. He wanted to believe that they could work things out, that Garrick was right and that they could figure out a future together. He wasn't sure he trusted that as much as Garrick did, but as sleep claimed him, he clung to the idea that maybe, just maybe this could work out.

Chapter Twenty-One

Plop. Garrick woke up to sixty-odd pounds of dog wiggling her way between Rain and him, interrupting a sexy dream and causing Rain to make a startled noise and roll away from Garrick.

"Cookie! I was having such a good dream too." He shoved at her bulk but couldn't move the stubborn beast. In the dream, everything had been back to normal between them, no big talk looming, no hard questions or lingering awkwardness, and he wouldn't have minded staying in that happy, floaty place a little longer.

"Oh yeah?" Rain opened an eye. "Tell me about it?"

"It'd be more fun to show you, but I think *someone* isn't going to let up until we take her o-u-t."

Proving him right, Cookie wiggled, tail thumping against the mattress.

"I think she can spell now. Why couldn't you rescue a dumb and lazy dog instead of this one who thinks she's part rooster?" Sitting up, Rain stretched, covers pooling in his lap, and bare torso giving Garrick all sorts of ideas that he wasn't going to be able to do anything about.

"I'll start the coffee if you want to get dressed and find the leash." Still in boxers from the night before, Garrick transferred to his chair.

Cookie leaped off the bed, racing out of the room.

"Damn. I think someone missed me."

"She's not the only one." Garrick squeezed Rain's bare ass as he passed.

"Good. Can I borrow a T-shirt? I think I've got shorts here somewhere."

"Help yourself. We need to get you your own drawer."

"Careful. I might go getting the idea you want to keep me around."

"Hey." Garrick pulled him into his lap. "I do want you around. A lot. I'm not offering to be nice or practical. I want you to keep stuff here. I want *you* here, as long as you want to stay. I fucked up in thinking I could let you go without it gutting me."

"Yeah, well, walking away, that gutted *me.* I've done a ton of thinking since our fight, and you're not the only one who fucked up, but I can't deny that you hurt me when you pushed me away."

"I'm sorry." Chest aching, Garrick pressed a kiss to his neck. "I want you to trust me again. I want to do what it takes to get back to that place. I know it's going to take time and probably some space too, but I'm willing to do whatever you need to regain that trust."

"Thanks." Rain dropped his head against Garrick's shoulder briefly before Cookie was back, dragging the leash Garrick's dad had left on the kitchen counter. "Okay, okay, silly dog. I'm getting dressed."

He pushed off Garrick's lap and went to rifle through the dresser. Garrick missed his closeness but was okay with a reprieve from the heavy talk.

"Not that I don't miss your ponies, but I like seeing you in my shirt," Garrick said a few minutes later when they were both dressed and in the kitchen, Rain in an old triathlon shirt over his own silver shorts.

"Okay, caveman." Rain kissed the top of Garrick's head, and for a moment at least, things between them were back to a light, easy place.

They set off toward the park at a fast clip, Cookie pulling Rain ahead and making conversation tough until they reached the pull-up obstacle along the park path.

"You don't have to do a full workout," he told Rain, who was eying the bar. "God knows you've been working hard the last week. Go easy on yourself."

"Maybe I don't want easy." Frowning, Rain rattled off an impressive ten pull-ups before returning to Garrick and Cookie.

"What *do* you want?" It wasn't lost on Garrick that he probably should have started with that question back during their initial argument. He'd made a lot of assumptions, assumptions his conversation with his dad had underscored, but now he was much less sure. More importantly, he was trying hard to not let his own fears get in the way of listening to Rain, actually trusting him, the way he wanted Rain to trust him as well.

"That's a good question." Rain walked farther, face creased as if he was thinking hard, before collapsing onto a bench near the sprinkler pad. "I know what everyone expects me to say—you included."

"Maybe fuck others' opinions. You've never let people stop you from doing what you want in other areas. And yeah, I'm guilty of assuming I knew best, but I'm willing to be wrong here." Garrick parked next to him, letting Cookie flop at their feet.

"Good." Rain's mouth quirked, but his eyes stayed wary.

"Also, if it helps, I don't think there's an answer that's necessarily a deal breaker for us as a couple—

that's the part I wasn't seeing clearly before. It's not all or nothing."

"How do you figure? Seems to me like there's a really clear choice—here versus there, you versus alone." Rain kicked at a rock near the bench.

"Maybe we're both thinking about this wrong. It doesn't have to be so black and white. I meant what I said the other day—me and Cookie, we'll wait for you, as long as it takes. Go, chase the opportunity. There'll be a place here for you when the season ends."

"You hate long distance." Shrugging, Rain studied the opposite side of the park where two women were jogging, perfectly in step with each other, each footfall synchronized like a footwear ad. Why couldn't he and Garrick find the conversational equivalent of that kind of synergy?

"Well, I didn't say it would be easy. Or preferable. But it also doesn't have to be a permanent state of affairs. There's a universe where you get the job, love it, and maybe I come to you." He'd been thinking about that option for days now, but saying it aloud for the first time, his pulse still sped up. "I'm not tied to the smoke jumping job anymore. Dispatch or fire admin type jobs are going to be easier to come by wherever you land next."

"But you love it here. This is where you grew up. Your dad is here. It's your home. You've got your dream bachelor pad."

"You're not wrong about loving it here. And it would be complicated to move, sure. And it'll always be home, but I also don't want it to be an excuse for not going for what I truly want." Taking a deep breath, he took Rain's hand, squeezed it. He could admit now that when he'd been younger, he'd clung a little hard to those excuses, and he wasn't going to make the same mistake again. "And what I want is you. Us. A chance at a future. That's why I mean it when I say that I'd follow you. If you need to go, I'm not going to be the thing stopping you, but I would like to be the person at your side for the ride."

"Wow. That... You want me that much? To leave everything if that's what I really wish?"

"That's how much I *need* you, yes. Wanting you was never the issue. You were right when you said I was afraid you'd break my heart by leaving eventually no matter what. But you make me want to be brave on a lot of different levels. And part of that is admitting that maybe my dreams have changed."

"Exactly." Rain exhaled hard but didn't pull his hand away. "That's what I've been wrestling with. Trying to figure out how to explain precisely that. Dreams change. Like, maybe at the start of the summer I did want to make a hotshot crew. I wasn't lying about that or about wanting an adventure, wherever the universe wanted to send me. But then the weeks passed, and working out became less about a ticket away from this place and more about spending time with you. I thought less and less about the job potential and more about us."

"I like spending time with you too. Hey, you even got me knitting." He laughed, then sobered because this was an important point. "But I want you to have everything you want—adventure included."

"That's the thing. I always thought I'd have to go away to find the perfect adventure. Away from the co-housing community where I grew up. Away from Portland when the right situation didn't materialize there.

Away from here because I was bored at first with nothing to do. But the more I think about the future, the more it seems like maybe staying—like actually putting down roots somewhere—that might be its own sort of adventure."

"I don't disagree, but you're twenty-three. I'm not saying you're wrong or trying to say I know your heart better, but settling down…that's a big decision. It's taken me a lot of years to get to that point myself."

"Maybe not all of us are on the same timeline." Rain gave him an arch look, and okay, Garrick could be honest with himself now that maybe Lisa leaving had been more of mutual thing, neither of them truly ready for that kind of commitment. He'd had a lot of growing up and maturing left to do to get to this new place where he could handle the sort of relationship and feelings that came with caring for someone as deeply as he did Rain.

"Point taken. But even if you don't need as many years as I did to figure out what you truly want, it's okay to want to have fun and follow your whims and take different risks and gain unique experiences. There's nothing wrong with your drive for adventure, even if that leads away from here."

A group of birds flew up from beyond the basketball courts, heading out for parts unknown. Hard as it was to picture a life away from this place, what Garrick wanted most of all was for Rain to have the opportunity to truly grow and flourish, find his wings, whatever that ended up looking like for him.

"And if it doesn't? If it leads me right back here? Maybe I had it wrong all along, and my dreams don't have to all be about thrill seeking and adrenaline rushes."

"You'd be passing up a great opportunity though. That's not nothing." The birds circled back around, playing now, dancing in the early morning air.

"It would be a risk, sure, but so is going." Now Rain was the one to squeeze Garrick's hand, holding on tight. "What if what I've been searching for has been right here all along? Do I really need to spend another year or five learning that before we both trust it? Waste all that time?"

Huh. This wasn't the response Garrick had spent all week anticipating. He didn't want to try to talk Rain out of conclusions he'd reached when he'd said he'd listen and trust Rain to know his own mind, but he also didn't want to be too fast in taking Rain up on the staying option. Taking a breath, he pulled Rain a little closer.

"Trust me, I know better than most how life can change in an instant. And I don't want to waste time either. And the worst thing for me wouldn't be leaving this place. It would be missing out on my chance to have you. Yeah, there's still that possibility that maybe some-day you'll go and not take me with you, but I want to at least be open to going, to compromising, to not simply letting you walk away and take my heart with you. Be-cause that much *is* a given—you've got my whole heart now, no matter what."

Nodding solemnly, Rain swallowed audibly, holding Garrick's hand that much tighter. "And if I believe you care that much, can you believe me when I say that I don't want to put you in that position? Not right now. Can you trust me enough to let me stay?"

"That's really what you want? No hotshot crew?" The pair of joggers were back, circling the path, not quite so in sync, but laughing at each other, clearly having a great time. Maybe that mattered more than how in step they'd been earlier. Garrick spared them a smile as they passed.

"My crew here needs me. Our boss is gonna be out awhile recovering from a mild heart attack. Bosler needs me on the radio. Yeah, maybe the work isn't the most exciting a lot of days. But I want to see the summer through. You asked me what I want, and that's what I want. To stay. Space, like you said, but not from you. Space to figure out what's next for me. When the boss got ill, all I kept dwelling on was how I never got my EMT certification when I had the chance. I want to think more about my path forward, how I can best help people and also meet my own needs."

"That sounds really wise. Mature. You don't need all the answers about your future right now." As much as Garrick wanted things settled with a clear plan, he had to admit that Rain's more pragmatic plan had certain benefits too. "I only want a chance to be part of it with you, whatever you end up deciding."

"So we're not simply a fling?" Throwing Garrick's words back at him, Rain raised an eyebrow.

"We never were. That was me being scared. And a jerk." Rain's emphatic nod made him laugh before continuing. "I honestly did think I was doing the right thing, but that's not the best excuse. Next time, I'm going to listen more."

"Good. And me too. I was…quick to assume the worst about you. I didn't listen the best either."

"I didn't exactly make it easy. And this is me saying sorry and doing what you requested and asking you for more. Asking you to not settle for something less than the real relationship we both want and deserve."

"I'm not going to. I want it all. That's why I'm staying too—I know you cared enough to let me go and now you're brave enough to offer to go away with me, but I want to stay. See what we have together. See if we can truly build a future together here."

Woof. Having had enough of their stopping and talking, Cookie let out a series of barks along with a long-suffering look for them both.

"Cookie approves of my idea." Rain leaned in and brushed a fast kiss over Garrick's cheek.

"Can't let Cookie down." Giving Rain's hand one last squeeze, Garrick took the brakes off his chair. "And I want that too. It's frankly a little terrifying, but losing you would be way worse. So yeah, I'm willing to do what it takes to make that future happen."

"Excellent." Beaming at him, Rain pointed at the path ahead of them. "Race you to the next obstacle?"

"Always." Laughing, Garrick wheeled hard as Rain and Cookie jogged alongside him. It might not always be this easy, and there was still an awful lot to work out, plenty of uncertainty, but at least they were together. They could deal with all the unexpected bumps and turns in the road as long as they had each other. He'd meant every scary word he'd managed to utter too. He cared about Rain, more than he ever had anyone else, and he was willing to do his part to make sure that they got the future they both wanted.

Chapter Twenty-Two

"Are you sure your dad is cool with this?" Rain asked as he stuffed towels in a bag in Garrick's living room, afternoon sun filtering in.

"This as in us coming to swim? Or his offer to grill mushroom caps for you instead of steak? Or your awesome new swim trunks? Or more in general, like is he okay with us as a couple?"

"Uh. All of that. I'm weirdly nervous."

"You? Nervous?" Garrick captured him around the waist, hauled him into his lap. "You do know that he figured out weeks ago that we're sleeping together, right? What's changed?"

"Everything." Embarrassed at his strangely emo turn, Rain buried his face in Garrick's neck. This was silly, but he still couldn't stop the flutters in his belly. This outing, their first in public so to speak since their reunion, felt momentous somehow. Maybe it was how everyone, Grandma and Garrick's dad included, seemed to still expect him to move on. Grandma had merely nodded and made a sort of skeptical clucking noise when Rain told her they'd made up. It felt like no one was rooting for him to stay.

Worrying about stupid shit made him weirdly antsy

about simple things like this invitation to come for dinner and a swim.

"I get that everything feels different now. Maybe we *are* different." Garrick tipped Rain's chin up with gentle fingers so that he could give him a soft kiss that went a long way to quieting Rain's butterflies, especially when he pulled away laughing. "Maybe we're like morphing superheroes or something. You're growing blue horns and I'm—"

"Dork." Joining him in chuckling, Rain shoved at his shoulder, but Garrick didn't release him. "You know what I meant."

"I do. Sorry. Couldn't resist. And I know you don't believe me, but despite his old-school ways, Dad really does want me happy. He's not going to make trouble for us because you *do* make me happy, and he knows that."

"You sure you're happy?" Maybe Rain needed to hear it again, a few dozen times, and then he could start to believe in it more.

"Just ask Cookie." Garrick gestured at the dog, who was already by the door, leash in her mouth, tail wagging because she sensed a car ride. "She's so much calmer and perkier with us together. And I might not have a tail to shake, but that's me too. When you're not here, it feels like I'm missing something essential, like I'm a stack of kindling without the spark."

Garrick's pretty words made Rain's skin heat and he kissed Garrick's cheek. "I dunno. You might look cute wagging. And feel free to lick my…whatever."

"Ha." Garrick playfully swiped at Rain's face with his tongue. "Seriously, though. You make me happy in so many little ways with your jokes and kindness and caring."

"My caring? It feels like you're always the one taking care of me. All week you had food for me even when it was late, and you spoil me in lots of other ways."

"That's exactly it. I love taking care of you. It's quite possibly my favorite thing in the whole world, and it's not that I think you need it or that you're not capable of taking care of yourself, but I love that you let me. I think I was looking for something like this—someone like you—a very long time. It's like I had all these little cracks, and us caring for either other, that fills them all in, makes me warm and cozy inside."

"So you're saying I'm like caulk?" Rain had to joke or else Garrick's sweet speech was going to make him overwhelmed, make this tightness in his chest unbearable. And it wasn't that he didn't believe Garrick was sincere, but Garrick being this open about the depth of his feelings was…something. Something good, but also scary, wanting him this much, wanting to be wanted like this, and being worried it was all going to tumble down if he did or said the wrong thing.

"Hey, I never promised to be a poet." Garrick kissed him again, slow and gentle. "All I'm trying to say is that you're special. Special in general and special to me specifically. And I do think others can see and appreciate that specialness—like my dad."

"I heard you on the phone with him the other day." Rain finally admitted to one of the real sources of his discomfort. It hadn't been an angry call at all, and it had ended with the invite, but there had been definite skepticism in the part Rain had overheard. "He thinks I'm going to leave. And I know Grandma does too. She's been teasing me like I'm… I dunno…a fickle kid,

I guess. Like this is another whim and I'll change my mind soon enough."

"So? Prove them wrong." Giving him a tight squeeze first, Garrick locked eyes with him. "And I meant what I said the other day. If you do go, I'm going to follow. You're not getting rid of me so easily."

"Good." He tried to let Garrick's conviction chase away his doubts.

"I only want you happy. And I think that's where the others are coming from too. Everyone wants you to find that thing in life that makes you the happiest, whatever and wherever that might be."

"I did. I found you." He held Garrick's gaze this time, willing him to understand. Maybe he hadn't found a profession for himself yet, but he'd found Garrick and Cookie and a place here, and that was something, something real and tangible.

"Damn. I love you." Garrick's tone was almost reverent, and it made a bubbly sensation race up Rain's spine.

"Seriously?" They'd been dancing around the words for days now, talking about how much they cared and how they wanted this to work out. Sweet words and sweeter kisses, but not this exact wording, not yet.

"Told you. You're special and I want to keep you around, whatever I have to do to make that happen. Yeah, I love you."

"Thanks." It wasn't the same as saying the words back, but it was all he could seem to manage, throat tight and brain whirling. Love…that was a whole different level. He was still trying to wrap his head around Garrick caring enough to be willing to think about leaving his home. Love. That implied a permanence and an even greater depth of feeling that Rain wasn't entirely sure what to do with. It wasn't that he didn't *want* to say the words back, but somehow he couldn't.

Garrick frowned slightly, but if anything, he held Rain tighter. "I mean it. And I love all of you. Not just your smoking new swim attire."

"You do have good taste." Relieved that Garrick was giving him a change of subject to cling to, he forced his voice to be light and easy. Remembering Rain's disdain for standard swim trunks, Garrick had surprised him by ordering this set, close-fitting powder blue shorts with Rain's favorite pony character on one leg and a rainbow on the other, and a matching rash guard shirt. It might not be as sexy as skinny-dipping, but it was more than satisfactory as socially acceptable swimming attire for public.

He liked the shirt part a lot because it was the combo of bare chest and baggy board shorts that he'd never much liked. It wasn't so much that he'd craved a more femme option as that he wanted to feel more like himself, and this new outfit did that. All that was missing was his usual mindset of not giving a fuck for others and their opinions. He needed to stop worrying about whether Garrick's dad approved of him. Garrick swore that Rain made him happy. Heck, he said he *loved* Rain. He needed to focus on that, not stupid worries.

That in mind, he stole one more kiss then hefted himself off Garrick's lap. "Come on, Cookie. Let's load up."

Once they were underway, Garrick fiddled with the stereo volume before speaking. "I've been thinking. And talking to Stephanie at PT yesterday too. I think I'm going to look into trading in my old truck, get something more compatible with hand controls and easy loading of the chair on my own."

"That makes sense." Rain didn't want to make too big a deal out of this decision, but he was well aware that this was another large step in Garrick accepting the permanence of his situation and making plans for his future accordingly. "I don't mind being your chauffeur, but I can see where you'd enjoy driving again. Be able to set your own hours at work. You should do it."

He tried to be way more upbeat and pragmatic about this than he'd been about the special leash for Cookie. Garrick independent was a good thing, and like Grandma had said, even if a person had the ability to do something on their own, they could still choose to do things together simply because they wanted to. Like Garrick might still ride with Rain sometimes, and Rain was going to work on trusting that he'd want Rain around regardless of need.

"Yeah. I'll need lessons, and it might require a trip to Portland to find the right vehicle, but I think it might be worth it."

"Your dad will probably cheer you on too. You'll be able to do some of your own grocery shopping, get your endless supply of eggs and protein powder." He gave an exaggerated shudder to make Garrick laugh.

"Hey now. The drinks I make myself aren't *that* gross."

"Yeah, they kind of are. But it's okay. You're cute and I lo—*like* you anyway." He had to stop himself from the casual use of the L-word. If he hadn't been able to get the word out back when Garrick had been waiting for it, Rain wasn't about to toss it in as an oh-by-the-way in an ordinary conversation either.

"I like you a lot too." Garrick gave his thigh a fond pat before Rain made the turn for the country road that led to his dad's place. This wasn't his first trip out this way as he'd picked Garrick up from here a couple of times, but this was the first invitation he'd had to a meal. Damn it. Now his flutters were back, which Garrick seemed to sense, because he added, "You're damn easy to like. Just ask Cookie."

"Cookie likes anyone with biscuits." He snort-laughed, but it did work to relieve a little of his antsiness. "Your dad is maybe a *little* more discriminating."

"He called me this morning to verify what you can eat. Twice. Maybe he's nervous too. It'll work out, baby. You'll see."

"Okay."

"And you deserve a nice dinner and swim after the week you've had on clean-up duty. Everyone's noticed how hard you've been working. Ryland and Adams both remarked on it yesterday. You've really stepped it up with your boss out."

"Yeah, well, Bosler's a pretty good role model, even if he does get cranky sometimes."

"And he understood when you told him you were staying?"

"Yeah. Like Grandma and your dad though, I think he believes I'll regret it, but he simply shrugged and said there's always next year. Competition for a hotshot crew here will be tight though. Speaking of, Zeb keeps making noises about wanting to know my training regimen. I'm telling you, you could make extra dough as a personal trainer."

"Have Zeb meet us at the park some morning. No fee. I enjoyed doing a plan for you, but not sure I want to make a career out of it. Your friends are always welcome at my place, though."

"Oh, I'm not sure he's a *friend* yet, but he's at least not as skittish around me. Even let me get away with cursing the other day. Guess sharing a tent for a week has a tendency to make unlikely bonds."

"That it does." Garrick laughed knowingly.

"And who knows what I'll end up doing as a winter job." He pulled into the long gravel drive for Garrick's dad's small acreage, horses grazing in the pasture closest to the road, house and outbuildings farther back.

"Whatever you end up doing, you're going to be good at it. You can do anything you want, and I'm going to support you no matter what."

"Thanks. That means a lot." He let Garrick get away with stealing a fast kiss after he parked, and he almost said it right then. Those words. The ones he knew Garrick was waiting for. But then his dad was bustling out of the house and the moment passed. Or maybe he chickened out. Either way, no words were said, and they drifted away from heavier topics to lighter subjects like whether to let Cookie go off-leash with the farm dogs, a pair of older mixed hounds who were world-weary cowboys to Cookie's youthful energy and sparkly accessories.

Eventually, Cookie did get them to run and play with her before she settled under a lounger while they hung out by the pool. If Garrick's dad had an opinion on Rain's outfit, he kept it to himself, humming happily as he grilled, same habit that Garrick had when he cooked. It was cute, the way Kenny and Garrick were so similar and so close to each other. Seeing them together, side by side, debating how to season their steaks, it was easier to believe that maybe all his dad really did care about was that Garrick was happy.

When he went inside to get a soda from the kitchen, he saw a row of pictures of little Garrick on the wall in the hall—T-ball and football and holidays through the years. Lots of sports and horses and gap-toothed smiles.

"Had him up on a horse before he could walk." Kenny came up behind him carrying an impressive platter of vegetables. "And I'm just saying this once. Y'all can raise a pack of socialist vegetarians. But they're gonna learn to ride. Some things are nonnegotiable."

Dazed, Rain followed him back out to the patio. Kids. Huh. That was…unexpected. And almost as scary as Garrick saying the L-word and professing a willingness to follow Rain's dreams, whatever they were. But it wasn't an entirely unwelcome idea either, and he tried to figure out what the appropriate response was.

"Dad. What did you do to Rain?" Garrick called from where he was floating in the deep end, arms resting on a small inflatable raft. "He looks like you've been telling some of your ghost stories."

"Just letting him know that my grandkids, they're gonna know their way around a horse."

Garrick's slow blink was comical. Oh good. Rain wasn't the only one caught off guard. "You mentioned *kids* to Rain?"

"Well, yeah." Kenny shrugged as he arranged food on the grill. "You told me he's sticking around. Figured I better get my bid for grandkids in while y'all are still in that lovey-dovey phase where you might want to make an old man happy. Speaking of, I've got a lead on a horse about to retire from a program down in Klamath Falls. Sweet girl, used to wearing an accessible saddle and working with wheelchair users. Think you'd be interested in saddling up if she comes here for her golden years?"

"You deciding you need another horse is the least surprising part of this whole conversation." Garrick laughed. "And you're right. I've missed riding. I didn't want to talk about it much because it felt like one more thing I couldn't do anymore. But maybe it's like driving—I can get it back if some adjustments are made."

"Exactly." Forget kids and words he hadn't yet said and uncertainties about the future. He was so damn proud of Garrick right then, proud of all the ways he was reconfiguring his expectations. His willingness to adapt made Rain all the more sure that maybe they could weather all those uncertainties together.

"I'll ask Stephanie what muscles we can work on so I can use an accessible saddle. But, Dad, you need to stop scaring Rain." He gave a nod in Rain's direction. "Baby, ignore him. He finally got grandkids from my sister. He knows perfectly well that my spare room is a gym."

"I didn't say no." Rain drank in Garrick's slack-mouthed, wide-eyed expression before he dove into the pool, a perfect swan dive that probably surprised Garrick about as much as his words. But he wasn't saying them simply for effect—the possibility, once raised, was…intriguing. One of those many varied future paths they might find themselves on, and as scary as not knowing was, it was also damn exciting. Adventures waiting to be had.

"I like him." Garrick's father was laughing hard when Rain finally surfaced.

"Me too." Still shaking his head, Garrick captured him for a fast embrace. Again, Rain was *this* close to saying the words, but they had an audience, and somehow it was easier to joke about a future with kids than to utter three little words.

So he ate his weight in grilled vegetables and watched Garrick and his dad tease each other and let the last of that fluttery feeling drift away. This was going to work out. He might have to learn to ride a horse, but this would work out.

And as the evening light faded, a perfect once-in-a-lifetime central Oregon sunset of pinks and purples, he knew beyond a doubt that he'd found that thing that gave him purpose and made him the kind of happy everyone seemed to want for him and it was right here, the future lurking in each of Garrick's easy grins and loving looks. He'd spent years searching for the right shiny thing to run toward, but it turned out that what his soul truly wanted was a reason to stay. Everything else could figure itself out in the coming years. He had what he needed, right here.

Garrick's dad ducked inside to retrieve some marionberry sorbet for dessert. He wasn't gone more than fifteen seconds before Garrick was stealing another kiss, and suddenly the words came startlingly easy, gliding over his tongue like he'd said them a thousand times before.

"I love you too."

"Yeah?" Garrick grinned broadly. "Dad didn't scare you away?"

"Nah. It's going to take a lot more than some horses to scare me away."

"Or grandkid talk?"

"Even that. I'm sorry I didn't say the words earlier when you did. It wasn't that I didn't want to. More... I'm working on believing that this is going to work out, that I'm actually going to get what I was afraid to let myself want. Trust. It's hard."

"I get it. And I'm right there with you. It's not easy to trust in the future, but I'm trying hard to not let fear hold me back from what my heart truly wants."

"And it wants me?"

"Always." This time when Garrick leaned in for a fast kiss, Rain gave a happy sigh and met him halfway. Neither of them might have all the answers, but he did believe with all his heart that they were better together and that his future, whatever it might be, was infinitely brighter with Garrick in it. Loving him was both the scariest thing in the world and the simplest, and like Garrick, he wasn't going to let his fears stop him from doing exactly that.

Chapter Twenty-Three

Winter Solstice

"Smile pretty," Garrick's sister urged from her position by the paddock gate as she held up a camera. Her family had arrived that morning, prepared to stay the holiday week, and Garrick's dad hadn't wasted any time in hurrying them all to the barn and horses. Rain was counting down until their solstice party that night, but he hadn't protested the idea of a short ride. The weather was too perfect to not be outdoors—crisp and clear and cold. Nothing like a soggy Portland winter, that was for sure.

"You sure you're okay riding double, Rain?" Garrick's sister paused her picture taking to get that worried-mom furrow to her forehead.

"Yup." Rain tightened his grip on Garrick's nephew. Kenny had the youngest in front of him, and it meant something to Rain that Kenny trusted him enough to let him ride with the other kid.

"He's put in the time this fall, learning the ropes." Garrick's dad's approval felt like the fleece lining of his jacket—warm and fuzzy. Learning to ride had been far more fun than he'd expected, and watching Garrick and his dad bond over the experience had been more than worth a few missteps along the way. "Old Blue stands around and pines for their visits."

"And the new horse seems to love Garrick."

"Dad's retirement program for her is practically a luxury retreat," Garrick joked, but Rain knew how hard he'd worked with his physical therapy to make riding in the adaptive saddle comfortable. "But Honey's a great horse. Being able to ride again, that's been awesome."

His tone was light, but his eyes were serious, an emotion there that Rain wasn't entirely sure how to name. It was similar to when Garrick had completed the purchase of his specially modified car, how he'd seemed proud yet vulnerable at the same time. Confident too, the way he talked to Honey now, a cowboy side Rain hadn't realized he had. And seeing him gain it back, well that had been one of the highlights of the past few months for Rain.

And far from rendering Rain unnecessary, sharing the progression of both riding and driving goals had brought them closer together. He'd wholeheartedly cheered Garrick's first solo drive, secure in his place in Garrick's life. It had taken a few months to get there, but he trusted now, on a deeper level than he'd even thought possible.

When their eyes met, he tried to tell Garrick without words how happy he was. Later, everyone would gather at their place, work friends, his family, and Garrick's. The prospect should be scary, but instead, all it did was fill him with a giddy sort of joy. *Their place.* Grandma had gently mentioned at a certain point that she wanted her spare room back, and he'd realized that it had been months since he'd spent the night there. So, he'd packed up his things and rather than live out of suitcases, he and Garrick had assembled a second dresser for the bedroom, and Rain had gotten to work on his holiday knitting and decorating projects, and that had been that. Shirley joined them for food several times a week, and Rain helped her whenever she let him, and together, they'd all fallen into a routine that worked for them.

"Tomorrow we can do a longer ride. You're off, right, Rain?" Kenny asked as he made a slow circle around the paddock, much to the little kid's delight.

"Yup. I'm working weird hours for the holidays. I volunteered for Christmas Eve since so many people wanted off for that, so I got today and tomorrow off. I wanted Christmas Eve anyway since that's the big party for our residents in the morning."

Surprising almost everyone, including himself, Rain had taken a job at a retirement community after the fire season had ended. His main job had started out as driving the community's shuttle van, but he'd quickly moved into filling in for an activities director out on maternity leave and doing whatever other odd jobs needed doing, like holiday decorating.

"Adams and Ryland better watch out if they want you for a crew next summer." Kenny laughed as he pulled up even with Rain's horse.

"Oh, I'm still working out with Garrick to be ready for a fitness test. My friend Zeb is too. The woman I'm filling in for will be back from leave, and there's a good chance I can work both places over the summer."

As far as long term, he still wasn't exactly sure what he wanted, but he was making his peace with not having all the answers yet. He'd come to really enjoy the work with his hand crew, and the thought of being back out there in some firefighting capacity come fire season made his insides dance. Anticipation, as it turned out, was its own adventure—having things to look forward to, things to return to, and things to try anew.

"Ready to head out?" Garrick asked as his sister opened the gate.

"Yep." Rain had seldom meant his agreement more. Lead or follow, he was in this thing for good now. He was totally ready to head out, see what the future brought them both.

"Doing okay?" Shirley paused in setting out food to give Garrick an appraising glance.

"A little sore," he admitted. His hip flexors were still getting used to the special saddle, and the kids had begged for a longer ride than initially intended. But damn, being up there on Honey, hanging out with his dad and the rest of the family, had been more than worth a little discomfort. He hadn't realized how much he'd missed riding until he had the chance to do it again. He hoped his dad knew how grateful he was to him for making that possible.

"Well, try not to overdo."

"Says the woman who's been baking all week," he teased. Garrick and Rain were hosting, but Shirley had been bustling about all week with preparations too. It was funny and more than a little surreal, seeing his once-dream bachelor pad transformed for a gathering of friends and family. He'd held plenty of parties here, but nothing compared to this. Endless strings of white lights twinkled both indoors and outside, the firepit was roaring on the back patio, and the table groaned with the ever-growing buffet as more people arrived.

Garrick's dad had contributed a fresh-cut tree, which stood in the front window, baby gate around it to keep Cookie from stealing the colorful ornaments Rain had produced—an eclectic mix of miniature stockings he'd knit along with discount store finds and a few additions from Shirley. Even Garrick had been goaded into crocheting little snowflake ornaments, something he'd found surprisingly hypnotic, a nice way to relax while Rain and Shirley worked on their holiday knitting projects.

"All this food looks amazing." Garrick's dad snagged a muffin from the basket on the table. Garrick couldn't remember the last time he'd seen his dad so happy, all the visitors and holiday prep rubbing off on him in a way they hadn't in years. He'd even made sure that there would be a veggie roast for Rain for Christmas dinner in a few days. Garrick's sister and dad would cook a big meal and the kids would get Santa presents, and Garrick couldn't wait to see his dad's place filled with the sounds and smells of the season.

"We made it!" Someone must have opened the door to let in Rain's parents, who arrived with yet more food for the table and hugs all around.

"Is there anyone you didn't invite?" Garrick's dad shook his head as he took in the gathering. Rain's brothers and Harper stood near their parents, while other friends like Bosler and Zeb mingled with some of Garrick's old crowd. "Surprised Rain didn't add some of his residents."

"Maybe next year." Rain's smile was wide and pleasure clear in his words whenever he talked about his new job. Every day he came home with fresh stories about helping this resident with groceries or that resident with hanging pictures, going above and beyond what the community paid him for. It wasn't a hotshot crew, but in a lot of ways, Garrick had never seen Rain happier, and he was so glad that he'd backed off and given him the space he needed to apply widely to different jobs as the fire season had ended. And if Rain's growing collection of muscles was any indication, he wasn't going to have any worries about making it onto a crew in the summer.

"Heck, it feels like half the town came as it is." Garrick gestured around the packed house. This was nice. More than nice. Felt like his chest could scarcely hold this much joy and happiness. And Rain wasn't the only one happy with work. Garrick had stayed on with the forest service after fire season had ended, helping Ryland and Adams plan for the spring controlled burns and working dispatch for winter crews. He was always going to miss smoke jumping, but there was surprising satisfaction in his new role.

And more than a little of that was having Rain and his bottomless enthusiasm to come home to. Even on boring paperwork days, he could look forward to some new recipe, some silly story or some new Cookie antics. Having this place truly become a home for both of them was a pleasure he hadn't seen coming and one he wouldn't trade for anything.

Leaving Rain to his family, he slipped on a jacket and wheeled out to check on the small group by the firepit. Linc had a steaming cup of coffee while Jacob was playing tug-of-war with Cookie and her new favorite toy, a fake leopard-print slipper Rain had produced recently. It was something of a private joke between them as it also matched a sexy leopard-print robe Garrick had

given Rain some weeks back, and the toy never failed
to make Garrick smile.

"There you are. Been waiting to catch you alone."
Linc gave him a smile. Garrick still wasn't used to how
much more his friend smiled these days, thanks largely
to Jacob. "We've got Jacob's family gathering on Christmas, so we're giving you your present early."

"I don't need a present," he protested.

"Yes, you do. Yours for us arrived yesterday. Nice
taste." Jacob laughed.

"That was Rain's doing!" He laughed because of
course Rain had remembered the threat about matching pajamas from their Pride double date and followed
through on it, finding ridiculous ones with paw prints
on them. And how damn amazing was it to be here now,
hint of snow in the air, Rain still around, to the point of
doing joint presents.

"Card said it was from both of you, and regardless,
this is for you." Linc pulled a white envelope out of his
coat pocket and handed it to him. Jacob stopped playing with the dog long enough to watch Garrick open
it, and Rain slipped out onto the patio right as Garrick
was reading the slip of paper inside.

"What? I don't understand." He looked at the three
of them, all of whom were studying him intently. "It's
a gift certificate for skydiving. But I can't…"

"You can." Linc clapped him on the shoulder. "I
found an instructor out of Reno who's a master at adaptive skydiving, even taking people with quadriplegia up.
He'll be in the area over New Year's. What do you say?"

"I…uh…" Garrick swiveled his head, gaze landing
on Rain, who had an expectant smile on his face. He'd
bundled up in a thick hand-knit cardigan and mittens

and looked even more eager than Linc and Jacob. "You were in on this?"

"Well, yeah. And I know a tandem jump isn't quite the same as a solo flight, but I know how much you've missed it."

"Oh…wow." All summer and fall, Garrick had worked on coming to terms with not returning to smoke jumping, letting go of the idea that he might never get to experience the high of free fall again. And now his friends were saying that some piece of that might be possible after all.

It was not without risks. But even knowing all those risks, he wanted to, could already feel the wind rising up to meet his face, the tug of the chute when it deployed, and the thump of landing. And yeah, tandem jumping was different, less control for him, but the idea that he could have even a little slice of all that back was intoxicating. As was the fact that Rain seemed to want that for him. He understood him so damn well, on a level that few others could.

"I do want to try. But only if you're okay with it."

"I'll be right there, cheering for you. I'll keep the coffee hot on the ground, and then we can all watch the video after."

All Garrick could do was nod at that because the idea of getting one more jump with Linc and Jacob…that was really something. Best present he could imagine from friends he wasn't sure he deserved and the person who already had his whole damn heart.

"Good. Can't wait. I'm getting more food. Jacob?" Linc ushered Jacob back into the house, leaving Garrick and Rain alone in front of the fire. A stray flake landed on Rain's sweater arm, and Garrick brushed it away.

"It's snowing. Hope it sticks." Rain's grin was warmer than the fire, more joyous than the music filtering out from the house, and there was enough mischief in it to have Garrick counting down to when the house might be empty again and they could crawl under the covers in their big bed and watch the snow falling together.

"Thank you." It wasn't adequate, but it was all he had.

"Well, most of the logistics was Linc." Rain waved away the praise. "I'm just your cheering section."

"And that's a lot. Everything. Knowing you're waiting for me..." He shook his head. "I've had plenty of reasons to jump before, but never such a good one to come back to earth for. You're something else."

"You were willing to wait on me or follow me if that's what I wanted and needed. I'm just returning the favor." Rain held his gaze. "And always. You go fly. Cookie and I will be right here. And who knows, if you make it look fun enough, you guys might get me to try it yet."

"I'd like that. And I like knowing you're here even more. You don't have to ever jump to prove something to me. I love you exactly how you are."

"Same. And this is a part of you."

"A part of my past," Garrick corrected, grabbing his hand. "You're my future. The future I never knew I needed this damn much, but I do. I love you for making this happen for me, but I love you for giving me my future even more. You give me hope, hope that the best parts of my life are still to come. And I can't thank you enough for that."

"How about you just love me instead?" Smiling, that

secret private pleased grin of his, Rain bent his knees so he could brush a kiss across Garrick's mouth.

"I can do that." And he could. And he would. Behind them, the house erupted with laughter, a joke they'd hear about later, but right here, it was only them and that wide-open future full of possibilities. Job changes. New hobbies. More pets. Lots of additional parties over various seasons. Trips. Promises they'd make and vows they might take. They'd grow and change, and Garrick honestly couldn't wait to see it. He pulled Rain down for another kiss, this one more lingering. This was his forever person, whatever the future brought, and he was going to keep on loving Rain through all of it.

* * * * *

Reviews are an invaluable tool when it comes to spreading the word about great reads. Please consider leaving an honest review for this or any of Carina Press's other titles that you've read on your favorite retailer or review site.

To find out more about Annabeth Albert's upcoming releases, contests, and free bonus reads, please sign up for her newsletter here or eepurl.com/Nb9yv.

Author Note

As I embarked on book two in this series, my research into the world of wildfire fighting and forestry led me down many new and fascinating paths. Like book one, rather than try to copy an existing smoke jumping base with its specific procedures, policies, ways of handling rookies and so on, I combined various bases into one fictional one. The especially eagle-eyed will note that I essentially replaced the Redmond, Oregon, base with my own, but mine is not intended to be an exact duplicate of theirs in any way. Likewise, Painter's Ridge is an entirely fictional central Oregon town.

While Garrick and Rain both work for the federal Forestry Department, the reality of modern fire management usually involves multiple agencies and interagency coordination at both the state and federal levels. In Oregon alone, fires frequently affect state, federal, and private lands, sometimes all in the same fire. Again, some of these details were simplified to allow the focus to remain on the characters and their growth and their story, but I did try to include as much realism as possible. Wildfire fighting is an arduous job that taxes the people who take it on, and many consider it a calling as much as a vocation. I tried to bring their amazing dedication and resilient spirits to the secondary as well as the main characters. I also tried to reflect the very real dangers the job brings. Garrick's injuries are far from uncommon because every year, brave and valiant people die fighting wildfires while others are seriously injured.

Garrick's injuries were another avenue of research for me, and I was fortunate to get amazing help in my endeavors to be as realistic and sensitive as possible. A large number of men with spinal injuries do struggle with sexual function, and I wanted to reflect that in a way that felt organic to this particular story. Likewise, it's a reality of healthcare in America at the present moment that insurance decisions play a huge role in prognosis and progress. I appreciate all the resources I consulted about Garrick's condition, treatment, and long-term prospects.

Finally, yes, central Oregon does have a small Pride festival! I fictionalized vendors and activities, but this area of the state is near and dear to my heart, and I tried to reflect its unique culture and vibe as much as possible. The area also features a number of pet rescues who work hard to serve the local community, and the problems in finding Cookie her forever home aren't intended to detract from the amazing work they do. The town of Painter's Ridge may be my own invention, but the area's geography and attractions absolutely helped to flavor the series.

Acknowledgments

As we continue this series, I am truly blessed with an amazing team supporting me, especially at Carina Press and the Knight Agency. My editor, Deb Nemeth, had the exact right blend of enthusiasm and careful critique. Her insightful comments encouraged me as always to dig deeper into revisions. Those revisions were also aided by invaluable beta comments from Edie Danford, Louise Auty, and Cathy Mullican. Wendy Qualls gave her usual amazing plotting sounding-board assistance, and her excitement for Rain's backstory in particular helped shape the ultimate direction for the book.

My behind-the-scenes team is also so appreciated. My publicist, Judith of A Novel Take PR, goes above and beyond with every release, and I am so very grateful to her. My entire Carina Press team does a fantastic job, and I am so very lucky to have all of them on board. A special thank-you to the tireless art department and publicity team and to the amazing narrators who bring my books to life for the audio market. A special thank-you to Abbie Nicole, who is new to my team and whose assistance to my writerly life is making a giant difference for me.

My family deserves special thanks for their cooperation and assistance. My life is immeasurably enriched by my friendships, especially those of my writer friends who keep me going with sprints, advice, guidance, and commiseration. I am so grateful for every person in my life who helps me do what I love. And no one makes that possible more than my readers. I can't thank readers enough for their readership and encouragement over the years. Your support via social media, reviews, notes, shares, likes, and other means makes it possible for me to continue to write stories that mean the world to me, and I don't take that for granted!

About the Author

Annabeth Albert grew up sneaking romance novels under the bedcovers. Now, she devours all subgenres of romance out in the open—no flashlights required! When she's not adding to her keeper shelf, she's a multi-published Pacific Northwest romance writer. The #Hotshots series joins her many other critically acclaimed and fan-favorite LGBTQ romance series. To find out what she's working on next and other fun extras, check out her website: www.annabethalbert.com or connect with Annabeth on Twitter, Facebook, Instagram, and Spotify. Also, be sure to sign up for her newsletter for free ficlets, bonus reads, and contests. The fan group Annabeth's Angels on Facebook is also a great place for bonus content and exclusive contests.

Emotionally complex, sexy, and funny stories are her favorites both to read and to write. Annabeth loves finding happy endings for a variety of pairings and particularly loves uncovering unique main characters. In her personal life, she works a rewarding day job and wrangles two active children.

Newsletter: http://eepurl.com/Nb9yv
Fan group: https://www.facebook.com/groups/annabethsangels/

*Coming soon from Carina Press
and Annabeth Albert*

*When two childhood sweethearts are reunited as
adults, intense feelings resurface, but first they
must battle old hurts and new dangers if they are
to have a future together.*

*Read on for a sneak preview of
Feel the Fire,
the next book in Annabeth Albert's
Hotshots series.*

Chapter One

"You want me to go *where*?" Luis paced the narrow length of his boss's office, ignoring the visitor's chair in front of where Rosalind sat. His pulse alternately revved and sputtered, struggling to keep up with the freaking live grenade Rosalind and the Forest Service had just lobbed into his life.

"Central Oregon. The Painter's Ridge Airbase is there along with an interagency hotshot crew and, of course, a large forest service office. It's a big operation."

"I know what's there." Even now, he could picture exactly what was there—endless sky, big ranches, surprising number of cowboys, and Tucker. But not the Tucker of his memories. Chestnut hair. Gap between his teeth. Floppy hair over his ears. Penny in his sneakers. That boy was gone forever, replaced by a fully adult Tucker, who undoubtedly had a happy wife, happy life, maybe a half-dozen kids by now, all with Tucker's damn smile. That boy—*man*—had roots as deep as a two-hundred-year-old fir in that area, and no way was Luis getting lucky by him having moved away or something.

"I had a feeling you might. You grew up near there, right?" She gave him an encouraging smile, sun glinting off her short gray hair. She was one of the few in the building with a window in her office. Usually he enjoyed visiting her and her collection of houseplants and stacks of forestry manuals, but not today.

"Something like that." His voice was probably terser than Rosalind deserved, as they'd been good work friends before she'd taken this promotion, but damn, he was still reeling. "I grew up in Riverside mainly, but we spent some years up in Oregon when my dad was transferred there to manage a new bank branch. All my family's back here in California now though," he added in case she was under the mistaken impression that he was pining for the area. No, he'd gotten all the pining out of his system years ago and all that was left was a bitter, ashy taste and a major distrust of toothy grins and careful promises.

I promise to write.

I'll wait for you. I'll wait forever.

You're the one. My one.

"Hmm." Rosalind's mouth twisted. "I'm not saying this assignment will be easy. Extended travel is never fun. And I'm sure your family will miss you. You're not seeing anyone right now, are you?"

Ah. There it was. The real reason Luis was being shipped north. In a large office with several fire behavior specialists, he might well be the best, but he was also the only single guy, only one without kids. And that made him expendable. This wasn't the first time the forest service had loaned him out to a region with great need—he'd spent a few weeks in northern California last year, and in Montana with the big national park fires the year before that. But fucking Oregon? That he wasn't prepared for.

"If I say yes, will that get me out of this?" He gave her his best smile, but she simply sighed.

"Sorry. I know this is short notice. But you'll get the travel per diem. If you're frugal with food, that can be a nice little bonus for you, maybe?" Her dark eyes pleaded with him to understand and not make her day that much harder. And anywhere else in the country and he'd already be back at his desk, making arrangements. But this was *Oregon* and he was going to dig his heels in.

"I'm not worried about the money. But you're saying this could be more than a couple of weeks. I've got…" He cast around for some good reason. His coworkers had softball games and kid day camps and family reunions this time of year, but he was rather low on excuses for himself. A hollow feeling bloomed in his chest as he tried to remind himself that he liked his life, liked his freedom from entanglements and encumbrances. After Mike, he hadn't wanted anything to do with domestic bliss, not ever again. And sure, he had a social life, but nothing he could point to as a commitment. Those he stayed away from. "The cat and—"

"You took her with you to Mendocino. I remember." Smiling, she shook a finger at him. He'd let her assume he was an indulgent pet parent instead of a guy stuck with someone else's cat who was reluctant to pay sky-high pet-sitter fees. "We'll make sure we find you a pet-friendly extended-stay place with a kitchenette. I know you like to make your own food. And assuming you want to drive it, I can arrange mileage too."

"It's thirteen hours, give or take." He'd had that number memorized for decades now, dating back to when it had seemed to matter with life-and-death urgency, each mile an endless chasm between him and what he really wanted. But now it was simply a scar, a wound he'd rather not acknowledge, let alone reopen.

"Do it over two days," she urged, apparently assuming that was him agreeing. "And come on, Luis, don't look at me that way. I wouldn't ask you if you weren't seriously needed. They've been shorthanded all season thanks to this hiring freeze we're all under, but now it's reached crisis level there with a maternity leave, a stroke, and an abrupt move. They're dealing with a much greater number than usual of spot fires."

"Arson?" He didn't want to be curious, but his neck prickled all the same.

"That's the working theory. They don't have anyone with your level of expertise right now. Their crews are overworked, and management is stretched thin. They need help getting through this peak of the fire season, and they need a specialist with your qualifications. So when an old friend called in a favor, I immediately thought of you."

The single guy. But he only nodded. He could tell when something was a losing effort, and trying to get her to send someone else surely was. Just like he'd been well and truly screwed at sixteen when his parents had moved back to California partway through his junior year.

They're making me go.

I don't have a choice.

I'm gonna miss you forever.

At least at thirty-five he was a touch less dramatic. He'd get through this. Somehow.

"You're exactly what they need."

Somehow, he doubted that. "Wasn't that you last

week complaining that I'm too headstrong and that I don't take critique well?"

"Oh that." Rosalind made a dismissive gesture. "I mean, you're the best fire behavior specialist I know of. It's why Mendocino asked for you last year. And it's why I know you're going to do excellent here. And I'm going to owe you. Seriously."

"Yeah, you are." He managed to keep his tone almost playful, not petulant, but it was a close thing. Her flattery wasn't unnoticed either—she'd known the mention of arson would pique his professional interest, and he did have an excellent reputation in his specialty of identifying and predicting how a particular fire would react to given variables like wind, weather, and type of response available. He was used to working with various incident commands and interagency teams of wildfire fighters, and he tried his best to be adaptable and good with crisis situations. In short, he'd be perfect for this job. But, *Oregon*.

Rosalind leaned forward, expression kinder now that he'd agreed. "Isn't there anyone up there you'd like to see again? Old friends?"

"Nope." He had a vibrant social media life but not a single Oregonian on his contacts list, hadn't for years now. Then, as Rosalind frowned because that was kind of harsh, he added, "I fell out of touch with my high school friends. I'll be okay though. No warrants for my arrest up there or anything."

"Better not be." She laughed and offered him the bowl of candy she kept on her desk. "This will work out. You'll see."

"Hope so." He crunched into a cinnamon hard candy, letting the heat fill his mouth and tamp down some of his reservations. Maybe this wouldn't be so bad. It was a big area. Fair number of people spread out through several small farming communities. And he hadn't checked—thank you, iron self-control—but chances were high that Tucker was off running his dad's ranch by now. Him and that smiling wife and half a dozen kids. He'd be way too busy to be concerned about what the forest service was up to. Luis would simply get a room for himself and Blaze and plant his ass there when he wasn't working. If he didn't have to see Tucker, this didn't have to be anything other than a pain in the neck temporary assignment.

"I'm sorry, we're getting *who?*" Tucker was usually all about getting through the morning meeting as quickly as possible, and he'd learned through years of working with Fred that too many questions would slow the boss down, lead to tangents and rambles and a lost morning he could have been working. And a lost morning meant being late getting out of here in the afternoon, meant another hasty dinner for him and the twins and grumbles all around. So he made a point of paying attention to the announcements and getting information right the first time, but this time he had to have heard Fred wrong.

"New fire behavior specialist out of California—Angeles National Forest is sending him since we're still under a hiring freeze and now down to a bare-bones operation. You know all that. You were complaining about overtime last week."

"I get that we need some more boots on the ground. But I've been working as burn boss the last several fires, and Garrick's coming along too. Would be nice if they'd send us some more admin support and not someone who's going to expect a leadership role."

"Don't get your feathers ruffled. You're both an asset to incident command, sure, but we need this guy's fire behavior experience, especially as it pertains to arson. He's got the analytical skills we can use and the experience to back it up."

"Glad they're finally taking the arson suspicions seriously. And what did you say the name was?" That last part was what he really wanted to know. He could deal with the problem of too many chefs in the kitchen, but he could have sworn Fred had said—

"Luis Rivera. Comes to us with great experience."

"Sounds good." He managed a nod, even as his head swam. *Fuck.* Maybe there were a lot of guys with that name in the LA area. Maybe it was some stodgy near-retiree and not the darkest, deepest pair of eyes Tucker had ever known. The voice, husky and earnest. The smile he'd never forget.

"Apparently he knows the area at least a little is what his boss told me on the phone."

And with that, Tucker's corn flakes and coffee turned to bricks in his stomach, a heavy weight he hadn't felt in eons. There might be plenty of guys with that name in California but there had only been one Luis Rivera in central Oregon, the one who'd left with Tucker's heart all those years ago.

"They're making me go." Luis's voice had wavered, *first time Tucker had seen him cry since he'd broken his arm back on a fourth grade dare, and even then, he'd been more mad than sad, all sputtering bravado. This was a level of devastation Tucker had never seen from his friend.*

His chest hurt, like he was some hapless cartoon character and his heart really had been cleaved in half by this news. Scooting closer, he wrapped an arm around Luis's slim shoulders, trying to be brave for both of them.

"You could stay with us to finish school. Share my room and—"

"I'm hardly your parents' favorite person." Luis's weighty sigh hit Tucker like that time a swing had slammed into his gut, because he was right. Tucker's parents weren't going to come charging in to save the day.

"I'll wait for you," he promised.

Only Tucker hadn't. And if it was that same Luis, well, there wasn't going to be any avoiding him. As shorthanded as they were, it wasn't like Tucker could claim some of his mountain of unused vacation days. Fred would want him working closely with this person. But maybe he could figure a way around—

"Should be here any minute."

Or not. Damn it. He needed time to sort himself out, time he apparently wasn't going to get because here came Fred's assistant, Christine, knocking at the conference room door, ushering in…

A stranger.

Not the boy Tucker had known. A *man.* One with a couple of flecks of gray in his dark hair, which was neatly styled, not all choppy and goth, and he had a lean, muscular build, taller than him by a couple of inches, not some scrawny kid. His shoulders were solid, a man who had known his share of heavy labor, and the biceps peeking out of his forest service polo said he kept that work up. The edge of a tattoo played peekaboo with his sleeve. Tucker's memory had miles of smooth tawny skin, no tattoos or scars like the one this guy had on his other arm.

But right when Tucker's shoulders were about to relax, the pit in his stomach starting to ease, the guy frowned, and Tucker would recognize that hard, defiant look anywhere. Luis's head tilted, revealing the familiar curve of his neck to his shoulder that Tucker remembered all too well.

"*Tucker?*" The Californian accent drew out the vowels in his name, an effect that could make him feel special and singled out when whispered on a starless night. But add a little disdain and a deeper timbre than Tucker recalled, and it made him feel like an unwanted extra in a surfing movie.

"Yeah." He nodded, head feeling untethered, like a helium balloon about to escape.

"What the—" Luis blinked, then drew his shoulders back, professional distance taking over, smoothing his facial features and softening his next few words. "Sorry. Wasn't expecting…"

"Y'all know each other?" Fred stood to greet the newcomer with a hearty handshake. "Now, that's just great. Small world, right?"

"Right," Tucker echoed weakly, unable to take his eyes off Luis. "Small world."

Too small. Especially considering that he'd once seen the miles between them as an uncrossable sea, a distance so great it made his brain hurt almost as much as his heart. Once upon a time, he would have given anything to end up in the same room again, weeks of working together looming, and now he'd trade an awful lot to avoid it.

"We went to school together a few years," Luis said dismissively, body-slamming eight years of best friendship to the ground, reducing everything they'd been to a chance acquaintanceship.

Tucker almost couldn't breathe and sure as hell couldn't get the words out to correct Luis. And even if he could find the power of speech, what the fuck was he supposed to say?

Nothing. That was all he could do, so he managed a nod without meeting Luis's eyes.

"Good, good." Fred continued talking, explaining the office management structure to Luis and asking about his drive up from the LA area, but Tucker's ears were ringing too loud to register Luis's answers. Luis was here, invading the office Tucker had worked out of a good decade plus now, never a problem. Now here Luis was after all these years, looking all grown up and pissed off and way, way too good to ignore. He might not be the same boy anymore, but he was a *man*, and that was possibly more devastating to Tucker's sanity.

Tucker had spent almost two decades working around wildfires, first on a line crew, then engine and hotshot outfits, paying his dues before moving into fire management. He'd worked hard on his reputation for being unflappable under pressure. No one wanted a burn boss who startled easily or who couldn't keep his temper. And after all that time on the front lines of fires, not much scared him anymore. Except maybe Luis and the prospect of needing to work alongside him and pretend that they hadn't once been everything to each other. And more to the point, Luis had every reason in the world to still be pissed at him, even after all this time. Tucker couldn't expect him to simply forgive and forget any more than he himself could.

As Fred talked, Luis kept glancing over at Tucker, mouth still twisting like he couldn't believe his rotten luck. Or maybe like he was expecting to wake up any minute from this bad dream. Lord knew Tucker felt the same way. *Wake up, damn it.* He had plenty of other stuff to worry about this summer more than Luis's sudden reappearance.

"So Tucker can show you around the office, introduce you to our support staff, show you where we keep the coffee." Not even looking at Tucker, Fred nodded like this was a done deal. "He'll bring you up to speed on our various projects. This is undoubtedly a smaller operation than you're used to, but we're family here. Everyone pitches in, and we get the job done, one way or another. You'll see. I've got a good feeling you're going to fit right in."

Tucker had the exact opposite feeling. And family or no, he wasn't exactly eager for their past to become office gossip. These were his work colleagues, people he'd do anything for on a professional level, although personally, he'd always kept to himself and he'd like to keep it that way.

But it wasn't like he could argue with Fred or volunteer someone else—that would only raise suspicion, start that gossip mill chattering. No, he'd have to face this head-on.

"Yup. I can do that." There. He sounded normal. Distant yet helpful even.

"I appreciate it." Luis spoke more to Fred than him, not bothering to glance Tucker's way until they were in the hall. Together. Alone.

Forget all his usual cool resolve. This was fucking terrifying. Every cell in his body took notice of Luis's nearness in the narrow space, the way he smelled like an unfamiliar spicy and citrusy aftershave, the way he was too big, nothing at all like Tucker's memories, tall enough now to glower down at Tucker.

"What the hell, Tucker?" Luis's voice was low, but the fury there was unmistakable. Yup. Two decades might have passed since they'd last locked eyes, but he was still angry.

Before he could reply, Christine came bustling down the hallway with a cheery "It's Selma's birthday today! There's cake in the breakroom. Make sure the new guy gets a piece."

"Sure thing." Tucker managed a nod her direction before she disappeared into the copy room right next to where they were standing. Goodbye chances of a long conversation he undoubtedly needed to have with Luis. What he wanted to say wasn't going to happen with an audience. Instead he took a deep breath and forced a hearty tone. "Let's start your tour there, then. Get you some coffee and cake. Follow me."

Luis's eyes narrowed like that was the very last thing he'd like to do. He opened and closed his mouth a few times while he darted his eyes to the copy room, posture tense until finally he exhaled.

"Fine. Lead the way." His tone was every bit as fake as Tucker's.

Damn. This was going to be a long-ass day of pretending things were fine. Wait. Long-ass *weeks.* Luis was here for weeks. And that meant at some point they *would* have to talk. It was inevitable really, and Tucker was already dreading it with his entire being. Hell, he'd live through the twins' colicky phase again if it meant avoiding having it out with Luis. But one glance at Luis's stiff shoulders and tight mouth told him no amount of bargaining with the universe would save him from Luis's barely controlled anger. Weeks. It was going to be *weeks*, and he might not survive.

Don't miss
Feel the Fire *by Annabeth Albert,*
available fall 2020 wherever
Carina Press ebooks are sold.
www.CarinaPress.com